SOMBER PRINCE

Book 1

MARINA SIMCOE

THE RIVER OF MISTS

Somber Prince
Joyless Kingdom

This book is a work of fiction. Names, characters, places, and incidents are a
product of the author's imagination. Locales and public names are used for
atmospheric purposes. Any resemblance to actual people, living or dead, or to
businesses, companies, events, institutions, or locales is completely coincidental.
Spelling: English (American)
Story Critique by NJ Torrance and May Sage
Editing by Cissell Ink
Proofreading by Owl Eyes Proofs & Edits
Cover image source Depositphotos.com
Cover Design by Marina Simcoe
No generative artificial intelligence (AI) was used in the writing or illustrating of
this book. The author expressly prohibits any entity from using this publication to
train AI technologies to generate text or pictures, including, without limitation,
technologies capable of generating literary and artistic works.
Somber Prince is the first book in the Joyless Kingdom trilogy. It contains graphic
descriptions of intimacy and discussions on adult themes. Intended for mature
readers.

Somber Prince

JOYLESS KINGDOM
BOOK ONE

MARINA SIMCOE

To my Captain,
Who isn't afraid of the dark.

DAWN

THIRTEEN YEARS AGO

"What do you want to watch?" I asked Elaine, tossing my schoolbag on the floor in the hallway.

Elaine was twelve, like me, and had been my best friend since kindergarten.

"I don't know," she said, putting her bag on the bench by the entrance. "Maybe that movie we started yesterday?"

She picked up my bag and placed it next to hers. No wonder my mom loved to have Elaine over after school. She was probably hoping that Elaine's good manners would eventually rub off on me too.

I kicked my shoes off, then drew Elaine by her arm to follow me into the living room.

Mom met us there before I had a chance to beeline for the TV.

"Please keep it down, girls." She pressed a finger to her lips as dad entered the room after us.

Dad had picked up Elaine and me from school on his way from work and would drive me to my dance class later.

"How is she?" He gave Mom a kiss on the cheek.

"Sleeping." She sighed. "Just fell asleep about twenty minutes ago."

Elaine leaned to my ear, whispering, "Ciana?"

I nodded. Mom was talking about my older cousin Ciana, who came to live with us two days ago, though not under good circumstances.

Ciana stayed in the guest room in the basement, and I knew she didn't sleep well at night. I'd heard her screaming, probably from nightmares. Last night, my mom had to run downstairs to calm her down.

"You know what? Let's go to my room." I tugged Elaine toward the stairs to the second floor of the house. "We'll watch something on my tablet instead."

She nodded and followed me, adjusting her glasses that tended to slide down her nose.

Ten years older than me, Ciana had always been the girl I admired to the point of worship. She was the daughter of my mom's older sister who passed away a few years ago. Ciana's father had raised her through high school on his own while the two of them would come to our house for every birthday and holiday.

I loved everything about my cousin. She had her dad's dark-brown skin and his curly hair, as well as my aunt's laughter and cheerful voice that used to sound through our house like a bubbling brook whenever she came over.

Not surprisingly, the most popular boy in school had noticed her and asked her out. Dylan seemed to do all the right things while they dated. He'd taken her to the movies. They'd gone danc-ing. He'd asked her to prom.

When Dylan left our small town to go to college after gradua-tion, Ciana went with him. I remembered how happy she'd been looking forward to a new adventure in the big city. Then her dad passed away, and she never came back, not even for a visit. Not even for Christmas.

About two years ago, Ciana called to tell us she'd married Dylan. When she was younger, she'd talked about the wedding she wished to have. She'd said our whole town would be invited, and she'd dreamed about wearing a dress with the longest train ever.

As it'd turned out, when she married Dylan, no one from our town had been invited, not even us, her closest family.

"How did she do today?" Dad asked Mom quietly.

I paused on the bottom stair, waiting for her answer.

"A little better, I think. We went shopping for clothes for her this morning and got her hair done. We talked a little. But she still refuses to speak about *him*." She shook her head. "I swear I should've strangled that piece of shit back in the city."

Elaine gasped at my mom's swearing, but I knew Ciana's husband deserved all that and more.

I remembered Mom growing more and more worried as Ciana's phone calls grew shorter and farther between. Then they had stopped completely. We hadn't heard a word from Ciana for an entire month. One day, Mom and Dad had packed their suitcases and driven to the city, leaving me at home with Melanie, my older sister.

I'd heard there had been a fight when they'd confronted Dylan. I'd learned the police got involved. I'd heard Dylan was no longer allowed to come anywhere near Ciana, which was a good thing. He must've done something bad to her. Because my smiling, bubbly cousin had been a sad, timid shadow of her former self ever since Mom and Dad brought her to our house two days ago.

"Is she still talking about the black smoke?" Dad asked quietly.

I strained my hearing to listen to their conversation, but Mom had no chance to reply.

An ear-splitting scream tore through the house.

Mom's face went as pale as the wall behind her.

"Ciana..."

Dad tossed his briefcase aside and sprinted for the basement door. I ran after him.

Ciana's terrified screams rushed from the basement when Dad threw the door open. She screamed like she was being murdered, and I hoped Dylan hadn't sneaked into our house somehow. Because then, my parents would surely kill him right there in our basement.

Dad ran down the stairs, skipping a few at a time.

Over his shoulder, I saw the closed door to the guest bedroom. Black, shadowy tendrils curled from under it.

Black smoke.

It was so thick, it looked like ink spreading through water. Then it suddenly constricted again, as if pulled back into the room.

"Ciana!" Dad shouted on his way to the door.

Her screams stopped abruptly, as if cut off mid-breath.

Dad slammed against the door, shoulder first, knocking the door off its hinges. Splinters flew all over the place.

"Ciana?"

I skidded to a stop in the doorway.

Her bed was unmade and empty. As my dad frantically searched the small room for my cousin, I watched the black licks of dense-like-ink smoke being sucked into the walls by some silent, invisible power.

Then, the smoke was gone.

And so was my cousin.

NOW

"Hey, keep it down!" Melanie, my older sister, stomped down the stairs into the basement.

I sat on the couch with Elaine who was staying overnight. We were watching a movie.

"What do you mean?" I snapped at Melanie. "The sound is barely on."

Melanie jerked her head impatiently, flicking back her shoulder-length hair, blonde like mine.

"Well, Dad wants to go to bed. He needs his teeth brushed and stuff." She gave me a pointed look.

It'd been years since Mom passed away from the same disease that had taken her older sister. A decade older than my mom, Dad had always said he'd go first, but fate had ruled otherwise. He'd never recovered from losing her so early, and with age, his mental health had deteriorated to the point that he could no longer live alone, needing constant care.

Melanie took a week off work to "help" look after Dad, but that didn't mean she actually did anything to help. I'd been Dad's one and only caregiver ever since he took a turn for the worse last year.

It made sense for me to take over his care. Melanie had a growing career in finance. I had nothing but odd dance gigs here and there, still trying to get a contract with a production company. Between the two of us, it seemed a more logical choice to put my dreams on hold and move back home to take care of Dad.

"I'll do it." I got up from the couch.

I stopped by the laundry room to get Dad's favorite blanket that I'd washed earlier that day. "Hey, where is Dad's Afghan blanket? I had it folded on the top of the dryer."

Elaine jumped off the couch. "Sorry, I put it in the guest room. I thought it was from the bed there. I'll get it."

A shiver of unease ran down my spine as Elaine ran into the guest bedroom.

It'd been years since Ciana disappeared. The police had never found her or any information about who took her. Dylan had pleaded guilty to the charges of domestic violence and abuse during their marriage, but he insisted he knew nothing about her whereabouts and had no contact with her after Mom and Dad had taken her from him.

I was the only one who'd seen the black smoke in her bedroom that day. Dad had been too focused on searching for Ciana to notice the bizarre thick shadows curling around his feet before they disappeared into the walls and the carpet. But I was only twelve back then. Adults had quickly dismissed my story about the smoke that came without a fire and disappeared without a trace.

The smoke hadn't been entirely odorless. I remembered it smelled like heat, like sand warmed up by the sun. But that had proven too vague for the authorities to take my words seriously or to do anything with that information.

Eventually, Ciana's disappearance had been tossed into the pile of unsolved cases, and life had moved on.

Nothing else had happened since then. The black smoke hadn't come back, and no one else had disappeared from our town. Ever since that day, however, I'd been avoiding the basement bedroom. I would only come downstairs to do the laundry, keeping the bedroom's door closed. When Elaine visited, we came to the basement to watch TV, so as not to disturb Melanie, who'd been working on a presentation for work, even though she was supposed to be on vacation this week.

"Is the blanket there?" I asked Elaine, staying a few feet back from the cursed bedroom.

Her high-pitched scream came in reply.

Panic exploded through me with a painfully familiar jolt of terror. It paralyzed me, rooting me in place.

"Dawn!" Elaine grabbed onto the door frame, the colorful blanket falling out of her hands.

A thick tendril of ink-black smoke wrapped around her waist, dragging her back into the room.

"What the fuck?" Melanie muttered in horror. Her stupor lasted for less than a second before she whipped around and dashed for the stairs up to the main floor.

Instead of following my sister, I ran to Elaine. I couldn't let the smoke take someone I loved away from me again.

"No!" I grabbed her arms and pulled.

A shadow emerged from the guest room, enveloping me from behind. The almost forgotten scent of heated sand wafted from it like a blast of desert air.

Dread creeped up my back as the shadow merged into a vague shape of a person, complete with two arms that wrapped around me tightly. They looked like tendrils of thick smoke but felt far more tangible than that. Solid and strong. Inescapable.

Another shadow separated from the darkness inside the room. It dissipated into a fine, black mist that blew across the basement, then solidified into a humanoid shape in front of Melanie, cutting off her escape.

"Get away from me!" she screeched, kicking at it.

The basement door slammed open.

"Children?" My father rushed down the stairs, tripping over his feet unsteadily. "What's going on?"

The shadowy shape in front of Melanie twisted at the torso. A long, curved sword emerged out of nowhere. The blade glimmered with red sparks, descending on my father. With a strangled, gurgling sound, he crashed down the stairs.

Dad's neck bent at an odd angle when he hit the ground. A dark-red puddle immediately formed under him. The pungent coppery stench of blood blended with the scent of the desert.

"Daddy!" I cried.

Horror and anguish gripped my chest so tightly I couldn't

draw a breath. My hands trembled, letting go of Elaine, and the shadows took her.

I flailed my arms, trying to grab on to the door frame or to the bed—anything that would keep me anchored in my house, in this world.

But it all slipped away from me. The room was gone.

All that remained was darkness.

Two

DAWN

Darkness thickened around me, suffocating like a heavy blanket. It crackled with odd yellow sparks. The sensation of energy gathering around me felt like a thunder storm about to erupt. It skimmed down my arms, slid over my face, and coursed through my veins like a physical presence, invading my entire being.

At some point, a pink shimmer joined the gold. For a while, it got easier to breathe. I felt weightless, floating in light and shadows that curled all around me in the pink mist. But I had no control over where I was going.

Then the darkness flooded my vision once again, and the heat rushed in. The sensation of weightlessness was gone. Gravity tossed me down to the ground. Hot sand scraped my hands and burned my knees through my pajama pants.

The darkness thinned but didn't dissipate completely. The night sky was above me. The bloated moon looked perfectly round, surrounded by twinkling crystals of stars among the feathery clouds.

I was outside. And I wasn't alone.

"To your feet, human." Someone yanked me up by my arm.

Disoriented, I tried to obey. I had no shoes on, and my socked feet sank into the hot sand. The carpet of our basement floor was gone.

Where was I?

The ground was black, just like the sky. Moonlight streaked the crests of sand dunes with silver.

As my eyes adjusted to the night, the surrounding me dark figures came into focus. Elaine was kneeling to my left. She patted the ground around her, likely searching for her glasses since they weren't on her face. I spotted their metal frame twinkling in the sand in front of me and picked them up.

"Here you go, Elaine."

"Thanks." She put them on, getting up.

Melanie spat the sand out of her mouth, climbing to her feet too. "What the fuck is this shit? What happened? Where are we?"

"You're in Alveari, the Kingdom in the World of Under," the person who had helped me up said.

Slightly taller than me, the person was dressed in a peculiar garment. It looked like a piece of fabric held with a belt in the middle around the waist. Half of the fabric draped down like a skirt, reaching just below the knees. The other half was lifted over the person's head like a cloak and secured with a clip around the head. The fabric opened in the front, allowing me to see the chest covered by bejeweled chainmail. It draped over a pair of breasts. This was a woman, then? Though her deep, powerful voice could've equally belonged to a man. Her skin was as dark as the night around us, and so were her clothes. Her gaze skimmed over the three of us.

"Who are you?" I demanded. "Take us back home." *Home...* Where we left my dad lying on the floor. Helpless and alone. "I need to go home. Now."

I whipped around. A hill rose into the sky behind me. A faint golden glow died on top of the hill, swallowed by the silver moonlight. Rare patches of grass and black rocks littered the side of the hill. On the right, down the hill, stood an odd dark structure. But there were no streets, no trees, no town—nothing I would recognize.

Elaine grabbed my arm while Melanie spat and cursed, trying to get the sand off her tongue.

"Where are we?" I whispered, my throat closing with dread.

"I already told you where." The strange woman's voice was edged with annoyance this time. "I'm not wasting my breath on repeating the same things if you don't care to listen." She glared at me, then squinted, peering at my face. "What's wrong with your eyes?"

Was anything *right* with anything at this point? But I brought my hands up to my face, quickly running my fingers over it. Other than the fine layer of sand covering every inch of my skin, my face seemed normal.

"What about my eyes?" I blinked.

The woman winced and glanced away. "They don't match."

"No. They don't. Never did."

I had heterochromia—one of my eyes was blue, the other brown. Most people commented on that when they first met me, though no one ever looked as disturbed or repulsed as this woman did. I had no idea how she even spotted my eye color at night or why it mattered so much to her.

I stepped toward her, fisting my hands to stop them from trembling.

"Will you explain what's happening here? How did we get here? Who are you and what did you do to my dad?"

Dad.

The last I saw him, he was...

I wished I could block that image out of my mind.

Maybe it'd been just a dream? A nightmare? Whatever was going on right now still didn't feel real.

"Time to get moving," the woman said, not answering any of my questions. "We need to get to Teneris before sunrise."

"To get where?" My mind was reeling, my head spinning. I thought I might get sick.

Melanie shook the sand out of her jeans and blouse.

"Who cares *where?*" she snapped. "I'm not going anywhere with these weirdos."

She gestured wildly with both arms, and I noticed several more figures surrounding us. Some of them were taller, with more masculine proportions, though all of them wore the dark garments and high leather boots similar to the outfit of the woman.

"What's going on?" Elaine asked the question that kept spinning in my head in a maddening loop.

The strange woman huffed impatiently. Raising her hand, she snapped her fingers. A few of the people came closer. They were considerably taller than either of us, with wider shoulders and broad chests covered by chainmail set with gems. Like the woman's, their faces were as black as ink or darkness. Only their eyes were light-colored, standing out like stars in the night sky.

The man who approached us first had two curved swords attached to the belt on his hips. The sight of the weapons flashed through my mind with the image of an identical sword raised over my father's frail frame.

"You attacked my dad," I croaked.

The woman turned to him. "Is that true?"

Grief and anger exploded through me, blowing any sense of self-preservation to pieces.

"You hurt my sick, old father. You bastard!" I launched myself at him.

Startled, he stepped back.

The woman acted quickly, grabbing my hands before I could land a blow.

"Tie this one up, Serus," she ordered to another man.

"Yes, my general." Serus yanked a coil of rope from his belt.

He had a pair of curved swords on each side too. All the men around us were armed like that. Anyone could've been my dad's attacker. Except the sword that had hurt him had appeared from a *shadow*. How was it possible?

My brain hurt. Stunned, I didn't even fight Serus as he tied my elbows to my waist from behind.

"Now get them on the camel." The female general tipped her head at the three of us. "We don't have much time to lose."

Serus grabbed me with one arm around my middle, easily lifting me off the ground before sweeping Elaine under his other arm.

Another man went for Melanie. She scowled at him, jumping back.

"I'm not going on no fucking camel!" Melanie ran.

The man suddenly diffused into the air, as if absorbed by the night. After a gentle swish following my sister, his shadow solidified in front of the running Melanie. She bumped into his chest at full speed and fell back onto her ass with a loud "oomph."

The shadow man calmly collected her, then tossed her over his shoulder as she kicked and screamed. He carried her over to the dark silhouette of a camel that appeared to be painted in ink against the velvet night sky.

"Let me go!" I kicked my feet, aiming for Serus, who took us to the camel too.

The animal emerged from the night like a mass of darkness, as black as the sand around us.

"Keep still," Serus grunted, adjusting his hold on me. "Or General Oskura will order me to tie your legs too."

He whistled, and the camel bent its front legs, kneeling to lower the caged seat that was mounted on its back. The beast appeared too dark and huge to be real, yet it moved its jaw, giving us a curious look as Serus shoved Elaine against its side.

"Climb," he ordered.

With a soft whimper, Elaine climbed the rope ladder hanging down the camel's side.

"You too." He slammed me against the animal's side next.

"How?" I bent forward, thrusting my bound elbows toward him. "My arms are tied, you asshole."

"And whose fault is that?" He shrugged, shoving his hand under my butt.

"Hey, get your hands off me!"

"Climb," he snapped, giving me a push up the camel's side.

"Come here, Dawn." Elaine grabbed me under my arms and pulled, helping me into the narrow cage on the camel's back. "We can't fight them," she added softly. "We need to find another way."

Cursing and swearing, Melanie climbed into the cage from the other side. The camel then rose to its feet, tipping the cage. Elaine and I rolled backwards. And Melanie screamed, grabbing onto the bars.

General Oskura whistled loudly, summoning three more camels from the darkness. Instead of cages, they had double seats framed by curtains. The general and her men climbed into the seats then, and our small caravan moved ahead.

Forming a line, all four animals headed into the night, taking us into the unknown.

Three

DAWN

"**W**here the fuck are you taking us, you shady assholes?" Melanie yelled.

She hadn't shut up ever since they'd shoved us into this cage. Shedding whatever class she'd so carefully cultivated while building her career in the city, she swore and cursed like a drunk sailor, calling our captors all possible kinds of names. I couldn't blame her. I'd do the same if my mind wasn't weighed down by grief.

The image of Dad falling down the stairs played in my head on repeat. Despite his fragile mental health, Dad was a survivor. He must be alive. I refused to think otherwise.

But if he survived, he'd be lying at the bottom of the stairs right now, drowning in his own blood, with no one to help him.

There had been so much blood...

The sword slit his throat.

A sob tore from my throat. Soft crying echoed it, coming from the corner of the cage where Elaine curled up into herself, wrapped in her long fuzzy sweater.

Deep inside, I knew Dad was dead the moment it happened.

The way his head bent when he hit the ground, the way the open wound gaped across his throat, the way his eyes remained open... My poor dad.

I cried openly now, and from my sorrow, anger rose.

They'd pay. Whoever was responsible for killing my dad would pay. I wouldn't rest until I brought them to justice. We had laws for a reason. Murderers and kidnappers got arrested and prosecuted. These people would rot in jail. I'd make sure of that.

"They're not getting away with this," I muttered, my voice low but harsh.

"We're not on Earth anymore, Dawn." Elaine's words yanked me out of my vengeful thoughts.

"What do you mean?" I wiped my wet cheeks with my shoulders the best I could with my hands tied.

Elaine crawled closer and pulled on the rope, trying to untie the intricate knot that the shadow man made.

"Look around us," she said. "And look closely."

I sniffed, blinking tears away. We must've travelled for some time now. My arms were going numb from being tied for so long. My mouth felt dry, and Melanie sounded like she was losing her voice from all her yelling. The air had cooled somewhat, sending chills down my arms and seeping through my t-shirt.

Pressing my face between the cage bars, I did what Elaine told me to do. I looked closely, studying our surroundings carefully. And the more I looked, the bigger the dread grew inside me.

Black sand was uncommon, but not impossible in our world. I'd heard of black sand beaches on volcanic islands. There could possibly be a black desert somewhere on Earth too.

Except that the dunes here shimmered in the moonlight as if studded with diamonds. A breeze shifted the sand with the melodious sound of trickling water. The camels stepped softly on the desert floor, moving along the dunes like a flotilla of ships in the ocean. I'd never seen a live camel before, but I doubted they were normally quite as big or had such soft flowing fur like the one who carried our cage.

While Melanie screamed her head off and I was lost to anger and grief, Elaine paid attention. She listened and watched. And she was right. This wasn't our world. The creatures who took us weren't humans. I'd never seen a shadow wielding a sword before.

Cold fingers of fear creeped up my back and into my chest, gripping my heart.

"Where the hell are we?"

"We're not speaking English, either," Elaine pointed out in a voice hollow with fear.

The realization slammed into me like a wrecking ball. From the moment we got here, we'd been speaking the same language as our captors. Only when I listened to it closely, it didn't sound like any language I'd ever learned or even heard before.

"Oh God, Elaine..." I gulped, hyperaware of the foreign sounds forming in my throat as naturally as my mother tongue. "What's happening to us?"

Her long, shuddering breath was her only response as she kept tugging at the rope around my arms to no avail.

The ground appeared to rise on the horizon, blocking the starry skies. For a moment, I feared the desert was bloating, ready to explode or swallow us. As we got closer, I realized a giant hill stood up ahead. Overgrown with tall grass, the hill appeared to breathe like a giant animal in slumber when the grass moved in the breeze like waves of the ocean.

Terraces and balconies were built into the hill with gazebos draped in silver vines. Large, pale moths fluttered around the flowers on the vines. Their silver wings spread shimmering dust, leaving glowing trails in the air.

The hill was buzzing with life. People filled each terrace and balcony, mingling in groups and watching our small caravan approach.

Looking back, I noticed with surprise that the caravan was no longer small. Somewhere along the way, more camels had joined us. Now, the line stretched as far as I could see behind us. Some of the animals carried identical cages to ours, and all the cages had people inside them.

"What is this place?" I whispered, but no one in our cage could answer this question.

The camel stopped, and the men dragged us out of the cage.

Elaine kept close to me, her fuzzy sweater tickling the skin on my bound arms.

"Where are we?" she whispered.

"I'm more concerned with how to get the fuck out of here," Melanie croaked, standing next to us. Her voice had almost completely gone by now, but defiance was clear in her expression. "We need to find a way back, and the sooner the better. I have a very important presentation next week."

A presentation?

It took me a while to even understand what she was talking about. Was she thinking about her work?

That world—our *real* world—already felt so distant, as if a lifetime had passed. Even the horror of what happened to my father was slowly slipping away, like it'd happened in a nightmare that had already passed.

A tall gate of carved wood and metal opened in the side of the hill on the ground level, and a few riders exited. The one in the front rode a snow-white camel, which instantly set him apart from the rest. Like the others, he also wore a skirt-like garment, a chainmail over his chest, and boots. But his clothes were slightly different.

Both layers of this rider's skirt were down. The black fabric shone with emerald green in its folds, flowing down the sides of his camel like liquid malachite. The high side slit exposed his leg from the short boot all the way up to his muscular thigh. The mesh over his chest had more gems than metal. It draped from his neck and shoulders down past his ribs, with the precious stones glistening in the moonlight.

As he rode ahead, his long hair streamed in the breeze like black ink, held by a thin golden circlet on his head. In the mass of his hair, several thin braids sparkled with golden rings spread evenly along their lengths.

The general approached the rider and bowed her head.

"Greetings, Your Highness."

Your Highness?

This was a prince, then? Did he have the power to let us go?

The prince swept the caravan with his gaze. Moonlight bounced off his golden circlet. Two black spikes rose on each side of his head like horns. At first, I thought they were parts of his headdress. With another puff of the breeze, however, one of the spikes flicked like a cat's ear would twitch in annoyance when touched.

They couldn't be his ears. Could they? Everything that had happened to us tonight was unbelievable. At this point, I could almost accept that this man had long, pointy cat ears.

The general unclipped her head cover and shrugged the fabric off her head and shoulders, revealing a pair of long, spiky ears of her own. Tall and pointy, they stood upright, like the ears of a Doberman or a German Shepherd. Only unlike the lovable appearance of the dogs, the ears made these people look fierce and menacing. Like they were alert and ready to attack.

The prince turned his white camel back toward the gate, and General Oskura followed him.

Her men prodded us, urging us to move. "Come on. Let's go."

Serus shoved his hand in my back. I tripped, almost losing my balance. Somehow, I regained it but lost my patience instead.

"Go where?" I snapped. "Where are we? What is this place? Who the fuck are you? And what do you want with us?"

Serus huffed, hiking his chin up. "We are the shadow fae of Under. This is the City of Teneris. It belongs to Prince Rha."

"Did you just say 'fae?' And what's Under? What does it mean?" Little of what he'd said made sense.

Elaine squinted at the giant hill in front of us.

"This doesn't look like a city," she muttered.

"Teneris is one of the most thriving cities in Alveari, second only to Kalmena, the Queen's City," another man said. "If you do what's expected of you, you can be very happy here."

"And if we don't?" Melanie rasped.

Her question remained unanswered as they ushered us through the gate.

Four

DAWN

Incredibly, Teneris truly looked like a city inside. It had cobblestone streets, multiple-story buildings, and a large open plaza where they brought all of us who had arrived with the caravan.

Instead of streetlights, tall, glowing columns illuminated the place with soft, yellow light. Intricate mosaics covered the floor of the city square that wasn't actually shaped like a square but like a hexagon, with each corner leading into a narrow side street. The yellow clay walls of the buildings edged the plaza. On their roofs, the tall grass swayed, making the city look like a giant hill from the outside. An *anthill*, I thought, looking up at all the openings, windows and balconies of the two-story walls surrounding the city plaza.

It truly was a different world. A place from a dream. Or from a nightmare.

"Maybe that black smoke in your basement made us all hallucinate?" Elaine speculated out loud, echoing my own misgivings and disbeliefs.

Oh, how I wished that was the case. That all three of us had just passed out from some weird hallucinogen seeping from the walls of our old house. Someone would find us lying on the floor soon. They would air the place. We'd wake up and go on with our normal lives that might not be great but were real.

A big problem was that this world also felt real. Unlike in a dream or a hallucination, the events here occurred continuously and in a logical order, with no time or space jumps. All my senses absorbed my surroundings in a regular, realistic way, even if the surroundings seemed as fantastic as if conjured by a feverish imagination.

Behind her glasses, Elaine's eyes darted around the plaza, taking it in. "I really have no other explanation for any of this."

Neither did I.

Please, let it all be just a hallucination.

Everything inside me—confusion, fear, even grief—hung suspended in anticipation of waking up.

Meanwhile, they herded us into the middle of the hexagonal plaza, along with other humans. The shadow people placed all of us shoulder to shoulder, forming a line. The people in line appeared to be adults, some younger than us, some older. There were men and women of all races here. Some wore pajamas or sleepwear, like Elaine and I. Others were dressed in street clothes that seemed to come from all over the globe. One woman wore a sari. A stout man had a wool coat and a fur hat on. Two younger girls had light dresses and thong flip-flops on their feet.

It appeared the shadow folks had just dashed into our world and grabbed whomever they could get their hands on before heading out. Kind of like the way I did my grocery shopping twenty minutes before the store closed. And now, I desperately hoped these creatures weren't intending to eat us.

What *did* they need us for?

A tall man sauntered onto the plaza, and I recognized the rider of the white camel. He'd left his camel elsewhere but retained his royal attitude and the regal posture.

General Oskura marched up to him. "Eighteen, Your Highness. Eight males. Ten females. All here, as per your order."

He nodded, slowly moving his gaze along our line, as if surveying his new property. In long strides, he moved down the line, giving each of us a brief glance.

The closer he got to me, the harder it was to breathe.

"As per your order," the general had said.

It meant this man was the one who sent the shadows to take us. He was responsible for everything. For the black smoke invading my house. For our kidnapping. And for my father's death.

Anger bubbled in my chest. It rose to my throat, making my face burn and my heart pound hard against my ribs.

The prince stopped in front of me abruptly. Every muscle in my body tensed in his proximity. Rage coursed through my veins, scorching hot like lava. But my hands were tied, literally.

"Why are you tied?" he asked me.

"Ask your goons," I gritted through my teeth. Refusing to look at him, I stared at the plaza past his bicep.

"General Oskura, why is this one tied?"

Not waiting for the general's reply, he slid a curved dagger out of the sheath on his belt. With his hand on my shoulder, he gently rotated me with my back to him, then cut the rope in one smooth movement.

The moment I was free, I pivoted to face him. The earlier numbness blew away from my emotions like a morning fog. The pain of loss sliced through me, sharp like a blade.

"You killed my dad!" I slapped the royal cheek so hard, pain reverberated through my palm and up my arm.

His eyes grew wide from shock. His irises were such a pale yellow, they looked almost white in the stark contrast to his coal-black skin.

I brought my arm back again in hopes of landing another blow. Sadly, the element of surprise was no longer on my side. The prince grabbed my wrist. Then, shoving his dagger back in its sheath, he preemptively grabbed my other wrist too.

"*That* was why she was tied, Your Highness," the general informed him, shooting me a reproachful look.

The prince towered over me, holding my wrists in his hands. His black pupils narrowed to pinholes, and his shapely lips pressed into a thin line. He clearly wasn't used to being slapped and didn't appreciate it in the slightest.

"Don't ever do that again." His voice was low, but every word was weighted with power and meaning.

I had no doubt he could kill me as easily as I'd slapped him. It surprised me he hadn't done so already. But I was too angry to care.

"You killed my father, you asshole," I hissed in his face.

"I've never met you until tonight," he replied evenly. "I'm certain I never knew your father, either."

"One of them slit his throat," I choked out, jerking my head in the direction of his people standing nearby. "And you were the one who sent them."

He held my gaze steadily for another moment. His eyes moved between mine, back and forth. He flinched as if repulsed. Suddenly, he released my wrists and stepped back, avoiding eye contact now.

"My prince," the general lowered her voice, but they stood close enough for me to hear her. "This was a public insult to you. She needs to be punished."

He frowned, no longer looking at me at all. "Put her in a separate room from the rest."

Pivoting on his heel so fast his skirt swirled in the wake, he marched out of the plaza without a single glance back.

Five

With a flick of my fingers on my way from the plaza, I summoned Oskura closer. She caught up, matching my step.

I crossed the covered inner-court garden toward the palace. The guards opened the palace gates of ornamental gold for us. From the spacious main hall, I turned into the corridor leading to my private rooms.

The pale, ill-tempered Joy Vessel refused to leave my mind.

"That woman has extremely disturbing eyes," I voiced my concern out loud.

Oskura easily kept up with my pace, walking by my side. "Are you talking about the human who dared raise her hand to you?"

"Yes. What's her name?"

"No idea, Your Highness. But I agree, her eyes are disturbing."

I winced, recalling the gross imbalance. "One is blue. One is brown."

"That is awful." Oskura grimaced in disgust. "My apologies, Your Highness. The men clearly didn't pay attention, otherwise they would've never brought her here." She paused for a moment, as if thinking of a solution. "I can gouge one of them out. Which one would you like gone? The blue or the brown one?"

My general had a direct way of thinking and the ability to solve problems quickly, which was beneficial on a battlefield, but not so much in matters of delicate nature like human Joy Vessels.

Oskura rubbed her chin. "Though with one eye, there'd be no symmetry, either."

"No. There wouldn't be." I pinched the bridge of my nose, remembering Oskura meant well. She usually did, even if it came out wrong sometimes.

"But if we got them both out—"

I raised my hand, halting her bloodthirsty plans in their infancy.

"Please leave her eyes alone. There'll be no gouging. Can you just explain to me why they are the way they are? Is she sick? Humans are generally weak. I've heard they get sick easily."

"I don't know, my prince. My apologies. I noticed her eyes too late. We wouldn't have taken her otherwise."

That was understandable. I couldn't blame Oskura for the rush.

"You had no time to be picky. The portal was open only for a few minutes." I waved a dismissive hand, entering my dining room.

The sky behind the arched window had already lightened with the approaching sunrise. It was time to secure the palace for the day and go to bed. Things would have to wait until the next night.

"Bring her to dine with me tomorrow."

"To dine?" Oskura stared at me in bewilderment. "My prince, the human publicly insulted you. She needs to be punished, not fed dinner in your royal presence. It'll set a poor example for other Joy Vessels."

I rolled back my shoulders weighed down by the heavy jewelry piece over my chest. Oskura was right, of course. The human raised a hand to me in front of my entire court. Whoever hadn't seen it, surely heard the ring of the slap as her hand connected with my cheek. The spot still burned, as did my ego. No one had dared insult me like that before, not even my mother.

I adjusted my braids over my shoulders. Each thin braid had six round golden clips positioned at even intervals along its length. Six braids. Three on each side of my head, with the rest of my hair upbraided and unbound. A perfectly even, symmetrical arrangement. Unlike that human's face.

Curiosity nudged at me to find out the reason behind her misfortune.

"Besides," Oskura continued, "she clearly hates you. She'd be useless as a Joy Vessel, anyway."

That sounded like a challenge, sparking the urge to prove her wrong.

"Bring her anyway. She'll dine with me. But make her the first to be fitted with the *leilatha* harness. That'll be her punishment."

Oskura eyed me skeptically. "Hardly a punishment, Your Highness, considering how much pleasure it brings to fit the harness."

"It brings an equal amount of torment too."

"Any amount of pleasure is worth every amount of pain," she retorted quickly.

I couldn't argue with that. Pleasure was rare and treasured higher than gold. A human might view it differently, but either way, putting the *leilatha* harness on her would not be the punishment equivalent to her offense.

My curiosity about her far superseded my desire to punish her, however.

"She said her father was killed. Is that true?"

Oskura frowned, then squinted, wrinkling her nose. She'd been the general of my army for eight years now, ever since I'd left Kalmena, my mother's city. But Oskura had been my loyal friend and my right hand for many decades. By now, I'd learned all her expressions, including the face she made when she was stalling, knowing I wouldn't like the answer.

"Is he dead?" I demanded.

She heaved a breath. "Yes."

"Who killed him?"

"Serus," she said reluctantly. "But he said he was startled. He didn't expect the old man to show up."

A soldier in my army, a member of my personal guard, living in my city with the full access to my palace should not get that easily startled, especially by an old, weak human. I expected far better self-control from my people.

When the queen banished me to Teneris, this city was nothing but a bump in the desert with a confusing system of narrow caves underneath. It served as a trading post for unlawful desert dwellers, overrun by poverty and crime.

In eight short years, I'd turned Teneris into a prosperous city, a true jewel of the desert, run by law and order. But for the laws to work, they had to be enforced.

"My orders were not to kill anyone," I reminded my general.

She dropped her gaze. "Yes, Your Highness."

I paused, hating what I was about to do. But the balance had to be restored. The human was right to demand justice.

"This isn't Serus's first offense, is it?" I asked.

"No, my prince," Oskura admitted. "It's his second instance of disobedience that resulted in lives lost."

That was enough for me to decide.

"I want his head."

Oskura hesitated, but only for a second. She knew better than to argue.

"As you wish, Your Highness."

Six

DAWN

"I can't even yell anymore," Melanie complained in a husky voice, rubbing her throat.

"Which may be a good thing. No point in aggravating them," Elaine muttered, sliding a cautious glance at the guards. They led us down a narrow street along with the rest of the captured people. "Pay attention to where they're taking us and memorize the way back."

Memorizing our way back would allow us to return to the city gate if we got a chance to escape. But then what?

The desert lay between us and the hill where our journey began—the desert as vast as the ocean. Even if we found a way to cross it without getting lost, I had no idea how to get from that glowing hill back home.

Hopelessness weighed down on me. I envied Elaine's pragmatic optimism and Melanie's unwavering stubbornness. Still, I looked around, trying to memorize the streets with all the turns we were taking, if only just to orientate myself in this place.

The buildings in this hill-city were only two to four stories high. But when looking up from the narrow streets that were barely wide enough to accommodate two horses riding side by side, the walls around us seemed taller than they were. Some buildings connected through balconies or had an overhanging of grass on the roof that completely obscured the sky above. Very little sunlight could get in here. I imagined the streets remained mostly in the shade throughout the day.

"I think it's best not to scream, guys. And no punching anyone anymore." Elaine gave me a pointed look. "At least until we figure out what's going on here. We need them to explain how they brought us here, so that we know how to get back."

Elaine had always been the voice of reason.

"I didn't punch him," I muttered. "It was just a slap."

Not that it changed anything. I had assaulted the man in power, and I didn't even have it in me to regret it. I felt tired and worn out by all of this. I shut my eyes tightly for a moment before opening them again.

Elaine touched my hand gently. "I don't blame you for slapping that guy. He seems to be in charge around here. And if so, he's responsible for everything that happened to us and to your dad."

She sighed, dealing with her own emotions. Elaine knew my dad for almost as long as I did...

I shook my head, stuffing the devastating thoughts so deep inside me, they'd hopefully remain buried for a while. I couldn't think about my dad right now. Not if I didn't want to break into tears again.

"What do you think they'll do to us?" I asked instead.

"Isn't that obvious?" Melanie scoffed. "They're going to rape us all and make us their sex slaves."

Elaine sucked in a breath in horror, her eyes growing wide. A woman behind us giggled, obviously overhearing us. Melanie hadn't tried to be quiet, speaking as loud as what was left of her voice would allow her.

I glanced at the woman behind us. Her copper-red hair was pulled up into a messy bun. Freckles generously sprinkled her nose and cheekbones. She looked about Melanie's age, a few years older than me.

"What are you looking at?" She met my eyes straight on, hiking her chin up in defiance. "They won't need to 'rape' me. I'll fuck them myself."

Elaine gasped again, and Melanie huffed, rolling her eyes.

The woman slid her gaze down the back of the guard walking in front of us.

"A nice ass like that? Why not?" She shrugged.

The three of us followed her in eyeing the guard's backside. It was a nice one, I had to agree. The fabric of the guard's skirt streamed down his hips, highlighting the curves of his muscles in a rather appealing way as he walked.

All our captors looked conventionally attractive. Tall and lean, they stepped softly, moving gracefully like shadows along the street. But they were still our captors. And at least one of them was a murderer who slit my dad's throat.

"You." A guard grabbed my arm suddenly. "You come with me."

My heart leaped to my throat. "Just me? Why?"

"Me too!" Elaine lunged after me. "Take me with her. We're together."

"No." The guard stopped her by extending his arm between us. "Prince Rha ordered to put her in a separate room. Alone."

Assaulting royalty had its consequences. The question was, how dire?

I fisted my hands in my pajama pants, frozen in place.

Elaine clung to the guard's arm, pleading. "We can't be separated. We have to stay together. Please."

She couldn't move his arm even by a hairbreadth. The man was as strong as a steel fixture, and seemed just as unfeeling.

"Do you wish to join her in her punishment?" he asked.

"No!" I blurted, finding my voice at last. "She had nothing to do with it. Leave her alone. I'll go."

I couldn't let them hurt Elaine for what I had done. Another guard dragged her away.

"Dawn!" she screamed before the guard shoved her into the crowd that quickly absorbed her and moved away.

"Come." My guard tugged my arm, leading me through an arched door in the wall to our right.

"When will I get to see my friend again?" I asked, hating how small my voice sounded.

"Will *I ever see her again?*" was what I wanted to ask but was too scared to hear the answer.

"If you wanted to stay with your friends, you should've thought about it *before* raising your hand to His Highness Prince Rha."

The prince deserved it and more. A slap wasn't nearly enough for everything his people had done to us. But I kept my mouth shut, fearing the consequences.

The guard took me down a narrow corridor with mosaic floors and yellow clay walls.

"You'll stay here." He stopped in front of the door with a long, narrow opening on the bottom.

"What's this? A jail cell?"

He shrugged. "What did you expect? The royal chamber?"

If the royal chamber belonged to their precious prince, then no, I definitely did not want to be taken there.

The guard unlocked the door and stepped aside to let me in.

"Your *leilatha* harness fitting is tomorrow. First thing after breakfast," he said.

"My *what?*"

But he already locked the door behind him, leaving me alone in a small room with a hexagon shaped floor. Smooth yellow walls with rounded corners surrounded me. Instead of a traditional bed, a raised platform was in the middle, with a mattress and some bedding.

After the noise of the crowd out in the streets, the silence in the room felt unsettling. Loneliness crushed me. I sank to the mattress and buried my face in my hands.

How was I supposed to get out of this?

How did I get here in the first place?

The smoke, the shadow people, and this whole world felt surreal. But not entirely new.

I'd seen this smoke before, in the same place where they'd taken us from, in my parents' basement. Years ago, Ciana was taken. And now I wondered if what happened to us had happened to her too.

Did she survive all these years?

Maybe there was a way for me to find her here. I just had to survive whatever was waiting for me tomorrow.

I WOKE up to the sound of wood sliding along the marble floor. Someone pushed a tray under my door, and it took me a few moments to remember where I was.

The jail cell.

Inside a hill city.

Because I slapped their prince.

Because he sent his people to kidnap me, my sister, and my best friend. And because one of them killed my dad...

Fear and sorrow slammed into me anew, squeezing my chest so hard it hurt. This hadn't been a dream or hallucination. The cell hadn't disappeared. I didn't wake up back in my bed in my parents' house. I was still here.

My stomach spasmed at the sight of the tray with a plate of food on it and a painted water bag. Someone had brought it here.

I jumped out of bed and rushed to the door.

"Hey!" I slammed my palm against the carved-wood surface. "Is anybody there?"

The door remained locked, and no one came in. No one

replied. I heard no movement behind the door either. It was like the food tray had materialized on its own. But the shadow people moved so soundlessly, maybe I just couldn't hear their footsteps?

Disheartened, I used the toilet in the niche in the wall, washed my face with the clean water from the pitcher on the stand next to a large painted bowl, and brushed my teeth with the toothbrush provided along with other toiletries in the basket on the shelf under the bowl. For a jail cell, this was a rather neat one and stocked like a hotel room.

I moved automatically, going through the motions. But I'd cried myself to sleep. My eyes felt sore and puffy, and I hadn't had anything to eat ever since we got to this cursed world. If I had to face something horrible today, I might as well do it with my face clean and my stomach full.

Grabbing the tray from the bed where I'd left it, I examined the food. The plate held a generous pile of warm, tasteless mush. Whoever made it hadn't bothered putting any salt in it, not to mention any added flavor. The corked skin bag held some cool, clean water. Refreshing, but hardly satisfying.

Not knowing when my next meal would come, however, I ate and drank it all. The moment I placed the tray with the empty dish on the floor next to the slit in the door, it disappeared, pulled out into the corridor.

"Hi?" I said tentatively. "Who's there?"

The door opened suddenly, making me jump. General Oskura stood behind it, flanked by two of her men. The third man slipped away quietly, taking my tray with him.

The general had traded the long boots she wore in the desert for a pair of soft shoes with flat soles. Her dark, flowing skirt was a little longer today, reaching her ankles. Other than the bejeweled chainmail on her chest, she remained topless, just like the two men who came with her, and just like their prince was last night. The only visible difference was the size and pattern of the stones in their jewelry.

I opened my mouth to ask some of the many questions roaming my mind.

"Good morning—"

"Evening," the general corrected.

"Evening? Did I sleep through the entire day?"

"Yes, like everyone else did," she dismissed. "It's time for your fitting, Sweet One."

The *fitting* had been mentioned before, only no one had explained to me what that was.

"What is it exactly?" I asked. "How is it done?"

"You'll see," she replied evasively, gesturing for me to get out of the room.

I grabbed on to the door frame, not in a hurry to leave the relative safety of the room where I'd spent the day. "When can I see my friends again? Where are they?"

She pursed her lips, clearly displeased by my stalling.

"All human Joy Vessels are fine and well taken care of. We have to go now. The Joy Guardians are waiting."

Following her quick gesture, the guards grabbed my arms and pulled me out into the corridor. I tried to dig my feet into the ground, but my socks easily slid along the floor tiles, providing no resistance against the guards dragging me after the general.

Worry vibrated through me, making my voice shake as I fired questions at her.

"Who are the Joy Guardians? Or Joy Vessels? Are they going to do the fitting? What are they going to *fit?* And how? Will it hurt? Why do you have to do this to me?"

The word "joy" was tossed around quite a bit here. Only nothing about this world made me feel *joyful* so far.

General Oskura threw an annoyed glare at me over her shoulder.

"You will get your *leilatha* harness today," she said in a clipped voice. "It is pleasurable but also extremely painful, I've heard. You're getting the harness first, before anyone else, as the punishment for the disrespect you showed to Prince Rha last morning."

Her explanation only increased my anxiety.

"What do you mean? Painful and pleasurable are opposite things. They can't be both at once."

"You'll see," she repeated with a shrug, then opened a door that led us into a covered garden.

Dark-green vines climbed up the lattice of carved arches. Small fountains bubbled in the niches in the walls. Tiled walking paths ran between small ponds and narrow streams with colorful fish playing in the water.

It presented such a drastic change after the narrow corridor with bare walls. As worried and distracted as I was, I couldn't resist a quick glance around.

"It's lovely here," I muttered, wishing I could just stay here instead of going wherever they were taking me.

"The gardens in Teneris are some of the best in the kingdom," the general said with pride. "They're the result of hard work under the direct supervision of Prince Rha."

The prince who stole people also liked to plant gardens? Go figure.

"Almost there, Sweet One." The general urged us to keep walking with a beckoning gesture.

Why did she call me "sweet one" when I'd behaved in a way quite the opposite of sweet? It sounded ominous, like she was referring to the taste of my flesh, not my character or my behavior. A cold shiver of apprehension ran down my spine.

God, please don't let them eat me.

My knees grew weak as we approached tall golden gates in an arched doorway. Behind the gates lay a hall with a high, vaulted ceiling.

The general marched ahead and across the hall, explaining to me over her shoulder. "Joy Guardians will build the connection between your *leilathas* and our tendrils."

"My *what* and your *what?*" I struggled to free my arms from the guards. "Listen, I'm not taking another willing step unless you tell me exactly what's going to happen."

The guards could have easily forced me to move, like they'd done before, but they stood back, taking their hands off me. The general huffed a breath, looking irritated.

"*Leilathas* are the magical receptacles for our tendrils." She placed her hands on my shoulders, then slid them down my arms. "They will be placed here." She gave my arms a light squeeze, just above the elbows. "And here." She tapped the back of my neck and a spot lower down my spine. "Through them, we will be able to savor your joy with you."

Lifting my shoulders, I shrank away from her touch. "And what if I don't want to *savor* anything with you?"

"But you will," she replied confidently, pushing yet another door open. "That is your only purpose here."

The guards stepped behind me, cutting off my only route of escape.

A group of six people waited for us in the room. Three men and three women gathered by the window with the view of black sand and starry skies. It was night again. The general didn't lie when she said I'd slept through the entire day.

A lattice of hexagons arranged in a honeycomb pattern stood in front of the window.

They sure liked hexagons in this place. Then it dawned on me. Teneris wasn't an anthill but a beehive. And if I was the "sweet one," then I must be about to get stung.

Dread tightened around my chest like a steel band. With my eyes darting around the room, I frantically searched for an escape. Maybe I could break through the glass in the window? Only I'd have to make it past the six people on my way to it first.

"Greetings, Joy Guardians." The general gracefully brought both arms forward, giving an elegant bow to the group by the window.

The Joy Guardians returned her greeting, casting curious glances my way. All six wore skirts that looked like they were made from melted gold. The fabric streamed down, hugging their hips and legs and leaving their arms and torsos bare. The metal mesh over their chests was made of golden hexagons, also connected in a honeycomb pattern. The mesh was decorated with black and yellow stones set in a unique pattern for each person. Their hair was shorter than of anyone else I'd met here so far. It was pulled up and twisted into intricate knots on top of their heads.

The Guardians moved closer to a long, high table in the middle of the room. One of them lit the thick yellow candles that were arranged into a pyramid on the stand nearby.

A female Guardian turned to me. "Greetings, Sweet One."

"Welcome to Alveari Kingdom," a man echoed in a warm tone of voice.

Another woman brought her hands up in a smooth gesture. "You will have to disrobe from the waist up."

I crossed my arms over my chest.

"No, I won't." I shook my head, inching backwards, only to bump into the hard chests of the two guards behind me.

A female Joy Guardian pressed her hands together in front of her with an expression of utter serenity. "It'll be faster and possibly less painful if you don't fight us."

"You can't expect me to just let you do whatever you want to me," I snapped, not coming any closer.

Her arms suddenly appeared to be dissolving just below her shoulders. Black smoke curled out from each arm in a pair of tight spirals. The spirals grew longer, solidifying into agile, snakelike appendages that stretched down past her knees.

"What the hell are those?" I croaked in horror.

The long, black things lifted. Two more appeared from behind her. The ends of all six unraveled into tendrils of dense, black smoke.

The tendrils.

The general had said something about them before.

Were they going to put those things on me? To burrow them under my skin to "savor" me?

Panic sliced through me. I screamed in terror, pivoting on my heel.

"Let me go!"

I pounded with both fists against the chests of the guards who stood in my way.

"Hush now." The woman's voice sounded from behind me. Black tendrils slithered around my wrists. Getting hold of my arms, the smoky appendages moved them aside and away from the guards. "Yours is not the worst fate, child. It's best for you to learn to be happy here."

"But I don't want to be happy. I can't! Definitely not here."

"Nonsense," she said, using her tendrils to turn me around. "Happiness is the heart's deepest desire. Everyone longs to experience joy. You're one of the lucky ones who can. Why deny it to yourself?"

A man held up something constructed from wide black ribbons and studded with golden star-rosettes.

Was that the harness that they all kept talking about?

In my struggle, I tripped over my feet, and I would've fallen had the woman not held me with her tendrils.

"If you don't want to cooperate, we'll do it without your help. But it will be done," the woman cooed, uttering the threat as if it were words of comfort.

"It has to be done," a man echoed.

Another woman cut my t-shirt and my bra off me with a small dagger.

"You ruined my clothes!" I cried, trying to cover my breasts with my arms.

"You'll get new ones." They pried my arms away from my chest and laid me out on the table like on a sacrificial altar. "Be still now."

The rest of the Joy Guardians released their tendrils too. They slapped them like ropes around my arms, legs, and torso, immobilizing me. My heart raced so fast it echoed in my skull.

"Now, let's slip this on," one of the women said, gesturing to the man with the harness. "We'll be done in no time, Sweet One," she said in a sing-song voice. "Just lay still."

She sounded kind, as if she was helping a child get dressed in the morning. As if she was putting cozy socks on my feet, not some devious contraption that was designed to do god-knows-what to me.

They threaded my arms through the two loops of ribbons on each side, then closed two other loops, one around my neck, the other one just under my breasts. The soft ribbons lay flat and snug against my skin. The cold, metal rosettes pressed against my arms and my spine.

"Now relax your body and *feel*." A male Guardian pressed a hand on my shoulder, urging me to stay down. The rosettes on my back scraped against the hard, black metal of the table-altar.

I breathed rapidly, staring at the high vaulted ceiling where the painted wooden beams met in a hexagon in the middle. Small white, orange, and green tiles made a pattern inside the hexagon. Counting the green tiles in my head, I prayed all of this would be over soon.

So far, nothing hurt, but the loss of control was unnerving. I couldn't move a muscle, tied with the solid, black ropes of their tendrils.

Resting their fingers on the edge of the altar, they murmured softly. I listen to the words they recited in unison. It sounded like a call to gods I'd never heard of.

"Nelinu, God of Darkness, lend us your magic to reach the realm unknown. Help us connect to the hidden world of her emotions."

"Melas, Lady of Night, the First Priestess of Joy, guide your Vessel. Let her feel."

The altar appeared to hum. The metal stars on my harness vibrated against it with a soft clinking noise. A golden glow rose from the altar, arching like a sarcophagus around me.

"What's happening?" I whimpered, but they didn't hear me, lost to their chants.

Their eyelids hooded their eyes. Their features relaxed as if in meditation. The glow shimmered in the candlelight. It looped to the stars of the harness. The metal warmed, then heated, searing my skin.

"It burns!" I screamed, jerking in the hold of their tendrils.

But the Joy Guardians wouldn't let me move.

I was trapped. Burning alive.

The physical pain grew unbearable. Everything hurt, even the sight of the candle flames. I shut my eyes. The metal burned through my skin, melting into my body. I howled, gritting my teeth.

In addition to the physical pain, something darker and far more sinister gripped me from the inside. The pain of loss. The agony of grief. Sadness so dark it was mind-blinding. The emotional torment was deep and all-consuming. Tears streamed down my face, but they brought no relief. For there was no relief from this devastating anguish.

The emotional pain proved far stronger than what was happening to my body. I no longer cared about the burn from the harness. My heart and my very soul were wrenched out of my chest. With that came terror. It shook me with incomprehensible horror.

There was no escape. I believed I would die, plunged into the deepest abyss of despair, when a hand landed softly on my shoulder.

"It will pass," a deep male voice said soothingly.

I held on to his words like to a lifesaver while being tossed around in the ocean of pain and sorrow. Finally, the swells of both seemed to grow smaller, receding.

Pain gave way to anger. It raged through me like a wildfire, devastating in its hatred and violence. I thrashed in the tight loops of the tendrils, roaring until my throat hurt. I clawed at the hard surface of the altar with my nails, wishing it was flesh I could tear through and destroy.

Mad. I had gone mad...

"It will pass." His words echoed in my mind.

It would end. All of it would eventually pass. It had to. Only I feared it would take my sanity along with it.

As the pain receded, rage ebbed, too, giving place to less intense emotions. Though those were still highly unpleasant.

I felt weak, small, and insignificant. Helpless and useless to everyone, even myself. I felt frightened, and timid, and filled with self-loathing. Then a swell of shame rolled in. Mortification made me shut my eyes tighter. It burned my face, urging me to hide, but I couldn't move my arms to hide behind them.

The warm, soothing hand never left me. It squeezed my shoulder slightly, as if in support. And I followed its lead, allowing hope to take hold inside me. It filled me with optimism, banishing shame.

Warmth spread from my face down my body. My muscles relaxed. There was no more pain anywhere. Instead, a tingling sensation scattered along my skin. It brought anticipation that pricked inside my chest like gas bubbles popping in sparkling wine.

The anticipation fanned into excitement. Tiny sparks of desire peppered my skin like phantom kisses. Relaxation rolled over me in a wave of shivers.

The supportive hand on my shoulder stroked my skin. The sensation of the touch spread through the rest of my body with light pleasure, as if a feather boa was running over me, from my head to my toes.

I inhaled deeply. The desire built up steadily. There was no teasing, no desperation, no fear. Confidence glowed warmly in my chest. I felt like I could do anything. I could move mountains, swim across the entire ocean, and cross a desert. Nothing was impossible. I felt strong inside and out. Comfortable in my own skin, in every way.

I released a breath with a soft moan. The loops of tendrils loosened around me, allowing me to stretch. Pleasure tingled through my muscles. Desire grew stronger, coursing through my veins unimpeded. It flooded my core.

The feeling grew from within me. It needed no stimulation from outside. But the hand on my shoulder added to the excitement. I arched my back, moaning as lust grew and ebbed on the way to its peak.

Freeing my arm from the loops of my restraints, I grabbed the hand on my shoulder and shoved it down to my breast. His touch had guided me through the worst, and I wished to feel him as intense pleasure rocked through me.

Ecstasy exploded through every cell of my body. The orgasm went on forever. I moaned, bending my legs. My toes curled, digging into the metal surface under me. My thighs trembled.

As the physical pleasure ebbed, the purest joy filled me. I fell back to the altar, luxuriating in the utter bliss that flooded my veins like warm, sweet honey.

I found myself stroking the hand on my breast, the two of us —the faceless stranger and I—floating in the warm, puffy cloud of complete euphoria. It lasted long enough for me to appreciate every aspect of both physical and emotional fulfillment, a state I didn't recall ever reaching before.

It made me feel invincible, and I didn't want it to end. Sadly, reality slowly creeped back into my awareness.

"It's over now," the same deep voice said. The voice that had been my beacon through this intense, insane journey. The voice that I only just recognized now.

I snapped my eyes open.

The light golden eyes of Prince Rha gazed down at me. He blinked when met with my stare.

"You!" I seethed.

Anger returned, wiping my feelings clean of any lingering bliss. This man was responsible for everything, including what they had just put me through. He'd ordered it. And now, he'd come to watch my torment, probably enjoying the show and my tears.

The Joy Guardians' tendrils fell away from me, and I jumped from the altar. My head swam with dizziness, and my muscles felt like cooked noodles, nearly sending me crashing to the floor.

"Careful." The prince grabbed me under my arm, but it proved not enough to keep me upright. He had to hold me around my waist to stop me from falling. "The fitting can be strenuous on one's mind and body."

"No kidding," I scoffed. "Yet you had no qualms about forcing me to go through with it."

He held me to him, firmly but gently. "Such is your purpose."

"And your punishment," General Oskura chimed in from the door.

I glanced her way briefly, but my awareness remained on Prince Rha's arms holding me and the fact that I was topless. Other than the black ribbons circling my neck, arms, and under my breasts, I didn't have a stitch of clothing above my waist.

What was worse, I'd just experienced the longest, most amazing orgasm, with the prince's hand on my naked breast and a whole bunch of strangers in attendance. I desperately wished for the floor to part and swallow me whole. Sadly, that didn't happen. and instead my mortification boiled over with rage.

"Let me go." I tried to shove the prince away, but it was like moving a wall.

"If I do that, you'll fall," he stated matter-of-factly. "I'll carry you back to your room."

He made a move to lift me into his arms, but I pressed my hands into his shoulders, pushing away from him as hard as I could. "No, not you. Anyone but you."

His eyebrows moved closer together, forming a deep groove between them. Those golden eyes of his narrowed. The moment I made eye contact, however, he immediately glanced away.

"Fine," he conceded. "General Oskura will take you back. Will that be acceptable to you?"

The general came forward. I nodded, and the prince backed away, letting the woman take me. Instead of simply helping me walk, she lifted me into a cradle hold with one arm under my shoulders and the other under my knees.

Before we could leave, however, the prince stopped us by lifting a hand in a regal gesture.

"What would you like for dinner in the morning?" It took me a moment to realize he was asking *me.*

Was it supposed to be a joke?

"Are you serious?" I glared at him, but there was not a shadow of a smile on his lips.

"Yes." He spoke as if it was a normal thing for us to have dinner together.

I opened my mouth to say something snappy to decline, but then changed my mind. Since he asked, why not put in an order? The more ridiculous an order, the better, especially after the nasty, tasteless stuff they had served me for breakfast.

"All right. I'll take a caprese salad, with shrimp cocktail as an appetizer. A filet mignon with balsamic reduction and truffle potatoes for the main course, and crème brûlée with fresh rasp-berries for dessert, paired with red wine, the best that you have."

I flicked my wrist nonchalantly, as if ordering a meal like that was a normal occurrence for me. In reality, I'd never seen truffles in my life, and I'd only tried filet mignon once at a posh dinner party I'd gone to with a guy I'd dated at some point.

The prince looked unfazed by my over-the-top demands, however.

"Have a good rest." He inclined his head, letting the general take me away.

Seven

DAWN

Weak and trembling, I curled into myself the moment General Oskura placed me on my bed. I didn't remember how she left my room or when I passed out. But I woke up thirsty and ravenously hungry.

Sitting up in bed, I tried to gather my bearings. The memories of the "fitting" assaulted me. I groaned, hugging my arms, but I couldn't feel the harness under my palms.

Did I dream it all up?

Sitting up straighter, I inspected my left arm. Sadly, it hadn't been a dream. The harness was there. Black ribbons of shimmering velvet circled each of my upper arms twice. One loop was above my elbow, the other one just below my shoulder. There was also a ribbon under my breasts around my torso. One would be around my neck, too, but I couldn't see that one without a mirror.

I didn't actually *feel* the ribbons either with my hands or on my skin. I scratched against the one on my arm, trying to get a finger under it, but it was no use. The ribbon had melted into my flesh to the point that it appeared painted on my skin now.

The golden-star rosettes twinkled in the yellow light from the glowing ceiling. When I twisted my arm, I felt a gentle press of the ornate metal filigree against my muscles. However, when I touched a star, I felt nothing but my skin.

"How do I get rid of it?" I asked myself.

A food tray slipped under my door, snapping my attention to it. Sadly, it held only a water bag with not even a morsel of food.

"Hey!" I knocked on the door. "Can I have something to eat, please? I'm starving."

Instead of a reply, tendrils of black smoke snaked through the cut-out in the bottom of the door. A jolt of fear sent me back to my bed with a cry. I crawled away from the door as the smoke rose and the shadows grew, forming a figure.

I recognized him as one of the men who'd accompanied General Oskura to my harness fitting earlier.

He raised his hands in a calming gesture. "Don't be afraid, Sweet One. I'm not going to harm you."

He sounded kind, speaking with a concerned expression.

Still, I stayed where I was. "Then why don't you use the door like people do when they *don't* come to abduct anyone?

I grabbed a blanket from the bed and covered my chest. Since they'd cut my clothes, I had nothing to wear but my socks and pajama pants. My nudity didn't seem to bother the guy, however. On the contrary, he gave me a confused look, as if wondering what got me so rattled.

"I can't open the door with the tray in the way." He pointed down. "But you said you were starving, which is a serious concern. I had to get in. Are you all right?"

Was he really worried I might pass out without food?

"Well." I rubbed my forehead with the hand that wasn't holding the blanket to my chest. "It's just an expression. I'm not quite dying from hunger yet."

"Good." He seemed satisfied. "Can you wait until dinner, then? Your enjoyment of the meal will be higher if you wait. His Highness will appreciate it."

"What does *he* care about my enjoyment?"

I almost forgot I'd been personally invited to dinner by the prince. Was it still the same day, then? Or the same night? Time seemed to be all over the place lately.

"Are my friends coming to dinner too?" I asked with hope.

I was not looking forward to seeing the prince again, but if Elaine and Melanie were there, I could possibly suffer the royal company too. Also, getting some food sounded enticing. I was so hungry, my words seemed to echo in my empty stomach.

"No," he crushed my hope. "Prince Rha requested *your* company only."

"Really? That's odd."

There was no reason for the prince to favor me over the others. If anything, I'd given him plenty of reasons to avoid me at this point. First, I'd slapped him, then I had an embarrassingly intense orgasm while clutching his hand, and after that I pushed him away.

Unless the invitation to dinner was not a favor but something else? Another form of punishment maybe?

"Why me?" I asked cautiously.

The man shrugged. "Who knows? Maybe His Highness wishes to get to know you better?"

"Is that what he said?"

He tilted his head, looking at me as if I were a clueless child.

"No. Prince Rha does not confide in me about the reasons for his behavior. We don't share meals. But you will. That'd be your chance to ask him all your questions."

He had a point. Maybe His Highness would be more forthcoming with information over some good food and wine?

"Fine," I said. "No need to be snarky."

The man raised his eyebrows in surprise. "I wasn't trying to be *snarky.*"

"It must be a natural talent then," I quipped, but then raised a hand in a gesture calling for truce. There was no need to antagonize this man when I could use an ally in this place. "Sorry, I don't want to be snappy or mean. I'm just hungry and feeling crabby, I guess. What's your name?"

"I'm Sigid." He bowed. "I'll be a Joy Vessel Keeper in the *sarai* once I complete my training."

He seemed proud of that position, so I nodded in support, although I didn't really understand what he was talking about. Hunger tugged at my insides, making it hard to focus on anything else.

"Nice to meet you, Sigid." I adjusted the blanket around my torso.

The locals obviously didn't mind running around topless, men and women alike. But I didn't even have their mesh jewelry to cover my chest with.

Sigid seemed nice, putting me at ease, so I asked, "Can I get something to wear, since my shirt was ruined?"

"I will see to it, Sweet One."

That weird form of address scraped against my nerves.

"Can you call me Dawn, please?"

He inclined his head respectfully. "As you wish, Joy Vessel Dawn."

"No." I winced. "Just Dawn, please. When you say 'vessel,' it makes me think of a jug."

"Not a jug, but a chalice. You are a magnificent vessel filled with the purest of joy."

"Except that I'm a person, not a dish. And I don't feel all that joyful, to be honest."

"It is my duty to provide you with anything you need to change that," he said with another bow.

Anything.

Except for freedom, my friends, or any food. What did it leave me with?

"How long did I sleep? What time is it now?" I ran a hand through my matted hair. It used to be in a bun when they snatched me from my house. But now, it must be resembling a bird's nest, built by a very messy bird unable to focus on the task.

"It's just about six hours past midnight," Sigid replied. "His Highness chose to have dinner at seven in the morning. I'll come back for you then." He turned to leave.

Dinner in the morning? It didn't make sense. But then what did make sense here?

Clutching the blanket around me, I scrambled off the bed after him.

"Wait!"

With his hand on the door handle, Sigid gave me a questioning glance.

"Do you wish to change the dinner time?" he asked. "Move it sooner, maybe?"

"No. I'm good." Despite my hunger, I wasn't in a hurry to see the prince. "Seven o'clock is fine. But..."

I dropped my gaze to my feet. My once white socks were now dingy gray and filled with sand. I'd been wearing them and the same pair of pants for a while now. The black sand of the desert seemed to infiltrate every fiber of my clothing and every crevice of my body.

"Can I have a bath? Or do you want me to attend the royal dinner smelling the way I do?"

Sigid leaned toward and sniffed tentatively, as if trying to determine whether the package of meat he'd kept in his fridge for a while was still any good. Obviously, it wasn't, as he wrinkled his nose in repulsion.

"You're right. The smell is offensive."

"Thanks for noticing," I retorted, not sparing on sarcasm. "You're so charming with your compliments."

His expression turned to confusion. "I paid you no compliment. You do stink."

Clearly, sarcasm was not his language, just as a sense of humor wasn't one of his qualities.

"Alright," I brushed it off. "So, can I have a bath?"

"You absolutely should." He nodded. "Follow me."

He picked up the tray from the floor and opened the door.

"Why do you even bother with doors?" I asked, following Sigid through a maze of narrow corridors. "Why don't you just move around like a smoke, the way you did when you came into my room?"

"Turning to shadows is taxing. It requires magic and concentration. Walking can be done without much thought, allowing for a conversation." He gestured between us in demonstration. "Besides, moving as a shadow can be disorienting. Prince Rha's warriors train hard to be able to use their magic in battle."

It was hard to deny that magic existed in this place since I'd seen it with my own eyes as people dissolved into shadows.

"Do they actually go into battles? Or is that what you call their kidnapping missions?"

"Both," he replied calmly.

We crossed another gorgeous indoor garden on the way. Then, Sigid led me through a set of carved wooden doors into a room so large, for a moment I believed we'd arrived outdoors until I saw a high ceiling cut in rock and realized we were inside a cavern. The air here was thick with moisture and filled with sounds of bubbling water. Steam rose from several pools of various sizes and from the intricate water features lining the walls.

"What is this place?" I looked around.

"The palace baths." Cupping my elbow, Sigid took me to the nearest pool. "Take your things off and put them here." He pointed at the mosaic ledge of the pool before going to fetch a bunch of vials and jars from the bamboo stand nearby. "I'll wash you."

"You'll what?" I clutched my blanket tighter around my body.

My modesty might be unfounded, considering this guy had already seen me topless earlier at the harness fitting, but "washing" me meant he'd have to put his hands on me. Besides, the palace baths weren't empty. We weren't the only ones here. The shadow people strolled along the tiled paths between the pools.

Some washed in the waterfalls cascading down the walls. Others had conversations in groups, wading through the shallow parts of the streams.

"You're not touching me," I hissed to Sigid quietly. "And there are way too many people here for me to undress. Don't you have a private bathroom with a shower somewhere? It doesn't have to be an entire swimming pool."

"Prince Rha has a private bathing area underground. I can put in a request for you to bathe in his—"

I stopped him by lifting a hand. "Um...no thank you. Let's keep the prince out of it. I'll bathe here, but I'll wash myself."

If I had to choose between Sigid and Prince Rha as my bathing companions, I'd go with Sigid. At least this guy wasn't the mastermind behind all the kidnappings and murders.

"All right," Sigid replied, arranging the bottles of toiletries along the ledge by the pool. "Could you explain to me, please, what about me washing you makes you uncomfortable?"

"Do you really not get it? You honestly think there is nothing weird about a man rubbing oils and soaps onto the naked body of a woman he's just met?"

"Not if a woman is a Joy Vessel, and the man is a trained Keeper. Taking care of you is my purpose. I also fail to see how gender has any relevance in this case." He tipped his chin at the other bathers in the area. "There are people of all genders here."

True. Looking closely, I realized this was a mixed crowd. Men and women mingled easily. Most wore only a narrow strip of fabric tied around their hips and no jewelry to conceal their chests. They seemed completely unaffected by each other's nudity. There were no heated glances thrown between them. I caught no signs of erections bulging behind men's loin clothes. Things appeared rather calm, helping my anxiety subside.

Sigid watched me with growing impatience. "Or if you no longer wish to bathe, we can just leave. I have no orders to wash you before the dinner, anyway."

"No. It's fine. I do need a bath. Just pass me those things, please, and let me know what every one of them is for. I don't want to end up washing my hair with a shaving cream or something."

"There is no shaving cream. We aren't werewolves. The only hair we have is on our heads."

"How convenient." I took a furtive look at his arms as he handed me an uncorked bottle.

His skin appeared matte, absorbing all light like fine velvet, but it emitted a slight shimmer as he moved. My hand itched to touch him, but I held back, afraid that it might come across as an invitation for him to touch me back.

Sigid didn't look like he cared either way, however. He seemed impatient and mildly annoyed by the delay.

"Here." He shoved the bottle closer to me. "This is to clean your skin."

"Thanks." I dropped the blanket from around me, then shoved my pajama pants down my legs.

I watched Sigid as I stepped out of my clothes. He slid a curious glance down my naked body, pausing on the trimmed triangle of hair between my legs.

"Yeah, well…" I cleared my throat, turning toward the pool. "We do have hair in more places than one."

"I see." He didn't sound particularly interested.

His light-green eyes flicked to the large ornate fixture hanging on the opposite wall. Black sand trickled down a maze of glass tubes mounted to a polished gold plate with shiny movable parts.

"We don't have much time before dinner," he said with urgency.

"What is that thing?" I pointed at the glass-maze fixture. "A wall clock?"

"Yes. And according to it, we need to hurry if you want to make it to the royal dinner on time."

I didn't care about making it on time. But I also saw no point in stressing poor Sigid out.

"I'll be quick," I promised, sliding into the pool.

Crossing his legs under him, he sat on the ledge and handed me another bottle from his collection.

"This one is for your hair... *Wherever* you have it."

I smiled, taking the bottle from him. "And here I thought you had no sense of humor."

The bottle contained a clear, odorless liquid that lathered pretty well when I massaged it into my hair.

"Now, rinse it with this." He handed me yet another small jar.

I did as he said. Between washing and rinsing, I cast cautious glances at the shadow people around me. But after some initial interest in my sudden appearance in their midst, no one paid me much attention.

"So, you're a Keeper?" I asked Sigid, hoping he'd be a little more forthcoming with the answers than anyone else had been so far.

"Yes, I will be a Keeper of Joy Vessels soon."

"And a Joy Vessel is me?"

"Yes."

"How does one become a Keeper of Joy Vessels?"

"How?" He flicked one long, pointy ear, looking a little surprised by my attention to his person. "Well, I used to look after the royal camels. But with you coming to Teneris, Prince Rha needed someone to tend to his new *sarai*."

For now, I chose to ignore the fact that skills of looking after cattle proved to be so easily transferable for him to look after humans.

"And the *sarai* is?" I asked instead.

"That's all of you, the Joy Vessels. It's also how the part of the palace called where you'll live. It's nice there," he offered helpfully. "You'll like it. *Sarai* has one of the most beautiful gardens in Teneris."

"So, only humans can be Vessels?"

"Humans and everyone else from Above."

"Above where?" I automatically glanced up at the arched ceiling over us.

"Other kinds of fae live in the planes above us. There is the World Above, with several kingdoms like Lorsan, Dakath, and others I don't really remember. No one I know has been up there. Then there is the Sky Kingdom, which is even higher than those places."

"Other planes? I'm not sure I understand."

I thought "fae" was just another word for fairies—tiny magical creatures with wings—and either way, they were supposed to be *imaginary*.

It'd be so much easier if Sigid, the rest of his people, and this entire world with all its different "planes of existence" had turned out to be just a hallucination after all. But the longer I stayed here, the more I feared there was no waking up from this. This world was far too solid and real to be a mere hallucination, though its magic certainly had some dream-like qualities.

"Aren't fae supposed to be in the forest? Living in mushroom circles or something?" I asked.

Sigid looked at me as if I'd eaten some very questionable mushrooms myself and was talking nonsense.

"In Nerifir, all sentient creatures born with magic are called fae as opposed to animals who wield no magic and, well... humans." He cast an apologetic glance my way. "Look, the shadow fae are here." He held his left hand in front of his chest, palm down. "Gargoyles, sirens, and others are here, in Above." He placed his right hand, also palm down, just above his left. "And Sky Kingdom is here." He moved his left hand from under the right one to over it. "Three planes of Nerifir," he concluded triumphantly, obviously proud of his explanation.

"So, everyone in Nerifir has magic and can turn to shadows?"

"No, just the shadow fae." He glanced at the sand clock on the wall once again before continuing, "Other fae's magic is different. Sirens have water powers. Gorgonians turn people to stone just by looking at them. Sky fae can control light."

It all sounded too fantastic to believe. Except that I'd witnessed some pretty fantastic things lately.

"And us, humans, have no magic. It's unfair, don't you think?"

He stared at me with his eyes wide open. "But you are the most fantastic beings, Dawn. You have something that's even better than magic. Humans possess the most exquisite ability to feel joy."

"Do you mean that fae can't?"

"The shadow fae cannot."

"We will be able to savor your joy with you," General Oskura had said when taking me to the harness fitting.

"Is this why they put this on me?" I touched a ribbon on my arm. No matter how hard I rubbed it with soap, it still didn't come off. "The tendrils... Do you have them too? Or just the Joy Guardians?"

A shudder ran down my spine at the memory of the tight loops holding me on the table. Sigid glanced down at his arms, but nothing appeared from his smooth, velvety skin.

"It's not allowed to release tendrils in the presence of a Joy Vessel without permission from His Highness," he said. "But yes, we all have them."

I rubbed my upper arms. An uneasy feeling unfurled in my chest like a dark shadow.

"Sigid... What's Prince Rha going to do to me at dinner?"

Upon my mentioning the prince, Sigid's gaze snapped back to the wall clock.

"Are you done with the bath, Dawn? Because we really should be going now."

"Almost." I rubbed some more odorless soap on my shoulders, thinking of a way to get some more information from him. But he jumped to his feet, already on his way to get a towel from a woman passing by with a stack of them.

How could fae be real?

"Are you immortal?" I asked Sigid the moment he returned with a towel for me. "Fae usually are, aren't they?"

He gave me an incredulous look. "Of course not. Immortality

is a curse. Who'd want to remain stuck in the same world forever?"

"So, you can be killed then?"

"That's a sure way to move on to another world." He nodded. "We're more resilient than humans, but a weapon of Nerifir iron is usually very effective at killing a fae, especially if it hits a vital organ or is left in the wound for a while for the iron to poison the blood stream—" he cut himself short, giving me a suspicious glance. "Why do you need to know that?"

I smiled, trying to put him at ease again.

"Don't worry, I'm not planning an assassination. I'm just trying to learn as much as possible about your world. Remember, I didn't ask to come here. The least anyone could do would be to explain things to me, but no one has even told me even how it was possible for us to get here from our world."

"Oh." He rubbed behind his ear. "It's not easy to travel to the human realm from the World of Under. The Joy Guardians had recently discovered an ancient ritual that opens a portal between our worlds. It allows our people to cross the realms as shadows, then bring humans here without a change in time if it's done as a round trip through the same portal."

"This wasn't the first time the portal has been opened, was it?" I prodded a little further. "You've come to our world before."

"Right." He nodded.

My heart leaped in my chest. I knew it. The shadow fae were the ones who had taken Ciana all those years ago.

"Are there more humans here, then? Other than those who came with me?"

"Not in Teneris—" Sigid was interrupted by the melodious clinking of the wall clock.

The glass labyrinth rotated with a series of sounds, sending Sigid into a frenzy.

"We need to go." He opened the towel, urging me to get out of the water. "Quickly, please. We can't possibly make the prince wait."

I didn't care about the prince waiting, but I didn't want to get Sigid in trouble. He'd been honest and forthcoming with me, and I'd actually enjoyed his company.

"Fine," I sighed, getting out of the pool and stepping into the towel. "Let's not try the royal patience then."

Eight

DAWN

"All right, here we are." Sigid blew out a breath.

He seemed nervous, leading me to a set of wide double doors decorated with geometric designs made from pieces of hammered metal.

Two guards stood on each side of the doors. As we approached, they crossed their long, curved swords in front of us, blocking our way.

"The Joy Vessel is here by Prince Rha's invitation," Sigid announced.

The guards gave me a once-over before withdrawing their swords and opening the doors. The moment I stepped over the threshold, the doors silently closed behind me, leaving Sigid outside.

"Wait." I shoved both hands against the metal relief of the doors.

Then, an appetizing aroma reached my nostrils, making my stomach spasm. I hadn't eaten since that tasteless breakfast before the harness fitting. At this point, I felt like I could eat the prince himself, with or without truffles. The hunger didn't ease the trepidation buzzing inside me, but it gave me the courage to turn around.

The room was long and spacious. In addition to the glow coming from the ceiling beams, tall candles in the pyramid-shaped holders illuminated the space.

Prince Rha reclined in a pile of cushions that were artfully arranged on a wide, low platform between two huge, shuttered windows. Two men on either side of the platform fanned him with feather fans on long handles. Dressed in a long flowing skirt of midnight blue, his chest jewelry glistening in the candlelight, the prince presented a truly regal picture.

"Good morning," he greeted me.

I did not like the guy. I had good reasons to hate him. But my breath hitched at the sight of him. Like a black panther resting in a tree, his posture held that quiet, confident power that often proved far stronger and was more appealing than a loud bravado.

"Um...hi," I squeezed out.

I knew very little about the man who held my freedom in his hands and found myself intrigued, wishing to learn more about the ruler of Teneris. The realization unsettled me. I far preferred my initial feelings of dislike and resentment toward him.

"Join me for dinner." With an elegant hand gesture, the prince invited me to the long, low table that stretched between him and a floor cushion where the prince pointed for me to sit.

I smoothed my sweaty palms down the long skirt of my simple beige dress that Sigid had sourced for me, then took a few hesitant steps forward. The wonderful aroma of the food laid out on the table lured me in.

Shocked, I realized the prince had somehow gotten everything on the order I'd so haughtily placed with him earlier. Fresh sliced tomatoes were arranged in a circle with cheese and sprinkled with oil and herbs. Peeled prawns with their tails intact hung over the rim of a wide glass filled with greens and drizzled with red sauce. Filet mignon lay next to a generous scoop of mashed potatoes. I had no way of telling whether the potatoes contained any truffles, but they looked great and smelled amazing.

"You got it all," I said in bewilderment.

"Some things had to be substituted with local ingredients," the prince admitted. "But I hope the taste is still to your liking."

Among the plates on the table stood a large dish covered with a tall, silver dome that looked like it might contain an entire birthday cake.

"How did you even know what all these dishes were?" I inched closer to the table but didn't sit down yet.

It felt off, making me suspicious. Weren't we in a magical world here, in a different dimension, in a brand new to humans plane of existence? Where did the fae hear about caprese salad from, for example? Maybe the entire table was just an illusion, created by their magic.

"Teneris has recently acquired a chef skilled in cooking for Joy Vessels," the prince explained. "Besides, the human world and Nerifir aren't as different as you may think. A long while ago, both were one and the same, before the River of Mists flowed between them, breaking the worlds apart. We still are able to source most of the ingredients here." He gestured at the table again. "Go ahead, take a seat, Sweet One."

There was a lot of food here. It could easily feed all four of us in the room and then some. Though, there was only one place setting on my end of the table.

My stomach rumbled, urging me to forgo any doubt and just stuff it with all this delicious goodness. But my mind remained cautious.

"Am I the only one eating?"

"Yes," the prince replied.

"How about you?"

"I've already eaten."

"When?"

"At midnight."

I made a quick calculation in my head. "That was seven hours ago. Aren't you hungry again?"

"No. Unlike humans, we only require one meal a night."

"And only at midnight?"

"Yes."

"What do you do during the day?"

"We sleep."

I'd gathered that much since everything seemed to happen at night around here.

"Why?"

If my barrage of questions annoyed the prince, he didn't show it, explaining patiently, "Night is a far more agreeable time to stay awake."

Gathering his long legs under him, he rose from his silk cushions. The men on each side of him moved their fans away as he descended the platform and sauntered my way. He moved with feline grace, stepping softly in his short black boots. The high side slit of his skirt parted, displaying one long, muscular leg. A man wearing a skirt had never looked more attractive.

Alarmed by the direction my thoughts were taking, I tore my gaze away from the prince's thigh and stared at my hands instead.

"You must be hungry," he said softly, standing just a step away from me. "You haven't eaten anything since breakfast. I made sure of it."

Resentment flared in my chest anew, and I desperately clung to it to distract myself from the view of his wide bejeweled chest and the strip of bare skin stretched over the well-defined abs of his midsection.

"You starved me on purpose," I stated flatly.

"Starved? The Head Keeper's advice was not to feed you anything before dinner so as not to spoil your enjoyment of the meal. Did that lead to starvation?"

There was not a drop of sarcasm in his voice. If it were, I would've taken it as an invitation to snap back. But the genuine concern in his words sounded almost comical, like he really believed I could die from skipping lunch.

"Why is my enjoyment of the meal so important to you?" I asked in turn. "Is it because you want to *savor* some of it too?"

"With your permission, yes," he replied.

Black wisps curled out of his upper arms. They spiraled through the air, braiding themselves into the long tendrils.

I swallowed hard. No matter how much I tried to prepare myself for this, the sight of the black smoke snakes was terrifying. What I did not expect was Prince Rha talking about my permission.

Did I hear him right?

"Will you really not touch me without my permission? Don't we all belong to you already? Isn't that why you stole us in the first place?"

"Joy cannot be stolen," he replied. "If a Vessel is forced, their joy dies. It can only be shared willingly."

That made a lot of sense. Still, unease pricked along my spine as I kept my eyes on the black, flexible appendages that curled around his arms and snaked from behind his back.

"What happens to the unwilling Vessels?"

"Why resist?" he murmured. "Most humans from your group have accepted their purpose already."

"Have they?" I squinted at him suspiciously.

"Why would they not? As my Joy Vessels, they're taken care of, provided with food, shelter, and clothing. Their senses will be stimulated to experience joy and pleasure. All they have to do is let us experience it with them."

I hugged my arms, covering the golden rosettes on the ribbons with my hands. "Why can't you feel it yourselves?"

Probably in response to my defensive stance, his tendrils relaxed a bit. They were no longer reaching for me, which calmed down my nerves a little.

"Shadow fae weren't created the same way as other dwellers of Nerifir," he explained.

"What makes you so special?"

"We were never meant to be people. At the beginning, the World of Under wasn't even supposed to be another plane of existence. It was a dark, isolated place where the souls of the undeserving landed after death before earning their passage to the afterlife. The World of Under was guarded by shadows—chaotic, tumultuous, and wild. Until the First Priestess of Joy arrived, born of night. She brought us together, let us experience pleasure, and built the kingdom with us."

"The Alveari Kingdom." I remembered the name.

"Yes. Today, it is governed by Queen Abeille, my mother. We have come a long way from the shadows of the past. We've gained physical bodies, skills, and the ability to reproduce. But the highest emotions of joy and pleasure are still unavailable to us."

"Why is that?"

"Because euphoria, joy, and pleasure all come from the divine. But my people are not meant to come close to the gods. The World of Under is the farthest from them."

Whether the story of the shadow fae's origin was true or simply a myth, their lot in life didn't seem fair.

"So, you're saying that humans are closer to your gods than you are?" I wondered.

"You're allowed to experience the highest of joy, my dear. Joy is a blessing bestowed by the divine. So yes, you are closer to the gods than we are."

I eyed his tendrils that undulated slightly, hanging from his arms like tight, flexible ropes.

"What exactly do you want with me, Rha? Do you want to find out what joy is?"

To my surprise, he shook his head. "I know what joy is. I've felt it before."

"But you just said you're incapable of that."

"On our own, we can't experience it. We can only feel such emotions through someone else or through the Joy Source in the temple where the Guardians have been collecting it for many millennia."

"They collect joy?" My brain was swelling with so much to absorb. "How is that even possible?" Then, I answered my own question, "Let me guess. Magic?"

Why not? In the kingdom where people dissolved into shadows, why not have joy collected and stored in a jar somewhere?

"Yes, magic," he confirmed. "Joy used to be collected from the fae from Above ever since our kingdom first came into existence."

"Have you been kidnapping sirens, werewolves, and such?"

"Well, no one would come to the World of Under willingly. So..." He shrugged, an uncharacteristically casual gesture for his royal persona.

"So, you've been stealing people for ages."

"Yes," he admitted simply, without trying to justify or excuse it.

I stared at him in disbelief. "You've been kidnapping people, then stealing their joy."

"*Sharing* into it," he corrected, as if that made any difference. "Joy is a necessity in everyone's life. It balances sorrow."

I crossed my arms over my chest.

"And how has it been working out for you with all the abductions?"

His smooth brow furrowed. "The World Above has sealed our shadow tunnels. As did Sky Kingdom. We have never been welcomed anywhere in Nerifir, but now we're physically unable to travel to Above."

"Is that why you switched to abducting humans instead?"

Once again, he shamelessly admitted, "Yes."

"Is that your new plan now? Keep hauling my people over here daily?"

"No. Traveling to your world is not that simple. The River of Mists that connects Nerifir with the human realm doesn't stream through Alveari Kingdom. Using the ancient magic of our gods,

Joy Guardians opened a portal to connect to the river, which in turn took us to your world and back."

And also turned my entire life upside down.

I sighed. "You feel absolutely no remorse over what you've done, do you?"

"Remorse?" He seemed shocked. "Over what? Joy Vessels have a far better life here than anywhere else. Nothing is required of them, and every effort is made to keep them happy. Whatever you'll ask for, I will do my best to deliver."

He flicked his wrist at the lavishly set table, as if a fancy meal could make up for everything that his soldiers had done to me and my family while following his orders. Anger dowsed my hunger.

"You kidnapped me. You killed my father. And now, you expect me to just happily eat here with you? Well, I've got news for you, *Your Highness*. I've got no joy to share with you. You'll get nothing from me. You might as well send me back."

He heaved a long breath, folding his arms across his broad, bejeweled chest.

"I'm sorry about your father. I really am. I didn't wish for that to happen."

"And yet, he's dead." I bit down on my lip to stop it from trembling and squeezed my hands into fists.

He took a step toward the table. "Sadly, I cannot bring your father back. But I want to help you deal with your loss."

"I don't need your help." I hugged myself again, shrinking away from him.

He lifted the high dome from the large serving platter that I'd assumed held a cake. Instead, a dark sphere rested on it.

A head?

"What the fuck is this?" I muttered, backing away on shaking legs.

It was a severed head of a shadow fae. Its pointy ears tipped backwards. The eyes and the mouth were closed. The long, braided hair was wound around the stump of the neck like spaghetti noodles around a fork.

The mental comparison to food made me gag. But the illusion was that much stronger due to the black smoke rising from the dead head like steam. The wisps of smoke appeared to lift the particles of the skin, flesh, and hair in some bizarre decomposition process, leaving gaping holes in the flesh.

My stomach churned. Thankfully, it was completely empty. Otherwise, I'd throw up all over Prince Rha's fancy skirt and fine jewels.

"It's the head of the man who killed your father," he explained calmly, as if presenting me with a head of cabbage he grew in one of his beautiful indoor gardens. "Your father is now avenged."

The pungent stench of fresh blood reached me, mingling with the aroma of the food. Nausea rose to my throat, unstoppable.

"I've got to get out of here…"

Gripping my throat with my hand, I shoved the doors open and ran.

Nine

RHA

I kept holding the silver lid over the platter with Serus's severed head. The Joy Vessel had fled, leaving me stunned.

There were two ways I'd envisioned this moment would go. Either the human would cry from gratitude. Or she would smile, filled with gratitude. Either way, she'd be grateful.

Now, it didn't seem like she was.

Humans were still largely unknown creatures, unpredictable in their emotions. But I expected this Joy Vessel to experience some relief from her sorrow after seeing her father's death avenged.

Instead, she was clearly upset.

Why?

The question nagged at me. It buzzed in my head like an annoying fly and would likely deprive me of sleep if I went to bed now.

I couldn't go to bed. I needed answers.

I needed them now.

And I was going to get them.

Tossing the lid aside, I stormed out of the room and took a

course toward the human's bedroom. It was farther from my rooms than the *sarai* of Joy Vessels. On the way, my confusion had plenty of time to grow into irritation. By the time I shoved a hand against her door, the irritation spiked into anger.

"Why?" I demanded, as the door to her room flew open.

The human squeaked in shock at my sudden intrusion but recovered quickly.

She hiked up her chin, as if accepting a challenge. "Why what?"

I realized I had so many more questions than just one.

Why aren't you grateful?

Why don't you feel relieved?

Why did my gift upset you?

And why is my disappointment so great now?

Why was I looking forward to our dinner with so much anticipation?

"Why did you run away?" I asked instead.

Her weird, mismatched eyes opened wide, unsettling like always. But I didn't look away. I had to see her face to read her expression. I longed to understand her.

"What did I do wrong?" I insisted, reining in my anger.

She made a strangled sound, as if choking on her own breath. "You really have no idea?"

"I presented you with the head of your enemy. It's an honorable gesture."

"Best present ever." Her voice was flat, her pale skin turning even paler.

"Do you not appreciate it? Revenge should bring satisfaction. It eases the pain of loss. A life paid for a life. It creates balance."

Balance was the most important state of mind. It helped reach the highest feelings my kind were capable of—contentment and satisfaction.

Her expression turned somber. She gazed at me intently, as if trying to understand me too. I held still under her scrutiny, even as the look from her mismatched eyes made my skin crawl with unease. Nothing about this woman seemed balanced—neither her appearance, nor emotions.

"Two wrongs don't make it right, Rha," she finally said.

Her use of my name without the title or honorifics was highly disrespectful, but I didn't correct her. She didn't sound like she was mocking me, and I had a more important thing to focus on—this conversation.

"Two deaths don't create a life," she continued. "Killing my father's murderer will not bring my dad back."

"But what would lessen the pain of loss for you?"

Her chin trembled, and her eyes turned glossy with welling tears. She broke our eye contact, glancing aside.

"Right now, it feels like nothing will, but they say time heals all wounds. So..." She snapped her gaze back at me, as if spurred by a sudden thought. "If you really want to make it better, let me go. Release us. Let me and my friends go back home."

That could never happen, of course. But it shocked me that for a fraction of a second, I actually wished there was a way to fulfill her request, just so I could no longer see her tear-filled eyes.

"I'm afraid it's impossible."

"Why not?" she insisted, her cheeks flushed with energy from the idea. "Whatever you did to get us here, do it in reverse. Have the Joy Guardians open another portal."

"Only the queen can give that order."

"Ask her, then. She is your mother, isn't she?"

The sweet little Joy Vessel was clearly under the impression that being the queen's son meant having access to that woman's favor. How badly she was mistaken.

"I cannot send you back," I stated. "It requires strong magic to open a portal and then to keep it open long enough for a person to pass through. The power that Joy Guardians used for that is finite. And for now, it has all been used."

"How can it be 'used'? Isn't magic supposed to be...well, all-powerful? Can't they make some more of it?"

It intrigued me how much her knowledge of the world differed from my own.

"Do you know so little about magic?" I asked.

She blew out her breath, running a hand over her face.

"I'm still trying to wrap my mind around the fact that magic even exists. Honestly, it'd be so much easier if it turned out I was just dreaming about you and all of this..." She waved a hand around the room. "It's just too hard to absorb it all, you know?"

She looked lost and more vulnerable than ever. My heart pinched with compassion. It couldn't be easy to be uprooted like that, especially since she likely hadn't even been aware of Nerifir before coming here.

"I take it humans don't know about the existence of other worlds?" I asked.

"No. Most of us are just happy to stay in our own little bubble, thinking our kind is the only one in the Universe, utterly unique and unmatched."

"There is a certain satisfaction in ignorance," I agreed. "Learning new things carries a risk of upsetting one's view of the world and consequently one's state of mind."

She gave me a puzzled look, like I was a source of questions to her, the way she had become to me.

"What's your name?" I could no longer think of her as simply a Joy Vessel. She'd become unique to me, different from the rest.

"I'm Dawn."

The sound of that word scraped against my nerves like metal on glass. "Really?"

She tilted her head. "Yes. Why?"

Her name was horrible. Almost as bad as her eyes. It represented that unpleasant time of day when the sun was about to rise and start scorching the black sands of the desert with punishing heat.

She kept staring at me, expecting an answer, but I could no longer hold back my curiosity.

"What's wrong with your eyes?" I finally asked.

She blinked. "My eyes?"

"They don't match. Are you sick?"

"Oh, that..." She brushed a strand of hair away from her face. "No. It's not a sickness. Just a condition. It's called heterochromia. It's harmless, in my case anyway."

"So, there is no cure?" I tried to conceal my disappointment.

The more time I spent with her, the more stimulating I found her company. But I would prefer not to be continuously unbalanced by her appearance.

She gave me an unimpressed look.

"There is no need for a cure. The color of my eyes doesn't bother me. Does it bother you?"

I sensed a challenge in her voice, feeling that an honest answer might not be well received by her. Yet I chose to be honest, anyway.

"It's unsettling. Any imbalance in the world is unnerving, but a visual one is the most apparent."

Her forehead furrowed. She crossed her arms over her chest defensively. Yet she looked more puzzled than angry.

"What is it with you and the need to *balance* everything?"

"Contentment is the highest positive emotion that shadow fae are capable of," I explained. "There is a feeling of satisfaction in achieving balance and symmetry."

"I see. So, you find my 'asymmetrical' eyes offensive? You know what?" She plopped on her bed, looking exhausted. "You don't have to look at me. You don't even have to be here. Why did you even invite me for dinner if all you wanted to do was to present me with the decomposing head?" A shudder ran across her shoulders.

Her mentioning the dinner reminded me she still hadn't eaten anything. My intentions were to make this morning as pleasant as possible for her, but now she risked going to bed hungry.

"You have to eat," I said. "Please, return to the dining room with me. I'll order Serus's head removed from the table if it offends you."

I shouldn't have mentioned the head. She shuddered again, her expression closing off completely.

"Thanks, but I'll pass." She bent down and untied the straps of her sandals, then kicked them off her feet. "Can you leave, please? I'll just go to bed and hope once again that all of this will disappear like a bad dream when I wake up."

STARLIGHT, my camel, walked steadily along the foothills of the city. She was significantly smaller than the pack camels used by caravan merchants, which made her perfect for one rider. I also appreciated Starlight for her calm disposition and steady gait. Her unusual white fur made her stand out against the black sand of the desert at night, which would make me an easy target in a battle against raiders from the desert. But we weren't going into a battle, just on a short ride out of the city.

I steered Starlight around the slanted wall of Teneris. The above ground part of the city stretched wide and long. It would take us days to ride along its entire circumference, which the city guards did regularly.

Oskura and I were surveying only a section of it tonight. I just wished to feel the cooling air of the desert on my skin. Starlight's steady gait always helped me think. Since last morning, however, all my thoughts had been going in the same direction, and the ride hadn't helped me figure out why.

"Have you ever met someone disturbing to look at?" I asked Oskura. "Yet you couldn't get them out of your head to the point that the only thing you can think about is your desire to see them again?"

Oskura glanced at me sideways from under the cover over her head. The night breeze was light, but it brought a steady stream of fine dust with it. Both my general and I had the top layer of our garments pinned over our heads for protection from the sand.

"Sure," she said. "Remember that ugly slimy lizard I stepped on during our patrol once? It whipped its tail around my leg, burning me with its toxic slime. The lizard was pretty gross to look at, I'd say. And yes, I couldn't stop thinking about it as I lay burning with fever for days, waiting for the poison to work its way out of my leg. I never stopped wishing to see that bastard again so that I could kill it."

Not quite what I meant, though perfectly in character for my general.

"But what if it wasn't a lizard, but a person? And she wasn't gross or slimy, but just...difficult to look at, and—"

"And instead of whipping you with a slimy tail, she slapped you with her hand?" Oskura finished for me, giving me a knowing look.

I rolled back my shoulders under her stare.

"Have I become that obvious?"

She shrugged. "You've been more silent than usual, Your Highness. And the two times you spoke to me this evening were both about that disorderly Joy Vessel. Also, she's the only human whose name you cared to learn."

I realized I hadn't even thought about asking for the names of the others.

"We've wronged her, Oskura, and I can't figure out how to fix it."

"Time rights all wrongs. She just needs time to heal."

Wise words. Only they failed to put my concerns to rest. How much time did Dawn need to adapt to her new life in Alveari Kingdom? I hoped it wasn't forever because every second of her unhappiness brought my feelings into turmoil that I couldn't quiet.

"What if she never recovers?"

Oskura rubbed her chest through her beaded armor. "She is not the only Joy Vessel you have. There are plenty of others in your *sarai* that are far more agreeable than her. I'd say, give them all a chance before choosing a favorite. You may develop a greater preference for someone else's joy."

That was the most puzzling thing—I hadn't even tasted Dawn's joy yet. I longed to feel it. But more than that, I wished for her to have joy in the first place.

Following the curve of the city, we slowly circled back to the main gate. The moment it came into view, I knew something was wrong. A tight group of guards gathered a few paces away from the gate. More of my warriors blocked the access to the city in a defensive formation, their weapons drawn and ready.

"Something is happening there," Oskura muttered, drawing one of her swords. She made her camel move faster, hurrying toward the gate.

As fast as Starlight could be if needed, it wasn't fast enough for me. I had to be at the gate now.

With a long breath in, I willed my body to dissolve into wisps of shadows. By the time I breathed out, I was at the gate—my body, my clothes, and my weapons solidifying into their shapes once again.

A bout of nausea hit my stomach. The distance was too great to travel as a shadow to leave me unaffected. The transformation left me disoriented and weak. My head was spinning, blending the faces of the city guards into a blur.

I blinked, rooting my feet into the desert floor. I'd trained all my life to transform and recover quickly. By now, I was able to successfully do it everywhere, even in battle. I just needed a moment to ground myself for the world to turn upright again.

"What's going on?" I asked the leader of the guards on duty.

"Your Highness." He bowed his head. "A desert dweller tried to enter the city with a merchant caravan. But we apprehended him."

"Just one man?"

Desert dwellers were a nuisance. Before Teneris became mine, they had grown to think of the city as their own. Many refused to bend to my rules and left, but they never abandoned organizing raids on the city to steal supplies and terrorize my people.

One man wasn't much of a concern, however. Unless he was a spy or an assassin on a mission, a part of a bigger plan.

"He's dead!" someone yelled from the crowd of guards.

"Dead?"

The guards stepped aside, allowing me to see the man on the ground. His throat was slit wide open. A black dagger of Nerifir iron lay next to his hand. Dark blood gushed from his wound, the edges of the cut flesh already fraying with shadows of decomposition.

The man was certainly dead. The question was *why?*

"Who did this?" I cast a glance around the circle of somber faces of the guards.

"He did it himself, Your Highness," one of them replied.

"Grabbed the knife and slit his own throat before we could stop him," another one added.

"Why would he do that?" I pondered.

The first guard rubbed his neck, looking uneasy. "I told him we'll have to question him."

"And I said that Your Highness would want to speak to him too," the other guard said. "That's when he pulled out the knife."

I saw confusion on their faces, not guilt. They must be telling the truth, puzzled by it like I was.

Oskura climbed down from her camel. Starlight had come with her.

"Looks like he chose death over the chance of meeting you, my prince," my general pointed out.

I knew I wasn't favored by desert dwellers, but none of them had killed themselves before just to avoid seeing me.

Oskura kneeled by the decomposing corpse. "Do you know this man, Your Highness?"

I looked closely at the dead body. His hair had been cut to shoulder length, like that of Joy Guardians. But desert dwellers often cut their hair, and some even shaved their heads, not bothering with braids or following the court fashion. His appearance bore no other signs of a Joy Guardian, however. He was dressed in rags and wild animal skins like a desert thug of the lowest class that he probably belonged to.

There was nothing particularly threatening about the man. Yet his behavior demanded an explanation.

When Oskura lifted the blood-stained dagger to examine it, I spotted something in the sand underneath.

"What is that?" I crouched as she scooped out a cluster of succulent yellow flowers using the tip of the blade. Their thick stem was crushed, with some flowers torn or missing.

"It's a golden hyacinth." Oskura flinched, tossing the cursed plant away with the blade, without touching it.

The juice of the predatory flower had been used in the assassination plot against the queen that ended up taking my father's life. Since then, Queen Abeille had forbidden to plant, harvest, or sell the golden hyacinth or to use its juice in any form.

There was no place for it in my city.

"Did he bring it with him?" I questioned the guards, only no one knew the answer. They just shook their heads and shrugged apologetically.

"It may've been here before him," Oskura offered.

The golden hyacinth grew wild in the desert. No number of royal orders could stop that. It could've been growing nearby and brought here on the hoof of a horse or the foot of a camel. The thug didn't necessarily pose a threat to Teneris.

Yet my skin pricked with warning. Dropping the cover from my head, I strained my hearing and scanned the horizon for any signs of danger.

Oskura stood next to me.

"If he planned an assassination," she said quietly, "he would've sought a meeting with you, not killed himself at the prospect of one."

Unless it wasn't me who he'd been after.

I gritted my teeth. Had I gotten here earlier, would I've been able to stop him from slashing his own throat? Probably not. Still, I wished Starlight had been just a little bit faster on our way back.

"He knew I had the means to get the truth out of him. Or maybe he was also creating a distraction." I turned to the leader of the guards. "Where is the caravan that this man arrived with?"

"In the city, Your Highness. The owner is well known to us. She's a widely respected woman."

"I need to talk to her and to everyone who accompanied her."

"Yes, Your Highness."

"I want more guards at the *sarai*," I said to Oskura. "More Joy Vessel Keepers too."

She tilted her head. "Should we move Dawn there? She's still in isolation."

What I really wanted was to move that particular Joy Vessel to my private rooms, to keep her safe and sound underground. Maybe then, this maddening vibration of worry about her would ease in my chest.

But would that be wise? Or would it feed the affliction I couldn't even identify myself?

Something about Dawn was off center, and it wasn't just her appearance. Her anger came from dissatisfaction and imbalance that I had a feeling might run deeper than the sadness from being taken away from her home or even from the death of her father. Any imbalance unnerved me, urging me to fix it.

Oskura arched an eyebrow. "You really want her as your favorite?"

That couldn't be the reason. The purpose of favorites was to enjoy them. Dawn had said it herself—she didn't have much joy to give. I couldn't develop an addiction to something I hadn't even tasted yet.

I just wanted to keep her safe.

"No, but put Dawn together with the rest," I said. "We'll improve the security for all Joy Vessels in the *sarai*."

Addiction or not, it was best to stay away from that woman for a while. My general was right. I should take the chance to get to know the others.

DAWN

Atray slid under my door a few minutes after Prince Rha had left my room that morning. I'd already brushed my teeth, getting ready to go to bed. But at the smell of food, hunger returned with a vengeance.

I ate it all—the prawns, the steak with the fancy potatoes, and the dessert, licking the spoon after finishing the crème brûlée. The joy from eating all this food was all mine since Prince Rha wasn't here to "share" it. But it didn't bring me the satisfaction I expected.

Rha must be disappointed that our dinner didn't go as he'd planned. It might've been better for me if it went more smoothly. Maybe I should've worked on gaining his favor, then he'd help me locate Ciana or even find a way to get us all back home.

I sighed. Did I blow my chance? Or had I even had a chance to begin with?

Apparently, the prince found my appearance "unsettling." With seventeen other more "symmetrical" people in his possession, it was safe to assume I'd never see the prince one-on-one ever again.

That thought shouldn't have upset me. But I realized I would've liked a chance to talk to him again, even if our opinions differed.

He had a calm, *balanced* way of explaining things with reason and patience. He'd been forthcoming and seemed genuine in his answers. And he had that smooth, deep voice that soothed my frazzled nerves, making a conversation with him rather enjoyable, despite the difficult topics we had discussed.

I wished I could ask him more questions. Too bad another dinner invitation was highly unlikely after this morning. My best bet now would be to question Sigid when I saw him again. I also had to find Elaine and Melanie. Everyone had assured me that the Joy Vessels were well taken care of, but I needed to see them to believe it.

I shoved the tray with the empty dishes back under the door, then brushed my teeth again. As I lay in bed, the image of the dead head rose in my mind, black smoke rising from it like steam from a roast. My stomach spasmed with disgust, threatening to expel the delicious dinner I'd just had.

Yet the prince seemed to honestly believe this was an excellent idea for a present. And while talking with him, I made an effort to see it through his eyes.

This was a different world. With different customs. Rha thought he was doing me a favor by beheading one of his men to avenge my dad.

He even said he tried to ease my suffering, as if my feelings somehow mattered to him.

Except that it'd changed nothing. The death of his murderer didn't bring my dad back. And now, there were two dead people instead of one.

The balance that Prince Rha was striving for just didn't exist.

WITHOUT A CLOCK or a window in my room, I had no idea what time it was when I woke up. My sleep cycle had been all over the place here, which added to the lingering feeling of being constantly disoriented.

Was it evening or morning?

Time for dinner or breakfast?

It didn't help that the shadow fae functioned on a reversed cycle to what I was used to. They stayed awake during the night and slept during the day.

The breakfast tray wasn't there, however. I got up and got dressed in the clothes I wore yesterday—a long beige dress made from light, cotton-like material, a pair of underwear, and a soft comfortable bra. The shadow fae wore no clothes above their waists, but it was nice of them to have those for someone like me who would rather not run around topless.

As I was fixing the straps of my flat-sole sandals around my ankles, a knock on the door came.

"Dawn? Are you awake?" Sigid called from behind the door softly.

"Yes. Awake and fully dressed. Come in."

The door opened, and Sigid poked his head in. "Did you sleep well?"

As he entered, I slowly backed away to the far wall. Sigid's tendrils were out. All six of them hung limply, almost reaching the floor. A wide, dark-metal clip circled each tendril at the base, close to his skin.

I swallowed hard, my throat turning dry at the sight of them. "I thought you weren't allowed to release those when humans were around."

"Right." His left ear twitched, and he scratched behind it. "But I was just sworn in as a Joy Vessel Keeper earlier this evening," he announced proudly. "All Keepers have their tendrils clipped."

"What does that mean?"

"The Nerifir iron in the clips disables our magic. We can't use the tendrils." He flicked a finger against one of the clips with a burst of red sparks from the metal.

"That...doesn't sound right. And you agreed to that?"

He nodded. "It's a great honor to work in the *sarai* with Joy Vessels. The clips are just a minor inconvenience. Their use has a good reason behind it. The Keepers have unrestricted access to the Joy Vessels. Some may be tempted to take advantage of that. It's best to eliminate the temptation from the start. This way, we also can no longer transform into shadows, which further puts the Joy Vessels at ease. Most of you seem to find our transitions unnerving."

I definitely was one of those who found their dissolving into shadows unsettling. Still, having Sigid's natural abilities restricted because of that didn't seem fair.

He looked proud of his new status, however.

"You no longer need to feel frightened of me, Dawn," he assured me in an upbeat voice. "Come, I'll take you to the *sarai*, to your friends."

That made me perk up at once.

"Really? I can see them? Is my punishment over then?"

"Prince Rha wants you to move in with the rest."

"Does he now?" I wondered what had changed his mind. But I didn't wonder for long. Whatever it was, it allowed me to see Elaine and Melanie again, and that was all that mattered. I looked around for my things, then realized I had no things to pack or to take with me other than the clothes I was wearing. "Let's go then."

Sigid led me out of the room and down the corridor.

"So, am I free to go anywhere I want now? Or do I need you to accompany me everywhere?" I asked.

"You can go anywhere inside the palace, as long as you let the guards or the Keepers know. If you wish to go out into the city, you'll have to be accompanied by guards and at least one of the Keepers."

"Do I need that many people to keep me from running away?"

He shook his head. "There is nowhere to run past the city, Dawn. The desert is murderous during the day. And even at night, you wouldn't get far on your own. You need the guards to keep you safe in the city, not to stop you from running away."

"To keep me safe from what?"

"From being stolen," he said matter-of-factly. "Joy Vessels are rare and precious."

"How many times can a person possibly be stolen?" I exhaled a humorless laugh.

Sigid didn't smile. Granted, it was a sad joke, but I'd never seen anyone laugh in this place. Smiles just didn't seem to be a part of the shadow fae collection of expressions.

"Well, you'll be the safest in the *sarai*." He stopped in front of a pair of ornate gates that were guarded by six men on each side.

The guards opened the gates for us without question.

"Welcome to the royal *sarai, Dawn,* the living quarters of the Joy Vessels," Sigid announced.

"So, it's something like a china cabinet? For the *vessels*?" I snorted a laugh.

Once again, Sigid didn't laugh with me. Granted, it was a silly joke. But he didn't even crack a polite smile.

"Something like it, I suppose," he said with a straight face, then gestured for me to enter. "Come on in. All the humans are here already."

We entered a large open garden with an intricate system of fountains and waterfalls in the middle, complete with cushioned seating and loungers in between. Silver moonlight shone between the beams crisscrossing the open space high above the garden like the roof of a gazebo. The golden light of glowing columns positioned evenly along the mosaic paths illuminated the place.

Bamboo lattices with pale vines lined the walls of the buildings that surrounded us. The walls rose up two stories high and had balconies with vines and flowers draped over the railings.

Large, colorful moths noiselessly glided between the vines and the flowers. Their delicate wings fluttered fast, spreading a shimmer in the air.

"What a gorgeous place this is!" I couldn't hold back the admiration.

"Joy Vessels are treasured in Teneris," Sigid said. "The *sarai* is well-maintained to keep them happy."

I spotted my sister in the lounger by one of the fountains the moment she saw me.

"Dawn!" She jumped from her seat and rushed to me. "Are they releasing you from jail? Or is it some kind of trick?" She glowered at Sigid.

"Not a trick. I can stay here now. Right?" I confirmed with Sigid, and he nodded. "See? I don't have to go back." I gave her a hug. "How have you been?"

She freed herself from my arms.

"Oh, it's horrible, Dawn. They say we're to stay here forever. No one is allowed to leave—" She threw another glare at Sigid. "Hey, can we have some privacy here?"

"Certainly." He stepped back with a bow. "Breakfast will be served soon."

"Oh, take your breakfast and shove it," Melanie hissed at his back.

Taking me under my arm, she led me to the loungers by the fountain.

"Dawn! You're back!" Elaine bent over the rail of a balcony on the second floor. "Wait. I'll be right there." She disappeared into the room for a minute, then ran out from an arched doorway on the main floor.

Both Melanie and Elaine were dressed in long, silky tunics, like all the other women lounging around the fountains and waterfalls. Men also wore the same tunic-dresses. Though at least one of them, a stout man with a rope-belt tied under his solid potbelly, had on a pair of pants under his tunic.

"They released you!" Elaine flung herself into my arms.

She still wore her fuzzy brown sweater, hugging it around herself like usual despite the balmy night. The sweater felt even fuzzier and smelled as it must've been recently washed.

I pressed her to my chest tightly. It felt like hugging a warm, fuzzy teddy bear. Comfort and relief spread through me, warming my heart.

"Are you okay?" I asked my best friend. "How has it been?"

"We're good, everything considered—" She cut herself short, staring at the black ribbons of the harness around my arms. "They did it to you too?"

"And to you?" I couldn't see her arms inside the sweater but spotted a sliver of black velvet around her neck.

She nodded quietly. "Most have been talked into getting it. Promised all possible kinds of fine things."

Melanie's arms remained ribbon-free, however.

"What?" She jerked her chin up, catching my questioning stare. "I didn't let them touch me."

Elaine giggled. "She kicked a Joy Guardian in the shin so hard, he howled."

"You all should've put up more of a fight." Melanie shrugged. "Now, you're stuck with those ugly black things on your skin."

"I didn't know the harness was optional," I replied.

In my case, it certainly hadn't been. General Oskura had escorted me to the fitting personally. And that woman didn't look like someone who could be stopped by a kick in the shin. Neither did the Joy Guardians when they tied me to the table. But in my case, the procedure was presented as a punishment. I was not "talked into it."

"You're just too weak, Dawn," Melanie stated. "Always have been. And now, you have those black ugly things on you for the rest of your life. You'll have to cover them up like tattoos every time you go for a job interview."

In my line of work, I went to auditions, not interviews, but I didn't correct her. Did it even matter now? When I wasn't sure if I would ever get a chance to go to either one again.

"Do you think we'll ever go back?" I asked.

Melanie pressed her mouth into a thin line, determination shining in her eyes.

"Yes, I very much intend to go back. I have a lot waiting for me at home. My entire career depends on my presentation next week. And I'm certainly not giving my manager an excuse to fire me for absence. She already hates my guts and will use every opportunity to get rid of me. And Dad, you know... His tax payment is due and..." She blinked, her hard expression wavering, but only for a second. With a short breath in, her voice strengthened once again. "I need to go back, Dawn. I need to settle his affairs. There is no one else to look after that but me."

She was right. My practical, responsible older sister was always right.

I stared down at my hands folded in my lap, thinking back to the conversation I had with the prince last morning.

"Rha said the portal they used to bring us here is now closed."

"Rha?" Elaine squinted at me through her glasses. "Since when are you on a first-name basis with the crown prince?"

Melanie brushed her aside, leaning closer to me. "You spoke to the prince, Dawn? When?"

I nodded. "He...um, tried to have dinner with me yesterday."

"Just you?" Elaine kept peering at me intently.

"Yes."

A new interest sparked in Melanie's expression. "Was it a date or something?"

"No. Of course not. Nothing like that. He...he presented me with the head of the man who killed Dad." My voice dropped.

Melanie gasped. "He did *what?*"

Elaine squeaked in horror, gripping her throat.

"Yeah..." I rubbed my forehead. "That was his idea of justice, or closure, or whatever the heck he thought that was. He found the killer and had him beheaded, then served his head to me quite literally on a silver platter."

Melanie grimaced in disgust. "The man is sick."

Elaine looked like she was about to throw up.

And I...

I thought about the explanation Rha had given me. A life for a life. I stood by what I'd said to him about two wrongs not making it right. I didn't agree with what he did, but I understood why he did it. And I accepted it. I accepted that his intentions weren't evil.

I said none of that out loud, however, afraid it'd sound like I was defending the prince.

"You have to be careful, Dawn," Elaine warned quietly. "We all have to be careful around them. Just because they have been taking care of us doesn't mean they aren't capable of hurting us if it suits them."

"But have you been taken care of?" I asked. "How is life in the *sarai?*"

"Could be better." Melanie made a face, plopping into the closest recliner. She lifted an ornate metal goblet from the edge of the fountain and took a drink. "This is plain water." She lifted the goblet to me. "That's all we've been drinking here. They feed us some tasteless shit three times a day, or a night rather, since we're supposed to stay in our rooms during the day. They even close the sky off with solid shutters from before sunrise until after sunset." She pointed at the opening over the garden where the stars twinkled between the criss-crossed beams. "Like we aren't supposed to see the sun or something."

Elaine sat down on the lounger across from Melanie, pulling me by my hand to sit next to her.

"They brought us new clothes yesterday and asked us a few questions each."

"What kind of questions?"

"Like how we feel about coming to their kingdom," Elaine replied.

Melanie huffed. "I told them exactly how I felt about them and their shitty kingdom. I didn't 'come' here for a visit. I was forcefully brought here. This is forceful confinement, which is a crime."

It was a crime where we came from. But our laws didn't apply here, which made trying to apply them here useless. Our entire system of comprehending life had to be adjusted in order to understand this world.

"But are they treating you well?" I asked.

"The guards can be bossy sometimes," Elaine replied. "But the Keepers are friendly. They seem to try making us comfortable. I asked if I could keep my sweater, and they washed it for me." She stroked down a soft sleeve.

The stout man I'd noticed earlier bent over the fountain pool and splashed some water on his face and neck.

"The assholes didn't give me any pants," he complained. "I had to yell at them to make them find me some."

"I'm surprised they found any, since they don't wear pants themselves," I replied.

"Yeah, well, I'm not running around with my ass bare like they all are around here." He gave me a once-over. "You're the one who punched their head guy, aren't you?" He wiped his wet hand on the side of his tunic before offering it to me. "Hi. I'm Kostya. It's short for Konstantin."

"Hi." I shook his hand. "I slapped the prince, not punched him." For some reason, it felt important to clarify.

He shrugged. "Same difference. What did they do to you for that?"

I realized that there hadn't been much of a punishment for me for assaulting the crown prince of the kingdom. I had spent two days and a night in a room by myself and was fed a lavish dinner. I had the harness put on, but Kostya had one too. His sleeveless tunic left his arms bare, displaying the black shimmering ribbons with golden rosettes just like mine.

"She was kept away from us," Elaine answered instead of me. "This is her first time in the *sarai*."

"Well, great to have you here." Kostya slapped my shoulder,

rather hard. "Keep your hands to yourself from now on. Next time, you may not be so lucky."

With those parting words of wisdom, he sauntered away.

"Yeah, well, you keep your hands to yourself too," I muttered, rubbing my shoulder that ached after his slap.

I stayed with Elaine and Melanie by the fountains. A few other people, men and women, came by to say hi to me. Some had seen me in the lineup in the courtyard and remembered my slapping the prince. Some just saw a new face and came to introduce themselves.

"There seem to be people from all over the world here," I said to Melanie and Elaine between the visits.

"Yep," Melanie agreed. "Kostya is from Russia. Lucia is from the States." She gestured at the redhead who'd said earlier that she'd have sex with shadow fae willingly. Lucia was now stretching on a grass mat on one of the balconies, gracefully bending her voluptuous body in what looked like various yoga poses. "There is a married couple from Lebanon, two girls from China, a man from South Africa, and someone from Croatia, I think. But I can't remember who. It's hard to tell since we're all speaking the same language here."

That was such a weird thing. I still could speak English, only I had to make a mental effort to do so. Speaking the shadow fae language came more naturally now.

"It's like the shadows appeared in several different places simultaneously in our world," Elaine explained. "They grabbed a bunch of people at random, then came back here."

"I think that's exactly how it happened," I agreed. "And it wasn't their first time, either. They've come before."

Elaine glanced at me in understanding. "Ciana? Do you think they got her? The smoke in her bedroom was the shadows, wasn't it?"

A few years ago, I had finally talked to Elaine about my cousin's disappearance, including her complaints about the black smoke beforehand. Clearly, she'd thought about it too and put two and two together.

"I believe they did," I said. "They have more humans in the Alveari Kingdom, but not in Teneris."

Melanie listened to our conversation with heightened attention. "How do you know?"

"I talked to one of the Joy Vessel Keepers," I said.

"The Keepers wouldn't answer our questions about anything like that," Elaine complained. "They said they aren't allowed."

"Well, the guy I talked to wasn't really a Keeper yet," I said. "He was just training to become one. Maybe he didn't get the memo? I want to talk to him again, to get more info about the magical portal they had created between our worlds and about the other humans. I have to find out more about Ciana too."

Elaine sighed. "Let's just hope no one briefs that guy about the Keeper's code of silence before you get a chance to speak with him again."

Worry seized my heart. Sigid had been cautious before. But now, I'd probably never get him to answer any of my questions anymore.

Melanie eagerly shifted on her lounger. "Listen, who needs that Keeper anyway, if you have the prince? Ask him."

I winced. "I don't *have* the prince."

"But he seems to like you."

"Why would he?" I laughed in disbelief. "I slapped him, remember? That's literally the only physical contact we've had."

But my sister wasn't that easily discouraged.

"Yes, and after that, he invited you for a dinner date and presented you with the head of your enemy. The prince is clearly into you. Maybe he likes being slapped?" She mused. "Maybe he has a thing for being dominated? People in a position of power often do, by the way. A former CEO of the company where my friend used to work got busted visiting a dominatrix regularly. She had him wear diapers and spanked him. He was a married father of three, earned millions in his job, and paid some random woman big bucks to degrade him." She wiggled her eyebrows. "Maybe the shadow prince wants you to spank him too?"

I rolled my eyes, trying to ignore her nonsense, but she wouldn't give up.

"Hey, all I'm saying is that if he has a thing for you, we should use it to our advantage. Ask him questions. Get him to talk to you about the portal. Make him open it again. Maybe he'll let us go."

"Do you think I haven't asked him already? He said it's not up to him."

"Well, ask him again. But this time, be a little more like..." She gave me an assessing look. "You know, sweet and sexy and stuff."

I thought about the palace baths and how indifferent everyone seemed to be about nudity, including mine.

"I don't think the prince cares about sexy," I said. "I don't think anyone in this world cares about sex, to be honest. Shadow fae can't experience joy, which probably excludes sexual pleasure for them too. The most positive thing they can feel is something like contentment or satisfaction. They often find it in things like balance and symmetry. Like their art." I pointed at the mosaic around the fountains. "That must be the reason for all these geometrical patterns everywhere."

"How do they reproduce, then, if they don't have sex?" Elaine asked.

Melanie waved a hand at her. "Of course they have sex. They look too much like humans to pollinate like flowers or grow their babies in cocoons."

The gate to the *sarai* opened, letting a group of the Keepers in, flanked by a few palace guards. The Keepers wore similar sandy-green skirts like Sigid, who wasn't with them. Their tendrils were fully extended but clipped, hanging limply down their backs and arms.

"Those black hoses of theirs creep me out." Elaine shuddered.

"What do they want now?" Melanie muttered.

One of the Keepers stepped forward. Unrolling a pale-yellow

scroll in his hands, he started reading names from it. After naming six, including Kostya and Lucia, he stopped.

"The Joy Vessels whose names I've just read, please, come with us," the Keeper said. "His Highness Prince Rha extends his royal invitation for you to join him and his guests for the midnight meal."

Elaine audibly exhaled, likely relieved that her name hadn't been called.

But Kostya eagerly stepped forward. "Fuck yes. Are they finally going to feed me something better than the watery clay they call food in the *sarai?*"

Lucia left her balcony to come down into the gardens.

"What does he want us there for?" she asked the Keepers.

Another man, whose name must be on the list, joined them. "To feed us, I hope, because I won't let them do anything else to me other than that."

"Nothing else will be necessary," the Keeper assured the man.

The guards opened the gates again, and the Keepers escorted the six people out. All six, I noticed, had their harnesses implanted.

Melanie stirred uneasily, rubbing her bare arms. "Dawn, please do whatever it takes to convince the royal asshole to send us back home. Seduce the bastard if that's what it takes. Fuck his brains out. But get us out of here."

"I don't think he's interested in fucking me, Melanie, even if the shadow fae do have sex," I said. "He doesn't even like the way I look. He finds it 'unsettling.' Not that I want anything to do with him, either."

"But we have to go back home somehow. I have a life to return to. I can't waste my time here, living like a lab rat under a lock," she groaned, spearing her fingers through her hair. "*Make him interested.*"

This was not a life I wished to have either, but what could I do about it?

"Believe it or not, I have no power over Prince Rha. And now that we have no business left between us, I don't think he'd ever want to see me again. Look," I pointed at the gates closing. "He didn't even invite me for lunch with the rest of them."

I should be glad that he didn't. I *was* glad, wasn't I? There was absolutely no reason for me to want to see him or talk to him ever again.

The prince's deep voice echoed through my memories. Calm and measured, it always sounded soothing, even when he was angry.

God knew I could use some calm in my mind right now.

Eleven

DAWN

The six people invited to the royal lunch returned a couple of hours later. I'd just settled into a room next to Elaine's. She and I were having a drink of water on my balcony when Kostya strolled into the courtyard. He grunted with satisfaction, petting his belly.

"Finally, a decent meal of roast with all the trimmings, washed down by a pretty good wine." He made his way across the courtyard and disappeared into the building, probably going to his room for a nap, to help him digest all that good stuff he'd just eaten and drunk.

The other people quietly followed him through the gate. A man and a woman chose to stay in the courtyard, joining a small group of women. Lucia made her way to a long cushion by the fountain right under my balcony.

"Are you okay?" Elaine asked her, leaning over the railing.

"Yeah, fine." Lucia stretched on the cushion under the moonlight.

A few other women gathered around her, eager to hear what

she had to say. Elaine and I exchanged a look, then headed downstairs and into the courtyard, too, both curious.

"What did they do to you?" a woman asked Lucia.

"Fed us, played music for us. The prince gave me this." She stretched her arm, displaying a wide bangle made from filigree honeycomb with a golden bumblebee in the middle.

Elaine touched the bee. "It's pretty."

"Prince Rha gave it to you?" I asked, trying to sound casual.

"Yes. They say that honey represents the sweetness of Joy Vessels."

"How?" Elaine eyed the bracelet.

Lucia shrugged. "I don't know. Maybe because shadow people can't really taste honey without us?"

If they could taste it, they likely couldn't enjoy it the way we could since they didn't feel joy. Only now had I started to understand all the implications of a life without joy, when even the smallest pleasures were out of reach.

"Is that why they call us the Sweet Ones?" Elaine wondered.

"As long as they don't decide to eat us at some point." Melanie cringed.

"What else did they do?" another woman, Lin, asked. "How did they share your joy?"

Lucia winced, glancing aside for a moment. "They... Well, they used their hose thingies."

Elaine paled. "How?"

Melanie stilled. I stared at Lucia, waiting for her to elaborate.

"Here." She tapped one of the golden rosettes on her arm. "They call these *leilathas*. They attached their smoke ropes to us here while we ate."

"Did they eat something too?" I asked.

"They did. All of them at the table. There was the prince, the Head Councilor, that general woman who brought us all here... Then, there was some old woman too. I didn't get a good look at her because she was wearing a cloak that covered her head-to-toe. And two others, I forgot who they were, some important people from the Royal Court, I guess. They all sat on floor cushions at a long, low table. We sat behind them, with our food trays in our laps. Then, they used our *leilathas* to plug in their hoses, or ropes, or whatever they call them—"

"Tendrils," I offered quietly.

Everyone's eyes turned to me, but I had nothing to tell them other than what they already knew.

I cleared my throat and, for some crazy reason, asked, "Did the prince have his tendrils connected to you?"

Why did it matter?

Why would I even care?

I didn't know. But Rha connecting with Lucia, combined with him giving her a bracelet, would be significantly more than what I wanted to happen between them.

I felt an odd wave of relief when Lucia shook her head.

"No. The Head Councilor did. The prince had Kostya, I think."

"How did it feel to have them attached to you?" Elaine asked Lucia.

"It's weird at first." Lucia winced again. "But not painful or anything. Then, after a while, I even forgot the Head Councilor was there at all."

Lin sighed, looking relieved. "Well, if that's all they use these things for, it's not so bad, I guess."

Melanie pursed her lips. "Not so bad? But what do we know about any long-term effects of those? What if there are some long-term consequences?" She tapped a black ribbon on my arm. "What voodoo magic did they use to implant these in your skin? What if it gives you cancer?"

"Or slowly sucks our souls out," Lin's companion said with a mournful expression.

Lucia sat up on her cushion, looking uneasy.

"I should go," she said, before leaving the courtyard.

Lin and her friend moved away too.

"They should've fought it, instead of selling out for a promise of better food," Melanie said resolutely. "You too, Dawn. You should've fought them when they put that thing on you."

I rubbed my arms, remembering my futile struggle against the Joy Guardians. They had never given me a choice.

"I tried to fight," I said.

"Clearly, not hard enough. Honestly, you should be more of a badass in life, at least when it comes to standing up for yourself."

"Melanie," Elaine intervened, "you don't know how it happened to Dawn, you weren't there."

"But I was there when it *didn't* happen to me," my sister snapped. "And you know why it didn't? Because I didn't let it happen. You guys are just all pushovers. You too, Elaine."

"Well, thanks a lot." Elaine got up. "I'll see you later. I'm going to get some more water."

"See?" Melanie pointed at Elaine's back as my friend retreated. "The moment shit hits the fan, she runs away."

"Feels like a smart thing to do," I disagreed. "Shit has a tendency to smear and spoil everything."

"Running away from arguments doesn't solve anything."

"Neither does arguing over the things that we can't change."

"I can change them. And I will." Melanie's confidence didn't waver. "You two can remain stupid about this all you want. But I will survive this. And I will go home. With or without you."

Elaine didn't return to us after getting her water. I found her on the balcony of her room later.

"Sorry," she apologized, as if I'd blame her for running away from Melanie's verbal abuse. "Your sister can be a little too much in large doses."

"I know." I sat in a pile of cushions next to her.

"I agree with her about going back. I just don't see how screaming about it all the time is helping anybody. If anything, it'll just alert the guards and the Keepers, and they'll watch us more closely."

"So, you'd leave if there was a chance?" I asked.

"Of course I would. I'm worried sick about my mom and dad.

They know I wouldn't just run away like that. They must know I've been taken or worse, they probably think I'm dead. Remember how stressed your family was when Ciana disappeared?"

I remembered. How could I ever forget? There was no one to stress about me, though. Mom was long gone. And now, Dad was gone too. Grief weighed down on me, crushing like a mountain, and I rushed to change the subject before deep sorrow would consume me.

"They say we're allowed to go in the city as long as we get a proper escort of guards and Keepers," I said.

"Really?" Elaine perked up. "We should do it. We should see more of the city. Maybe we can find a way out then?"

Maybe, but outside of the city, there was only hot, dry desert. And we also needed to have the portal open first. But I didn't want to dampen Elaine's enthusiasm about the walk by reminding her of our inescapable situation.

A little while later, the Keepers returned with dinner. They carried in trays of plates with greenish beige paste, something like mashed peas or lentils.

"Yay, food," Elaine said flatly, getting up.

I followed her. "Looks gross, but I feel hungry enough to eat it."

We walked out into the yard again, where the Keepers were giving out the plates with the mush. Before I could get one, however, a guard rushed in.

"Don't eat that!" He positioned himself between me and the Keeper with my dinner.

I jerked my hand away from the plate. "Why not?"

Now, everyone in the courtyard was staring at us. The spoonfuls of green mash hung suspended in the air on the way to people's mouths.

"You're coming with me," the guard said. "His Highness wants you to have dinner in his rooms."

It was a good thing I hadn't gotten a plate yet, because had I held one, I would've dropped it in shock. The prince wished to dine with me? After what happened the last time?

Did I hear it right?

"What does he want with me?" I wondered as my heart skipped a beat.

Elaine gripped my arm. From the corner of my eye, I spotted Melanie making her way toward us.

"He wants you to have dinner with him," the guard repeated, looking slightly irritated by my delay.

"I guess the joy he got from Kostya at lunch has worn off already," Elaine quipped. "He needs a refill."

I'd learned a little more about the prince and his world during our last conversation. I doubted he got anything out of it, however. At the end, I'd even kicked him out of my room, despite it being located in the city he owned. He really had no reason to expect any joy from me.

"Are you sure it was *me* he asked for?"

I had a hard time believing that the prince would want to have anything to do with me. Didn't he make it clear that he found even looking at me uncomfortable?

The guard waved at me to follow. "Come. Prince Rha has a busy schedule. We can't make him wait."

Kostya materialized next to us. "I'll come if she doesn't want to. I can't eat this shit you serve us here."

The guard raised his hand, keeping Kostya at bay. "Prince Rha asked for Dawn. And only for her."

Melanie grabbed my elbow. Her hot whisper hit my ear. "Seduce the bastard, sis. Make him send us back."

Twelve

DAWN

I walked into the same room I'd been in last morning. But the prince wasn't here. His seat on the dais piled high with silk cushions was empty. The two servants with fans were also missing. Only a group of musicians played a pleasant melody from the low platform by the wall to my left.

There was no food on the table. Instead, a gorgeous dress from flowing silk printed with a geometrical pattern in gold and dark orange was spread over the tabletop.

Two tall windows, one on each side of the royal dais, were open. The opportunity to look outside was a rare treat in Teneris, and I found myself drawn to the night view of the desert framed by the open window panes of stained glass.

A slight movement by the window on the right caught my eye. It was as if the air shifted slightly or the shadows undulated, stirred by the flames of the candles burning in tall holders along the walls.

"Good morning, Dawn," Prince Rha's voice greeted me.

He stood by the open window. His dark frame blended with the night, his golden eyes like a pair of twinkling stars in the sky.

"Oh, my God," I gasped in surprise from his sudden appearance, pressing a hand to my chest as my heart seemed to leap to my throat.

"Did I startle you?" He took a step my way.

"Have you been standing there all along? Or did you just appear out of nowhere?"

Either way, he looked like a part of the night, blending with it seamlessly.

"I've been waiting for you," he said, stopping right in front of me.

"Why?" I asked. "Why did you want to see me?"

For once, he held my gaze steady, looking like he might be asking himself the same question.

"When it comes to you, I have a persistent feeling that our conversation isn't finished," he finally said. "And it bothers me, like a grain of sand trapped in my shoe."

It stunned me how accurately he'd described my own feelings toward him.

"But we've hardly spoken," I said. "And not even under pleasant circumstances."

"Well, maybe that is the problem, then? The conversation we need to have hasn't happened yet. We need to talk."

The intensity with which he looked at me made it hard to focus. But I came here with an agenda. I had questions that needed answers.

"Very well, Rha. Let's talk." I crossed my arms over my chest. "For starters, tell me about the other humans living in Alveari Kingdom. You've been abducting us for some time. There must be quite a few *Joy Vessels* around."

If the topic I chose surprised him, he didn't show it.

"Not as many as you may think," he replied. "There are eighteen of you here, and twenty-four in the queen's *sarai* in the city of Kalmena. That's all."

Hope stirred in me again.

"Do you know the names of those in Kalmena?"

"No. I've never met them. I left Kalmena eight years ago, long before the queen's vessels arrived."

That didn't add up. Ciana was taken thirteen years ago. Rha would've still been in the queen's palace at that time.

"When did they arrive in Alveari Kingdom?" I asked.

"About a month ago. Four weeks before you did."

"Four weeks," I exhaled, as my hope was fighting my disappointment. "But have there been other abductions before that? About thirteen years ago, give or take?"

"No. The portal to your world has only been opened twice during our known history—last month and about two days ago."

"That's it?"

"That's it," he confirmed, crushing my hope.

The disappointment felt excruciatingly painful, but it was all my fault. Ciana was never here. I took a far-fetched assumption and let it grow into hope. But hope was dangerous. It hurt when it died.

Concern crossed Rha's handsome features. "What's wrong, Dawn? You seem upset."

I touched my face absentmindedly, then smoothed a hand over my hair. I'd twisted it into a high bun earlier, but now found a loose strand and tugged at it while working on regaining my composure.

"I'm fine." I wasn't ready to talk to Rha about my life back home. He didn't need to know about Ciana, especially since she wasn't in this world, anyway. "I'm just..." I let my voice trail off, unsure what to say.

"Hungry?" he asked helpfully.

"Um...maybe a little." I rubbed my chest, hoping the tightness inside would ease.

"I'll have the dinner served at once then." He turned to the table then saw the dress he seemed to have forgotten about already. "How do you like this dress?" He tilted his head, clearly curious about my reaction.

"Is it for me?" I stared at him. "You got me a dress? Why?"

Once again, he appeared startled by a simple question. His mouth opened as if to reply, but he didn't seem to know what answer to give me.

"Well..." His left ear twitched, and he scratched behind it, glancing aside. "I thought you might like the color. It's bright."

The regal, confident crown prince suddenly looked flustered. He also seemed tortured by anticipation while waiting for my answer.

"It's pretty," I said to put him out of his misery. "I like it very much. Thank you."

He released a breath. "I hoped you would. Gold suits you. It matches your hair."

I hid a smile, thinking about how much thought and probably time he'd put into choosing the dress by using only logic because he knew nothing about my preferences.

"Do you want me to wear it?" I offered.

"Now?" He blinked his long eyelashes at me.

I shrugged. "I can change before dinner."

I glanced at the musicians, the only people in the room with us. Some of them stared at me with various degrees of curiosity. But just like from the shadow fae in the royal baths earlier, I sensed no sexual interest from them. Just like in the baths, I could've easily disrobed in their presence, but something held me back from shedding my clothes right then in there.

"It'd be lovely. If you wish," the prince agreed, resting his golden eyes on me.

A warm shiver of awareness ran down my body, and I realized why it wouldn't be easy for me to undress in this room. The musicians might not matter, but the thought of taking my clothes off in front of Prince Rha made my cheeks heat up with blush. Unable to hold his stare, I dropped my gaze to his short, embroidered boots.

"Is there a place where I can change in private?" I asked.

After a brief spark of confusion in his eyes, he nodded.

"Follow me."

Swiping the dress and the metal belt that came with it off the table, he swiftly moved to a door on the right. I followed him to a much smaller room behind the door.

Like so many living spaces in Teneris, it had the shape of a hexagon. Two adjacent walls had tall windows with the stained-glass panes folded to the sides. Outside the windows was a patio with a swing bench. It had a wide, cushioned seat held by chains with ivy vines threaded through the chain links.

"Whose is this?" I gestured at the swing.

"Mine," Rha replied.

"Yours? You...swing in it?" I smiled, trying to imagine the prince swinging like a kid, kicking his feet up in the air, his skirt and his hair flowing in the night breeze.

"I find it relaxing," he explained.

Of course, Rha wouldn't be kicking and laughing while swinging. He'd do it slowly. *Relaxing.*

And now, it was easy for me to envision the prince reclining in the cushioned seat, reading a scroll while pushing himself with a foot off the ground in a slow rocking motion. It suited him, in his constant strife for inner and outer balance.

A low table stood by the windows, with floor cushions next to it. The pile of the cushions formed a cozy seat that seemed like it'd be a comfy place to spend a morning in.

Flat multi-colored pieces of rock and stained glass lay on the table, arranged into a partially finished design. It looked like a snowflake, with perfectly symmetrical rays spreading from the orange hexagon in the middle.

"Is this also yours?" I asked.

"Yes."

"It's beautiful." I admired the symmetrical pattern of orange, green, yellow, and white pieces, arranged in a design far more complex than any puzzle I'd seen.

"It's not finished yet," Rha said.

"What will you do with it once it is?"

"I'll take it apart, add more pieces, remove a few, then start anew."

I looked at him in astonishment. "Then your puzzle will never be finished."

"Once the project is finished, the satisfaction from it wanes quickly," he explained. "The process of finding the best place for each and every piece is what creates a more stable and longer lasting contentment."

"You prefer the process of getting to the goal to actually reaching it?" I asked, trying to figure out this man who proved to be a challenging puzzle himself.

He stared at the pieces on the table for a moment. "Figuring out the pattern can be maddening. But the more difficult it is, the more satisfying it is once it actually happens."

He spoke with his usual calm confidence. But something had shifted in him the moment we had walked into this room. His wide shoulders seemed a little too stiff. His jaw was set hard, and the look in his eyes turned guarded as he watched me move around the room.

I had a feeling that this place was special to him, that it was his private place where not many people had access to, and I feared he might view my presence here as a violation of the rules.

Not wishing to prolong his discomfort, I reached for the dress in his hands.

"I'll be quick—"

My gaze fell on the cushions. Two round, yellow eyes stared back at me from the shadows inside the seat.

I gasped in surprise and gripped Rha's arm.

"There is...something here, in the cushions."

A black cat raised its head, watching me closely. The nearly perfect spheres of its eyes squinted into almond shapes, then further narrowed into slits, eventually closing as the cat seemed to doze off again. Its black fur blended with the shadows so completely, if the animal hadn't looked at me, I wouldn't have noticed it at all.

"This is Zala." Rha touched my shoulder reassuringly. "She won't hurt you, not unless you're the size of a rodent."

"You have a cat?" Somehow, that felt like the most unbelievable thing about the prince of the world of shadows.

"It's more like she has me," he corrected. "Zala showed up here one fine night, several years ago, and chose to stay."

"She adopted you." I smiled. "That's what cats do."

He didn't return my smile. Shadow fae generally seemed to lack that facial expression. But his features relaxed as he stared into the dark void in the cushions where the shape of the sleeping cat was absorbed by shadows.

"Are there cats in your world?" he asked.

"Yes, of course there are cats. I had one when I was little. An orange tabby."

His eyebrows rose in surprise. "An *orange* cat? What a fantastic creature."

"There was nothing overly fantastic about our Whiskers." I laughed. "Maybe just the amount of food that big boy could consume in one sitting. You don't have orange cats in the Alveari Kingdom?"

"No. All cats are black here. Some say the shadows that roamed the desert many millennia ago split. Some of them became people. Others turned into creatures—black camels, black scorpions, and black cats. With time, gray and even white variations occurred. But orange?" He shook his head in disbelief. "I've never heard of cats of that color before."

A part of me wished I could stay here the entire morning, with Rha and his cat. But I still believed that my presence in this room was an invasion of his personal space. I'd come here just to change.

"Well, I'll be quick." I reached for the dress again, but Rha held it up, ready to put it on me instead.

"Take off the dress you're wearing, and I'll help you put this one on," he suggested casually, clearly oblivious of my reason to request privacy.

Did he really feel nothing?

Not even if he saw me naked?

"All right," I said, slowly raising my skirt in a sudden desire to test him.

He watched with his usual serene expression as I lifted the skirt higher before taking the dress off over my head.

Dropping the dress to the floor, I was left wearing only the undergarments that Sigid had given me—the short underwear and the bra with straps crisscrossing on the back to leave the rosettes of the harness exposed.

Tilting his head to the side, Rha studied my body with similar interest as he'd studied my face before.

I was wearing more clothes now than I had in the baths, yet I felt more exposed here than in a room full of people. My skin tingled under his attention. Heat rushed to my cheeks and echoed with a soft throbbing between my thighs.

Lifting my eyelashes, I met Rha's eyes and...didn't find even a spark of desire in them. He studied me with keen curiosity, but nothing more.

I should be relieved by that. And I was. Mostly. I even felt safer with him now, knowing there was no risk of any sexual aggression on his part. At the same time, there also was a slight tug of disappointment in me that I couldn't quite explain.

"Can I have the dress now, please?" I stretched my hand.

Instead of handing it to me, however, he slid the garment over my head. The cool silk skimmed down my body, caressing my skin. The edge of the skirt draped over my hip on one side. As Rha straightened it out for me, the back of his fingers stroked down my naked thigh, but the caress didn't feel intentional.

The cut of the dress left my back exposed. The neckline dipped in the front, draping over my chest. With deft, quick fingers, Rha laid out the fabric folds over my breasts, looking completely oblivious to my nipples hardening under his touch.

Now I really needed to know. If shadow fae felt no pleasure, did they still have sex? And if not, how did they reproduce? The idea that this handsome prince was never meant to come undone with desire depressed me.

Satisfied with the way the dress fit me, Rha took the belt next.

It was made from interconnected golden hexagons. Leaning over me, he circled me with his arms to bring the belt around my waist.

He smelled like desert sand heated by the sun with a trace of sweet honeysuckle. One of his thin braids fell on my shoulder. As he straightened, moving away from me, I picked the braid up, letting it slide between my fingers. The unbraided portion of it at the end tickled my skin. I caught it, raking my fingers through the ends.

"It's soft." I smiled. "Your hair looks thick and glossy. I didn't expect it to feel like silk."

His eyes darted to mine. Black smoke curled from his upper arms in tight spirals, reaching for me. Alarm zapped through me. Dropping the braid, I leaped away.

The back of my legs hit the table with the puzzle. It tipped, sending the pieces raining down to the floor.

I watched in horror as the perfect lines of Rha's snowflake design broke and deteriorated.

"Shit!" I gasped, grabbing the table.

But it was too late. Only one of the six rays remained. But it was now so crooked, even I couldn't look at it without cringing. I could only imagine what this mess did to Rha's sensitivity of a perfectionist.

"I'm so, so sorry." I crawled on my knees, picking up the tiny pieces.

There were so many. I tried to fit them back in place, but only a highly sophisticated software program could possibly recreate the complicated pattern this man had going there. I frantically shuffled the pieces along the table, only making it worse.

Two large hands carefully covered mine, halting my fidgeting.

"Hush, Dawn." His voice was soft and soothing, like a gentle breeze. "Calm. Breathe."

"I'm so sorry, Rha. I ruined it..." My breath caught in my throat. Tears burned my eyes unexpectedly. My heart raced so fast I feared it would give out. "I always ruin things. I'm good at messing up. Everything. All the time. Not so good at fixing anything, though."

Panic rushed over me. It was no longer just about the puzzle. All my life seemed to be broken and crumbling, lying in pieces at my feet, and I had no idea how to put it back together again.

He took my hand in his and carefully unfolded my clenched fingers, one by one. The pieces I'd clutched in it fell out. Their sharp edges left red welts in my palm.

"Just breathe, my sweet," Rha murmured, gently rubbing my palm with his thumb to soothe the pain.

"You spent so much time putting it together, and I..." My lips trembled, with words hurting my throat like shards with sharp edges.

"I'll put it together again. It's not about the result, remember? The value of a puzzle is lost when it's solved and finished. Its purpose lies in the process of figuring it out." He took my other hand, letting me drop the pieces clutched in there, too, then massaged my palm. "It's not worth getting so upset over. I'll come up with another design, possibly a better one. Breathe, Dawn, just breathe."

I did. Listening to his deep, even voice, I focused on each slow breath I took.

The stress of the past few days had built up and blew up into a panic attack. I'd never had one like this before and didn't immediately know how to handle it. But Rha helped. Somehow, he knew what I needed to do. Breath by breath, my heart rate slowed down a little.

Holding my hands, Rha was sitting on the floor, and I didn't remember when or how he'd sat down with me.

The sight of the colorful puzzle pieces strewed around on the floor brought another wave of guilt in me.

"Rha, I didn't mean it," I muttered apologetically.

"I know," he said simply.

I wished I could bottle up his voice and keep it with me for whenever I needed to calm my nerves again. Nothing else had such a soothing effect on me before.

"My tendrils scared you," he said. "Can you tell me why you're frightened of them? Is it because of the way you were taken? Or of what you had to go through during the harness fitting? Or maybe you're afraid I'll violate your emotions by sharing into them?"

"All of the above," I admitted, amazed by how accurately he'd hit all the points.

He understood what I'd been through. He knew. But what surprised me the most was that he cared. Rha might not be able to *like* anything, but he clearly *disliked* me being upset.

"They are gone now. See?" He turned his arm for me to see his skin unmarred by any smoke or shadows. "I wasn't going to harm you. You were playing with my hair, and I just wished to know what you felt when touching me."

"Oh." I dropped my gaze.

Maybe it was better that he didn't know what I felt when touching him and especially when he was touching me.

"I'll tell you what..." With a finger under my chin, he brought my face up, forcing me to meet his eyes. "I will not release my tendrils again in your presence. Not until you ask me to."

That sounded great, but...

"But then, what do you need me here for?"

His forehead furrowed at my question that he didn't seem to have an answer for. As easily as the prince spoke about my emotions, he appeared to struggle to articulate his own feelings toward me.

"To have dinner with you," he finally said, getting up from the floor and offering me a hand. "Come. I know you're hungry." He helped me up.

As he led me into the dining room, I tried to imagine going through life without joy. For me, it'd probably be the little, everyday pleasures that I'd miss the most. Like the early morning breeze coming through the open windows right now and the floral scents it brought. Like the silky caress of the fabric against my body. Like the intriguing presence of this man in the room with me.

For the first time ever, I fully realized how utterly deprived the life of the shadow fae must be. Without joy, they could've let the rage and despair take over. But instead of killing off their own race in anger or even just sitting around feeling sorry for themselves, they went on. They built a civilization. They evolved. They existed. They lived, even without the ability of ever enjoying life.

"What keeps you going, Rha?" I asked. "What gets you out of bed every morning? I mean every *evening?*" I smiled when correcting. "I mean life isn't easy, not even for a prince, I imagine. What helps you when you're feeling down, since there is no joy or pleasure that would lift you up?"

"Duty has been my main motivation in life," he said. "My people depend on me and the decisions I make. That's what helps me rise every evening and keeps me working through the night. But this evening..." he paused, glancing at me. "This evening, I woke up, thinking about you."

"Me?"

"Yes. You're an enigma to me Dawn, a puzzle that may never be solved. Unexpected and unpredictable. My feelings are all over the place when I'm with you. They change so quickly and in such illogical patterns that I never know what to expect. Which proves oddly stimulating. I've been looking forward to seeing you all night."

"But you didn't bother to invite me to your midnight meal?" I didn't mean to sound this bitter.

I hadn't even wanted to see him at midnight. But the words were out now. And he arched an eyebrow, probably trying to decipher their true meaning that I wouldn't even admit to myself.

"The midnight meal was a state affair," he explained. "Its purpose was to show goodwill to the city officials by sharing the joy of my Vessels with them. By doing so, I hope to strengthen their cooperation in protecting the *sarai* as much as they protect the rest of the city. But I didn't wish to share *you* with anyone else."

A corner of his mouth jerked up, then the other one followed, stretching his lips into a...*smile?*

Was that what he was trying to do? It was hard to be sure. The expression was clearly too new for him to execute it perfectly.

"Rha, are you smiling?" I asked uncertainly, as my breath hitched. My chest expanded with the enormity of seeing a smile on a face that likely had never displayed one before.

"Did I do it right?" he asked, his shapely mouth returning into its naturally somber expression. "I noticed that you smile when you say something nice or friendly, and I wished to better convey my desire to have you all to myself. Somehow the words alone didn't feel adequate."

Was he really teaching himself how to smile for my sake?

What was I supposed to do with that?

It was not supposed to happen, and I had no business feeling as warm and fuzzy as I suddenly felt.

"You did good," I said softly. "You have an amazing smile, Your Highness. I look forward to seeing you practice it more often."

I sat down on the floor cushions in front of the table.

The musicians picked up their instruments. Servants closed the tall windows with thick shutters, getting ready for the sunrise.

As if following some invisible sign, the doors to the room opened and servants carried in dishes with food. They set them all on my side of the table while Rha took his place on the dais again, and a servant placed a single crystal goblet of water in front of him.

"Is it really enough to eat only once in twenty-four hours?" I wondered.

"It's enough to restock everything my body needs," Rha said.

I resisted a closer look at his body, but I'd stared at it enough to know it was well "stocked" in all the right places.

Servants placed an appetizer of flaky fish and veggies in front of me, and my willpower evaporated. I grabbed a fork and dug in. Only after I'd taken a few bites did I look up at Rha again.

His tendrils remained hidden. He reclined sideways in the cushions, his chin resting on his hand.

The dinner felt very one-sided with only me eating. The one way Rha could participate in it would be to allow him to use his tendrils, but a shiver of unease ran down my arms at that thought.

He'd asked me what made me so afraid of them, and I realized it wasn't the fear that had made me shrink away from him the last time, but the memory of it. The terror I'd felt when the shadows had come for me and then when the Joy Guardians had restrained me was still fresh in my mind, but I wasn't afraid of Rha. I believed him when he said he didn't want to hurt me.

A servant put an appetizing dish of meat with rice and vegetables in front of me. Another one brought a metal pitcher with a long, thin neck and a curved spout. He poured a glass of dark, fragrant wine for me while the prince continued to nurse his glass of water.

"You're not drinking, either?" I lifted my glass.

"No. I can't get drunk and can't appreciate the flavor. It'd be a waste of wine for me to drink it."

I took a tentative sip. The wine coated my tongue with the flavor of fruit and nuts. Just like the food, the wine tasted exquisite.

"He could enjoy it, too, if you let him." The thought rushed through my mind.

I tried to ignore the pinch of guilt that came with it. But I had to admit the dinner would've been far more enjoyable for me, too, if Rha shared it with me in some capacity. There was a reason why food played such a huge role in social interactions. A dinner was meant to be shared.

"What is this meat?" I asked instead, searching for a distraction from my unsettling thoughts.

"Lamb," Rha replied. "I took the liberty of ordering for you this time. But if you prefer the food you had yesterday—"

"No, it's good." I took another bite. "It tastes great. I was wondering, though, where did you get shrimp or fish in the middle of the desert? And so many different vegetables too?"

"The same place we get water from. Underground."

"You grow vegetables underground?"

"The orchards and vegetable gardens have openings to the surface since plants require constant sunlight. But the animal farms are lower underground, along with people's dwellings."

"You have farms and houses under there too?" I gestured with my fork at the floor.

"The entire city is below us, Dawn. People prefer to live away from the scorching surface with its daily sandstorms. Underneath, it's cool and quiet."

I stared at my plate, trying to imagine houses and even entire animal farms buried under the desert floor. "So, Teneris is an anthill, after all."

"An anthill? You can say that, I suppose."

"With farms, houses, and giant kitchens that produce all this fancy food?"

"There is only one kitchen in the palace," Rha corrected. "And I wouldn't say it's giant. The food you're eating is only prepared for humans. As Joy Vessels, you're the only ones who can appreciate it, anyway."

"What do *you* eat then?"

"The same thing that's served in the *sarai*."

"The tasteless mash and boiled meat, really?" I made a face. "That's what the Royal Court eats?"

He shrugged. "It all tastes the same to us. Why waste time and effort to prepare anything complex and flavorful?"

I sipped my wine, pondering his words. The lack of joy affected every aspect of the shadow fae life.

"If you took a drink of wine," I asked, "what will you feel? Will it taste like water to you?"

"No. I'd feel its taste, the bitterness, and the burn. But I won't enjoy the flavor or get intoxicated from it the way Joy Vessels do."

"But that sucks. You really have no fun. Not even the artificial exhilaration of getting drunk."

I set my empty glass down. A servant made a move to refill it, but I declined. Getting drunk on my own held no fun for me, either.

"Are there many things that bring you joy, Dawn?" the prince asked.

"Other than food and alcohol, you mean?"

"Yes." He looked expectant.

"There are some... Let me think." I drizzled a little honey over the plate of fruit dessert to buy some time. It was hard to remember the last time I felt truly happy. "To be honest, it's been a while since I felt 'joyful.'"

"Why is that?"

Did I really want to discuss my entire life with him? The problem was, Rha had turned out to be an excellent listener. I came here to ask questions, but he ended up being the one gently prying the door open to my innermost thoughts and feelings.

"Dancing," I said, evading his last question. "Dancing makes me happy. When I dance, I feel the purest of joy."

His golden eyes opened wide. He looked even more shocked than when he'd first learned about the existence of orange cats. "I didn't know you danced."

"Do you dance too?"

"No, but I've heard of it."

"You've *heard* of it?" I stared at him in bewilderment. "Rha, please don't tell me you've never seen a dance performance."

"But I have not."

"You're lying," I gasped.

"Why would I lie?"

"I don't know. But... How could you never have seen a dance?"

It was beyond my comprehension. For me, dance was everywhere. I lived and breathed it, even when offstage. I followed all the great performers. I was aware of every dance production in the country and almost the entire world. I constantly had choreography ideas running through my brain, accompanied by music playing in my mind. I danced in my head, even as I hadn't stepped a foot on a stage in many months now.

It might be the wine rushing through my bloodstream, but I couldn't stand the idea of someone being so completely deprived of the joy that dance had given me over the years.

"That's so wrong, Rha." I climbed to my feet. "We need to fix it."

The music playing in the room was too slow. I knew the classic ballroom styles, of course, and danced them all at competitions when I was younger. But my true passion had always been contemporary dance. It allowed for the best expression of emotion for me. And now, I yearned to move.

"Can we play a little faster, boys and girls?" I asked the musicians.

They paused in confusion. I assumed they were here entirely for my benefit, since Rha couldn't feel the pleasure that music brought. The musicians' execution had been flawless but soulless, like by someone who had meticulously learned to play an instrument and hit all the right notes at the right time but derived no joy from the result.

"May I?" I took a string instrument from the hands of a woman on the stage and plucked the strings in a high-tempo tune. "Hear this? Faster, like that. Can you do it, please?"

She took the instrument from me and dutifully repeated the notes and the tempo I'd just played.

"There you go." I nodded in encouragement as others followed her lead, picking up the speed.

I grabbed the wrist of a man with a large tambourine in his hand and hit the tight skin of the instrument with my other hand.

"Just like this, please." I set the tempo on the tambourine before giving the control back to the man. "Keep going."

Tapping my foot to the new rhythm, I directed the musicians with my hands. "You're doing great! Now keep holding it."

I glanced back at Rha over my shoulder. He'd already ordered the servants who'd served my dinner to move the table all the way to the opposite wall, making space for me in the middle of the room.

I considered the choreography for a moment, then decided to do what I often did when dancing purely for pleasure. I dropped my eyelids, shut my overthinking mind out of it, and let the music take me.

Blood rushed through my veins with energy. The soft-sole sandals allowed me to glide easily over the marble floor. The flowing skirt of my dress fanned out like a butterfly wing as I raised my leg in an arabesque, then swirled like a flower blossom with my turns.

I lost track of time and even the awareness of the place I was in. It'd been so long since my last dance, even longer since I danced simply for the sake of it, without the pressure of an audition or competition.

I started this for Rha but ended up doing it for me. The tightness in my chest eased. Tension drained from my muscles. My very soul appeared to soar, lifted by the music.

As I came out from yet another spin, my gaze fell on the prince in his seat. His head was tilted in the way he did when he tried to understand me. He tried. But he couldn't. Because he simply couldn't feel the way I did.

"Come here." I gestured for him to come closer.

"I don't dance," he warned, but got up from the cushions and stepped down from the dais, probably led by pure curiosity.

"I know." I took his hand, drawing him closer. "But just try with me. Please."

I waved at the musicians to slow down. As the tempo dropped to that of the waltz, I took Rha's hands and placed them on my waist.

"It's best to start slow," I said. "Just do what I do. Watch my feet and follow my lead."

I kept it simple. Placing my hands on his wide shoulders, I

mostly just swayed side to side, shifting my feet along the floor. With his innate feline grace, he followed easily. So, I moved my foot back in a waltz step. Again, Rha was able to keep up without any obvious difficulty.

"You're doing great, Your Highness." I smiled. "It's like you were born for this."

"The principle of it is similar to a sparring practice, which I do routinely."

"Are you training to fight?"

"Maintaining my skills, mostly. I finished the initial training decades ago."

"Decades? How old are you?"

"I'm sixty-three. How about you?"

"I'm twenty-five. Talk about an age gap!" I laughed nervously, trying to adjust my idea of him. It wasn't easy, since he didn't look like a sixty-three-year-old man. Rha was lithe, strong, corded with muscles, and with hardly any lines on his face.

"Fae live to about five hundred years, Dawn. Physically, we fully mature in our twenties, and our bodies stop aging shortly after. We resume visible aging only in the last years of our lives."

"Five hundred years is a long time to stick around."

However, I didn't feel jealous of his long lifespan. Centuries of living without joy didn't seem that appealing to me.

What was it like?

What was Rha feeling at this very moment, for example?

His long eyebrows moved closer in concentration as he focused on following my steps. He heard the music, but it didn't permeate his very being like it did for me. He moved his feet, but it didn't send a thrill through his body. He held my waist, but he didn't feel light-headed at the contact the way I felt.

Even the wine had no effect on him, while it filled me to the brim with bubbly effervescence.

No. I did not feel jealous of the shadow fae's centuries of life. I'd rather live the few short decades I had, finding joy in every single moment of my existence. I realized how often I'd taken those little sparks of joy for granted and vowed never to do that again.

I tossed my head back and closed my eyes, reveling in the moment. My hands lay on Rha's shoulders. His warm skin stretched over his hard muscles. The cold chains held the bejeweled mesh of his breastplate. I moved my hands away from the metal, shifting them closer to his neck and under the soft curtain of his hair. Cupping his nape, I stroked his skin with my thumb.

He leaned closer. I opened my eyes, finding his face tilted above mine. There was that familiar intense curiosity in his eyes, like he was trying to dissect my brain, or crawl under my skin and take over my senses.

It felt unnerving, like always. But it was also...tempting. I wished for him to learn what he so desperately wanted to know.

Emotions guided me, not thoughts. I rose to my tiptoes. With my hand on the back of his neck, I brought his face lower to me.

His lips parted. Sharp, white fangs peeked from under his top lip. Only a few days ago, the sight of him would've sent me away screaming. But now, I moved closer until there was no space left between us.

My lips touched his, and he didn't stop me. Holding still, he kept his hands on my waist and let me tangle my fingers into his hair, press my body to his, slide my lips between his. I breathed his warm scent, savoring his taste of far-away spices. A soft moan left me, getting trapped between our joined lips.

Then, I realized that the pleasure was all mine—all of it. Rha gave me free rein to his body, but he played no part in the kiss. He felt nothing.

I shrank away quickly. "I shouldn't have done that."

His hands flexed on my waist, however, keeping me close. His golden eyes flicked between mine, his gaze trapping me even more effectively than his arms. We were no longer dancing. My feet rooted in place.

"Yes, you should," he murmured. "And you should do it again, only..."

His arm twitched. True to his word, however, not a wisp of a shadow peeled from his skin.

"You want to feel it?" I croaked.

"I'd give what's left of my life just for a tiny taste," he admitted, earnestly.

I wanted it for him. I really did.

"Alright." I drew in a deep breath. Bending my arm, I moved it forward, offering the two star rosettes on it to him. "Let's do it."

"Are you sure—"

"Do it, Rha." I thrust my arm his way. "Before I change my mind."

Black tendrils spiraled from his arms, faster than I'd ever seen them appear before. The smoky ends of one caressed up my body. Gold sparks crackled in the smoke as it aligned itself with the glistening rosette of the ribbon on my left arm. Rha paused it there, giving me a chance to stop him.

I gave him a tiny nod instead.

And that was all he needed.

The tendril's ends slipped in the openings of the rosette on my arm. Black shadows curled around it, as if in a hug. It appeared to sink into my skin and deeper, into the muscle tissue underneath, into the bone below, into the very essence of my soul.

The intrusion wasn't painful, but it was absolute. It knocked the air out of my lungs and tripped my heart. My head swam, making me sway on my feet.

Sliding his hands to my back, Rha pressed me to him tightly.

"I've got you."

"Do them all," I said into his chest. "All at once."

I closed my eyes, not watching the shadows emerge and twist into tendrils. Three more of them connected to the openings on my arms. Two others fused with my body from the back, one on my nape, the other one a few vertebrae down my spine. I felt pressure at the points of their contact. But the effect of the connection spread through my entire body.

Rha slid a finger under my chin, lifting my face to his.

"What do you think?"

"It's like…" I heaved a breath, searching for words. "It's like you're hugging me both from inside and out."

It did feel like a touch, as if he embraced my emotions the same way his arms held my body. The bizarre sensation buzzed through me, leaving me feeling slightly out of control.

"Should I withdraw?" He asked, searching my eyes.

He felt it too. He felt my unease. He knew how flustered I was inside, no matter how hard I tried to keep my cool on the surface. There was no hiding from him anymore.

"No." I shook my head. "Stay." I pressed my forehead to the precious stones of the jewelry piece over his chest and took a few deep breaths, slowly adjusting to him being closer to me than anyone had ever been before. "Feel with me, Rha."

I asked for this because I wanted him to experience joy. And now, I had to give it to him.

"Will you kiss me again, Dawn?" he asked softly, making me smile as I lifted my head from his chest.

I cupped the side of his face and skimmed the sharp ridge of his cheekbone with my thumb. His hair draped down, tickling the back of my hand. I raked my fingers through it, pushing it away from his face. With my other hand resting on the side of his neck, I rose on my tiptoes again and kissed him.

This time, when I slid my lips against his, he immediately moved his lips in response. When I tentatively stroked the bottom one with the tip of my tongue, he darted his tongue out to touch mine. As I melted against his chest, he grabbed me tighter, leaning over me so hard, we both staggered on our feet to regain our balance.

My breasts pressed into the hard jewels on his chest. My heart pounded against his. Holding me to him with one arm, he sank the fingers of his other hand in the hair on the back of my head. My mind appeared to float away. I moaned into his mouth. And this time, a soft, deep groan came from his throat in response.

His reaction proved more intoxicating than wine. Heat

coursed through my veins, spreading through my body and beyond. It filled me to the brim, then spilled over into the tendrils attached to my back and arms.

Gold shimmer swirled around us both, like tiny transparent fireflies. Or maybe the shimmer was in my mind—beguiling and invigorating.

The intensity proved overwhelming. I jerked away, needing to catch my breath.

His chest rose and fell rapidly too. His eyes were wide open. Wonder, excitement, delight, and desire burned in them brightly, as if all his senses had awoken at once.

He darted his tongue out, licking his lips.

"What is that, Dawn?" he demanded. "What is it that you feel when you kiss me?"

As if I could accurately explain what exactly caused my heart to pound and my stomach to flutter as if filled with a kaleidoscope of manic butterflies.

"Joy?" I blurted out the first appropriate word that came to mind.

"Joy from what? What caused it?"

"You." There was no other explanation.

Thirteen

DAWN

By the time I made it back to the *sarai*, it must've been close to noon already. The opening over the courtyard was closed with solid wooden shutters. Only a few splinters of sunlight pierced through them.

I lifted my face to the shutters above, catching a rare tiny ray of sun on my skin. Thoughts and feelings twisted inside me in a tangled web. I'd kissed the Crown Prince of Alveari Kingdom, a shadow creature from the world I never knew existed, and kissing him was wonderful. It'd been both fun and sensual, and something I hadn't experienced with anyone else before. And I told him so. I told him he brought me joy.

Then, the most wondrous thing happened. The somber prince of the joyless kingdom gave me a genuine, happy smile and said, "No one has ever called me *enjoyable*."

The moment I had finally scraped enough brain cells to remember that I should know better, I'd pulled away, and he'd immediately let me go. I didn't even need to voice my intention to leave because he'd sensed it. His tendrils had quietly slipped out of the *leilatha* sockets of my harness, and he released me from his arms.

My feelings about all of it remained jumbled, but I smiled at the warmth of sunshine on my face.

From the corner of my eye, I noticed a movement on one of the balconies. Some of the humans must be up. Or maybe they hadn't fallen asleep yet. Either way, I didn't feel like talking to anyone right now. Bending my head down, I quickly crossed the yard and went to my new room.

It was more than twice the size of my previous cell. The low platform with bedding was comfortable. Six bed posts held a black canopy over it. Stretched like a batwing between the thin bamboo rails, the canopy blocked the glowing ceiling, creating a dark, comfy place for me to sleep.

Still, I didn't sleep well that day. Every time I dozed off, shadows would haunt me. They reached for me from the darkness, like gnarly, grabby fingers, startling me awake. The most distressing part of the nightmare was that I couldn't decide whether to run from the shadows or into them. I didn't know where the danger lay and whether my heart would lead me to or away from it.

After tossing and turning for hours, I gave up on sleep completely. I got up, put my new dress back on, grabbed a glass from the stand next to my bed, and went out into the courtyard.

It was evening already. The Keepers were opening the shutters above. The dark sky behind the lattice over the courtyard was streaked with the deep burgundy of the dying sunset. The palace was getting ready to resume its busy nightlife.

"Hey." Melanie sat next to me on a ledge of the fountain, as I was drinking my water.

I hadn't even noticed when she'd come out. But my thoughts had been twirling around the shadow prince.

"Did you just return from the royal dinner?" Melanie gave my new dress an assessing look.

"No. I came back hours ago."

"Hours?" She clearly didn't believe me. "But isn't this new? A royal gift?" She fingered the skirt of my dress.

"Yes. And it's the only clothes I have, so..." I shrugged.

"Where is the dress you had on when you left last morning?"

"Listen." I huffed, losing patience. "What do you want to know?"

"Did you sleep with him?" she blurted out. No one could ever accuse Melanie of beating around the bush.

I groaned, rolling my eyes.

Yawning and sleepy-eyed, Elaine shuffled over to us.

"Morning... I mean *evening*. Or whatever..." She hid another yawn behind her hand. "How are you both?"

"Dawn had dinner with the prince," Melanie reminded her.

"Oh, that's right." Elaine no longer looked sleepy. Instead of a yawn, a hiccup jumped out of her mouth. "So, how did it go? Did you guys have sex?"

She definitely said it too loudly. The sleepy faces of other occupants of the *sarai* were now looking down at us from the balconies.

"No," I said firmly and just as loudly for everyone to hear. "I had dinner with him. Just like the others had lunch. That's all." Then I lowered my voice. "I came back just after sunrise and went to bed. I just got up not so long ago. But sure, go ahead, make up stories." I waved a dismissive hand at Melanie.

My sister wasn't easy to dismiss, however.

Shifting closer, she grabbed my hand. "Did you talk? What did you find out? Will there be another portal? When?"

I'd already told her that Rha wasn't the one who could open the portal or even to order one to be opened. Still, shame crept up my neck and over my face in a wave of heat. I had not discussed the portal with him again or tested his willingness to help us leave. Instead, I'd spent the time dancing and kissing him.

Melanie read the answers to her questions in my expression and huffed.

"Come on, Dawn. You spent all this time with him, with the man who kidnapped us and killed our father—"

"Rha didn't kill Dad," I said quietly but firmly.

"Whatever. He ordered it."

"He didn't. His orders were not to kill anyone."

She stared me down, her hands on her hips. "He cut off a man's head and served it to you for dinner. Only a psychopath would do something like that."

I kept quiet this time. Rha had presented me with the dead, decomposing head, exactly a day before I kissed him. I should probably be disturbed more than I was by that.

Melanie groaned in frustration. "Why couldn't *I* be the object of this creep's attention? I would not have missed this chance to get some useful information. But you..." She gave me a disappointed look. "You've always been selfish and irresponsible."

Anger heated inside me. It wasn't fair. Yes, I blew it with the prince. But for her to dismiss my entire life like this because of one misstep? I couldn't accept that.

"I'm irresponsible? Melanie, I put my career on hold to look after Dad, so *you* wouldn't have to take a break with yours."

"Your career?" she scoffed. "You don't have a career. What you do have are some odd gigs here and there, in productions that are barely a step above school plays."

My cheeks burned even hotter, but no longer from shame. Now, I was furious.

"It's my work you're talking about. My life's work. I've been dancing since before you even knew what to do for a living."

"Taking dance classes is not 'working for a living,' sister," she snapped back. "In fact, it's the opposite of that. Do you know how much Mom and Dad paid for that little hobby of yours over the years? I bet your entire dancing to date hasn't earned that money back yet. And do you know how much Dad's care cost?"

"I was the one taking care of him, remember? Unpaid."

"Yeah? But who paid his living expenses? His utilities? The property tax on the house?"

"His savings paid the bills," I said with some uncertainty. Melanie had been in charge of the financial side. I only had a vague idea about Dad's expenses.

"His savings wouldn't have lasted long. And then what? Who would've had to pay for all of that? Me." She punched her chest. "I always knew it'd be me, Dawn. All you have are a big heart and a trusting nature, neither are good for paying bills. Why do you think I've been stressing out so much about keeping my job? Because if I lost it, we all would be fucked."

The fight left me. Anger fizzled out, flooded by grief and the realization that Melanie was my only family left. What we argued about no longer mattered because Dad was gone. And we were so far away from that world and that life.

Placing my elbows on my knees, I dropped my head in my hands. Melanie heaved a sigh and stopped screaming, too. What was the point of arguing about things and people that were no longer there?

She leaned over me and lowered her voice. "Listen, maybe not all is lost yet. How did it go with the prince? What did you do?"

"I kissed him," I whispered.

I regretted my words the moment they left my mouth. Our kissing was no one's business, especially since I hadn't even had a chance to wrap my own mind around what was happening between Rha and me other than me getting excited in his company and him gobbling my excitement right up.

But the words were now out. Elaine heard them too. And Melanie latched on to them like a tick to a stray mutt.

"You kissed him?" She exclaimed loud enough for others to hear. "Did he like it?" She pressed a hand to her chest. "Thank God you're not completely useless. Maybe you will get another chance with him after all. Did he say if he wanted to see you again?"

"No, he didn't."

Before she could yell at me again, the Keepers entered through the gate, carrying trays with our breakfast.

Elaine drew air through her nostrils. "It smells nice."

Melanie eagerly turned to face the Keepers. "Cinnamon? Or something like...what's that thing? Cardamom? Cloves? With nutmeg? God, I'd kill or fuck someone for just a drop of flavor in my food."

A pleasant scent of something incredibly appetizing drifted from the breakfast dishes. Like starved-for-brains zombies, we all shuffled toward the Keepers, following the delicious smell.

Kostya was the first one to grab a bowl from the tray.

"Oh, yeah!" he grunted with satisfaction, sniffing the creamy porridge. "Finally."

The porridge glistened with golden butter. Dark brown spices were sprinkled on top, emitting the wonderful aroma.

Before even leaving the line, Melanie put a spoonful in her mouth.

"Mmm." She closed her eyes, savoring it.

Elaine nudged me with an elbow. "Did you do that?"

"What? No? I wish I did." I accepted a bowl from Sigid. "This is wonderful. But what happened? Why the change?"

"Prince Rha ordered all meals for Joy Vessels made to their fullest enjoyment," Sigid explained.

"Why?" There was no one here to share our enjoyment from the food.

Sigid shrugged. "Because joy is precious and should not be denied."

Elaine shot me a glance. "Maybe you did have something to do with it, after all."

The only thing I did was let him feel the excitement that he caused in me.

Lin strolled by, cradling a breakfast bowl in her hands.

"Looks like the prince is celebrating a great date he had." She gave me a sly glance.

Lucia licked her spoon. "That must've been a hell of a kiss Dawn gave him. I can't wait to see what he does once she fucks him."

I blew out a breath. "I'm not—"

"Hey, I'm not complaining." She stuffed another spoonful in her mouth.

"Come, Dawn." Elaine hooked her arm into mine. "Let's go sit over there."

She led me to the sitting cushions under a flower arch. I crossed my legs under me and finally tried our breakfast.

"Shit, it's really good," I moaned with my mouth full. "But you know I didn't kiss him for this."

"I know," Elaine agreed, eating with gusto. "But does it really matter? Do whatever you want. There is no one to judge you. Just be careful not to fall for him."

Melanie joined us, plopping down on the cushion next to me.

"Not bad, hey?" She tipped her chin at my porridge. "The Keepers say they'll also bring coffee later. Apparently, the head chef fucked up the first pot. That guy from South Africa, what's his name?"

"Sipho?" Elaine offered helpfully.

"Right. He went to the kitchen to help the chef brew another one."

Elaine finished her breakfast and licked her spoon. "I'm surprised the kitchen staff even managed to pull this off after cooking nothing but tasteless gruel for most of their lives."

"It's because we aren't the only humans in the kingdom," I said.

Melanie snapped her gaze to me. "You did learn something more from him, didn't you?"

"Not much. And I would've told it to you sooner if you didn't start yelling at me. But there are twenty-four humans in the queen's palace in the city called Kalmena. They came about a month ago."

"And before that?" Elaine asked.

I shook my head. "That's it. There aren't any more, just them and us."

"But Ciana would've come here years ago."

"I guess she didn't." I sighed. "Rha said the portal had only been opened twice in all known history of the kingdom. Once, when they kidnapped us. And another time was a month or so ago."

"So, the queen has twenty-four. But how about her husband, the king??" Melanie asked.

"Rha didn't say anything about the king. His mother is the ruling queen. I'm not sure if she even has a husband."

Melanie pursed her lips, clearly disappointed in me once again.

Elaine studied the remaining porridge in my bowl. "I wonder where they get all this food from."

Her random comment was clearly meant to change the subject and discharge the heavy weight of Melanie's disapproval hanging in the air.

"Well, the city is located largely underground." I said, taking the chance she gave me. "Rha said there are entire farms there with houses and such. The shadow fae don't like sunlight or the heat of the day. Many prefer living under the surface."

Other inhabitants of the *sarai* moved closer, overhearing my words.

"An underground city? It sounds fun." Lin elbowed her friend in excitement.

"That'd be neat to see," her friend agreed.

"Do they have a food market there?" Kostya eyed my half-eaten breakfast. "The porridge was nice, but I could use more."

I offered him my bowl, and he grabbed it with a happy grin.

Sigid came by to collect Elaine's empty dish.

"Hey Sigid." I touched his hand, getting up. "You said we're allowed to go into the city with an escort, right?"

He scratched behind one of his long, pointy ears.

"I did say that, yes."

"Does it mean you can take us on a trip to the city? We'd like to visit an underground market please. Is there such a thing?" I asked.

"Sure. When would you like to go?"
I glanced at the people around me. "When?"
"How about right now?" Kostya boomed.
Sigid nodded. "I'll arrange it."

Fourteen

DAWN

Elaine looked up at the ceiling that arched high above the street. "Are we underground already?"

I didn't even notice when the glowing ceiling replaced the night sky as we walked along a street that slightly sloped downwards.

The eighteen of us had been broken into three groups of six to make it more manageable for our escort of Keepers and guards. Elaine and Melanie were in my group, as well as Lucia, Kostya, and a man named Sipho. I knew his name from Elaine and that he'd been abducted from South Africa, but he wouldn't talk to me when I'd tried to introduce myself. I didn't judge. We all had things to work through after being snatched from our past lives so abruptly.

Sigid came with us, too, along with a female Keeper and two male guards.

"It doesn't feel very different here," Melanie noted. "The streets outside are just as narrow as here. And the lighting is almost the same."

In addition to the silver-blue glimmer of the moths fluttering around, the street was illuminated by the golden light from the ceiling and the glowing columns of the buildings.

"Those ceiling tiles are really bright." Kostya squinted at the light.

"It's a naturally glowing stone," Sigid explained. "We mine it deep under the city. Its glow varies by location and can be enhanced with magic. No matter how bright it is, however, its light doesn't hurt our eyes the way sunshine does."

People hurried along the street, squeezing past our group. We encountered a few riders on horseback and a couple of merchants with camels in tow. All of us had to practically flatten ourselves against the walls of the surrounding buildings to allow for the camels with bundles on their backs to pass by.

"They're on the way to the market," Sigid said.

We followed the black camels to a wide, open space that was divided into rows by thick columns supporting the high ceiling. Merchants' stands formed perfectly straight rows along the columns. The noise here and the high energy of the market felt invigorating after the stagnated quiet of the *sarai*.

"Stay together," Sigid instructed, as the guards took their positions ahead and behind of our group. They held out their weapons, keeping the crowd at bay as we moved along the aisles.

"So, where is the food?" Kostya searched with his eyes the wares displayed in the stands.

Clothes of natural colors and geometric prints lay folded or hung draped over horizontal bamboo rods inside the stalls. Various weapons and household tools lay on the tables. Sandals, boots, and bejeweled armor were sold here too. There were a few stalls with bags of grain or baskets of vegetables on display. But I didn't see anyone who sold street food, nor could I smell any.

Scents of fried street food and candied treats had been a common feature of any fair or outdoor market back home. I'd taken it for granted before. And now, it felt like something important was missing.

"There is a food stand." Sigid gestured at a merchant up ahead.

The table of the stall held neatly wrapped packages the size of a sandwich. It was impossible to see what type of food they held through the gray parchment paper, and they weren't signed or labeled either.

A man approached the stand. He looked like he'd either just come from the desert or was about to go out there. The top layer of his long skirt-garment was lifted over his head and pinned to his hair, draping down his shoulders like a cloak.

"Five, please." He handed to the merchant a shiny hexagonal coin in exchange for five wrapped packages that he promptly stuffed into the satchel hanging on his side.

"What are these?" Kostya leaned over the table, taking a sniff. "They smell funny." He wrinkled his nose. "Couldn't be any good."

The woman merchant tilted her head, giving him a mixed look of curiosity and disdain.

"Humans," she scoffed. "Do you always sniff things? Like dogs?"

Kostya straightened his back, staring her down.

"Does your food always stink like shit?" he snarled, very much like a dog she'd likened him to.

She yanked a dagger out of the sheath on her belt so quickly I had no time to blink.

"Don't you dare!" She launched at Kostya over her table. "No one talks like that about my food."

Our guards crossed their swords in front of Kostya, shielding him from the merchant's wrath.

Sigid lifted his hands in a pacifying gesture, cautiously shifting forward.

"The Joy Vessel meant no offense, good woman. Please accept my apology." Sigid quickly ushered Kostya and the rest of us past the food stand and into a different aisle, away from the woman with the dagger.

"Wow," Elaine muttered under her breath, tossing a cautious glance over her shoulder. "And here I thought shadow fae were cold, unemotional creatures."

I held on to her sleeve, afraid of losing her in the crowd. "They come of all kinds, I guess, just like any other race or species."

Granted, Kostya had been a pest, but that woman should probably invest in a porch swing or some puzzle pieces to help her manage her temper. That made me think of Rha, of him holding my hands while helping me through my meltdown, and of our kiss. A warm glow spread through my chest, and I caught myself smiling.

Melanie suddenly bumped into my back.

"Hey! Watch it!" she yelled at someone behind her.

I turned to see the man who'd just bought the food from the high-tempered merchant. He gave Melanie a quick bow and briefly squeezed her hand.

"My apologies, Joy Vessel," he said softly before promptly disappearing into the crowd.

The guards slid closer to Melanie, but the man was already gone.

"Are you okay?" I asked her.

She threw a confused look in the direction where the man had gone.

"Yeah... I'm good. He tripped, I guess, and pushed me."

"Were you hurt?" one of our guards enquired.

"No. I'm fine," she assured us.

When the guard turned away, she opened her palm with a piece of paper rolled into a tight tube lying on it. Her forehead furrowed in confusion as she opened it.

"Did that guy give it to you?" I asked, keeping my voice down. "What does it say?"

Her eyes moved over the paper, then she quickly rolled it back and slipped it into her bra top.

"It's nothing." She waved me off. "Just some stupid prayer for our souls or something like that."

"Why are you keeping it if it's nothing?"

"Am I supposed to litter?" she snapped at me. "If you see a trash bin, let me know."

Kostya kept glaring in the direction of the food stand we'd just passed.

"What kind of food is that bitch selling?" he asked Sigid. "It stinks."

"It smells like boiled goat meat and raw turnips or possibly cabbage," Sigid corrected calmly. "It's unseasoned, with no added scent of spices."

Lucia cringed. "She sells boiled, unseasoned goat meat? How does she even stay in business?"

"Well, that guy bought five portions from her," Elaine pointed out. "He clearly didn't mind the taste or the smell."

"Neither the taste nor the smell matter to us, as long as they aren't those of rot," Sigid explained. "The meat is usually mixed with cooked grain and shredded vegetables. It's then pressed into packets to save space. It's perfect to take on the road or as a quick midnight meal when one is on the go. And it provides enough sustenance to last until the next meal."

For shadow fae, functionality won over taste and flavor. With pleasure not being a factor for them, food didn't need to smell enticing or taste delicious.

"Is that what the Royal Court eats too?" Melanie asked with disgust. "Unseasoned boiled goat?"

Sigid nodded. "Among a few other things, but the variety isn't nearly as large as the list of foods for the Joy Vessels."

One had to marvel at the versatility of skills of the royal chefs who, after years of boiling meat for their prince, managed to create a perfect crème brûlée for me when I had obnoxiously ordered it.

After browsing the aisles for a while, Melanie talked me into trading my golden belt for a necklace for her.

"You can get another belt if you play your cards right with the prince," she insisted. "But it's not like I'm going to get any royal presents anytime soon."

"And whose fault is that?" Lucia chimed in. "If you think you're too good for the *leilatha* harness, what's the prince supposed to give you presents for?"

"He can take his presents and shove them in the same place where he can shove that harness," Melanie retorted. "I'm not letting anyone mutilate my body like that."

"But you're perfectly okay with your sister 'mutilating' *her* body in order to get you that necklace?" Lucia obviously wasn't one to back down.

"It's fine, honestly. I don't mind." I tried to stop the argument before it would blow up into a fist fight, or worse. Melanie had always been pushy. And in Lucia, she seemed to have met her match.

"I'm sick and tired of her I'm-better-than-all-of-you attitude." Lucia fumed. "Like she should get a medal for not letting them put that thing on her."

Melanie propped her fists on her hips. "You just feel gross now that they harnessed you up like a horse."

"What if I don't mind being 'harnessed up?'" Lucia yelled. "What if I like staying in Teneris? Not everyone hates it here as much as you do or is as grossed out by their food as that chauvinistic oaf is."

"Hey! Watch it, bitch," Kostya protested.

"Oh, shut up." Lucia waved him off, staring my sister down. "I worked two soul-sucking jobs, lost my apartment, and slept in my car for weeks before the shadow fae took me. So, I'm not going to apologize or feel bad about liking it here. Now I have a roof over my head and regular meals, whatever the food may be. I don't have to deal with obnoxious assholes trying to grab my ass while I'm mopping the floor in the diner after a nine-hour shift. I don't have to clutch a knife in my hand in case someone breaks into my rusty car while I sleep between my shitty jobs. And if all these gloomy fuckers want from me in return is to share my happy mood to cheer them up, so be it."

Melanie rolled her eyes so hard, I feared they would stay deep in her head somewhere. She sucked in a long breath, ready to keep screaming, but Sipho, the quiet man in our group, spoke before her.

"I don't have a harness either," he said softly. "They never put one on me."

His calm voice seemed so out of place amidst the heated argument, we all turned to him at once. Looking uncomfortable in the spotlight of attention, Sipho shrugged, spreading his arms aside.

"It's true," he said.

Shoving his long-sleeved tunic off his shoulder, he presented us with the view of his ribbon-free dark-brown skin. Unlike most of us, Sipho had been wearing long sleeves, making the lack of harness unnoticeable until now.

Sigid cleared his throat. "The Joy Vessels in the *sarai* of Her Majesty Queen Abeille all got their *leilatha* harnesses within a day of their arrival. The intense experience of the fitting left some of them traumatized and unable to experience joy for a long time afterwards. Having learned about that, Prince Rha ordered not to put a harness on those of his Joy Vessels who weren't ready to accept one."

Elaine leaned to my ear. "Were you ready when they did it to you? I'm not sure I was, but I didn't fight them."

"Mine was meant to be a punishment, remember? For slapping the prince?"

No one had asked me for my consent before putting the harness on me. But now I wondered if that had been the reason for Rha coming to my fitting and for him keeping his hand on me to guide and support me through it all. As if after ordering the punishment, he'd wanted to make sure it didn't "traumatize" me.

I sighed, shaking my head. That man kept a delicate balance while treading a fine line between being ruthless and kind.

Then it occurred to me that without the harness, I would've never seen his real smile.

My thoughts remained with Rha on our way back to the palace. And when we entered the courtyard, my thoughts seemed to materialize, taking the shape of the prince sitting on a floor cushion by the main fountain. Surrounded by a small group of men and women, he held a scroll open in front of him.

My heart skidded, then leaped at the sight of him.

"How many warriors does the queen want me to send to Sumakis?" Rha asked the people he was with.

An elegant woman sitting to his right replied, "The High Lady of Sumakis requested from the crown at least a thousand for the adequate defense of her city. Queen Abeille trusts you will provide that number."

"She trusts me, does she now?" There was bitterness in his voice and in the hard set of his mouth.

I took in a long breath, calming my heart.

Just be careful not to fall for him, Elaine had said.

Falling for my captor with a harem full of people like me for his enjoyment would be beyond stupid, even for someone like me who was prone to making bad decisions.

Rha raised his head as our group entered.

"You're back," he said simply, rising to his feet.

The Joy Vessel Keepers took a knee. The guards bowed their heads. Not as well-versed in the etiquette of Teneris Palace, the rest of us just kept staring.

Rha's eyes found me.

"I've come for you, Dawn."

Everyone turned to me. Melanie's elbow jammed into my ribs as a reminder not to fuck it up this time.

The prince stepped closer, holding out his hand to me. "Will you share the midnight meal with me?"

Butterflies rose in my stomach, swirling in a crazy dance as I placed my hand in his.

I was not going to fall for him.

DAWN

"**I**s it going to be just you and me again?" I asked Rha as he led me into his dining room for our midnight meal.

The room was empty, save for the musicians in their usual places on the low stage by the wall. They nodded to me like they would to a good acquaintance.

"Yes, just you and me," Rha replied. "I find the presence of others distracting when I'm with you."

"Distracting in what way?"

"I need all my senses to absorb and process everything that's happening when you're near me. I have no attention to spare for anyone else."

Was it a compliment or a complaint? There was no change in his voice and no smile accompanied his words. It could possibly be the nicest thing anyone had ever said to me. Or he meant that I was a handful and a lot to handle.

My sitting cushions weren't in their usual place by the table. This time, they had been arranged behind Rha's dais, with a low stand placed in front of them.

"We'll share a meal but not the table?" I asked.

He nodded. "It's easier for the tendrils to connect in this position while we're eating."

So, he was planning to eat with me this time. Only in order for him to do that, he'd have to face the door while I'd be staring at the wall between the windows behind him. A great meal that would be.

"What's wrong?" he prompted when I didn't sit down.

"Does it feel right to you? Eating together with our backs turned to each other?"

"That's a limitation not of my making," he replied. "The tendrils are too short to reach over the dais and across the table. Unless you prefer I keep them hidden."

I didn't doubt he'd do that if I asked him to. But I was looking forward to sharing the meal with him, and I no longer no longer wanted to deny him the simple pleasure of enjoying it with me.

"That would defeat the purpose of having lunch together, wouldn't it?"

"Not exactly," he disagreed. "I find your mere presence in this room satisfying already."

"Is that why you personally came to the *sarai* for me?" Against my best intentions, my cheeks warmed, and something fluttered in my stomach once again.

"I severely dislike the unsettling feeling your absence causes in me."

I lowered my head, hiding a smile.

"You know what it sounds like, Your Highness? It sounds like you missed me. And if I dare venture a guess, I'd say you like me."

The man clearly had no idea about flirting. His expression remained unchanged as he stared at me batting my eyelashes at him.

"Liking someone or something falls in the range of emotions beyond our reach, Dawn. Now that you're here, I simply feel content."

It might not sound like much, but content was the highest positive emotion he could feel. And he felt it when I was here.

"I'll tell you what. Why don't we get rid of this thing?" Holding up my skirt, I shoved the heavy table out of the way with my foot. It slid only a short distance over the mosaic floor with a loud screech.

"Whatever are you doing, Dawn?" The prince stared at me like I'd completely lost my mind.

"I'm rearranging things here a little. Give me a hand, will you? This table might be low, but it's too heavy for me to lift on my own."

He gestured for one of the musicians to come closer. Together, they easily lifted the long, massive table.

"Where do you want it?" Rha asked me, looking more intrigued than upset by my manipulation of his personal environment.

"Over there?" I pointed at the spot by the opposite wall. "Just out of the way for now. Thank you."

While they moved the table, I brought my sitting cushions to the front of the royal dais. Then I put the stand that was supposed to serve as my personal table between my seat and Rha's.

There would still be a significant distance between us. His dais wasn't high, but it was wide, not allowing me to move the table much closer to his cushions.

As the musician took his place on the stage again, Rha sauntered toward me.

"Would it be terribly disrespectful to ask you to sit on the floor with me?" I asked carefully, keeping in mind that disrespect to his royal persona carried a punishment.

"Why do you want me on the floor?"

"You see, I can't move the table any closer because of this platform. But if you sat on the same level as me—"

He raised a hand in warning, stopping me mid-sentence.

"A Crown Prince is never on the same level as anyone else. Just below the queen, he's elevated above the rest."

"I see. Though it sounds like a lonely place to be."

He flicked his wrist at the musicians. "Leave us."

Obediently, they stopped playing, took their instruments, and exited the room.

"That is the place of the Crown Prince when he's in public," Rha clarified with a mischievous glint in his eyes. "In private, no one needs to know what the prince does, do they?"

A smile tugged at my lips.

"No. They do not," I agreed.

"Let me just get them to bring the food in first," he said. "Then you can place me wherever you like."

After the servants brought the dishes in and left, I grabbed one of the cushions from the royal dais and threw it on the floor by our little table.

"Will this work?" I asked and added with a smile, "I promise not to tell anyone how low you have fallen, Your Highness."

He inclined his head, arching an eyebrow, but there still wasn't a hint of a smile on his face.

"You don't find it funny, Rha, do you?"

"I appreciate the play on words as well as the double meaning of the phrase."

"But you're not laughing."

He spread his arms aside. "I never laugh."

"Well, I've seen you smile already. Not all is lost. Here." I tapped the *leilatha* on my left arm. "Stick your things in here. You're far livelier with my emotions in you."

His tendrils unwound immediately, like tightly wound springs that got finally released. They uncoiled straight down before reaching for me.

My bravado thinned at the sight of these smoky, snake-like appendages eagerly undulating toward me. I raised my hand in a defensive gesture, and they stilled, frozen in motion.

"Are you alright?" Rha asked with concern.

"Just give me a minute..." I pushed the words through my tightened throat. "Let's sit down first."

I sank onto the cushions, with Rha taking his place across the table from me. There was barely enough space on the small table for all the dishes that the servants had brought.

Roasted duck with crispy skin lay on a bed of fragrant rice. Plump dumplings were served along with long noodles. Skewers of marinated and grilled meat were arranged on a platter. And a flaky white fish dish looked like either a soup or a stew.

Everything smelled amazing, especially as compared to the food on the single plate placed in front of Rha. It held a pile of cooked grain like barley or farro, next to two handfuls of chopped meat and a heap of shredded pale vegetable, either a squash or a turnip. His food had no sauce, no herbs, not even a glint of oil or butter, and I doubted it even had salt.

"Is that what you normally eat?" I asked.

"This and a few other things, depending on what's available." He speared a piece of meat on his fork, put it in his mouth, and chewed. His expression didn't change. He didn't pause to savor, just chewed and swallowed, then reached for another piece.

"Wait." I stopped him, pointing at the tendrils resting at his sides like lazy snakes. "You can use these now. Just, don't shove them in too quickly, please, and I'll be fine."

The "snakes" stirred, lifting off the floor. Two of them moved closer to me. I held still, as if they were wild animals, curious but potentially dangerous. Their ends unraveled like wavy tassels. The wisps of shadows fanned over my skin as Rha moved them up my arms. A chilling sensation scattered with goosebumps over my body.

I halted my breath, bracing for the invasion. But he held back. Only one tendril touched the *leilatha* rosette on my left arm. Like a gentle lick of a tongue, the shadows slipped in, and the tendril connected.

"You're still scared," Rha said. "Why?"

"I'm not scared."

"Apprehensive."

"A little," I confessed. "Maybe. Wouldn't you be if you were in my situation? Would you let someone get under your skin freely like this to invade your feelings and roam through your thoughts?"

"I cannot read your thoughts."

"Thoughts and feelings are connected."

"Not as much as you think."

"Ha!" I lifted a finger. "If you can't read what I think, how do you know what I'm thinking about?"

He shook his head with a sigh. "Dawn, you've just told me your thoughts about that."

"Did I?"

"You stated—quite adamantly, I should add—that thoughts and feelings are connected."

"But aren't they? We think about how we feel. Like I would think that you have a charming smile, and I'd feel the attraction..." That sounded too much like a confession, so I made a weak attempt at back-pedaling. "Purely as an example, of course."

"You do feel attracted to me," he said as a matter of fact.

If I wanted to fool him, I should've done so before his tendril tapped into my feelings. And now, he certainly got the whiff of my mortification too.

"But I never knew it was because of my smile," he added, *smiling*.

Holy shit. Breath caught in my throat. It was an amazing smile —bright, a little crooked, with a cheeky glint of a fang.

I glanced away, feeling slightly winded.

"I should smile more often." Rha's quiet voice reached me across the table. "The effect it has on you is exquisite."

His remaining five tendrils moved closer to my harness.

"Go ahead." I shifted both arms forward to meet them.

One or six, what difference did it make? Rha was deep under my skin already, in more ways than one.

He connected them all through my arms and my back. Shadowy tendrils reached into my emotions like fingers. For a moment, their intrusion felt overwhelming, but the uneasy feeling quickly settled into the background. I felt Rha's presence, but it was similar to holding someone's hand. It required no concentration on my part, easily allowing me to do other things, like eating or talking.

"Alright." I picked up a piece of the fried duck on my fork. "Shall we?"

After putting the meat in my mouth, I focused on the bouquet of flavors bursting on my tongue, savoring the texture of the succulent meat in combination with the crispy skin. I did it in such detail for Rha's sake, I realized.

His eyes closed slowly. He tilted his head back, basking in my pleasure. I made it last for as long as I could before swallowing.

"It's good, huh?" I licked my lips.

He opened his eyes, staring at me in wonder. "I've never tasted anything like it."

"Well, you had lunch with Kostya yesterday, didn't you?"

"Kostya loves his food. But not like this. You..." He looked like he was searching for words before speaking again. "It must be your attraction toward me. It gives a unique flavor to your pleasure. It feels like bubbles are bursting all through my body. Look." He thrust his arm toward me. His coal-black skin was pebbled with tiny goosebumps. "It's never happened before."

I laughed, trying to cover up the awkwardness. It came from realizing how well he was aware of my liking him.

Of course, he picked up on that too. "You're enjoying my company, but you seem almost ashamed of that fact. Why?"

Why?

Because I shouldn't be this enamored by my kidnapper. I should be interrogating him for information that would help me and the others escape, instead of wasting my brain power on figuring out how best to please him with fried duck.

God, it was really good that he couldn't read my thoughts.

"Well..." I said. "Feeling attracted to someone generally makes people more vulnerable, doesn't it?"

"It does? How?"

"Fear of rejection, for one."

That was a lie. I didn't fear Rha rejecting me. A part of me—the sane, practical part—even wished it would happen. Then I could go on my merry way to plot our escape with the others in the *sarai* instead of sitting here and melting at the rare sight of his smile.

He frowned in confusion. "Why would I ever want to reject you? You are the only one who stimulates me both mentally and emotionally in ways that no person has ever done before and I believe never will. You are a unique treasure, Down. And I was incredibly fortunate to find you."

He sure had a unique way of delivering compliments. If it was wrong, I couldn't help it—his words sent a wave of warm pleasure through me, and Rha exhaled slowly, luxuriating in it.

I focused on what was happening that very moment—we were having lunch together, and it felt...nice.

What harm could come from the two of us simply enjoying the food?

I lifted the next piece of duck on my fork.

"Okay, let's eat, then. You too." I tipped my chin at his plate.

"What do you want me to do?"

"I want us to take the next bite together. Ready?" I waited until he speared another piece with his fork. "One, two, three." I put my fork in my mouth at the same time as he did his. "Mmm." I savored my food while Rha clearly was enjoying his. "What is it that you're eating, anyway?"

"A boiled desert snake," he said after swallowing.

"Oh..." I tried not to imagine what it tasted like, completely unseasoned too. "Why don't you eat the duck with me? There is enough for both of us."

He shook his head. "It won't taste much different to me than the snake. It's what *you* eat that matters."

When I thought I couldn't possibly eat another piece, Rha moved a small bowl with dessert my way.

"Try this one," he said. "Dried apricots soaked in honey. They say it's good."

I lifted an apricot on my spoon. The golden honey dripped from it in thick, shimmering drops. A sweet, nutty aroma teased my nostrils. Amazing flavors exploded on my tongue when I took a bite. Sweetness coated the inside of my mouth.

"Oh God," I moaned in pleasure. "They are right. It's so good."

A blissful smile played on Rha's lips as he watched me from across the table. I licked the honey off my lips.

"You should try it." I lifted my spoon with another apricot to his mouth.

"It'll be—" he started.

But I didn't let him finish. "Hey, we'll do it together. This way, you'll feel both the texture and the taste."

Taking a clean spoon, he humored me by grabbing an apricot from the bowl and bringing it to my mouth too.

"Three, two, one," I counted down before opening my mouth for his spoon to slide in. At the same time, I moved my spoon into his mouth.

We chewed together with our gazes linked across the table. I tried to focus on the taste but got distracted by a drop of honey escaping from the corner of his mouth. It glistened against his ink-black skin like a golden dewdrop, tempting me to taste it.

I could reach over the table and swipe it off with my thumb. But what I really wanted was to use my tongue to lick it off. I flicked my gaze to the table between us. As small as it was, it stood in the way.

Not taking his eyes off me, Rha shoved the table away, sending the half-empty dishes to the floor.

"Why did you do that?" I gasped in shock.

"You wanted it gone."

"You said you couldn't read my thoughts."

"I cannot. But I have a feeling you want to come closer." Hooking an arm around my waist, he drew me onto his lap. "And I want you here too."

I pressed both hands against his chest. "What if your feeling is wrong?"

He darted his tongue out, licking that tempting honey drop off his bottom lip. "Then why are you feeling happier here in my arms than you were over there?"

"Happier?" I squinted at him skeptically.

He nodded confidently.

"More excited. Exhilarated even. Anticipation is buzzing through you so strongly, I feel its vibration with all my senses." He leaned so close over me, I could smell the honey on his breath. "Kiss me, Dawn. Kiss me like you did yesterday. I've been dreaming about that kiss ever since."

His lips hovered a hairbreadth away from mine, but he wouldn't close the distance.

"Why don't you kiss me yourself?" I challenged.

"Because it feels better when you do it. There is no bitterness or apprehension in your emotions when you know you have control."

Oh, that was so true. I hadn't even realized it. But Rha sensed it. He gave control to me, and I accepted it. Cupping his face with my hands, I gently brushed my lips over his. He parted them eagerly, taking everything I gave.

He tasted of honey and apricots—the best dessert after the meal we'd just so thoroughly enjoyed together.

I rose on my knees, sinking my fingers into his long, silky hair. Somehow, our kiss grew deeper, and I didn't know whether it was my fault or his. He wrapped his arms around me tightly. His tendrils flexed, bringing me even closer to him. He slid a hand up my back. Pleasure rippled over my skin in the wake of his touch.

"You like it," he groaned against my mouth. "You like my hands on you."

It wasn't a question. He knew. He felt it all. And he kept exploring. His fingers pressed between my shoulder blades, dove into the hair on the back of my head, then slightly tugged at the roots, learning my response to each action.

"Here," I croaked, grabbing his hand and moving it to my breast. "I want you here."

His palm pressed against my hardened nipple through the fabric of my dress. Desire zapped through me. Rha hissed in pleasure, squeezing my breast hard. I whimpered in pain, and he immediately let go, leaning away from me.

"Too much?"

"A little." I smiled at the terror on his face. "We humans are delicate creatures. Shadow fae are so much stronger than us. And well, you just have big hands." I took his hand in mine. It was big but elegant, with long, deft fingers. "Maybe you should try again?" I shrugged my dress off my shoulder. The soft fabric slid down my skin easily. "Like this." I trailed the tips of his fingers along my collarbone.

My skin tingled from his touch. Hooking a finger under my bra strap, he tugged it off my shoulder and down my arm, past the tendril connected to my body.

The bra top slid down, freeing my breast. I sucked in a breath at the brush of cool air against my skin. A shiver of pleasure ran between my shoulder blades.

Rha paused his gaze on my pebbled nipple, then glanced up at my face.

"I'm not even touching you right now."

"I know. But the way you're looking at me..." I exhaled a soft moan.

"Is that all it takes? Just a look?" he marveled.

The right look. From the right man. At the right time. Yes, that was all it took for me to shiver in anticipation.

I leaned into his touch and kissed him again. He cradled my breast gently this time, massaging it softly. His thumb brushed by my nipple, and I whimpered at another zap of desire.

I'd had no wine with lunch, yet I felt drunk on his scent and his closeness. The heady sense of control made me believe I could stop any time. I could "quit" Rha at any moment. He'd stop if he sensed I wanted him to.

Except that right now, I wished for nothing of the sort. I wanted him to keep touching me. And he eagerly obliged.

"More," I moaned against his mouth.

He yanked the dress and the bra top down my other shoulder, then took my naked breasts into his hands.

I freed my arms from my clothes, peppering kisses along the sharp line of his jaw. Raking my fingers through his hair, I slid my thumbs up his pointy ears. Their cartilage was hard. No wonder I'd initially mistaken them for horns, but the skin on the outer side felt like velvet under my fingers.

He flicked an ear at my touch, and I jerked my hand away.

"Should I not touch these?"

The look in his eyes was dazed, glazed over with all the new sensations. His black pupils dilated larger than ever before.

"You absolutely should touch anything that brings you pleasure," he rasped. "My body is yours."

Because my pleasure was his. Literally.

I nibbled along the firm cord of a muscle on the side of his neck, dragging my teeth over his skin. A chain from his jewelry piece scratched my chin.

"I want this off." I tugged at it.

Without saying a word, he brought his hand back and unclipped the chain, sending the heavy chainmail to the floor. The hard, wide expanse of his chest was now all mine to explore. I roamed my hands over it, savoring the sensation of his warm skin under my palms.

"It's true, my prince," I breathed out. "You are extremely *enjoyable.*"

He mimicked my caresses, kissing my neck and stroking my chest. I tilted my head back, giving him more of my body to touch. More to learn.

"More…" I whimpered, rocking my hips against his hard abs.

"Tell me what you want, my treasure," he murmured against the side of my neck.

I leaned closer to his ear. "I want your mouth, Rha."

"Where do you want it?"

"Where your hands have been."

He tipped his head back. His eyebrows rose in surprise. Clearly, he had not expected that request.

"Have you ever heard of foreplay, Your Highness?" Why had I not considered that he hadn't? I felt like slapping myself. "Have you ever been with a woman before, Rha?"

"Like this? Never." With his hands on my back, he laid me down on the cushions. "With you, everything is for the first time."

He took my request quite literally, tracing with his lips every inch of my skin that his hands had touched. Once he reached my breast, he slowly made his way to the tip, then skimmed over it with his tongue, the way I'd done to his lips when we kissed. Rha learned things quickly and remembered well what he'd learned.

Pleasure skittered over my skin with a rush of warmth. I stretched on the cushions. Cradling his head in my hands, I steered him slightly, but then realized he didn't need directions from me. He felt my pleasure like his own.

Sucking a nipple into his mouth, he flicked his tongue over it. His sharp fangs scraped against my skin, but the zing of pain only spurred my desire. Sensing it, he didn't pull away.

I moved my hand to my other breast. And he quickly took over there too. While kissing one nipple, he let his fingers play with the other.

Desire spread through my body. Heat pulsed between my legs. I rubbed against his washboard abs, but it wasn't enough. My need grew, banishing shame. I slid a hand between us and slipped a finger in my underwear, pressing it to where I needed it most.

He exhaled sharply. My pleasure rocked through him with a shudder. I rubbed harder. I was so close that it didn't take long before an orgasm rolled through me. I closed my eyes, riding it with abandon as my moans echoed Rha's tortured groans.

When I opened my eyes, he rose over me on his arms, staring

at me in shock and wonder. His golden eyes opened wide, his black hair streaming over us like a shroud of darkness.

"Dawn, what was *that?*" he demanded. "I have no word for it. What did I just feel?"

How was I supposed to explain to a man nearly three times my age what an orgasm was?

I blew out a breath. "Well, we need to have this conversation, don't we?"

Rha sat up on his haunches between my open legs. I adjusted my clothes back in place, but when I tried to shift away, he drew me back to him. Sitting on his floor cushion, he placed me between his legs sideways. I leaned with my shoulder against his chest. The slit of his skirt opened, exposing his leg with thick corded muscles on his thigh.

My hip fitted snugly against his crotch, too snugly, meeting absolutely no resistance. There was no hard ridge of an erection between his legs, not even a softening one. No post-orgasmic wetness. Nothing.

I had a lot of questions. The topic was awkward, but we should be past any shame now. After all, he'd witnessed me come twice already, including that time on the altar with all the Joy Guardians present.

"Tell me, Rha, do shadow fae have sex? I mean, you have to reproduce somehow."

Unless they just multiplied in their shadow form by dividing into two, like amoebas.

To my relief, he said, "Yes, we have sex."

"How?" I pressed my hip a little harder into his crotch area. There definitely wasn't anything there. "Forgive me, Your Highness, but I don't believe you have...um, the necessary equipment."

"What do you mean?"

Clearly, being vague got me nowhere.

"Rha, do you have a dick?" I asked him straight on.

His eyebrows shot up to the circlet of his crown, and then...he laughed. It was a deep sound filled with mirth—*my* mirth because we remained connected through his tendrils.

"And you said you didn't laugh," I muttered, stunned.

Shadow fae could be happy. Or at least they could feel happiness, provided someone allowed them access to that emotion.

"Not normally, no." He shook his head, looking a bit shocked himself. "There are so many firsts with you, my treasure." He kissed my cheek. "To answer your question, no, I do not have the organ you call 'a dick' at the moment."

"Does it like...come and go?"

He grinned. I understood the hilarity of it. After all, he fed off *my* humor. But I was genuinely puzzled too.

"Rha, just explain it to me like I'm a kid. When two shadow fae love each other..."

The smile slid off his face. "Love has nothing to do with procreation, Dawn. It's best if it doesn't."

"That's right. I forgot, you can't feel love."

He looked taken aback by that. "Of course we can."

"How? Isn't love one of the highest pleasures out there? It's definitely higher than content."

"For humans, maybe. For us, it's one of the cruelest tortures known. Love means feeling a debilitating fear for the loved one when they're well and devastating anguish when they're hurt. I've heard that the agony of losing a lover is worse than death. People have lost their minds and ended their own lives over that. I would not wish love on my worst enemy. It's more terrible than a curse."

I believed I understood what he was saying. Love brought the highest pleasure. But it could also bring agony. For those incapable of feeling pleasure, agony was all that remained.

"Procreation, however, is just a physical function," Rha continued. "If a man spends enough time with a woman, his body reacts by creating all the 'equipment' necessary for when she enters her fertile cycle."

"And how often do your women enter that cycle?"

"About once a year."

"So, shadow fae only have sex once a year?"

"Yes, if they're married or bonded mates and are trying to procreate."

"And if they're not trying?"

He touched a strand of my hair on the side of my face. The gentle tickle of his fingers sent a flock of warm tingles through my chest, and he sighed with a smile.

"If the couple has been together for a while before the start of the woman's fertile period," he spoke softly, "they may fall into a mating fever, which usually spans about three days."

"So, you can only have sex once a year during those three days. And if you're not married or mated or whatever, you don't have sex at all?"

"Who would want to have sex for no reason?" He winced. "It's messy, often inconvenient, and always driven by instinct. It's nothing but a painful urge that needs to be taken care of or it'd drive one insane. It's best to avoid it unless absolutely necessary."

"Well... It is a bit different for humans."

"I've heard." He stroked the side of my face, probably to experience another rush of my pleasure from his touch. "Is that what just happened here? Was the pleasure we felt tonight of a sexual nature?"

The pleasure we felt.

The experience with him was infinitely more intimate than anything I'd ever shared with a man before because I didn't just share my body with Rha but also every emotion I felt while we remained connected.

"It was, Rha," I exhaled. "Welcome to your first orgasm."

He hadn't come himself. He didn't even currently have the body part necessary for that. But he'd experienced my orgasm as his own.

Rha touched my face, still exploring the effects of his touch on my emotions.

"What's this?" He rubbed a spot just above my lip on the right where I had a small birthmark. "It doesn't come off."

"And it won't." I giggled softly. "It's a birthmark. I was born with it."

"Just on one side?"

"Yes, Rha. Just on one side, specifically to offend your symmetry-loving sensibilities."

"You're such a chaotic mess, Dawn, inside and out."

That could be taken as an insult if it wasn't said in a reverent voice with a warm smile.

"Speaking of a mess." I gestured at the shoved aside table with the dishes strewn on the floor. "Who's going to clean this one?"

He paid no attention to the state of the room, keeping his gaze on me.

"I'm afraid no one can restore the order or clean the mess you've caused, Dawn, both in my dwelling and in my heart."

Sixteen

RHA

She was a splendid mess. A chaotic whirlwind of contradicting emotions. Her affection for me flickered like a candle flame in the breeze of doubts. But in those rare moments when it burned strongly, it was spectacular. And also spectacularly addictive.

All I wanted was to keep kissing her while I hunted for that spot between her legs that she'd touched before falling undone with the most intense, magical pleasure I'd ever tasted.

The doors flew open, however. Princess Alzali, my meddlesome cousin, slipped into the room uninvited. She'd arrived that evening with an order from the queen. I hadn't seen my mother for over eight years, and instead of coming to Teneris with a visit or inviting me to Kalmena, she'd sent Alzali.

"Your Highness." My cousin sank into a slow bow, visibly perfectly respectful. Never mind that she'd just disobeyed my order not to enter my private dining room while I was here with Dawn.

Alzali's orange eyes darted around the room, taking in everything. I was sure she didn't miss the dishes scattered on the floor, or my chest armor tossed aside, or me sitting on the floor like a lowly commoner with a Joy Vessel in my lap.

"Did I not say I would take my midnight meal alone?" I didn't try to keep the displeasure out of my voice.

Dawn stiffened in my arms. Unease and mortification oozed through my tendrils from her. She had no reason to be ashamed, but I had no time to explain it to her. Alzali had come here for a reason. Emboldened by the queen's order, she wouldn't leave until she got my undivided attention.

My cousin primly folded her hands in front of her.

"It looks like you're done with your meal, Your Highness. Unless you wish to lick the food off the floor?" She arched an eyebrow with a glance at the mess around the table.

"I should go." Dawn scrambled off my lap, leaving me no choice but to disconnect and retract my tendrils.

"You should, Sweet One," Alzali murmured, smoothly stepping aside and keeping the door open for Dawn to leave.

"Wait." I rose from the floor slowly, demonstrating I was not in a hurry to accommodate anyone who barged in on my private time with my Joy Vessel. "Dawn, please meet Princess Alzali."

"Princess?" Dawn nodded jerkily, looking confused and possibly frightened.

I could've strangled Alzali for her lack of manners.

"She's my cousin, the queen's niece."

"Nice to meet you." Dawn stretched her open hand toward my cousin.

Alzali kept her hands where they were, folded neatly in front of her. Realizing her greeting wouldn't be returned, Dawn dropped her hand to her side and repeated, "I should go. I'll find my way back to the *sarai*."

"No, you'll stay in my rooms from now on." I flicked my fingers at the guards waiting outside the door. "Take the Joy Vessel downstairs to the golden sitting room."

The bizarre death of the desert dweller at the gate to Teneris remained unexplained. I'd personally questioned the caravan's owner and everyone else who'd arrived with her, and still had no clear reason for the man to do what he did.

Maybe Oskura was right and there was no reason to worry. But when it came to Dawn, reason deserted me. I could barely wait for the Joy Vessels to return from the market. Racked by worry, I'd even moved my meeting with Alzali to the *sarai*, waiting for my Sweet One.

She looked at me with a silent question in her bi-colored eyes.

"You're staying here, Dawn. With me."

"But—"

"It's safer this way," I cut her off firmly. It wouldn't do for my Joy Vessel to contradict me in front of Alzali.

Thankfully, Dawn didn't argue any further. Tossing only a glare my way, she let the guards take her through the door and down the stairs.

Alzali followed Dawn with her gaze. "Did you find yourself a favorite? Already? You're much faster than your mother. The queen has twenty-four Joy Vessels but favors no one."

"Mother never favored anyone other than Father. Now that he's gone, I fear she'll never have another favorite ever again."

Alzali kept staring at the door behind which Dawn had gone.

"Her eyes don't match." Her shoulders moved with a shudder of repulsion. "Was that the best you could do, Your Highness? Is she sick? Or did she lose an eye, and it's been replaced by a hag with no skills?"

Irritation stirred in me. I didn't plan to choose Dawn. Like everything with her, it'd just happened without strategy or logic. Now that she was mine, however, any insult toward her applied to me too.

"What do you want, Alzali?" I snapped.

She jerked her head, looking appalled by my gruff tone. Personally, Alzali delivered her insults in the gentlest of voices, which only made them sharper. She flicked back her long hair that was gathered into a high ponytail held by a wide golden clip between her ears. Each ear was decorated with several earrings along the outer edge, interconnected by dangling loops of thin, golden chains.

"I came to Teneris with a royal order," she said, looking deeply offended. "But I was brushed aside in favor of a Joy Vessel. Could that not have waited?"

Spending time with a Joy Vessel certainly should've waited until the royal business was complete. But I simply couldn't stay away from Dawn for long.

I scrubbed a hand down my face. It was hard to concentrate with my thoughts swerving to her again and again. Even now, all I really wanted to do was to go to her. But the orders of the Queen of Alveari should not be ignored.

"Very well. Let's talk."

Alzali wrinkled her nose, glaring at the dishes on the floor. "It'd be best to have this mess cleaned up. Don't you think?"

Her voice remained gentle, which didn't make it sound any less condescending. It was not the way to speak to the crown prince in his own palace. But as the queen's closest ally and advisor, Alzali got away with things worse than that. In this case, I also had to admit she was right. The room needed a good cleaning.

Biting down on my irritation, I summoned another guard and gave a few orders. As servants filed into the room to clean, I headed toward my sitting room with a gesture for Alzali to follow.

"I never knew about this room." Alzali took a long, sweeping look around my private space.

I hated bringing her here. Other than the cat and a few servants who cleaned in here, no one entered this room but me.

It felt different from when I'd allowed Dawn to come in here to change into her new dress. Dawn had been observant and respectful, even when she tipped over my puzzle. Alzali's presence felt like an intrusion, prying into my personal life. But I'd rather have this discussion with her here than out in the dining room with the servants cleaning and listening.

"I already told you the queen can have the thousand men she's asked for," I said quickly, itching to be done with it as soon as possible.

"And who will lead them?" she enquired ever so politely.

As hard as she tried to hide it, I sensed her eagerness to lead my warriors.

Alzali leaned to pet Zala who woke up from her nap and now stared suspiciously at us both. Arching her back, Zala hissed then jumped off the cushions, evading the princess's hand.

Alzali jerked her hand away with a grimace. "This cat is feral."

"Hardly," I disagreed.

Zala might be a stray, but she loved to cuddle. She was, however, extremely discriminating about whom she granted the privilege to pet her. Flipping her tail up, the cat slinked out onto the patio between the open window panes. She'd probably bring back a jerboa or two before the night was over. Quite a few of them hopped in the tall grasses of the city's roofs and outer walls.

Alzali turned to me. "Can I report to Queen Abeille that her fearsome son will personally lead his men and women to execute her orders?"

Queen Abeille requested I send my warriors to assist the High Lady of Sumakis in fighting the desert dwellers who'd been raiding her city located on the outskirts of the kingdom.

Desert dwellers were rebels who had abandoned the strictly regulated life in a city in favor of the dangerous and often deadly existence out in the desert. They raided merchants' caravans to survive the harsh conditions outside. But that often proved insufficient, especially since the merchants had responded by organizing and increasing armed escorts. Now, the desert thugs resorted to attacking the cities. Sumakis was especially favored as an easy target.

The queen wished for me to fight the rebels, get their attacks under control, then catch and publicly execute their leaders. I'd done it before on many occasions and had been successful every time. But now... Now I had no desire to leave Teneris.

"My presence is required here," I said, not elaborating on the reasons, especially since the main reason was currently waiting for me in the golden room, and I hated making her wait for much longer.

Alzali humbly inclined her head, concealing her ambition behind her long eyelashes.

"It'll be my honor to lead your warriors for you."

As the next female in line for the crown, Alzali held the title of a princess, but she had no city of her own and no army. She was the heiress to her father's holdings, who was the queen's younger brother. But I'd long suspected Alzali had her sight set higher. Technically, her place was behind me in the succession line—she was the niece of the ruling queen while I was the queen's son. But as a female, Alzali's claim was strong enough to rival my own.

From the beginning of time, the Kingdom of Alveari had been ruled by a queen. There had never been a king, and many wished it would remain that way. Unfortunately for them, I was Queen Abeille's only child. She had no daughter.

Alzali laced her fingers together so tightly the skin on her knuckles turned from black to gray. It'd be a perfect opportunity for her to prove herself in action, thus adding another achievement to her list, which she then could use to fight me for the crown. I'd be a fool to give her the weapon she'd inevitably use against me.

"Oskura will lead them," I decided.

"Your lieutenant?" Alzali's lips quivered, but only for a moment. She regained her composure quickly.

"Oskura is my general now, has been for a few years. My warriors know and trust her. She will lead them to victory."

With her mouth pressed into a thin line, Alzali bowed her head.

"As you wish, Your Highness."

"I will assemble the best men and women and have them head out for Sumakis as soon as possible. It may take a couple of days."

"I will join them," Alzali announced.

It wasn't ideal, but there wasn't much I could do about that. I couldn't possibly order the princess to stay put or send her back to Kalmena. All I could do was make it clear to my warriors that General Oskura was in charge of this mission and that her orders superseded Alzali's.

"Very well then." I gestured at the door, signaling the end of our conversation.

Alzali left, maybe not entirely content but at least somewhat pacified. Tension drained from me, sending me down into the cushions.

With a muffled meowing, Zala returned, carrying a dead rodent in her mouth. She dropped it by my boot.

"It didn't take you long," I muttered, kicking the dead body away.

Zala jumped onto my lap, arching her back and rubbing her head against my arms and chest.

"Thanks for the present." I scratched behind her ear.

Peace descended upon me as the cat curled on my lap with soft purring vibrating through her small body. I stroked her fur, letting the calm relax my muscles. But for once, it wasn't enough. Since Dawn came into my life, I'd been craving emotions far more exhilarating than calm.

I craved chaos.

Seventeen

DAWN

The guards took me down a wide, winding staircase with an ornate railing. We descended into a huge, open cave. The place was so big, for a moment I wondered if we had come outside somehow.

The calming sound of a bubbling stream filled the cave. Stalactites of glowing crystal grew from the high ceiling above. A shimmering waterfall cascaded down the black rock wall, creating a stream that curved across the floor inlaid with colorful mosaic. Pale gray and dark purple plants grew in decorative arrangements between the rocks above the water.

"I had no idea that the underground could be this gorgeous," I muttered, stunned.

The air here was rich with moisture and filled with the aroma of the plants. Low marble benches stood along the stream, arranged in a way that presented the best view of the water for the person sitting on them.

"This way." A guard gestured for me to follow him down the path along the stream.

At the far end of the cave, the water ran under a wall of rock.

Two doors were carved into the wall on each side of the stream, connected by a narrow, arched bridge.

The guard opened the door on the left. "His Highness wishes for you to stay in the golden sitting room." He let me enter.

The ceiling and the walls in here were made of yellow clay. Long, thin crystals were laid in the shape of a hexagon in the center of the ceiling. They shone with a golden glow that spread along thin veins of crystals from each end of the hexagon toward the walls. The golden glow reflected with a shimmer in the silk cushions arranged on a slightly raised platform in the middle of the room. The platform was also shaped like a hexagon, with six carved poles rising from each corner. The poles arched over the platform into a structure resembling a gazebo. Light, shimmering fabric draped over the arches, framing a sitting area inside, and a mosaic of white and gold tiles decorated the floor.

The golden shimmer, along with the yellow walls, gold tiles, and butter-colored silk made the room indeed look as if made of gold.

Several servants entered behind us. The first few removed the cushions off the platform and the fabric from the poles. The ones following them carried in a thick round mattress and armloads of bedding.

Before I knew it, a large bed replaced the sitting area on top of the platform. Next, they brought in a black canopy that was stretched between long, thin spikes like an umbrella. They fitted it over the bed poles to block the glow from the ceiling for the person who'd be sleeping in the bed. And it looked like that person was going to be me.

I stopped one of the servants by catching the end of his skirt. "Am I to stay here until tomorrow?"

"You'll stay here for as long as His Highness desires," he replied.

Another servant brought in a huge basket filled with linens, towels, and toiletries. Setting it on the floor, he opened a door to the left.

"Your dressing room is here, Sweet One." He gestured into the adjacent room that held tall shelves and empty trunks with their lids open.

"Will Prince Rha come down here anytime soon?" I asked. "I need to speak with him."

"That is up to His Highness." He opened a door on the right. "This is the prince's private baths."

I poked my head out the door and momentarily stopped breathing at the sight of another giant cave. This appeared to be the continuation of the one before. The same underground river flowed from under the rocky wall. It spread into a wide pool with tiny islands that had been transformed into flower beds with plants, shrubs, and vines. Mosaic paths ran along both sides of the pool. Flat, polished rocks formed a path across the water to the other side with a set of wide double doors across from mine.

"You may freshen up here before going to bed after dinner," the servant said.

"Will I be allowed to go back to the *sarai* for dinner?"

"Prince Rha ordered it to be served here." He lifted the basket off the floor in the golden room. "Your spare undergarments and sleeping gowns are here, as well as soaps and brushes for baths. Tomorrow, we will deliver new dresses and anything else you desire."

After the servants had left, I sat on the edge of the bed. The longer I sat there alone, the more the pretty bedroom felt like a golden cage.

I didn't hear his footfalls. Moving soundlessly, like a true shadow, Rha appeared in the doorway a little while later.

"There you are." He looked relieved to see me.

"Where else would I be?" I got up from the bed, but he was already there, standing in front of me.

"Do you like the room?" He gently skimmed up my arms with his hands.

"It's beautiful, but—"

"Kiss me," he demanded, leaning closer.

I opened my mouth to reply. Impatient, he gripped my arms and covered my mouth with his. His tendrils unfurled, but he paced himself, connecting only one.

The kiss lasted but a second. He broke it off and frowned, his eyes searching mine.

"When I kiss you, it doesn't feel the same as when you do it. Do you always need to be in control to enjoy it?"

"Not always," I said quietly. "I like a man taking charge, too, but only if I know and trust him."

Concern shadowed his expression. "Do you not trust me?"

In our situation, trust was a complicated thing. I knew Rha wouldn't hurt me, that he would do everything to keep me safe, fed, and clothed. If I kissed him now, I trusted he'd do whatever it took for me to reach the most amazing orgasm ever. But many important things, I feared, would forever remain unsolved between us.

With Rha, I could never be free.

"I just don't feel like kissing at the moment." I bit my lip.

"Why not?" He wouldn't release my gaze.

"Will you eat another meal if someone puts a plate of food in front of you right now?"

"But I'm not hungry." He looked confused.

"Well, I'm not hungry for your kisses," I said. "Not when you sent me here without an explanation. Why can't I go back to the *sarai* with the others?"

"It's safer here."

"And the *sarai* is no longer safe?"

"Not safe enough for you."

"Why not?"

He drew in a long breath, running a hand through his hair.

"Because no place is good enough for me to keep my most precious treasure. My rooms on this level are protected by the ancient wards of magic. No one can come down the stairs unless I personally allow them in. But even here, it doesn't feel safe enough when I'm not with you. I wish I could put you in a vial and wear it on a chain around my neck, close to my heart. Maybe then, I would stop worrying about someone hurting you or taking you away from me."

He slid his hands up my back, bringing me closer. Tension locked my muscles. With a tendril connected to my arm, like an IV of emotions trickling from me to him, he sensed my mood immediately.

"What's wrong?" He ducked his head, trying to read my face.

"I'm not a jug or a vial, Rha. Not a *vessel* to be kept under a lock in a cave. I'm a person, born to be free."

"And do you think I don't know that?"

"It doesn't look like you do."

He narrowed his eyes at me like a man not used to his actions being questioned. I tried to free myself from his arms because standing inside his embrace while arguing felt weird. But he wouldn't let me.

"Don't go." A pleading note slipped into his voice. "I don't want anger to be the last emotion I feel from you before disconnecting."

"I'm afraid there isn't much else I can offer you right now, Your Highness. If it's positive emotions you're after, you definitely should disconnect for a while."

Still, he wouldn't remove the tendril.

"Tell me what I can do to make you feel better?"

I studied his expression carefully, trying to gauge how far I could push. But at the end of the day, what did I have to lose?

"If you really want to make me happy, Rha, let me go. Send me and my friends back home."

He flinched as if I'd slapped him.

"Is that what you really want? To leave me?"

The hurt in his voice was real, stirring my compassion. I splayed a hand on his bare chest. With his chain-link armor gone, it was just his warm skin, the hard muscles underneath, and the strong beating of his heart.

"Rha," I softened my voice. "We didn't meet under the best

circumstances. Your people stole me and brought me here to be your slave—" He stirred to protest, but I wouldn't let him. "What happened to me and the other humans happened without our consent. We did not want to come here. You can't argue with that."

He swallowed hard. "I'll give you anything you need to make your life with me better than it has ever been back in your world."

"Except that the one thing you won't give me is freedom."

I hoped so much that he'd contradict me, that he'd understand, that he'd prove I was more than just a "precious treasure" to him.

He groaned, raking his hands through his hair.

"I...I can't do it, Dawn."

I exhaled in bitter disappointment.

"You don't understand," he said quickly. "It's simply impossible to send you back exactly where my people took you from."

"Why?"

"We didn't simply use smoke tunnels like we did when traveling to Above. To connect to the human realm, the Joy Guardians had to use ancient magic to tap into the stream of the River of Mists."

"That's what I've been told. But why is it a problem?"

"The River of Mists is a magical entity that connects many worlds, including the human realm and Nerifir. The river is turbulent and temperamental. Some believe it has a mind of its own. If that's true, then it's also deliberately ruthless. Unless we use the same portal to travel both ways, the time changes. The portal you'd arrived through is now closed. If you try to return to your world, you will never come back to the same time."

"What time would I go to then?"

"No one can predict that. You may end up centuries before or after the time you had been taken from. The people you knew and loved would no longer be there. Even the place itself may not be something you'd recognize."

I eyed him suspiciously.

"Are you telling the truth? Because if not, if you're making it up just to keep me happy—"

"It'd be cruel of me to lie about something like that. Too cruel, no matter how desperately I wish to taste your happiness again."

Despair filled me, spreading through every fiber of my being like black tar. It weighed down on me, making it difficult to remain standing.

"Is there no going back then? No chance at all?"

Rha tightened his grip on me, helping me stay upright.

"There is always a slim chance that you'd be brought back close enough in time to resume your old life. The River of Mists may bring you centuries away from your time, but it could also be just months or even days."

"Is there any way to predict or influence that?"

"No, my treasure." He pressed his lips to my hair. "No way at all."

Which meant that even if we managed to open the portal somehow, we'd still be taking a huge risk going back.

"It means we're stuck here. Stuck forever."

Lifting me in his arms, Rha carried me to the carefully arranged sitting cushions by the wall and sat down.

"Is it so bad to stay here with me, Dawn?" he asked, placing me on his lap.

Cradled against his wide, warm chest, I found his lap a pretty good place to be. It was tempting to just give up. Like Melanie said, I had no grand ambitions in life. Going with the flow was what I'd always done. Why fight it now?

But what future lay ahead of me if I stayed?

In this world, I would never belong to myself ever again. I'd be a pet of the crown prince for as long as he would have me. I'd have to ask for his permission to leave the room, to take a walk, to see my friends. And when he grew tired or bored with me, I'd have to be ready to "share my joy" with whoever else he'd happen to have over for lunch that night.

How often could one be happy while locked up? What if I ran out of joy to share? Would he still keep me around? Or would he give me to someone else, since I was his property to do with as he pleased?

Through his tendril, Rha had access to the turbulence inside me. He ran his fingers over my hair, tucking a loose strand back into my bun.

"You're so close to trusting me, Dawn, but you keep fighting it. Whatever happens, I want you to remember you don't ever have to worry about anything. I'll take care of you."

I stopped short of thanking him. The reason he was taking care of me now had everything to do with him taking me from the life I had before.

He might be a gentle and caring captor, but he was my captor, nevertheless.

Eighteen

DAWN

I stayed in the golden bedroom for two days. Other than the servants bringing me meals, I spent most of the time alone. Rha would drop by often but only for brief visits.

He explained he was busy organizing reinforcements to send to the High Lady of Sumakis to help her defend her city from raids by rogue desert dwellers. Apparently, that was the order from the queen, delivered by Rha's cousin Alzali. She seemed polite and soft-spoken. But Rha's expression hardened whenever he spoke of his cousin. I sensed some tension between the two, in addition to some family troubles Rha appeared to have with his mother.

As curious as I was about his situation, I didn't question him about it. I had no business being involved in his life too deeply. I didn't need to get to know him any more than I already had. What I needed to focus on was my own situation.

I thought long and hard about what he'd told me about traveling between Earth and Nerifir, the portals, and the River of Mists. The process sounded complicated, but the repercussions seemed clear.

If Rha told me the truth, then we could never go back home. Not to our time, anyway. This was the information I absolutely had to share with Melanie and the others. Except that Rha was as stubborn as a bull when it came to my safety and refused to let me leave the golden room or allow any outsiders to visit me behind the magical wards guarding the caves. The only thing he'd agreed to was to let Elaine and my sister know through a Keeper that I was safe and had been moved to his private rooms permanently.

With the increased amount of activity in the palace and with the outside visitors being here, including Princess Alzali's escort from the queen's city of Kalmena, Rha acted outright paranoid, as if someone was about to take me from him.

On the third day, the isolation started getting to me. I felt displaced and restless, with no direction for the future and no goal in sight. With the lighting underground being the same day and night, my sleeping pattern had unraveled completely. I napped through the night and often stayed awake during the day when everyone else was sleeping. I had a beautiful wall clock in my room, similar to the one in the palace baths. But it didn't help much in regulating my sleep cycle.

Waking from yet another fitful sleep, I sat on my bed, feeling disoriented. Was it still morning, and I'd just gone to bed? Or was it evening already, and I should be getting up? Either way, I knew I wouldn't fall asleep again if I tried.

I climbed out of bed and threw on a light robe over my nightshirt, then shoved my feet into a pair of suede slippers. I used Rha's private bath cavern that also contained toilets artistically hidden behind plants and rock formations.

The double doors on the other side of the stream across from my golden room led to Rha's bedroom. They were closed, with him either still sleeping or maybe not there yet. I wasn't going to check. I hadn't been invited to his bedroom yet, and it was better that way.

Instead, I went out into the large main cave with the waterfalls. The entrance to the prince's private rooms was heavily guarded above, but there were no guards down here. All was quiet, only the sound of water rushing over the rocks filled the air.

The big cave made me feel less claustrophobic and confined. But I longed to see the sky.

I climbed up the stairs to the floor above and into Rha's private dining room. It was empty. I assumed the guards outside the doors wouldn't let me go out, so I turned into Rha's sitting room instead.

The cat lay curled up in the cushions, like a blot of pure darkness against the gold-and-purple silk. As I approached, she raised her head, squinting her golden-green eyes at me.

"You're not going to tell your master on me, are you?" I whispered to make as little noise as possible in the perfect quiet of the room.

She kept watching me as I made my way to the window. It was closed with shutters. The moment I opened it, the cat jumped off the cushions and beelined to me.

"Do you want to go out, kitty?"

A red and orange glow fell on my face when I moved a shutter aside. The vivid colors of sunset splashed across the sky. I yanked the window open wider, letting the bright hues spill into the room.

It'd been so long since I last saw the sky, even longer since I watched a sunset.

The cat slinked by my legs, her back rubbing against the hem of my robe. I followed her out onto the open patio.

The black desert sand crunched under the soles of my slippers. It covered the mosaic floor of the patio in a thick layer that almost completely hid the tiles from view. The sand must've been blown in during the day because I'd never seen so much of it here at night.

The patio was on the outer wall of the palace. It opened to the unobstructed view of the horizon and the spectacular sunset. The sloped wall ran downwards, overgrown with long soft grass. The wispy ends of it undulated like waves in the evening breeze.

The grass grew shorter as the wall descended toward the black desert floor far below. The sand broke the turf into patches and grassy knolls the further from the city it went, swallowing it completely just a few paces from the place where the city wall met the desert. Beyond that lay nothing but dry desert with its deadly daily heat and sand storms.

It wouldn't be too difficult to climb down the slanted side of the hill. One might even evade the guards that patrolled it. But then what? The dessert was the true impenetrable wall that kept people inside the city.

With a brief purring sound, the cat leaped on the banister around the patio then disappeared into the tall grass beyond.

I stared out into the desert where the ocean of black dunes replaced the gray waves of the grass of the oasis city.

As deadly as it was, the desert looked ethereally beautiful. The smooth ridges of the dunes wavered in the heat, rising from the scorched sand into the cooling air. The dying sunlight reflected in the grains of sand, making the desert floor look as if sprinkled with diamonds. But the sky presented the most magnificent sight, bursting with purple, orange, and red.

The lingering heat scraped against my skin harshly, but I tilted my face toward the light, desperate to hold on to the remnants of the day. Unused to bright light by now, I had to squint, but I wouldn't turn away.

The light was rapidly slipping away to disappear behind the horizon. Just like my past life had been shifting further and further away from me. With it, I was losing a part of me, never to get it back. And I didn't know whether to mourn or welcome that.

Was my life before the shadows took me worth to mourn it? As far as Melanie was concerned, it was a failure. I chose to do what I loved for a living, and it led me nowhere. It wasn't just Melanie's opinion, either. As supportive as my parents had been, at some point, they both had tried to talk me into finding a more reliable job that didn't involve dancing.

My life never fit into the mold of what conventionally would be considered a success. And now that it was gone, I felt more at a loss than ever. In the dying light of the sunset, all emotions were felt much more acutely.

As I stood there, on the border between day and night, between my disappearing past and worrisome future, sadness filled me, darker than the black desert. A tear rolled down my cheek, quickly followed by another.

"Dawn!" Rha's voice sounded from the window to the sitting room. "Thank gods, there you are."

I quickly wiped off the tears with the sleeve of my robe before turning around.

The prince stood in the open window, keeping to the shadows and squinting in the sunset's blood-red glow. He grabbed the upper layer of his skirt and drew it over his head. Holding the dark fabric like a shield against the sun, he ran out to me.

"You shouldn't be here, my sweet. The servants haven't even swept the sand after the storm yet—" He stopped, giving me a penetrating look. "What happened? You've been crying."

His tendrils weren't even out yet. We weren't connected at all, yet somehow he knew.

"Did someone hurt you?" His voice dipped with menace. "Tell me who?"

"No one hurt me. There is no one to hurt in retaliation to restore your precious balance. Just..." I swept the sky with my arm in a wide gesture. "Look at these colors. What do you see? Beauty or a disorganized mess?"

He peeked at the sky from inside the shadows of his fabric shield and grimaced.

"You hate it, Rha, don't you? You, just like everyone else, prefer the predictability of an order. A pattern. But what if it doesn't fit in any pattern or any order? What if I'm not shaped like a perfect piece for your puzzle and there is no place in your mosaic for me?"

"Dawn." He came closer and drew the fabric over both of us. "If only you knew how much it hurts me to see you upset."

His tendrils appeared, reaching for me.

I shook my head. "You don't want to feel this. There is really nothing pleasant inside me right now."

He paused the tendrils, but only for a moment.

"I'm just trying to understand you, Dawn. All of you, even your pain. Your feelings are chaotic. But I believe that the more time I spend with you, the better I can read them."

The smoky ends of his tendrils flared before fusing with the openings on my arms and along my spine. I inhaled, bracing for the intrusion. The more often he did it, however, the less intrusive it felt. By now, it was simply like opening a door and letting him in.

His handsome features pitched into a frown.

"I told you there's nothing pleasant in there," I said in response. "You really should listen sometimes and stay away for your own good."

He drew in a long breath, as if adjusting to the cacophony of emotions raging inside me.

"That's the problem, my treasure. I can't stay away, and I don't want to. You aren't just a piece of a puzzle, Dawn. You are the entire puzzle. One that keeps teasing me with a solution I don't think I'll ever find."

"I have a spoiler for you, Your Highness. There is no solution. If there was one, I would've already found it and used it to get my life in order."

"Has it not been in order then?"

I shut my eyes tightly for a moment before blurting out, "I'm twenty-five years old, which is 'a very ripe age' for a dancer, as someone put it at one of my auditions. But I feel like I'm still only trying to figure things out. Without much success, mind you."

"Twenty-five is so young, Dawn."

"I'm sure it is for someone like you. But in my world, there is a place in life one is kind of expected to be at by a certain age. Like I may not have a successful career yet, but I should be on my way to getting there. I may not be married, but I should at least be dating the right guy. I may not have children, but I should probably know where I stand on having a family. But I have none of it figured out. Nothing. I've been drifting through life with no plan and no direction, hoping things would fall into place one day. Only it's been going from bad to worse." I drew in a shuddered breath, suddenly feeling short on air. "When I look back at the years I've lived, Rha, all I can see are losses. First, Ciana and her parents. Then, Mom. Now, Dad... I've lost people close to me. And gradually, I've lost my confidence and sense of direction too. Dance was the only thing that has been constant, but even there I've failed to make any big gains. I followed my passion for the sake of passion, without a plan. That's not how things are done if you want to achieve success."

"Passion like yours is rare, Dawn, and should be treasured."

I huffed a bitter laugh. "Passion alone doesn't pay."

"But it does. In our kingdom, emotions that strong are valued above anything else. You are the rarest treasure."

I wondered why I was saying all of this to Rha, why I was confiding in the prince of darkness about my innermost insecurities. But then, I remembered he was the one intimately connected to me right now. He was literally swimming in all my emotions, and he showed no desire to get out. In fact, he seemed willing to dive even deeper, no matter how murky my inner world was.

"You sure are a glutton for punishment, Your Highness," I muttered softly, then ran a hand down my face, trying to collect myself. "I'm not even sure why any of it matters, anyway. That life is gone for me now."

With an arm around my shoulders, he led me over to the swing. He shook the sand off the seat cushion, then sat down, taking me with him.

"I sit here late in the evening or early in the morning before sunrise sometimes." He pushed off the floor with his foot, rocking the swing. "You're right about one thing, Dawn—all your worries are now in the past. As long as you're with me, I'll do the worrying for you."

If only it were that simple. But Rha wasn't a solution to my problems. He was a part of them.

"Coming here wasn't an escape from my past, Rha. Here, I gave up even more. I don't even belong to myself anymore, and I'm scared to lose the little I still have left. I'm scared that something worse will happen to everyone I care about. Sometimes it feels like all I have left is fear."

He stroked my hair, cradling me against his chest. Stoic, solid, reliable, like a pillar of strength amidst a storm. And I leaned on him, soaking up his support like a sponge. He didn't offer me any words of platitude, which was perfect. His silence proved more comforting than any words.

Darkness solidified around us as the sun sank deeper behind the horizon. My anxiety settled with the disappearing light.

"Sorry for dumping it all on you." I wiped my face with my sleeve again, taking a long, calming breath. "Not sure why I told you all of that. You probably don't even know what it's like to make mistakes. You're too calm and rational for nonsense like that." I lifted my head, sliding my gaze up his wide chest covered with precious jewels, to the muscular column of his neck, to his beautiful face with the proud chin, high cheekbones, and intense golden eyes. "You're perfect in every way, Rha. Of course your life is perfect too."

His shapely lips curved into a bitter smile. "Is that what you think?"

"It certainly looks that way."

"From the outside, it might."

I didn't want to know his story. I didn't need to get any closer to him. Physical attraction was more than enough to have between us, considering the circumstances.

Yet against my better judgement, I asked, "Isn't it true?"

"In a way, it is. I'm careful about avoiding making mistakes because I can't afford many. I already made one giant mistake at the very beginning of my life."

"Which is…?"

"I was born a boy."

I frowned in confusion. "How is that a mistake?"

"Alveari Kingdom has always been ruled by a queen. For the first time in our history, the crown has an heir, not an heiress."

"I still don't understand. Why does it matter?"

He rolled back his shoulders, sitting straighter. "For my people, tradition is everything. Contentment comes with stability. Changes are unsettling and often mean turmoil."

"Still, your gender shouldn't matter this much—"

"But it does. It means everything, to the point that many feel the woman in line to the throne behind me should be the next ruler of the kingdom, bypassing me."

"Who is that woman?" I asked.

"My cousin, Princess Alzali."

"The one who is in the palace, right now?"

"Yes. She's leaving tomorrow, with General Oskura and a thousand of my best warriors, to defend the City of Sumakis. I did not put her in charge. But even so, if she succeeds, it will further endear her to my mother, who already significantly favors Alzali over me."

"You're not close with your mother, are you?"

"No. Never was. I don't think she ever forgave me for being born a boy."

"But that's unfair. How is it your fault?"

"Maybe it's not. But we can't always help the way we feel, and the queen's animosity toward me has always been apparent." He remained calm. Only a glint in his eyes and a slight glow on his cheekbones betrayed his emotions.

"How about your dad?" I asked tentatively.

"He's been dead for over five decades now," he said in a hollow voice.

"I'm sorry…" I started, but words weren't necessary between

us when we were connected. He felt my compassion and in response brought my hand to his lips for a kiss.

"Father was the only real parent I had," he said. "He was a fierce warrior and taught me how to use a sword before I even learned how to ride either a horse or a camel. He never let me feel like I was lacking in anything. It hurt to lose him." He winced, rubbing his chest. "It still does."

I took his other hand in mine. "What happened to him?"

"He was killed with the dagger that was meant for my mother. I was twelve and remember that night well. It was a planned assassination of the queen, but Father took the dagger to his chest for her. The blade was poisoned with dark, ancient magic. Father never stood a chance to recover from that wound, but his body didn't turn to a shadow as it should have. His spirit remained trapped in this world. Held by the magic of the dagger, it wouldn't cross into the afterlife. The queen forbade anyone to touch it, keeping his body unchanged for over forty years—" He stopped abruptly and cupped my face. "You feel too strongly, my sweet. I shouldn't be sharing such things with you."

I hadn't even noticed when my breathing picked up and my heart squeezed tightly from the emotions rising in me while I listened to his story.

"It must've been terrible to live through that, Rha. I'm sorry it happened to you and your family. But I'm not sorry you told me. Have they caught the assassin?"

He nodded. "Mother had him tortured, then exposed him to sunlight for days. He was eventually beheaded with an iron sword. But in a way, he still won. The queen hasn't been herself ever since."

"Did she love your father?"

"Very much. They weren't bonded mates, but theirs was a love match. She never remarried. Neither does she have a companion. According to Alzali, Mother hasn't chosen a favorite from her Joy Vessels, either."

"Is it common to have a favorite Joy Vessel?"

Playing with a loose strand of my hair, he glanced at me. There was no longer any unease in his expression when our eyes met, just tenderness that sent a flutter of excitement through me.

"When it comes to humans, nothing is 'common,'" he said. "Your kind is so new to our world. There are no traditions yet."

There were only forty-two of us here. The first group arrived just over a month ago—

Suddenly, a realization hit me.

"Rha," I breathed out, afraid to hope again. "If crossing the River of Mists to our world affects time, does it also work the same when coming here? When two different portals are used? I mean, could the people that came here last month have been taken thirteen years before my group was?"

"Yes." That one simple word said in his quiet, even voice sounded like an explosion between my ears.

Ciana could be here, after all. She could've been here, in Alveari Kingdom, all this time.

I leaped to my feet. My sandals slid in the sand on the marble patio tiles, almost sending me back onto his lap.

"What is it, Dawn?" Rha got up too.

"Oh my God, Rha..." I tried to pace, but attached to him by his tendrils, I didn't make it far, spinning to face him again. "Do you know what that means?"

He spread his arms aside with a faint smile. "No, my treasure, I do not."

"My cousin was taken thirteen years ago from the very same place where the shadows came for us. I asked about that. But was told that the last and only known portal was opened just a month ago. You see? I asked the wrong question." I groaned, slapping my forehead with my hand. "Because I didn't know about the time warp thing then." I grabbed his forearms, digging my fingers into his skin. "Rha, do you know if one of your mother's Joy Vessels is named Ciana? She'd be... Gosh, she'd be younger than me now, because of that time leap. A beautiful woman, with a most gorgeous smile. She had thin, long, pink braids the day she was taken. And her skin is dark, but not like yours. It's brown, not black..." Hope rushed over me, strong like a current. I could barely breathe. "Please tell me she's here."

Could that be true? Was it possible after all the losses in my life, to get my cousin back?

Sadly, Rha shook his head. "I left Kalmena more than eight years ago and haven't been back since. I never met the queen's Joy Vessels and don't know their names."

"Is there a way to find out? Can I ask Princess Alzali, maybe?"

A muscle in his jaw ticked at the sound of his cousin's name.

"I'd rather you don't speak to her."

"Why not?"

"Alzali has a way to pry out more information than she gives, even when she's not the one asking questions. I'll tell you what." He wrapped his arms around me. "I'll speak to her myself. I'll be able to get what you need from her faster and hopefully with less damage to us."

"Thank you..." I pressed both hands to my chest, my heart racing in a wild gallop. "Oh, Rha, what if it's true? What if my cousin is really here?"

"I wish for it to be true." He pressed a kiss to the corner of my mouth. "And if your cousin is really one of the queen's Joy Vessels, I'll find a way for you to see her. Even if I have to beg my mother for an audience in Kalmena."

I took his face between my hands. "You'll do it? For me?"

My heart overflowed with gratitude. My chest expanded with too many emotions twirling in a twister. I didn't stop to analyze them all before pulling him down for a kiss.

He obliged, eagerly meeting my lips. His arms tightened around me. He inhaled deeply, breathing me in. His hand cupped my breast. The pad of his thumb circled my nipple, making it instantly hard. Desire pulsed through my body.

He leaned back, finding my eyes.

"You are hungry for my kisses now," he said with satisfaction.

His kisses had never been a problem. I always wanted him, even when I thought I should hate him.

"Are you still bitter about what I said two days ago?" I asked.

The look in his eyes turned smoldering with lust—*my* lust.

"Not anymore," he rasped.

"Then keep kissing me." I pulled him back to me.

Claiming my mouth again, he slid my robe and my sleeping gown off my shoulders, baring my breasts. The sun had set. The cooling air of the night brushed against my skin, pebbling my nipples.

The window to the sitting room suddenly opened wider. Two servants with brooms paused in the window frame, staring at us in hesitation. With a gasp, I threw my arms over my chest, my face flushing from mortification.

"Leave," Rha snapped at them, grinding his teeth. "Don't you dare come back here again."

Bowing their heads, the servants slipped away silently, taking their brooms with them.

Rha slid his warm palms up my bare shoulders.

"There is no need to feel ashamed of your pleasure, sweetheart. No one will ever judge you for sharing your joy with me. They can only be envious."

He trailed soft, gentle kisses down the side of my neck. I tilted my head back, giving him more of my neck to caress. There was not a part of me that didn't welcome his touch. My arms fell away from my chest, exposing my breasts to him again. He ran his fingers around the swell of each.

"You like my hands on you, but you love my tongue even more." He lifted me into his arms, bringing my chest to the same level as his lips, then sucked a nipple into his mouth.

I arched my back with a moan and wrapped my legs around him as he lay me down on the cushioned seat of the swing. He tore my sleeping gown down the middle, exposing more of my skin for his kisses.

Heat coursed through my body. Need pooled low in my belly, aching and begging for a release.

"You need more, don't you?" He slid a hand up my leg, hiking up my skirt. "Tell me, my sweet, where do you want me? Where did you touch yourself the last time?"

His hand moved up my thigh, his fingers probing and stroking. He brushed against my underwear, and I whimpered as another spark of desire zapped through my body.

"Oh, God...Rha..."

"Here?" He stroked me through the thin fabric.

I exhaled sharply. My muscles trembled.

"Here." He smirked confidently, tugging my underwear off.

Kneeling by the swing seat, he let his fingers dance around my opening. With his other hand, he massaged my breast, pinching the nipple and rolling it gently.

"Just like that," he exhaled, breathless with my pleasure.

Lost to his touch, I could no longer speak at all. He kissed the inside of my thigh. Once again, his fingers found my most sensitive spot. My hips bucked.

"Right there..." He narrowed his touch to that one point of pleasure. "Gods... This is divine."

Kissing down my belly, he brought his mouth where his fingers had just been and took my clit between his lips.

Air rushed out of my lungs. I gripped his hair, tangling my fingers in his braids. Raising my hips, I rode his tongue.

"Oh, yes..."

My need grew stronger, more desperate. But he matched it perfectly, licking faster and sucking harder until our shared pleasure crested and exploded with a mind-shuddering orgasm.

I panted, gripping his hair. His fingers dug into my thighs. He buried his face between my legs, riding my orgasm with me.

When I finally relaxed into the cushion of the seat, he rested his head on my belly, still kneeling on the sand-covered patio by the swing.

"How is it possible..." he panted, catching his breath, "to hold this much pleasure inside you? How is there any place for sadness at all?"

I relaxed my fingers, releasing his braids, then smoothed his hair gently. "It's all about balance, isn't it? You, of all people, should understand that. One can't always be happy. If they are, they've lost their mind."

Only this kind of balance was impossible to achieve for shadow fae. They felt sadness, anger, envy, and grief, without any reprieve of pleasure.

Rha had every right to rage against the unfair hand dealt to his kind, yet he was the most even-tempered man I'd ever met. He worked hard on keeping his composure, and I couldn't help but admire him for that.

I kept running my fingers over his dark, glossy strands, playing with the thin braids laid over his unbound hair. And I thought about this swing, the endless puzzle he'd been working on, and the soothing sound of the stream running through his rooms downstairs. He employed many devices and put a lot of effort into simply finding and maintaining his inner peace.

"I've been learning something, Dawn," he said. "There are emotions that are impossible to rein in. Wild and thrilling, they are the opposite of peace. They are chaos." He lifted his head, catching my gaze. "There is beauty in chaos too. And I don't want to live without it anymore. I need it more than peace. More than the air I breathe. I need you, my treasure."

"I love spending time with you too." It came out flat, compared to the passion of his confession. But he'd be leaving soon to go about his nightly duties of a prince. And I was facing many hours locked alone once again.

There was no balance in this relationship because I wasn't his equal and never would be.

I sat up on the swing and tugged my robe back up my shoulders and over my chest, which was left exposed in the torn sleeping gown. My underwear had been lost to the sand on the patio floor, so I just smoothed my skirts down.

He sat next to me on the swing, not retrieving his tendrils even as my post-orgasmic glow had faded.

"Tell me, what can I do to stop the sadness from taking over you again?"

I met his eyes. "Let me see my friends."

"All seventeen of them?" He didn't look pleased by my request.

"At least two. My best friend and my sister. They are the closest I have to a family now. You can't keep us apart like that."

I made my voice firm and my glare hard. But he would also feel the desperation and loneliness inside me.

He heaved a long breath, fighting his own inner battle.

"I won't allow your return to the *sarai*. I need to have you close. However, I will let your friend and your sister come for a visit."

"When?" I perked up with excitement.

"Tomorrow. They can join you for the midnight meal after Alzali and her people have left Teneris."

Nineteen

DAWN

The following evening was dragging torturously slow as I waited for Princess Alzali to leave and take her people with her, so that Rha would finally feel safe enough to let anyone enter the sacred golden bedroom with his most precious "treasure," aka plain old me.

It was ridiculous how much he fussed over me. I absolutely believed him when he'd said he wished he could put me in a locket to wear around his neck. There were moments when his adoration was flattering. But often, such an obsession felt restrictive and even smothering.

When the intricate sand clock in my bedroom finally indicated midnight, I felt too excited to stay in. Leaving my bedroom, I hurried out into the main cave and ran into Elaine and Melanie descending the stairs. Several guards escorted them, including Prince Rha himself.

"Dawn!" Elaine jogged down the stairs and straight into my arm.

"Oh, it's so good to see you." I hugged her tightly, my fingers sinking into the soft knit of her ever-present sweater.

Over Elaine's shoulder, I met Melanie's curious eyes.

"Not bad." She whistled, giving the cave an assessing look. "I can see why you don't want to come to the *sarai* anymore."

I released Elaine from my hug. "I'm not here by choice."

Elaine turned to Rha, but he held her gaze stoically, the same way he met Melanie's glare. Clearly, he was not going to apologize to my friend or sister for keeping me all to himself.

"Are you staying for lunch?" Melanie asked him with a snark.

Before replying to her, he turned to me. "Do you need me to stay, Dawn?"

"No. We're good," I said quickly. There was no need for his presence or for the tension it generated with my friends.

"Then I will not." He gave my guests a brief nod. "Enjoy your meal, ladies. The Keepers will take care of you."

I spotted a familiar face in the small group of servants behind Rha.

"Sigid? It's so nice to see you again. How have you been?"

The Keeper bowed his head. "I've been well, Dawn."

Rha arched an eyebrow, flicking a curious glance between the Keeper and me. Knowing his possessiveness, I half expected Rha to send Sigid away in a jealous fit. Instead, the prince nodded calmly.

"I'm wishing you joy, ladies." He turned, his skirt whipping around his legs. The side slit opened as he ascended the stairs, flashing his muscular thigh with every step.

"Well," Melanie turned to me. "He really wants to keep you *joyful*. Just look at this place. And it's all for you alone."

"Alone," I echoed. "Which isn't as great as you think."

Elaine's expression darkened. "Did he...hurt you?"

"What? No." I shook my head adamantly, refusing to let anyone think about Rha like that even for a second. "It's just boring, sitting here by myself. That's all."

Elaine wrapped herself tighter into her sweater, looking concerned.

"Elaine," I tried to calm her worry. "They can't hurt us. It's not in their interests, remember? They want us happy, so they can experience our happiness, too."

The servants brought in a low round table and placed it on a rocky island in the middle of the wide stream. The island was connected to the riverbank by a short wooden bridge with carved railings.

As the servants set the table with lunch dishes under Sigid's instructions, Melanie strolled along the path, surveying the picturesque waterfalls and the luscious flowerbeds between the rocks when Elaine and I joined her.

"So, are you happy here, sister?" Melanie asked. "Is the prince doting on you and catering to all your needs?"

Other than the confinement and isolation, I didn't have much to complain about. But the mocking note in her voice triggered me.

"Are you judging me for what I have no control over?" I propped my hands on my hips, widening my feet in a defensive stance.

She turned, facing me. "How much do you love it here, Dawn?"

I blew out an exasperated breath. "You speak like I chose to come here."

"But what if you had a choice? Would you even consider leaving here?" Her question didn't feel purely rhetorical. "Or is his dick worth forgetting who you are and where you came from?"

Anger flared like a rocket inside me. Melanie had always been so good at setting it off.

"He doesn't have a dick," I snapped.

That shut her up, leaving her staring at me with her mouth wide open.

Elaine gasped softly behind me. "What?"

We'd walked away from the island where the servants were arranging the sitting cushions around the table. Still, I lowered my voice, just in case.

"For the shadow fae, sex is just a task that they perform solely for reproduction. That's when their sexual organs appear. The rest of the time, they don't have any. They're not like us," I said softly, calming down a little. "They don't have sex for pleasure."

Elaine blinked, clearly stunned. "How do they pee?"

"*That* I don't know," I confessed. "I've never seen the prince naked, despite what you may think."

He, on the other hand, had seen me naked plenty of times already. He'd seen me. Touched me. Tasted me...

Heat creeped up my face at the thought of everything Rha had done to me so far. Oral sex was still sex. Rha and I shared an intimacy that happened only between lovers. I couldn't deny it.

Thankfully, Melanie didn't go into that kind of nuance.

"God, these creatures are so weird." She shook her head.

"Well, it looks like our lunch is ready." I ran a hand over my hair, glad to get out of this conversation. "Let's go eat."

"It's really nice here." Elaine smiled, relaxing on the cushions.

We finished eating. The servants had already cleared the table, leaving just a pot of tea with a tray of desserts.

I bit into a piece of jellied fruit puree and let it slowly melt in my mouth, savoring it just like I used to do when Rha shared lunch with me. He wasn't even here this time, but searching for pleasure in every moment had already become a habit for me.

Elaine poured some cream into her cup, then stirred a spoonful of honey in it. "I like the sound of the water. It's soothing."

"That's why Rha chose to have his bedroom here. He appreciates the peace and quiet of this place."

Melanie popped a sugar-roasted almond into her mouth, then

crushed it between her teeth. "And how much do you appreciate *him?* Even without a dick?"

Annoyance rose in me again.

"Why does it matter?"

"Because I'm afraid you like the man you have every reason to hate," she huffed.

If I really wanted to, I could find plenty of reasons to hate Rha. Only none of them seemed enough. I didn't hate him, not anymore.

Was it wrong? I didn't know, but Melanie clearly believed it was.

"What do you want me to do?" I shrugged. "Slit his throat in his sleep? I couldn't do it even if I wanted to. We don't share a bed."

"The problem is that you wouldn't do it even if you had a chance," she said.

"Honestly. Is that what you want? For me to assassinate the prince?" If so, she'd come to the wrong person.

She gave me a calculating look. "What I want to know is how much I can trust you."

"Trust me with *what?*" A cold shiver ran down my spine.

If Melanie was really plotting Rha's assassination, she shouldn't trust me at all. Because not only would I not help her, but I'd actively try to stop her. And if that was wrong of me, so be it. He did not deserve to die.

Melanie mulled over something, chewing on her bottom lip. Shoving aside the dessert platter, she leaned over the table toward me. "What if I found a way for us to leave here? To go back home? Can I count on you to come with us?"

My breath hitched in my throat. "Do you know the way home? How?"

She shook her head. "I asked you first, Dawn. Can I count on you, or would you rather stay here as the prince's pampered pleasure toy?"

But my sister didn't know what I knew.

"We can't return home, Melanie. Not to the same time where we were taken from. Time changes when one crosses from this world to ours unless the same portal is used. Since our portal is now closed, there can be years or even centuries between when they took us and when we'd come back."

Elaine frowned. "How do you know that?"

Melanie just scoffed. "Is that what *he* told you? And you believed him?"

"Why would he lie to me?"

"Because it's in his interests to keep you happy, you said so yourself. He'd tell you whatever you wish to hear, just to keep his favorite little Vessel filled with joy for him."

"Lying to me wouldn't make me happy."

"Oh, but it has," she argued. "Look at you, smiling and thriving in your underground prison. And now that he's convinced you there is no way out of here, you wouldn't even think about running away."

I tried hard to ignore the sting from the words she'd so masterfully darted at me. But Melanie was right about one thing. I could never be completely happy with the role of a royal "pleasure toy" for the rest of my life.

"But is there a way?" I asked. "Do you have an actual escape plan?"

She leaned back into the cushions. Tossing another nut into her mouth, she crunched the hard sugar coating between her teeth.

"Maybe," she said in a low, conspiratory voice of a spy or a mafia boss. "But I'm not telling you anything. Not until I'm certain you're not going to run to your prince with the info."

That stung like the snap of a whip.

"Melanie, I would never—"

She stopped me by raising a hand.

"Sorry, Dawn. But this may be our only chance, and I'm not going to risk it. It's enough to say that there are shadow fae who want the same thing we do. They want all humans out of their world."

"But that doesn't make sense. We're their source of joy."

Melanie tilted her head. "*Whose* source of joy are you, Dawn? Only a handful of them have access to the *sarai*—Prince Rha and some of his courtiers. That's it. The rest will never even see us."

"They have their ancient source of joy already—" Elaine started.

"Elaine," Melanie stopped her with a warning in her voice.

But my friend waved her off. "You may not trust Dawn, but I do. She won't betray us." She turned to me again. "Their ancient joy is kept in a temple with access for everyone. Some of the fae see us as a threat to their traditions and values. They're afraid we'll 'pollute' their ancient joy with our low-grade 'magic-less' one."

Melanie darted a cautious glance around the room. But there was no one close enough to hear us. The servants had taken the dishes away, and Sigid, with a couple of other Keepers, rested on the cushions by the stairs, keeping an eye on us from a respectful distance.

My sister leaned toward me, speaking hurriedly. "Swear you won't say a word to that precious prince of yours."

"I swear," I said firmly.

She hesitated for a moment, but then continued, "Some of the Joy Guardians aren't happy with us being here. They've collected and grown their Source of Joy for several millennia. Apparently, it all came exclusively from the fae they kidnapped from Above. Now, they fear that our plain, human emotions may end up mixing with their precious blob of magical joy and devalue it somehow."

"They collected joy in a blob?" It was hard not to laugh, even as Melanie's expression remained serious.

"As a blob, or in a jar, or pressed into bars, who cares?" She shrugged.

"They say it's in a temple, but we don't know in what form," Elaine clarified. "Shadow fae can come to the temple and connect to that Source of Joy for something like a blissful meditation. The Joy Guardians guard and protect it, hence their name. They gave a vow to guard it with their lives, and they seem to take that vow very seriously."

"How do you know all of this?" I asked.

Elaine glanced at Melanie before explaining to me. "There is a small but very determined group that wants us gone from Alveari Kingdom. They got in touch with Melanie the day we went to the city market."

Now I remembered. "That note the guy shoved in your hand, it was from them, wasn't it?"

Melanie nodded. "We have a chance to leave here, Dawn. The question is, will you take this chance?"

"I would, but..."

"Don't tell me it's because of *him*," Melanie huffed.

"No," I said quickly. "But Ciana may be here."

She exhaled slowly.

"Not that again. Dawn, sweetie..." Her voice softened. "I loved Ciana. Everyone did. But she's gone. You need to let go."

"But what if she's really here? We can't leave her behind."

"How can she be here?" Elaine asked. "The portal to our world was first opened just like five weeks ago."

"Yes, but if the time moves differently when one crosses the River of Mists, what happened a month ago here could've been thirteen years ago back home. Which means Ciana is here."

"Would she age thirteen years in five weeks?" Melanie looked skeptical.

"No... I mean, I don't know exactly how it works with this time travel..."

My sister rolled her eyes. "Are you even listening to what you're saying, Dawn? Time travel? Really?"

"This world doesn't work like ours," I argued. "You can't ignore the risks of going back. And we must find Ciana because if we don't, she'll be truly lost to us for good. Rha promised to find out if she's in Kalmena. He said he'll take me to see her—"

"What if he's lying?" Melanie sighed.

"But why would he?"

She threw her hands in the air. "Because you make it too easy for him by being gullible and naïve. He feeds you bullshit to make you happy, then eats your happiness like a snack."

My face flared with heat from indignity. There was only a three-year difference in age between us, and it drove me nuts when Melanie spoke to me as if it was at least half a century.

I opened my mouth to argue, but Elaine spoke first.

"We can't dismiss what Dawn said about time travel, Melanie. The people in the *sarai* have to know about it. Also, if Ciana really is here, we can't leave her behind. There's still time to find her."

"When are you planning to do it? How much time do we have?" I asked.

Elaine inhaled to reply, but Melanie stopped her.

"It's best if you don't know the details yet," she said to me.

"I promise you can trust me."

"Sorry, Dawn, but you're too close to the prince. One wrong word from you to him, and all our plans will be ruined. Also, who knows what he can fish out of you with those smoky snakes of his without you even knowing? We just can't risk it."

Rha couldn't read my thoughts, but he sensed my emotions so acutely. He'd been exceptionally perceptive even without connecting his tendrils to me.

Elaine took my hand. "You're all alone here, Dawn, away from all of us. Please, be careful."

"I'm safe," I assured her.

"Don't let your guard down," she insisted, still looking concerned. "The prince is enjoying you. But pleasure can be addicting. People often do horrible things to satisfy their cravings. Remember, no matter how much you may like him, he can't like you back. His kind is incapable of such a feeling."

Twenty

RHA

The Head Councilor followed me to the doors of my private dining room.

"What can I tell the emissary of Princess Alzali, Your Highness?"

Fighting the raiders of Sumakis proved difficult. A week after leaving Teneris, Alzali sent for help. Giving her what she was asking for would severely weaken the defenses of Teneris, which I couldn't allow.

"I'm not changing my answer, Head Counselor," I said firmly, stopping at the doors. "Alzali gets half the number of warriors she's asked for and not a single person more. Instead of wasting her time with pestering me for more than I can give, she could've asked the queen for reinforcements. She's had enough time for that."

I was confident in my decision, especially since the reports from Oskura about the campaign sounded far more optimistic than Alzali's grave predictions of doom. I trusted Oskura and her experience far more than anything coming from my cousin.

"Half," I repeated resolutely. "That's all she gets."

"But Your Highness—" The Head Councilor made a move to follow me into the dining room, which would be an intrusion I couldn't suffer.

I placed a hand on the man's bejeweled chest, stopping him in his tracks.

"We'll reconvene our discussion after the midnight meal if you so wish, my lord." I all but shoved the Head Councilor out, entered the room, then shut the doors behind me.

The servants were setting dishes on the table and arranging the cushions for both Dawn and me. Except that Dawn wasn't at the table. Normally, she'd be here, waiting for me already. The sight of her smiling face always made the world seem like a better place.

"Where is my Joy Vessel?"

Before anyone could give me an answer, the exit door swung open again. With irritation bursting through my chest, I whipped around, ready to teach a lesson to the obnoxious Head Councilor who'd obviously forgotten his place.

Instead of him, however, the Joy Vessel Keeper Sigid entered the room. He carried a large basket filled with clean, gauzy material. A leather water bag was tucked under his arm.

I'd sensed the ease with which Dawn held herself around this particular man. They must've become friendly back in the *sarai*. So, I'd assigned Sigid as Dawn's personal Keeper. Now, this man's only task was to make sure Dawn was comfortable and in need of nothing.

"Do you know where Dawn is?" I demanded.

"Dawn asked to be excused from sharing the meal today, Your Highness. She isn't feeling well."

Alarm sliced through me like a blade.

"What happened? Is she in her bedroom?" I pivoted to the staircase that led to the lower level, then rushed down three stairs at a time.

Dawn was hurt. How? Why? Who dared touch her? There was no time to question the Keeper. I had to see her myself.

I barged into her bedroom without knocking.

"Rha?" Dawn was sitting in her bed.

My throat all but closed with worry at the sight of her. Why was she still in bed? She had on a light beige robe over her sleeping gown. Her golden-yellow hair was pulled back with a tie.

She was not smiling. And that fact disturbed me more than anything.

"What happened?" I dropped to my knees by her bed and grabbed her hand. She squeezed my fingers gently, but her other hand was already outstretched toward Sigid who'd followed me to her room.

"Oh, you're a savior, Sigid." She practically moaned when the Keeper handed her the water bag. Sliding it under the covers, she pressed it to her stomach and collapsed back into the pillows. "I'm feeling better already." She rolled her head to face me. "Sorry, I'll have to miss our lunch. It's that time of the month, you know? The first day is always the worst for me. Tomorrow should be better."

Her explanation was completely lost on me.

Desperate to know exactly what she was feeling, I let out my tendrils and slid them up her arms toward her *leilathas*.

"Oh no." She swatted a tendril away. "Trust me, darling, you don't want to feel this. Cramps are nasty."

"Please, let me." I held out a tendril.

She shrugged. "Alright. Suit yourself, but I've warned you..."

I connected a tendril, just one, which would muffle her feelings for me. Yet the pain came in like a punch. It churned my insides, as if a fist gripped my organs low in my belly and twisted them in a merciless torture. The agony spread down my thighs and resonated with a crippling pain in my back.

I yanked my tendril out, gasping for breath.

Dawn shook her head. "I did warn you, didn't I?"

"What's happening to you, my sweet? Who did this to you?" I gritted through my teeth in murderous thirst for revenge.

Was it a curse? Did someone try to poison her? Whoever it was, their heads would roll.

"What are you talking about, Rha? I'm on my period, that's all." She glanced up at Sigid, who stood by the bed with his basket. "What else did you bring?"

"More pads." The Keeper held the basket out to her.

"More? Honestly, Sigid, how many pads do you think I need? I already have enough gauze to stock a field hospital during a bloody battle."

My muscles seized with dread. "What does she need the gauze for?"

"To absorb blood," Sigid replied.

Blood.

The word exploded through my brain, turning my vision red and blurry.

"You're bleeding, my treasure? Where?"

She squirmed, looking uncomfortable.

"Well, if you don't know already, I'd rather not tell you *where.* Sigid?" She raised a pleading gaze to the Keeper. "How come you knew what I meant when I told you what happened when your prince acts like he's never heard of a woman having her period?"

"What kind of a period?" I frowned, moving my focus from my favorite Vessel to her Keeper.

"The normal, regular kind," she said. "Well, mine might be a bit heavier than some, even after I got my IUD, but still nothing to freak out about. It's normal."

"How can the pain you're feeling be normal?"

I couldn't believe it. I didn't understand how she could even still talk with that agony rocking through her body.

"It was new for us too," Sigid replied. "The Joy Vessel Keepers from Kalmena shared the knowledge they'd gained about humans from the queen's *sarai.* Then, Joy Vessel Lucia further enlightened us on the matter when she had her period a week ago. We are well prepared to handle the situation now."

As Sigid took the basket to Dawn's dressing room, she looked at me with sympathy. "You don't look so good, baby."

Baby.

From the mouth of anyone else, I'd take it as an insult, punishable by public whipping. When Dawn uttered the word, however, it came with a warm note of tenderness in her voice. It made me wish to be closer to her. I climbed onto her bed and lay on my side, propped on an elbow.

She caressed my cheek. "I'm fine, promise. You worry too much."

How could I not worry when she was suffering?

When Sigid returned from the dressing room, I ordered, "Fetch the royal hag at once. Tell her to brew the tea she makes for the wounded in battle. And if it so much as upsets my Joy Vessel's stomach, the hag will die. I'll also make sure her death is not a quick or an easy one."

"Yes, Your Highness." With a bow, Sigid left.

Dawn rolled her head on the pillow, meeting my eyes. "You've been so sweet to me that I often forget how ruthless you can be."

"I don't punish without a reason. But if someone harms what's mine, they'll pay dearly for it." I stroked the side of her face. "You'll feel better soon, my sweet treasure. The hag's brew has eased the pain of many gruesome wounds."

She looked at me as if I indeed were a babe. "I'm not wounded, Rha."

"But you're bleeding." I guided her face to me for a kiss.

I rarely kissed her first. It felt far more exhilarating when she initiated it, then it often led to us both panting in the heat of her climax. But I didn't kiss her to feel her pleasure this time. I did it to comfort her.

Afterwards, she put her head on my shoulder as we lay side by side.

"You're so cuddly today." She fidgeted with one of my braids. "Does it bother you so much that I'm in pain?"

It did. I'd much rather endure it for her if it were possible.

"I wish I knew a spell that would release you from all pain, my treasure, for as long as you should live."

"That's probably the nicest thing anyone has ever said to me." Her smile was warm and enticing.

My tendrils itched to connect to her again, to taste the feeling that had caused it. But I remembered the excruciating pain.

I considered myself a brave man. I'd survived many bloody battles and endured pain from deep wounds and gruesome injuries. But I would never again willingly subject myself to the pain of a human woman's "period." *That* was not caused by a wound, apparently. It couldn't be healed, just endured. It made no sense, but the thought of Dawn suffering wrecked me.

"Come with me." I scooped her from her bed and into my arms.

"Where?" She wrapped her arms around my neck.

"To my bedroom."

"Oh." She exhaled a soft giggle. "For Netflix and chill?"

"What?"

"It means sex, Rha. In my world, when a man invites a woman to his bedroom, he probably hopes to have sex with her."

"Will having sex alleviate your pain?"

"Not likely." She sighed. "Also, I'm not in the mood for it right now."

"Then no, we won't have sex. I have a few things to do, and I just want you close when I'm doing them. My bedroom is bigger than yours."

"Then, can I grab that warm water bag Sigid brought for me, please? It does help."

I bent over the bed for her to grab the water bag. She clutched it to her belly like her life depended on it.

"We'll eat in my room," I said, carrying her over the rock path across the stream. "What would you like to have for your midnight meal? Tell me, and I'll churn the sands of the desert to source it for you."

She giggled, burying her face in the place between my neck and shoulder. "No need to be that dramatic, Your Highness. It doesn't have to be anything fancy. I just feel like something soft, warm, and sweet. Rice pudding, maybe? With raisins and cinnamon. Is there rice pudding in Teneris?"

"I'm sure the head chef can make it happen. You will get your rice pudding, my treasure. No matter what."

Twenty-One

DAWN

It'd been ten days since I moved to Rha's private rooms underground. During this time, we'd made it a habit to have lunch together. He'd join me for dinner whenever he had time to spare. And we even got to dance again, twice.

But this was the first time ever that I entered the bedroom of the Crown Prince of the Alveari Kingdom.

He didn't lie when he said it was bigger than mine, quite a few times bigger. Colorful mosaics decorated the floor and ceiling. Each of the six walls held a recessed, arched niche. Five of them were painted with murals of some epic battles. One had an intricate waterfall that trickled down a system of different sized vessels tilted at various angles. The bubbling sound of water filled the room that held a couple of sitting areas and a huge hexagon shaped bed.

In addition to the canopy above the bed, Rha also had panels of carved wood positioned around it like a fence. The two panels in the front had been moved open, and he carried me up the platform, then placed me into the plush bedding carefully before moving the panels a bit further aside.

"Why do you have these?" I asked.

His left ear twitched as he answered, "This room is too big. Without the screens, I feel like I'm sleeping out in the open, which isn't very relaxing."

It was dark and cozy behind the screens under the canopy. The large bed was like a small room on its own.

"I see." I nodded. "I like it better this way too."

Sigid knocked on the open door tentatively.

"Your Highness, the royal hag is here."

With Rha's permission, a hunched over figure entered, shrouded in a dusty-gray cloak. I'd seen the royal hag before once or twice, always in passing. If the fae of Alveari Kingdom were shadows, then she looked like nothing more than an apparition, moving like a patch of gray fog.

The woman seemed shorter than an average shadow fae with her back permanently hunched over. Mists seeped through her shroud like smoke escaping the embers hidden within. However, when she approached the bed, I sensed no heat emanating from her body. Instead, chills brushed my face.

She carried a small bronze tray with an earthenware pot on it next to a wide mug.

"Greetings, Your Highness. I brought the tea for your sweet Joy Vessel," she said in a soft, rasping voice.

"Thank you, Grandmother." Rha seemed at ease around this spooky woman whose appearance gave me the creeps.

He poured some steaming liquid from the pot into the mug. The hag took it from him. While the prince carried the tray with the pot to a side stand by the bed, the woman leaned over me, handing me the mug.

"Here you go, Sweet One. I made it mild, like for a baby. It won't put you to sleep but will soothe your ache."

Among all the chaotic feelings I had for the prince, one was firm—I trusted him to keep me safe. His protectiveness often felt restricting and isolating, forming a shield around me. But I felt safe behind that shield. It kept any potential danger at bay. Rha would never let this woman in here if he didn't trust her completely, and it gave me all the reassurance I needed.

I took the mug from her.

"Thank you...um...Sorry, I don't know your name."

Her pale-yellow eyes glistened from under her hood. Her face was lined with deep wrinkles. She looked old, unlike all the other fae I'd met in Teneris.

"Call me Grandmother, like everyone else does," she said.

"Thank you, Grandmother."

As she withdrew her hand, the wide bangles around her arm shifted, revealing a tattoo inside her wrist. It was a picture of a black scorpion inside a golden hexagon. Our gazes crossed before she yanked her hand away from me, hiding it in the midst of her gray cloak.

"If Your Highness no longer needs me, I wish to retire back to my rooms." She bowed to the prince.

With a nod, Rha dismissed her. The woman left, relieving me of the eerie feeling in her presence. I drew in a breath, then took a sip of the dark, sweet tea she'd brought.

"She's not really your grandmother, is she?" I asked Rha.

"No, not in the way that binds through blood. But Kanjie has been with my family for centuries. When I left Kalmena, she came with me to Teneris and has been here ever since."

"How old is she? She doesn't look like any of you."

"No one knows a hag's age. All hags look like they're nearing death. But in their case, it's often only an illusion. A hag gives up her youthful looks in exchange for magic that is stronger than even the queen's."

"Yet the hags are the ones who serve the royals, by the looks of it."

"Hags don't care about ruling over people. They don't need riches, love, or a family. What they crave is respect, and they get most of it when serving powerful people."

"So, she's like a healer at your court?"

"Mostly, yes. But Kanjie also lends her magic to priests and Joy Guardians whenever needed for the good of Teneris."

Servants brought in our lunch, as well as armfuls of scrolls and papers for Rha to go through, and a wide flat box that they put on a side stand. Rha ate his boring snake meat quickly, then got busy poring over the long scrolls and stacks of papers.

I devoured the yummy rice pudding with raisins that the head chef created to my order, then drank some more of the hag's tea.

"How are you feeling?" Rha asked, lifting his head from the paper he was reading.

He sat on a thick floor cushion by a low round table that was littered with scrolls. Though "littered" was the wrong word to describe anything where Rha was concerned. There was always a system in anything he did. The scrolls on the table in front of him were grouped into neat piles. The papers were also arranged in stacks and lined up in some order only he could understand.

I leaned to the side to deposit my empty mug onto the stand.

"I'm feeling much better. Thank you. The royal hag knows her stuff. The tea is working already." I spotted the flat box that the servants had brought in with our lunch. "What's in this box?"

"Oh, that..." Rha put down his paper and got up. "It's from my jewelers. I asked them for specific gemstones."

With his usual feline grace, he strolled to the side table, picked up the box, then placed it on my lap.

"What do you think?"

I ran my fingers over the collection of blue and brown gemstones laid over the black velvet. Smoothly polished or cut with facets, they shimmered and sparkled in the dim light under the canopy over the bed.

"These are gorgeous."

"Hm." He took his chin in his hand in thought. "Maybe you can help me put them into a design for a necklace."

"Who is the necklace for?"

"You."

"Me?"

"Yes. You said you like these stones."

"I do…" I stroked the precious rocks. "They are beautiful. Too beautiful. And there are so many of them. How big is that necklace going to be?"

"I may not end up using all of them, only those that will fit into a pattern. But it should be a good size when it's finished. Not too heavy to weigh on your delicate neck and shoulders, but big enough to make a statement."

That intrigued me.

"What kind of statement are you going for?"

"I want the world to know what you mean to me and how much I treasure you," he replied without a moment of hesitation.

I tried to ignore a flutter in my chest somewhere in the area of the heart. "And how are you planning to express that in gems?"

He climbed on the bed next to me and raked his fingers through the stones in the tray.

"I ordered turquoise, moonstone, opal, sapphire, brown agate, and golden-brown onyx—all are the colors of your eyes."

My breath hitched. I hadn't even realized the colors of the stones meant something. But of course they would. As a shadow fae, Rha derived no pleasure from aesthetics. For him to appreciate anything—be it a color, a fabric, or a picture—there had to be a logical meaning behind it.

I tilted my head, peering at him from under my eyelashes. "I thought you disliked my mismatched eyes."

"I used to find them disturbing," he admitted. "Sometimes, I still feel like there are two people looking at me instead of one. A blue-eyed and a brown-eyed one. They may even have two different personalities. I know you're at war with yourself at times."

I sure had enough doubts and insecurities to last for two people and more.

With a finger under my chin, he turned me to face him. "But I don't dislike your eyes, Dawn. I don't dislike anything about your appearance at all." He glanced at the rocks in the box. "I used to avoid using flawed pieces in my designs. But now, I think their imperfections don't make them any less perfect. They make them unique and worthy of a special meaning."

"Is that what you want me to help you with? To find the perfectly imperfect stones?"

"No." He placed a kiss on my cheek. "It turns out I'm very good at finding flawed treasures on my own. But I need your help in arranging the gems in a design that pleases you."

"What if it's something asymmetrical?" I teased.

"As long as you like it. And yes, I suspect it'd be asymmetrical. Your emotions don't fit into any predetermined pattern."

"Hmm," I moved the polished rocks along the velvet lining of the box. "What if we don't do anything geometrical at all, but do...swirls maybe?" I lined the stones into curvy lines. "Blue and brown, like sky and ground..."

"...twirling together in a day storm," Rha added.

"...or in a dance." I finished in one breath.

Our eyes met. A shiver ran down my arms. Rha touched his chest with a sigh that echoed mine. Something sparked between us, an emotion that I was sure he felt, too, even without his tendrils connecting us.

I turned away, breaking our eye contact, and cleared my throat, shifting the rocks in the box.

"We can arrange them from the darkest to the lightest. Ombre effect." My voice sounded a little rough. "See, like that? What do you think?"

The wisps of tendrils appeared from his arms. He placed a hand on my thigh, as if trying to connect with me through touch first. I turned my arm to him, craving an even closer connection with him.

"It should be fine now. The pain is almost entirely gone. Here you go." I aligned a *leilatha* on my arm with the frayed end of his emerging tendril. "We may as well have fun together while working on the design, right?"

Tentatively, as if tasting the water of a treacherous stream, he connected the tendril. The hag's tea had done its job. My cramps disappeared. The backache was now almost gone too.

Rha connected the second tendril, then swung the rest of them over me, connecting to my other arm. I felt a gentle prodding at my back and leaned forward to allow him the access to my spine.

"Good?" I eyed him.

I felt comfortable with him this close, both physically and emotionally. It was like hugging a warm blanket around me. Peace flooded me, relaxing my muscles and soothing my soul.

A smile stretched his lips as he inhaled deeply, breathing in my inner peace.

"It's just perfect, my treasure."

Twenty-Two

DAWN

About a week and a half after my period ended—finally easing Rha's worries about me potentially bleeding to death—I invited the entire *sarai* over for dinner.

Rha generously offered his private dining room for my soiree while he was out with General Oskura. The general had just returned from Kalmena where she and her warriors had been honored by the queen for the successful defense of the City of Sumakis from the desert dwellers.

We were having a fun dinner with music and wine. Everyone seemed to be enjoying themselves.

"These guys are good," Kostya pointed with a half-eaten lamb leg at the musicians on the stage. "They won't replace a TV or my laptop. But still better than nothing."

Other than the humans and the musicians, there were also a few Keepers in the room, including Sigid, of course, who had become my personal shadow, keeping a watchful eye on me from a distance and anticipating my every wish.

After the servants had cleared the dishes of the main course and brought in dessert, Melanie shifted closer to me.

"Is that new?" She pointed at the giant bib-necklace that covered my entire chest.

Although it wasn't as big or as heavy as some that shadow fae wore, it still required two golden chains that crossed over my shoulders and under my arms to hold it in place.

"Yes. It is." I splayed a hand over the cool surface of the precious gems.

It took Rha and me several days to arrange the stones. Then, the royal jewelers put them in the elaborate setting of strands held together by golden links. The result was truly unique.

"Is that a picture of a storm?" Melanie tilted her head, squinting at the swirls of blue and brown.

The turquoise, moonstone, and onyx of shades from the deepest dark chocolate to coffee with cream created a truly stunning piece.

Elaine peered at the necklace from across the table. "It's beautiful. But it doesn't look like the typical designs that shadow fae wear. They prefer geometrical shapes. This one gives me some Van Gogh vibes. Did the prince give it to you?"

I nodded. "We designed it together."

Elaine's eyes narrowed behind her glasses. "You two spend quite a bit of time together, don't you?"

As the head of the busy city with a large population, Rha didn't have much time to spare. But every free moment he got, he spent it with me. Now, when he wasn't around, I had that annoying restless feeling like something was missing. But I sensed neither my friend nor my sister would like to know that.

Melanie threaded her arm through mine, sparing me from having to reply to Elaine.

"Three days, Dawn," she whispered excitedly. "The portal to our world is going to be open again in three days."

The news came like a bucket of cold water dumped over my head.

"It's actually going to happen?" I muttered.

"Yes. Apparently, the queen gave her permission to acquire

more Joy Vessels for Princess Alzali to celebrate her recent successful campaign, or battle, or something like that. But Joy Guardians will open the portal a day early for us to get the fuck out."

"Why would they go against the queen's orders?"

"Because they don't want us in their precious kingdom and certainly don't want to bring any more of us in."

I chewed on my bottom lip as so many emotions swirled inside me, but I couldn't accurately name any of them. I had no idea which one to pick or which way to lean.

"It'll be the last portal possible between our worlds for a very long time, Dawn," Melanie added.

"What do you mean?"

"That'll be it, sister. Apparently, the portal can only be opened three times, four weeks apart each time. That's what that magic spell can do in our lifetime. That's our only chance, Dawn."

"How do you know this?"

She gave me a smug look. "I have good sources."

"What makes them good? How do you know you can trust them?"

"I don't trust anyone. But these people aren't doing it for you or me. They're doing it for themselves. They want us out, and that's just fine with me."

The room appeared to spin in a slow, maddening circle. I knew Melanie had been working on an escape plan. I thought I'd be ready when the time came. But the finality of it all hit me hard.

"It really is now or never, isn't it?" I exhaled.

Lucia met my gaze from across the table. She looked like she might know what we were talking about, but she didn't seem enthusiastic about the subject.

"Is everyone coming?" I asked Melanie.

"It has to be everyone from Prince Rha's *sarai*. They want all eighteen of us out. Otherwise, they won't even bother with the portal."

That explained Lucia's mournful expression. She never made it a secret that she preferred the life in Teneris to the one she'd left behind.

"Melanie, do people know the risks when crossing back into our world?"

"They do," she assured me. "We talked about that."

Elaine, who was quietly listening to our conversation, nodded in confirmation.

I scraped both hands down my face. "And they're okay with the risk?"

"No one wants to be a slave, Dawn. Even if it's a pampered slave," Melanie said.

I dropped my gaze to my lap. Melanie was right. A cage was still a cage, even when it looked like a golden bedroom.

Silence settled over us, and Elaine broke it first.

"Kostya is quite excited about leaving," she said. "He can't wait to get all the modern conveniences back."

I glanced at the man she was talking about. He was finishing a second helping of meat and potatoes, looking quite happy with where he was for the time being.

"Does he know he may end up in the time way before electricity was even discovered?"

"He does." Elaine smiled. "But he decided he'd be the one to discover it and would make millions."

"So, everyone is really on board?"

"Yes," Melanie confirmed.

For some, I imagined, traveling to a different time period might present a chance to start anew—a hope to do better.

"How about you, Elaine? What do you think about going back?"

She fidgeted with a button on her sweater. "As long as there is a chance to get to our time, I think it's worth a try. My family must be losing their minds. I have to make an effort, you know? For their sake."

Pulling the sweater tighter around herself, she got up and

moved away from the table. I followed her with my gaze as she sat down on a floor cushion by the wall next to a Keeper.

"I still didn't hear anything about Ciana," I reminded Melanie.

Rha was meeting with General Oskura right now. But what if she still didn't have any news for me?

"I hope we hear something soon. But we really can't wait longer than three days." Melanie took my hand, her voice softening. "Imagine if we got back to the time when Mom and Dad were still alive."

My heart squeezed with longing. What wouldn't I give to see my parents well and alive again? For a moment, I even forgot that it would mean reliving their deaths all over again too.

"How would that work? Would we be kids again? Or would there be two versions of each of us running around?"

Melanie jerked her shoulder. "I guess we'll find out when we get there."

I poked with my spoon in the bowl with my dessert. The head chef started adding roasted pecans to the honeyed apricots and served them with whipped cream, making the dish even more delicious. This had become my favorite dessert, and of course Rha enjoyed it too. Eating it without him almost felt like a waste.

I glanced at Elaine. She was telling something to the Keeper while animatedly moving her hands. She laughed, probably at something funny in her story. In response, the Keeper's mouth stretched into a polite half-smile.

The shadow fae who'd been interacting with us the most had mastered that expression by now. They would smile when we did, mimicking our expression. But the Keeper couldn't possibly enjoy Elaine's story. What did he get from the interaction? Or did he simply endure it to indulge Elaine as a part of his job's duties?

The doors to the room suddenly opened and Rha breezed through. He entered noiselessly, like a shadow. Yet his presence immediately filled the space, bringing everyone's attention to him.

"Your Highness." The Keepers scurried to their knees, bending their heads in deep bows.

The musicians paused, bowing as well. The etiquette didn't require us to do the same. Still, all the humans bowed their heads, too, some deeper than others.

Rha's golden gaze skimmed over those present, finding me quickly. His shoulders dropped with relief at the sight of me. A smile tugged at my lips in response. I loved the familiarity we shared. It stretched between us like a silent greeting across the room full of people, no matter how far from each other we were.

He raised a hand, releasing the Keepers and the musicians from their bows. "Please continue."

He headed to his private sitting room and closed the doors behind him—calm, dignified, and regal like always. I knew him well enough by now, however, to spot an unusual tension in his stride.

"Dawn?" Melanie's voice reached me as if through a fog. "Are you listening to what I'm saying?"

I wasn't. Did she say something?

My thoughts remained with the prince. The dark silhouette of his tall figure was still imprinted in my vision as I stared at the door he'd disappeared behind.

"Um... Just give me a minute. Okay?" I got up from the floor cushion.

Melanie winced. "Are you really going to run after him? Wagging your tail like a lapdog?"

There was no point in arguing with her. I just shot her a glare before grabbing my dessert bowl from the table.

"I need to speak to him."

I FOUND Rha out on the patio with the swing. He stood with his back to the windows, facing the desert.

The night was dark, with at least an hour or so before the sunrise. The shape of him merged with the night sky behind him. The golden clips in his six thin braids glistened like stars. The breeze played with his long, unbound hair under the braids, blowing the strands against the sky along with the dark wisps of clouds.

His skirt was made from a black material that absorbed all light. But in the fabric's folds, the moonlight glistened with indigo and emerald green, making it appear liquid. It streamed down his trim hips, hugging his muscular legs with the breeze.

Prince Rha wasn't just beautiful. He was majestic, his presence effortlessly imposing. And standing against the night sky like that, he appeared godlike.

However, I'd learned to see beyond his appearance. I noticed the drop of his wide shoulders, the tight grip of his fingers on the stone parapet, and the way he hung his head, as if weighed down by worry.

Rha had made my pleasure his mission. And somehow along the way, his worries had become my own. Whatever bothered him concerned me too.

"Rha." I climbed out onto the patio. "Look what I've got for us."

He whipped around with his hair and skirt churning in a swirl.

"Dawn. You should be with your friends, enjoying your dinner."

"The dinner is almost finished. Just dessert is left." I held up the small earthenware bowl with honeyed apricots. "Care to share?"

He gave me a half-smile similar to the one the Keeper had given to Elaine—humoring but distant.

"Just look how good it is." I lifted an apricot on my spoon, letting the honey drip into the bowl in thick, golden drops. "I'm so looking forward to enjoying it." I stuck out an elbow, thrusting the *leilathas* on my arm his way. "Come on, darling, plug in."

Coaxed out by my persistence, the black tendril uncurled from his arm, then gently connected with me. A second one promptly followed while Rha's chest rose with a deep sigh.

"Let's enjoy it, my prince." I shoved the spoon with the apricot into my mouth. Sweetness and flavor exploded on my tongue. I hummed in appreciation. The first bite was always the best, and I was glad Rha was here to share it with me.

His eyebrows remained knotted into a frown, however.

"It's good, isn't it?" I asked, licking the spoon.

Something distracted him. And I didn't like it. It worried me, and my worry had obviously filtered through the tendrils to him.

"What is it, Rha? Please tell me. Or we'll just continue feeding on each other's anxiety in circles."

He took the dish out of my hands and set it on the parapet behind him.

"Come here." He opened his arms for me, and I stepped into his hug without a moment of hesitation. "I have some bad news, my sweet. I fear it will upset you."

His somber tone sent a chill down my arms.

He couldn't have found out about our escape plans, could he?

I slid a finger down one of his tendrils. "Maybe you should get these out of me then?"

He pressed the side of his face to my temple with his mouth just above my ear.

"I want to feel what you feel. I need to taste your pain, then maybe I'll know how to help you through it."

I couldn't feel his emotions the way he felt mine, but I read his voice. He sounded sad, not angry. He wasn't talking about the escape.

"What do you need to tell me, Rha?"

"General Oskura brought news about your cousin."

I gripped his arms, afraid to breathe.

"And?"

"She was a part of the queen's *sarai* in Kalmena."

My heart leaped inside my ribs so hard, I swayed. Ciana was here. After all those years, I finally found her.

Except that Rha's somber expression didn't let my hope grow.

"Why did you say *was?*'Is she not there anymore?"

He slid a hand up and down my back in a soothing motion. "No. There has been an attack on the queen's *sarai*. Your cousin escaped."

"Escaped?" I clung to this one word. "So, she's alive? We'll just have to find her."

"She escaped the city, into the desert. Alone. That was days ago."

"You don't think she'll make it?"

His silence grew, smothering my hope, before he spoke again. "A human wouldn't survive in the Alveari Desert even for a day. She was alone, with no supplies, no water, or any protective clothing. I'm sorry, Dawn. I wish I could let your hope thrive, but it'd be heartless of me to prolong it. Your cousin is no longer alive."

I drew in a shuddering breath, clinging on to him as the full meaning of his words slowly filtered in, absorbed by my brain like water dripping onto the desert floor.

No longer alive.

Dead.

Ciana was truly dead now, and it felt like I was losing her all over again.

It shouldn't hurt as much as it did. Ciana had been gone for thirteen years now. But I'd just gotten a new hope, and it was ripped out again, creating a fresh wound.

He kept stroking my back, and I pressed my face to the cool gemstones over his chest. A tear rolled down my cheek. I didn't want to cry, but if I couldn't help it, I'd rather do it right here, in his arms.

He kissed my hair.

"It will pass, sweetheart," he murmured soothingly. "Pain always has an end. Otherwise, none of us would ever survive it."

A shadow fae would know all about pain. He couldn't get

distracted from it by pleasure or muffle it by alcohol. If our roles were reversed, I wouldn't know how to comfort him without a connection through his tendrils. He derived no pleasure from hugging. Stroking his back would not soothe him.

I leaned back, searching his eyes. "How do you deal with the pain of loss, Rha? What do you do to make it better?"

"I wait," he said. "Waiting is the only thing we can do. Let time do the healing. 'After the storms of day, the calm of night will come.' Such are the words of the First Priestess of Joy. She was the one who gave us pleasure when my kind were nothing but shadows. She helped us become people. The Temple of Joy was built in her honor."

His calm voice flowed like water over rocks, soothing and comforting. I remembered he'd done it before. He'd talked me through the worst of pain during the *leilatha* fitting.

"It will pass," he'd said then, too, leading me through the torrent of emotions from agony to ecstasy.

"It will pass," I echoed, sliding my hand up his chest to his shoulders.

The familiar caress of his hair met me as I hugged his neck. I threaded my fingers through the silky tresses, finding his braids in them. My tears slowed down and stopped as I breathed deeply, focusing on every breath.

"Thank you, Rha," I whispered, raising my face to his.

"For what?"

"For..."

How could I put into words the feelings that I was ashamed to acknowledge, even to myself?

I was in Alveari Kingdom because of Rha. He gave the order to bring me here with the intention of using me. And he *had* been using me. Only at this point, it felt like he had given me so much back too.

His presence grounded me. With him, I felt calmer, stronger, more aware of my emotions and, because of that, more in control of them. I was far away from home, but I didn't feel lost. I accepted myself for what I was, partially because of how he made me feel—appreciated for simply being me.

"Thank you for being there for me when I so badly needed someone to care," I said.

He kissed my temple, gently brushed his cheek against mine, then found my lips with his. Rha rarely kissed me first. He preferred for me to initiate it. But now, his kiss grew deeper. With a groan against my mouth, he took my head between his hands. His hold grew stronger, and his kiss turned more desperate.

He staggered forward, forcing me to step back.

I grabbed his arms to steady myself.

Normally, he'd sense the slightest hesitation in me in response to his actions and pull back. But he didn't slow down this time, ravenously devouring me with his kiss.

I jerked my head back and out of his hands.

"Rha..." I panted for air to catch the breath his kiss had stolen. "Are you alright?"

He reached for me again, but then yanked his hands back. His eyes opened wide with alarm.

"Dawn. You need to leave." His tendrils fell away from me all at once. "Go. Now."

Heavy breathing rushed through his throat. His eyes darkened, the black pupils flooding the gold of the irises.

"What's happening to you?" I whispered as worry gripped my throat.

"Go," he growled.

I took a few tentative steps toward the windows, but that wasn't quick enough for him. Storming across the patio, he hooked his arm around my middle and dragged me through a window and into the sitting room.

"You need to go," he gritted through his teeth.

Fear squeezed my heart with icy fingers.

"What the fuck is going on?" I screamed. "Rha!"

Zala, the cat, shot from the cushions and out of the room.

Rha let go of me, but only long enough for us to catch our breaths, while we glared at each other.

"You need to be away from me, Dawn. Go to the *sarai*, with the others. Tell the Keepers to lock you in the room with the guards by the door."

"Why? What's wrong with you? Are you sick? Please, talk to me. What are you feeling?"

He drew in a long breath, taking a step away from me.

"Lust."

His skirt moved below his belt as if with a puff of breeze. The fabric billowed in the middle, right over his groin.

Understanding dawned on me.

"Is that the procreation thing you told me about? The one that shadow fae go through once a year?"

He rubbed his face, wincing in pain. "You must be at your peak, my sweet."

"Me? What does it have to do with me?"

"Everything."

I remembered he'd said that a couple who spent enough time together would eventually end up having sex. The woman would enter her fertile period, triggering a response in the man.

We had spent a fair amount of time together. Was I ovulating? There was no way for me to tell for sure. I didn't feel any different.

But Rha certainly did.

For weeks, we had shared everything, from food to his bed to our feelings. His body had attuned to mine perfectly. And now, it was reacting in a way it was designed to do.

"Come." He scooped me up again, shoving the door to the dining room open.

My dinner party had mostly dissolved by now. Melanie and Elaine were still there, having a conversation by the table. Sigid, the only Keeper left, was relaxing on the cushions nearby. Kostya was still eating, helping himself to a tray of baklava.

All four turned to us when Rha all but crashed through the door, carrying me in.

"Take her to the *sarai*," he ordered to Sigid, depositing me in front of the Keeper.

"Rha, wait…" I immediately pivoted back to him.

He stood his ground, his shoulders raised, his head low. His ears tipped back as if getting ready for an attack.

"Get away from me, Dawn," he rasped.

"But how are you supposed to go through this alone?" I grabbed his arm.

He hissed, tossing his head back as if my touch singed his skin, then shoved me toward Sigid.

"Take her away. Now."

Elaine rushed to us. "What's going on?"

Met with Rha's wild gaze, she trembled like a leaf but came to me anyway and placed a hand on my arm.

"Come with us, Dawn," she implored, softly. "Please."

But I couldn't leave. Rha's tall, strong body shook in agony. A glossy sheen of sweat coated his shimmering ink-black skin, making it appear liquid. His handsome features distorted into a grimace I'd never seen before, baring his fangs in a scowl. He fisted his hands so hard that dark droplets of blood glistened between his fingers, seeping from under his nails that pierced the heels of his palms.

How could I leave him like that, when he was clearly suffering?

"Go." I said to Elaine. "I'll stay."

Melanie sprung to her feet.

"Are you insane? Dawn, just look at him!" She made a face, staring at Rha. "What's wrong with him, anyway?"

"Mating fever," Sigid spoke softly, as if afraid to provoke a feral predator into an attack. With his eyes on Rha, Sigid approached me carefully and touched my hand. "We need to go, Dawn."

Rha's eyes narrowed, focused on the spot where Sigid touched me. A low growl vibrated deep in his chest.

"Jesus Christ," Melanie gasped. "Why would you want to stay

even for a second with this beast?"

"Let's go, Dawn. Please, before he hurts somebody," Elaine begged.

They had to leave, but I didn't want them to worry about me.

"Just go, guys." I jerked my chin up and cocked my hip, faking the confidence I didn't quite feel. "Maybe I want to be ravaged, okay? It's been a while."

Kostya had finally caught up with what was happening.

"Hey, sweet cheeks." He smirked. "If you're up for some fucking, come with me, and I'll show you what all these frigid bitches in the *sarai* have been missing out by turning me down."

Rha jerked his head in his direction. With a snarl, he leaped across the table to Kostya. The human shrank in fear. All bravado left him. He tripped and fell backwards, then tried to crab-walk away from the shadow beast pouncing on him.

Rha's attack was smooth and graceful, like that of a large, black cat. Landing on Kostya's chest, he raised his hand to strike.

"Rha! No." I scrambled across the table and slammed my side into him with force.

Physically, it barely had an impact. But he paused. His nostrils flared, as if hunting for my scent. He turned his head to me, letting Kostya scramble away from under him.

I held Rha's gaze, speaking to Sigid, "Take everyone out of the room. Now."

"Come." Sigid promptly ushered everyone to the door.

A roar ripped from Rha's throat. He lurched away from me, then staggered down the stairs leading to the lower level.

"Dawn, come. Quickly," Elaine urged from the door.

I glanced at her, then at the stairs where Rha had gone.

"Sorry, Elaine." I shook my head. "Please, go without me."

Twenty-Three

DAWN

I almost made it all the way down the stairs when Rha grabbed me and hauled me to him.

"I told you to leave!" He shook me like a rag doll. "Go!" He shoved me away from him. I staggered backwards, stopping only when my back hit the rock wall behind me.

His eyes roamed wildly in their sockets. His garment bulged at his crotch, the fabric undulating as if it concealed a caged beast straining to get free. A bright golden glow burst from above his belt.

Trepidation slithered into my chest, curling around my heart like an ice-cold tentacle. But there was also a spark of anticipation. My heart beat wildly. I couldn't possibly predict what would happen, but I wanted to find out.

"What are you going to do if I'm gone, Rha?" I willed my voice not to shake, speaking louder than was necessary. I tipped my chin at whatever hell was happening inside that skirt of his. "Will you jerk off your newly manifested dick until it falls off? Judging by how hard you're fisting your hands, you'll probably rip it off."

My voice was firm enough, but my body shook, rocked by the feeling similar to the one I had when skydiving for the first time. The unknown was terrifying, but it called to me, urging me to take that one crucial step off the plane, after which there'd be no return, no changing my mind.

"Leave!" he roared. "It's an order. I'll give you three seconds to get out. One—"

He didn't make it to three.

Not even to two.

He lunged for me. His nails scraped the rock of the wall on each side of my head as he caged me.

"Too late," he growled in his own defeat. "I can't give you even a second more."

I slid my trembling fingers down his chest.

"Let me see it, Rha."

I had to know what exactly I was dealing with here. I gripped his belt as he jerked back. The closure on his belt clicked open, and the shimmering material fluttered down to the floor.

He stood in front of me naked, save for the short boots on his feet and the jewels on his chest.

Coils of black shadows streamed over his hips and curled around his thighs. He didn't have a singular cock, but an entire cluster of them. Shimmering gold in the middle with those outside being coal black, they undulated between his legs like shorter versions of his tendrils.

Stunned, I had no words and simply stared at that. Trepidation vibrated through me with both fear and an odd sense of excitement.

Lifting a trembling hand to the black ribbon on my arm, I tapped the golden rosette.

"Feel me, Rha."

I didn't have much joy to share at the moment. But connecting to me would hopefully lend some humanity to the feral beast I was facing. I needed him to feel my fear.

But he shook his head, keeping his tendrils in.

"My control is slipping," he croaked. "I will use you, Dawn. I will hurt you. And I'd rather not feel what it'll do to you."

My breath stuck in my throat. My spine went rigid. With my back pressed to the wall, I had nowhere to run. He'd given me plenty of chances to get out. But I stayed. And now, it was too late.

At the same time, I had an odd feeling I wouldn't mind being "used" by him, that I could manage it somehow. That I could even enjoy it. The butterflies in my stomach fluttered in both fear and excitement. His growls resonated through me, eliciting tingles of anticipation.

If he couldn't control himself, I had to find a way to control it for him.

A shadow of deep sorrow moved across his face. Like he was already mourning what he hadn't even done yet.

"I can bear my own pain, my sweet. But feeling yours would destroy me."

Said softly, the words made him sound like the Rha I knew, and my heart swelled with compassion and affection.

I'd been conditioned to associate Rha with safety. It was hard for me to see him as a threat now. Even when he was growling, with his teeth bared and his hands fisted, I saw mostly his suffering, not anger.

"I won't fight you. You don't want to hurt me. Let's just enjoy our time together, like we've done so many times before." Trying to keep my hand steady, I reached for the cluster of the slim, glowing tentacles between his thighs. They fanned out like petals of a magical chrysanthemum.

He grabbed my wrist, halting my progress, and I met his burning gaze straight on.

"Rha, I can help you. I'm not in pain. Not in a frenzy. It doesn't need to be what it usually is between shadow fae. I'm a human, remember? We have sex all the time." I smiled with more optimism than I felt.

Peeling my back from the wall, I took a tiny step his way. I wasn't sure he understood or even heard my words, but he couldn't stay away anymore. Yanking on my arm, he pulled me into his chest.

The prehensile appendages between his legs snapped around my hand, ensnaring me. Firm but flexible and slick with a sheen of lubrication, they twined between my fingers and curled around my forearm. As thick as my thumb at the base, they tapered at their ends, stretching as long as my forearm. And there were a lot of them.

Rha groaned, grimacing in pain.

"Rha, baby, please *feel* me. Let me ease it for you."

He ran his hands down my arms, but his touch was unfamiliar. His fingers flexed, rigid, as if he were grasping for a lifeline while being carried out to sea. Gripping my hips, he slammed me against him.

"It hurts. Make it stop, Sweet One," he sounded delirious, lost to the agony of need burning through him. "Please, make it stop."

Clawing at the fabric of my dress, he tore the skirt in the front, then ripped through my underwear and lifted my leg, pressing his pelvis to mine.

I gasped as the slick tentacles between his legs brushed against my bare flesh. Probing, prodding, and searching, his feelers undulated between us. Their touch was smooth but persistent. The tapered ends fluttered along the sensitive skin of my inner thighs and stroked between my folds. Some brushed by my clit, sending a bolt of arousal through my lower belly.

"God, this is...weird," I breathed out, only instead of pulling away, I pressed closer. "But *good* weird."

The sensation was like nothing I'd ever experienced before, and I didn't want it to stop. Hooking an arm around Rha's neck, I moved my hips to press against him.

The short tentacles found my opening and sank inside, one by one, filling me. The stretch quickly proved too much. My inner muscles clenched at the intrusion.

"Not all of them at once, please." I jerked back.

But Rha wouldn't let me retreat, holding me in place. He growled like a wild animal, trying to rut, but there were just too many of his feelers for me to take. They all tried to fit inside, prodding and stretching me to the limit.

I reached between us and grabbed a handful of them. I was gentle. Still, Rha bellowed in pain, throwing his head back.

"Feel me, Rha. Feel me, now."

That was the only way I knew how to ease his pain. Shaking, he finally let his tendrils out. They sprung from his arms, shaking and reaching for me like fingers of a starving man for a plate of food.

"I need..." he groaned. "Dawn, I need you."

Gripping my hips, he lifted me off the ground, then pushed me against the wall while his tendrils connected to me all at once. I wrapped my legs around him, and he thrust inside me. I held on to the few feelers of his, keeping them outside of my body. They curled around my fist, rubbing against my clit with his thrusts.

Our connection absorbed all my senses. My nerves were on high alert, making me hyper aware and exceptionally sensitive to what he was doing to me.

His feelers undulated in and out of me, constantly rubbing, prodding, and caressing my body with an ever-changing kaleidoscope of sensations. Those that I had trapped in my fist fought against my grip. In their frantic struggle, they rubbed against my most sensitive spot, sending waves of intense pleasure through my core.

My thighs trembled.

Orgasm approached, fast and violent.

Rha buried his face in my neck as I gripped his shoulders with my free arm.

"Rha... I'm..." My climax slammed into me, closing my throat. My hips jerked against him.

He roared as pleasure—*my* pleasure—rocked us both.

My hands shook. My fingers relaxed, letting the feelers escape.

But Rha's body felt more tense than ever, trapping me between him and the wall.

Did it work?

Did he come too?

Or was it just the echo of my orgasm that had him roar and moan with me?

Judging by the rigid tension gripping his body, he didn't come. And other than the thin layer of lubrication from his slim tentacles, nothing else was on my hand.

They didn't withdraw from me. On the contrary, those I'd released from my grip tried to force their way in again.

"All of them, woman," Rha rasped, his voice dry and tortured from desperation. "I need them all inside you."

Twenty-Four

RHA

Need.

Want.

Urge.

Pain.

Mind-blinding pleasure.

Sensations I'd never known before racked me. Emotions slammed into me like punches.

The best ones, of course, came through my tendrils from Dawn.

The worst ones were all of my own making.

She took my face in her hands, forcing me to look at her. Her mismatched eyes held mine.

"Do you have to come from all of them at once?" she asked. "Is that what you need?"

"Need..." I echoed.

The word resonated through my brain, booming like an explosion.

Jagged red welts marred her delicate skin on the side of her neck. The parallel scratches unmistakably came from my fangs. Her dress fell from her shoulders in ragged strips, shredded by my hands and from the chafing against the rough rock wall against which I'd rutted into her. Her necklace was on the ground.

What had I done to my treasure?

What was I still going to do?

I was destroying her—the most important person in my life.

Yet I had no strength to let her go.

Pressing her to me, I headed to my bedroom. The feelers of my mating cluster snapped around her thighs, anchoring her to me.

"Where are we going?" she asked.

I couldn't release her anymore, couldn't let her run to safety. But I could at least try to make her more comfortable.

Need choked me, seizing my throat.

"Bed," was all I could say.

I stumbled across the bridge over the stream. Kicking the doors to my bedroom open, I made it across the room before depositing Dawn onto the bed as gently as I could manage.

Her pleasure had alleviated my pain somewhat, enough for me to make it here, but tension was gripping my limbs like iron. Pressure pulsed low in my belly, crippling to the point I could barely walk.

My hands shook as I reached for the only one who could make it better. Gripping her hips, I flipped her over on her stomach and hiked up the remnants of her torn skirt.

Need was all I could feel.

"I need all of them inside you, sweetheart. My whole cluster."

She pushed off the bed, rising on her knees in front of me, her back to my front.

"We'll do them all. But my way. Okay?" She reached behind her, looking down over her shoulder. Grabbing a handful of my feelers, she separated them from the rest.

Her touch sent a spiral of sharp pain through my body and a

wave of comforting warmth through my tendrils. The two didn't quite balance each other. But it gave me a reprieve to breathe.

"I'm ready, Rha."

And I couldn't wait any longer. My feelers sprang toward her, sliding into her opening again as if that was their home now.

She gasped for air in short, shallow breaths. Through my tendrils, I knew she was her usual hurricane of emotions. They were swirling in an anxious twister—a dark cloud of trepidation, a spark of excitement, a heavy weight of fear. But one thing stood out, strong and unshakable amidst it all—her trust in me.

She trusted me far more than I did myself.

I lost all control over my feelers. Most of them were already inside her. But a few that she trapped in her grip strained to get free.

"Oh God, this feels so strange." She arched her back, thrusting her backside into my front. "It shouldn't feel as good as it does, should it?"

A tremor of pleasure ran down her body. It echoed through me, giving me another reprieve from pain.

But it wasn't enough.

"More. More. More," pounded in my head.

I had to be inside her. My entire cluster. I jerked away from her, trying to free the remaining feelers from her fist.

"No." She stopped me firmly. "These don't fit. Not in the same place, anyway." She guided the remaining feelers higher, right between the half-globes of her backside. "Here, Rha. Take me here."

She unclenched her fingers, releasing the feelers. They sprung free, searching frantically until they prodded against her back opening.

"Yesss…" She released her breath, dropping forward and arching her back. "Yes, Rha. Fuck me in the ass, my darling."

Holding her hips, I thrust once. Slick and agile, the feelers slipped through the tight ring inside her from the back. They trembled and undulated, straining for a release.

With my entire cluster buried deep inside my woman now, I found my footing. I released a long shuddering breath, pulled out just a little, only to slam right back in again.

And after that...

After that, I remembered nothing.

I lost all awareness of the place I was in or of the woman I was with. The need filled my entire world, blinding me to everything else. My very existence shrank to the frantic thrusting, again and again, as my body demanded.

Harder.

Faster.

Someone screamed under me. Someone else's pleasure rolled through me. It blended with my need, creating the most incredible cocktail of agony and elation.

My muscles seized, my mind grew blank, and I thought I would die.

A feral roar rocked the room, shaking the walls of the underground caves. The roar was mine. It tore from my throat as my seed spilled from my mating cluster for the first time in my life.

Then the strength left me. My limbs shook, weak as the day I was born. I crashed forward, then rolled to my side. My eyes remained open, but I saw nothing.

A gentle hand brushed over my forehead, parting the curtain of my hair over my face.

"It's over." Her sweet, gentle voice sounded above me. "You can rest now."

I didn't feel my body. It appeared to remain floating somewhere, back in the world of pleasure and pain.

Her affection filtered through my tendrils, soothing my pain like a magical potion. Anchoring me in place. She cradled my head in her lap. Brushing my hair aside, she kissed my temple, then stroked along my ear. Her touch was gentle. Loving. Tenderness spread through my chest with a warm glow.

Wrapping my arm around her waist, I buried my face in her stomach, breathing in her familiar scent.

A shiver ran through my muscles with chills, and she pulled a sheet over me.

"We did it, Rha. We got through it. It's over now."

Nothing was over yet.

My poor little treasure didn't realize that it all had just begun.

Twenty-Five

DAWN

The mattress moved with Rha shifting from it, and it yanked me out of my nap.

"Greetings, Your Highness." Sigid's quiet voice reached me.

Something was deposited by the bed with a soft clank then the mattress dipped again as Rha climbed back in bed with me.

I stretched, opening my eyes. Rha was by my side, wearing a thin beige robe over his otherwise gloriously naked body. My own body ached as if it'd been tossed in a concrete mixer with a bunch of rocks. Helping a shadow fae through a bout of mating fever proved to be quite a workout.

"What time is it?" I murmured, rubbing my eyes.

A soft kiss landed on the corner of my mouth. Rha's warm breath fanned over my lips.

"What does it matter?"

Time hadn't mattered for a while now. Nothing did. For the past two days or so, our vigorous fucking alternated with leisurely love making, interrupted by bath breaks and meals at random.

Exhausted, we'd dozed off a couple of times, with most of Rha's mating cluster still inside me.

"How are you feeling, my sweet?" he murmured, kissing along my jawline.

His tendrils skimmed up my arms, their ends hovered over my *leilathas*, waiting for my permission. I nodded, and they connected at once.

"You're sore," he stated.

"No kidding, Captain Obvious," I croaked. "What did you expect?"

He heaved a sigh with a somber expression. "My expectations were far gloomier than this."

"Of course they were." I smiled and stroked the deep worry wrinkle between his eyebrows. "*Gloomy* should be your middle name, my somber prince."

He ran his hands down my arms, then over my ribs. I winced when he reached my hips.

"I hurt you." His expression turned even darker.

"Mhm." I shifted a little in search of a more comfortable position on my back. "It seems the gazillion orgasms you've given me came at a price."

He bent down to the floor. I heard the sound of water as he rinsed and wrung out a cloth.

"A gazillion?"

"Well, I lost count after seven, which happened after our first visit to the baths but before that first tray of snacks we ordered."

He gently dragged the warm, wet cloth over the bruises on my hips.

"What's this for?" I asked.

"It's a healing potion infused with herbs and spices to make you feel better. The royal hag sent it, following my orders."

While I'd napped, oblivious to the world around me, he'd come to his senses long enough to give some coherent orders. Impressive. The cloth felt warm and soothing against my flushed skin.

"Are you hungry?" He dropped the cloth back into the bowl. "Sigid brought some fruit as well."

"Are there any apricots?"

"He brought some fresh ones. Unless you want them soaked in honey?"

"No. Fresh is good too."

Rha opened an apricot, took out the core, then handed me both halves of the fruit. While I ate, he rinsed the cloth again, then parted my knees with his hands. I didn't protest as he cleaned my inner thighs, then gently dragged the cloth between them.

It felt too nice to stop him. I discovered I enjoyed being taken care of by Rha. After the long hours of messy, sweaty sex with him, I didn't feel awkward or self-conscious. His touch was gentle and caring, almost reverent, erasing the ache through magic.

He cleaned between my thighs, then gently dipped a corner of the wet cloth inside me. Excitement sparked in the wake of his touch. He circled my clit, and my inner muscles spasmed in anticipation.

A flash of desire must've leaped through the tendrils to Rha because he paused, holding the cloth in his raised hand.

"I'm good," I rushed to reassure him. "Keep going."

He rinsed the cloth again, then dragged it from my front to my back, cleaning between my butt cheeks too. I blushed at the thought of how much action that part of my body had gotten over the last couple of days, far more than it had in my entire life prior.

Parting my raised knees wider, he kissed the inside of my thigh. I relaxed even more under his caress, closing my eyes like a cat basking in sunshine.

His kisses dipped lower until his warm lips landed between my thighs.

"Rha..." I exhaled at the exquisite sensation.

His tongue darted out, flicking my clit.

I didn't think I had any more orgasms left in me. But I enjoyed his caress, letting him clean me with his tongue. He was thorough, like he always was with everything. And after just a few minutes, he got me moaning again.

I gripped his hair, lifting my hips. The tip of his tongue rubbed harder against my clit, reaping yet another orgasm out of me. I whimpered in pleasure, riding his mouth. And he gently lapped at me, guiding me down from the crest.

"All clean." He smiled, licking his lips, then pulled himself up my body.

"Come here." I curled against his chest, and he drew the ends of his robe over me to keep me warm.

"You like this."

"Orgasms?" I murmured. "Sure. Who doesn't?"

"No. I meant *this*." He draped an arm over me, tucking me into his big, warm body. "You enjoy me holding you. You love my kisses after sex, possibly even more than during it. You relish my touch." He ran a soothing hand down my back. "Your pleasure is bright and intense during sex. But afterwards, the joy of having me with you is warmer and ever-lasting."

I couldn't lie to him. He knew exactly what I felt. But I wasn't ready to confide in him, either. Or to confront my feelings for him.

Instead, I ran my fingers over the hard ridges of his abs and down to that fantastic thing he had happening between his legs. His slim, magical tentacles welcomed my touch, quickly curling around my fingers.

"This is supposed to be about you, baby. Not me." I kissed his chest, wiggling my fingers in his cluster.

"You and I are connected, my sweet. From now on, everything will always be about both of us."

His words made me pause. My fingers went rigid inside the cluster of his eager feelers.

It was just sex between us. It couldn't be anything more. Not when I was about to leave him, this kingdom, and this entire world—never to return.

I pressed my forehead to his chest, catching my breath while my throat tightened at the thought of leaving.

He slid a finger under my chin, directing my face to his.

"What's wrong, sweetheart?"

Damn him and his all-sensing tendrils.

"I'm good." I faked a smile. "Just tired. You've worn me out, Your Highness."

"That I have." He splayed a hand on my belly, stroking it with a dreamy smile on his lips.

I realized with a jolt of panic what he might be thinking about, what the purpose of mating fever was all about.

"Can fae reproduce with humans?" I asked carefully.

"Yes, but a child of a fae is always a fae. Ours will have shadow magic, just like me."

Ours?

Oh, God…

I couldn't let him think like that, not even for a second.

"No, Rha," I said gently. "It's not going to happen. I have an IUD."

He stared at me blankly. Why the hell did I think a fae would know what an IUD was?

"It's a device inside my uterus that prevents me from getting pregnant."

His eyebrows moved in confusion.

"You were ready to receive my seed, Dawn. I would not have gone into the mating fever otherwise."

"Right. Well. This version of the device doesn't stop the ovulation, it just prevents the implantation. There'll be no baby, Rha. I promise you."

He nodded thoughtfully. "I'm sure the royal hag can remove this device before the next time."

There was something new in his eyes when he looked at me. A different kind of longing—a longing for a future. Only there was no future for us. Letting him believe otherwise would be cruel. But what could I say?

In the end, I said nothing. I stroked his cluster as a distraction, running my fingers through the slick strands that reached for me as if magnetized.

"Dawn..." A warning sounded in his voice. "Don't. You need to recover, and I can hardly hold back as it is."

I ignored his warning.

"Tell me something, Your Highness. You need to come from all of them at once, right?"

"Yes."

Breathless, he rolled to his back, trying to get away from me, but I crawled after him on all fours.

"So, what if I play with them? With my hands?"

He rolled his head on the pillow. "It can't be your hands, my sweet. I need to be inside of you."

"How about inside my mouth then?"

He shot me an intrigued look. "Will you do something like that?"

"Why not? You've done it to me."

"But it's not the same."

"I see no difference."

He opened his mouth to reply, but I dragged my tongue along one of his feelers. The scent of him was stronger here—warm and sweet, like honeysuckle. The feeler glowed faintly. The bright light it'd emitted earlier had dimmed with Rha's last orgasm. The slick appendage trembled at my touch, then slinked into my mouth before I managed to close it. It didn't stop, reaching all the way into my throat.

I gagged, pushing the intruder out with my tongue, then jerked my head back.

"Are you alright?" Rha asked with concern.

I coughed, clearing the tickling sensation out of my throat. "Such a squirmy little bugger."

Rha raked his fingers through my hair. "Just let it be, sweetheart, while I can still control it somewhat."

I shook my head stubbornly. "I can't let it win."

He gave me an incredulous look. "Are you earnestly having a competition with my mating cluster?"

"We're not competing. We're wrestling." I grabbed a handful of his feelers in my hand, then straddled his thighs as if getting ready for a rodeo. "Though I have to admit, I've never wrestled with a dick before. Or a cluster of them."

He produced a strangled sound, something between a laugh and a moan. Using both hands, I tried to collect all his feelers, which wasn't easy. They squirmed in my hands, wiggling out of my grip. When I finally gathered them all into a bunch, their ends flared out, spreading in every which direction.

My struggle produced a result, however. By now, Rha's groin burst with the brightest golden shimmer, and my poor prince moaned and writhed under me in desperate need.

"I need to use you again, Dawn," he groaned. "And I can only hope you'll forgive me for what it may do to your body and soul."

I didn't mind being "used." But I also kind of wished to finish what I'd started with my attempt at a blowjob.

"Let me use you first, my prince" I blew a loose strand of hair away from my face.

Opening my mouth, I touched one of the feelers with my bottom lip. The moment it sensed an opening, its wiggling gained direction. It slipped into my mouth, and the rest of them followed.

I flexed my hands, holding the cluster firmly. Gathered together like that, it was as thick as my forearm, and just as long if the feelers held straight.

Oral would not have been a viable option at the beginning of Rha's mating fever when he thrust into me without control. The feelers would have probably choked me to death before he could've stopped himself. The threat was still real, and I proceeded carefully.

The feelers snapped together, forming a tight, thick rope aimed at getting inside me by any means necessary. I took their tapered tips between my lips. Rha growled and jerked his hips up in a thrust. But sitting on top of him, I controlled how deeply I took him.

Holding the whole cluster at the base, I slid my mouth up and down its length, taking it as deep as it felt comfortable, which wasn't very deep at all. I couldn't move far past the tapered tips. I played with my tongue between the feelers and sucked on their tips. They jerked and undulated, but I held tightly, not letting any escape.

Rha groaned, bucking his hips against my mouth. The feelers trembled against my tongue, then burst with flavors of honey and summer flowers. I jerked my head back instinctively. But Rha tasted so good—fragrant and with the mild sweetness of a dessert.

He came in spurts bursting from all feelers at once, and I couldn't swallow fast enough. It dripped from my mouth, running down my chin like flavored syrup. I wiped my lips, then examined my hand in the pale light under the bed canopy.

Golden flecks were suspended in the clear, fragrant gel of his seed.

"For fuck's sake." I laughed, licking my hand. "Did you have to be this perfect in and out? I mean, whose sperm looks this pretty and tastes so good?"

He rose on his elbows, watching me. A sheen of sweat plastered a few strands of his hair to his forehead.

I climbed up his body.

"You are by far the yummiest man I've ever tasted."

"Let me try." He drew me in for a kiss. "It's sweet." He licked his lips after kissing me thoroughly.

"Mhm." I nodded.

"You like sweet."

I nodded again. There was no use in lying. He felt how much I liked it. He knew how much I liked *him*.

What he didn't know was that despite it all, I was going to leave him.

Twenty-Six

DAWN

The following night, Rha's mating fever waned completely, and that day, I insisted on sleeping in my room. Alone.

Except that I didn't go to bed. I packed the few possessions I had accumulated in Alveari Kingdom, including anything of any value that could be sold or traded when we were back in our world.

I wore the priceless necklace that Rha and I had designed together. It was easier and safer to wear it than to carry it in my satchel. The gold of the massive setting and the gazillion precious stones would fetch a good price in practically any time period we might land. Except that tearing it apart and selling the pieces was the last thing I wanted to think about.

After dressing in the most practical clothes I could find, I sat on the bed and watched the silky streams of black sand rushing downwards through the glass tubes of the clock on my wall. The moment the last grain of sand would hit the bottom of the intricate system of curved, blown-glass tubes, the entire face of the clock would rotate one-hundred-and-eighty degrees and the golden bee on the top of the clock would move by a notch, indicating the passing of an hour.

By then, the sun would have risen, sending the shadow fae deep into the city and underground. And for me, it would be the time to finally leave Teneris and Alveari Kingdom.

After almost three days of fucking me on literally every surface of his bedroom and beyond, Rha had finally returned to his former calmer self. His mating cluster disappeared, and the frenzied need had passed. However, his protectiveness over me had only strengthened. He allowed me to leave his rooms only after I'd complained that being held underground at all times depressed me.

He had personally taken me to the *sarai* after breakfast, then left me under the supervision of an entire army of guards and Keepers.

In the *sarai*, I sat in Elaine's room with her and Melanie, as the others joined us in small groups to discuss the final details of our escape in privacy, away from the Keepers who congregated in the courtyard.

Melanie gave me a stern look before I left her room to go back to Rha. "I don't care if he gave you the fucking of your life, sister, you can't let us down."

"I won't."

Elaine gave me a hug.

"Whatever happens, we'll be free," she said, then gave me a penetrating stare, as if trying to read my thoughts. "You don't have to feel guilty, Dawn. He'd never see you as a person, only as his property. Otherwise, he would've freed you already. You owe him nothing."

Sitting in my bedroom now, watching the final rivulets of fine sand sliding down the glass tubes of the clock, I whispered her words again, "I owe him nothing."

I'd stayed in my room this morning because it was easier for me to leave without risking waking Rha up. But I was also relieved that I didn't need to physically untangle my body from his and that I didn't have to see him sleeping while leaving him. Because it would've taken so much more strength for me to leave him then, and I wasn't sure I'd be strong enough.

The clock clinked as the glass fixture rotated, bringing the downside up and the upside down. The golden bee moved with a soft, melodious sound that had lulled me to sleep for weeks. Today, it was my signal to leave here.

I slung the satchel over my shoulder and smoothed my skirt over the long pants I was wearing underneath. Padding softly in my short boots, I exited the room and closed the door behind me.

I climbed up the grand staircase to the dining room and opened one of the tall shutters behind the royal platform.

No longer used to daylight, I squinted in the bright glow of the rising sun. The early morning looked peaceful. The air still carried a trace of the night chill. The flying insects had hidden already, but the birds were chirping in the tall grass growing over the city.

I tugged the top layer of my skirt over my head in the local fashion and climbed out onto the patio. Bending over the parapet, I studied the slanted wall of the hill-city, searching for the best way down.

From there, there'd be nothing between me and the desert. Rha relied on wards and guards at the gate to keep intruders out of Teneris. But no one worried about keeping people in. The desert did a good job of it on its own.

Melanie and the others would be waiting for me just around the corner, at the start of the road from Teneris.

"The Alveari Desert is a dangerous place, especially during the day," a dry voice suddenly rasped behind me.

I jumped in shock.

Dread hollowed my chest as I whipped around to face a hunched-over figure shrouded in a dark-gray cloak. The royal hag stood inside the dining room, holding on to the frame of the door-window while keeping to the shadows of the wall.

"The world outside these walls is wild and treacherous," she chuckled, "especially for a sweet little morsel like you."

Keeping close to the banister, I wondered if I could just make a dash for it. Would she try to chase me, the frail old woman that she was? Surely, I would outrun her. But she could alert the guards. That would end my escape and likely harm the others.

"What do you want?" I asked, not moving from my spot.

"I want to give you these." From the flowing folds of her wide cloak, she produced a pair of tall boots, similar to those that shadow fae wore in the desert. "Those tender thighs of yours will need protection out there. I'm sure they suffered enough already during Prince Rha's recent mating fever."

She chuckled again. I found the sound repulsive, wishing I could toss the boots she held out to me back at her. The boots, however, seemed far more practical for traipsing a desert than the short ones that I had on.

But why would she care about me or my thighs? This felt like a trap.

"Do you want me gone from Teneris?" I asked.

"Not just from Teneris, Sweet One. I want all of your kind out of Alveari Kingdom. And don't you ever come here again."

If she wanted me gone, she wouldn't stop me. But I couldn't help feeling a pinch of offense at her derisive tone.

"Why?" I asked. "What did we do for you to hate us?"

She dropped the hand holding the boots. As much as I'd like to take them, I wasn't coming any closer.

"It's not what you do," she said. "It's what you are. Our First Priestess helped our shadows turn into people. Our ancestors built her a temple, and she filled it with joy, pure and precious. Joy Guardians pledged to keep it. They were supposed to preserve its purity. Instead, they allowed it to be polluted with that of humans."

She wrinkled her nose, looking at me with resentment like I'd personally spat into her precious, ancient joy.

"Fine." I stretched my hand out to her. "Give me the boots, and I'll get out of your hair."

She handed them to me. The scorpion tattoo on her wrist came into view again, and she didn't try to hide it from me this time.

"What does your tattoo mean?" I asked, kicking off the boots I was wearing and putting on the new ones. Soft and smooth like butter, their leather slid easily over my legs. They reached all the way up past mid-thigh, like stockings that would protect me from thistles in the grass and the sand in the desert.

She turned her wrist to better display the tattoo.

"This is the sign of the Watchers."

"Who are the Watchers?"

"The few of the Joy Guardians who realize their duty is not only to guard our joy, but to protect it from the likes of you. They are the ones who will take you through the portal today."

I wondered if the hag was one of her "sources" that Melanie had spoken about. With the access anywhere in the palace, the hug probably helped at least with the communication between Melanie and the Watchers.

"Are you one of them?" I asked. "Are you a Watcher too?"

She scoffed at my assumption. "I'm a hag, not a Watcher or a Guardian. I serve Prince Rha and can't plot behind his back. I gave you the boots because it's my duty to protect what's his."

"To *protect*, but not to *keep*, right?"

"Exactly," she smirked.

"So, you won't wake the prince when I leave then?"

"It'd be rude to wake him up, wouldn't it? The poor thing is exhausted after rolling in the sheets with you for days. You don't look too bad, though." She slid her gaze down my body. "Fit and well after helping to break his mating fever. And they say humans are weak."

I shifted my weight to another foot, eager to end this conversation now.

"Well, thanks for the boots, now if you'll excuse me—"

But she wasn't done yet.

"I won't wake the prince. But when he gets up in the evening and finds you gone, I'll have to tell him where you went."

"Do you?"

"He's my prince. I swore an oath to serve him," she said firmly. "When he asks, I won't lie. I'll tell him where you went, and he'll come after you to take back what's his. But if you make haste, he won't catch you."

"Alright then." I made a move toward the parapet, but she grabbed my hand, reaching out from the shadows of the room.

"I want you gone, Sweet One. But I don't want you dead. Once you leave the safety of Teneris, make sure you keep going and don't stop until you go through the portal. Do you understand? The desert is not safe for anyone, but especially for your kind. There are those who wish you harm."

The rasp was gone from her voice. It sounded surprisingly firm and smooth. Her grip on my arm felt strong. Now I believed that if I ran, she'd catch up with me easily enough.

Her warning sent a cold trickle of dread down my spine.

"It's not in the shadow fae's interests to harm us," I pointed out. "Why would anyone want to hurt us? You said it yourself. The Watchers just want us gone."

"The Watchers do. But there are also those in the desert who will try to stop you from leaving. And they mean harm."

She glanced back into the room over her shoulder and let go of my wrist.

"Now go."

But I didn't move.

"No. Tell me what you mean. Who are the people who want to harm us?"

She glanced behind her again, looking nervous, then leaned forward, squinting against the sunlight that pierced through the shadows under her hood.

"A scorpion is a deadly creature, Sweet One, but it's not as cruel as the golden hyacinth of the desert."

"A what?" I asked, confused.

She held my gaze with her pale eyes. "The hyacinth of the desert is sweet and fragrant, like the finest dish created for Joy Vessels. But do you know how it grows so lush in the dry black sands?"

"No."

"By preying on desert creatures and drinking their blood. Beware of the golden hyacinth and of those who wear it," she hissed with another worried glance over her shoulder, before shrinking back into the room and slamming the shutters closed.

Had the old crone overheated in the morning sun already and was spewing gibberish?

I stared at the closed window, not quite sure if I should pay any attention to what she'd just mumbled to me. Then I realized that whoever spooked the hag into leaving could spot me here soon. I had to leave.

I climbed over the parapet, then started my descent along the sharp slope of the city wall. The grass covered me entirely, its wispy ends swaying above my head as I slid and rolled down the wall. I grabbed its willowy stems for support, ripping them out of the sandy ground with their roots.

My legs shook from strain and my palms burned from gripping the grass by the time the black sand finally crunched under my boots.

I turned left and hurried along the wall to the spot where Melanie, Elaine, and the others waited for me.

"There you are," Melanie exhaled with relief, as if the weight of an entire mountain dropped from her shoulders at the sight of me.

"I said I'd come." I shrugged.

Elaine placed a hand on my shoulder. "You made the right decision, Dawn."

I *knew* I did.

I just wished I *felt* it too. But all I felt was doubt.

DAWN

I didn't look back as we ran across the sand toward the closest dune. Teneris was behind me. The awareness of it pricked the skin on my arms and my nape, but I didn't look back.

Only when all of us made it to the dune behind which our two guides waited for us with a small caravan of camels did I finally turn around to take one last look at the hill city.

It lost its shimmer in the daylight. The pale grass looked dirty beige instead of gray, and without the glow and sparkle of the moths, everything magical about its appearance was gone. But I knew the magic was still in there, as was its prince, who was sleeping right now, sprawled in his spacious bed all alone.

"Goodbye, Prince Rha," I whispered. "For what it's worth, I'll never forget you."

I'll miss you, my mind added for me. But I didn't repeat these words out loud, not even in a whisper.

Kostya panted nearby, catching his breath after the run.

"I'm not getting back into a fucking cage," he huffed, pointing at the high contraptions on the camels' backs.

"Those aren't cages." A guide lowered the rope ladder down

the side of the animal closest to us. "They are seats. For your comfort."

There were four camels. Each had seating for four people. That left two of us without a seat.

"Two of you will have to ride a horse with each of us," the guide explained. "We need to hurry. Climb up, everyone."

Melanie grabbed onto the ladder of the closest camel.

"Just imagine, guys, we'll be home by dinnertime." She sounded so cheerful, as if we were boarding a train that would take us straight back to our families.

Sipho brushed past her on his way to the next camel.

"The head chef is making goat cheese soufflé for dinner," he muttered under his breath.

Sipho had taken it upon himself to help in the kitchen with meal preparation. The head chef had recipes with detailed instructions, but only a human could do the taste tests to ensure the right amount of spices in a dish. Sipho seemed to have enjoyed working with the cooks and creating new recipes. But now, he climbed the ladder up to a seat on a camel's back, just like everyone else.

Covered head to toe with his long garment for protection from the sun, the guide reached to adjust a rung of the ladder for me to climb up after Melanie. The edge of his shroud shifted, and I spotted a tattoo inside his wrist—a golden hexagon with a black scorpion inside it.

"You're a Watcher," I said.

He didn't flinch, glancing at his tattoo with pride. "I am. And I will deliver you to your world where you belong."

Elaine and Lucia joined Melanie and me in the two pairs of seats facing each other. We had to wedge our knees between the knees of the person sitting across for all of us to fit into the bamboo contraption covered with a dense material for protection from the sun.

Our seats swayed side to side as the camel moved at a considerable pace, but Melanie fidgeted in her seat impatiently.

"They're too slow."

We moved at the same speed or even faster than when we'd first arrived at Alveari Kingdom. That night, however, no one was chasing us. Today, Rha could send his army after us at any moment.

Elaine placed a hand on my knee. "Are you okay?"

"Sure." I shrugged.

I wasn't the only one having mixed feelings about leaving, but everyone seemed to handle it well, and I wasn't going to act any differently.

"We should be at the portal in the afternoon," Melanie said. "With any luck, no one will notice our absence until late in the evening. And by then, we'll be long gone from this world."

The Keepers didn't sleep in the *sarai*. There were plenty of guards by the gate, but since Melanie and the others had managed to trick them, slipping away undetected, it was safe to assume their absence wouldn't be discovered until breakfast was served, which happened well after sunset.

"Was the prince asleep when you left?" Lucia asked with a lift of hope in her voice, as if wishing for Rha to come after us.

"As far as I know, he was."

Melanie pivoted to me. "You don't know for sure?"

"I stayed in my room this morning."

"Well." She nodded with a knowing look. "His fucking frenzy is over, I've heard. He didn't need you anymore."

"Melanie!" Elaine's cheeks flushed bright pink, and she squeezed my hand in support.

"That's fine." I brushed off her concerns for my feelings. "It's not like what she said is a lie."

Elaine glared at Melanie through her glasses. "Maybe. But there is no need to be mean."

Melanie had the decency to keep quiet this time, and I turned away, staring at the cloth that shielded us from the desert.

I couldn't see anything through the dark material. Not the desert, not the hill of Teneris, and I tried not to think about the crown prince sleeping in his bed. I tried very hard not to think about what would happen when he woke up.

Maybe Sigid would bring my breakfast and would let the prince know that I wasn't in my golden bedroom. Or maybe Rha would intercept Sigid by the staircase, as he'd done before, to serve me breakfast himself. Then he'd see I was no longer there.

Would he be angry?

Or worse—sad? Heartbroken. And not just because I left, but also because of the way I did it—sneaking out behind his back without even saying goodbye.

It had to be done that way. I couldn't raise suspicions and jeopardize the escape of the others. But my heart ached, nevertheless.

I couldn't break down in front of everyone, holding back tears with everything I had. But I already knew the pain of leaving Rha would never go away completely. No matter where I'd end up, I'd always miss his deep, soothing voice and the comfort of his arms. I'd miss him for as long as I lived.

"You all have to promise me one thing," Lucia broke the silence. "We go through the portal together. At least the four of us, if not all eighteen."

"How are we going to do that?" Elaine asked. "By holding hands?"

"Whatever it takes," Lucia insisted. "Holding hands or hugging each other if necessary. We need to stay together. And if we land back where we came from, I'm crashing on one of your couches until I'm back on my feet, okay? I'm not sleeping in my fucking car again."

Elaine gave her a faint smile. "No one knows where we'll land. We may end up so far in the past, you'll get a chance to marry a duke and live in a castle filled with hundreds of your own couches."

"Yeah, right. With my luck?" Lucia laughed, then said in a more serious voice, lifting a finger for emphasis, "But if any of you bitches do marry a duke or a prince or whatever, don't you get snotty and forget about the rest of us. Deal? We'll return to that world together, and we'll stay together."

"Of course," Melanie agreed.

"Deal." Elaine nodded.

The three of them then looked at me.

I slid a hand under the fabric draped over my head and shoulders and clutched a strand of my necklace. The cool, smooth surface of the stones felt familiar and comforting in my fingers.

"Yes," I said. "We'll stay together."

OTHER THAN A COUPLE of short bathroom breaks, we made no stops, moving ahead steadily. At noon, Melanie shared some snacks and water she'd brought with her.

I wasn't hungry, but the heat was getting to all of us. The fabric over the bamboo frame blocked most of the sunlight, but it appeared to trap the heat inside.

When I moved a corner of it aside, however, hoping to get some air, a blast of hot wind tore into our small shelter.

"Keep it down!" Melanie shouted.

I yanked the cover back in place, but the wind sandblasted the fabric walls from the outside, shaking the thin contraption.

"I guess that's why they shutter the windows and doors in Teneris during the day," Elaine said.

She had taken her sweater off long ago and tied it around her waist instead. But even with her wearing only a thin sleeveless dress, the skin on her arms had already beaded with a sheen of sweat.

I'd taken my boots off back when we'd just started on our way and dropped the top layer of my skirt from my head and shoulders. But listening to the sand scraping against the fabric from the outside, I grabbed my boots and pulled them back on. I'd rather be hot than have the skin on my legs sandblasted raw when we left our shelter.

The camel stopped suddenly. Our seats tipped forward, then to the sides. I screamed, grabbing on to the rickety frame, but all movement ceased quickly, and our seats straightened again.

The black fabric was lifted on my side, and a guide poked his head through. He had a scarf covering the lower part of his face. The edge of the fabric over his head hung low, leaving his eyes in the shadows.

"A storm is coming," he said. "The camels won't go any farther until the storm has passed. But we're nearly there. Come." He beckoned with his hand. "We'll walk to the portal."

"Great." Lucia groaned.

Elaine untied her sweater from around her waist and put it back on. Melanie pulled the top layer of her skirt over her head like the shadow fae did. I did the same, then used the hair pins to fasten the fabric to my hair and over my chest.

After all of us had secured our clothing in some way, Melanie climbed out and I followed. The moment I stuck my legs out, the wind blasted them with the shrapnel of sand. I silently thanked the hag for the boots.

Wind pushed the sand in swirls. Fine black dust filled the air, obscuring the sky and nearly completely blocking the sun. The guide made his way to the next camel lying on the ground with its legs folded under it.

"Did he say the storm was just starting?" I ducked under the cover of the fabric pulled over my head, but the sand was already grinding between my teeth. "Because this looks pretty stormy to me already."

"I guess it'll get worse," Melanie predicted somberly.

"The camels are smart," Elaine said, stroking the unusually soft, long fur of the otherworldly animal. Wind had already blown sand over one side of the camel, covering it half-way up. "It's best to stay put."

"Look!" Melanie pointed up the hill straight ahead of us.

Black rocks littered the ground. They got bigger and higher toward the top of the hill. On the side of the hill, two large stone columns tipped toward each other, forming an entrance to an unusual building. It was constructed from black rocks and shimmering yellow mortar. A golden hexagon stood upright on the tall spire over its pitched roof.

Pale sunlight filtered through the swirls of sand above. A thick sun ray shone straight through the hexagon and toward another one, a smaller hexagon mounted on a tall pole held by four Joy Guardians with their golden garments billowing in the storm.

The beam of light streamed through both hexagons as the Joy Guardians directed it to the top of the hill. A circle formed where the light hit the black sand of the summit. The circle grew like a golden halo filled with darkness.

The guide gestured at it. "The shadow tunnel. It'll take you to the River of Mists and then back to your world. The portal is opening. Let's go."

"I don't think these are the same Joy Guardians who put our harnesses on," Elaine said as we all headed up the hill, following the guide.

They couldn't be the same ones. From what the hag had told me, not all the Joy Guardians wanted us out, only those who called themselves the Watchers.

Melanie pushed ahead, fighting the storm. "Who cares? Let's just get out of here."

The wind slammed against us relentlessly. Filled with sand, it scraped at our clothes and any exposed skin like sandpaper.

"Should've done this at night," Lucia croaked, barely audible through the hauling wind.

"At night, the prince's guards would've easily caught us," Melanie pointed out.

"Might not have been the worst thing to happen to us," Lucia snapped under her breath.

The wind caught her words and shredded them to pieces

before they could reach Melanie. Which was probably a good thing. We didn't need another fight between these two right now.

The golden shimmer on top of the hill bloomed brighter. I didn't have to look up to see its glow piercing the dust clouds and shimmering in the sand around us.

"When we go through that thing," Lucia reminded us, "we'll hold hands, okay?"

"Yes." I was so focused on keeping up with Melanie that I hadn't noticed how I'd lost Elaine from my peripheral vision. "Elaine?" I turned around.

She was climbing the hill just a couple of steps behind us, with the others from the *sarai* close by. But something else caught my attention.

Dark spots emerged from the storm behind us, taking the shapes of riders on horseback. Unlike our camels who refused to move, their horses kept going through the storm, fighting the wind.

Melanie glanced back over her shoulder and paled at the sight of the riders.

"These must be the guards from Teneris. Run!" She scrambled faster up the hill.

"Come, Elaine." I waved at my friend to hurry up.

There was still a good distance between us and the riders. We could make it to the portal before they'd gained on us.

But then, the front riders suddenly dissolved into shadows, momentarily blending with the sand in the wind. The shadows reappeared right behind us, solidifying into people again.

These weren't Rha's warriors, I realized with horror. Their ragged, tattered clothes looked nothing like the sleek uniforms of Teneris.

A man was gaining on Elaine, promptly climbing the hill behind her. His skirt had frayed to rags along the hem. A worn animal hide protected his head and shoulders from the sun. His feral scowl made me shudder.

"Elaine, run!" I screamed.

She lunged after me but tripped in her hurry. The wind blew her hair across her face. Shoving it away, she knocked her glasses off. They dropped to the ground.

"Leave them!" Melanie yelled.

But I knew Elaine was as blind as a bat without her glasses. She needed them in any world we'd go to. Sliding in the sand and on the patches of pale grass, I headed down the hill to help her.

Elaine raked her fingers through the sand in search of her glasses as her pursuer closed in on her. She found the glasses the moment he grabbed her.

"No! Elaine." I leaped toward them and gripped her sweater. "Get off her!"

Baring his fangs at me, the man tossed Elaine over his shoulder. Her sweater slipped from my fingers.

His chest armor flashed in front of me as he turned. It was made from plain leather discs linked together with small silver rings. The thick stem of a cluster of yellow flowers was threaded through the metal links. The succulent petals of the flowers burst with nectar, looking like drops of golden honey.

Dread chilled my spine, paralyzing my limbs.

The hag's raspy voice echoed in my ears, *"Beware of the golden hyacinth and of those who wear it."*

The man ran down the hill, taking my kicking and screaming friend away.

"Elaine!" I made a move to go after them when Melanie grabbed my arm.

"Let's go, Dawn."

"They've got Elaine!" I yelled in anguish.

More shadows appeared among the humans who tried to make their way to the portal on top of the hill. Screams pierced the howls of the storm as the shadow fae started snatching humans, then dragging them back to their horses.

"We've got to go." Melanie tugged me up the hill. "We can't help anyone. We need to save ourselves."

"Did you know about this?" I screamed. "Did you plan for this to happen?"

"What? No!" She looked so appalled, it convinced me she was innocent. "I've no idea who these dirty punks are. But we can't wait. The Guardians can't hold the portal open forever. We need to move."

More horsemen appeared at the foot of the hill. I'd lost track of the one who had Elaine. He seemed to have dissolved into the storm, taking my friend with him.

"Melanie, we can't leave her."

"But we can't save her, either. Or we'll end up captured too. This is our one and only chance, Dawn. Come on."

Some of the horsemen headed toward the Joy Guardians who held the pole with the hexagon. One rider threw an axe, and it sank into the chest of a Guardian, right against his heart.

Another rider leaped from his horse. Without touching the ground, he became a shadow, then appeared next to the three remaining Joy Guardians. He raised a curved sword, then slashed across another Guardian's neck. Dark blood gushed from the wound, splashing over the man's golden clothes. His head rolled from his torso and bounced along the ground.

The heavy pole shook in the hands of the two remaining Joy Guardians. The golden glow of the opening portal flickered.

"Faster, Dawn," Melanie begged, dragging me with her to the top of the hill.

The thug with the sword raised it again, moving onto the next Guardian. A spear flew through the storm and hit the man with the sword in the back. More horse riders appeared. These wore the black uniforms of the Teneris Palace.

"The guards are here," Melanie gasped.

We were in front of the portal now. A light breeze blew from it with wisps of shadows. It felt refreshing against my face and so different from the brutal heat of the sandstorm.

Then, the ring of the golden shimmer around the portal wavered. The darkness inside it thinned. Held by only two Joy

Guardians now, the pole with the hexagon teetered and shook, breaking up the beam.

"No, please, no..." Melanie clasped her hand over her mouth, watching the portal falter.

The two Joy Guardians struggled to hold the pole in the upright position. But a shadow solidified next to them, taking the shape of a man. His shimmering black garment was held with a golden circlet on his head—the crown of the prince.

"Rha," I exhaled.

He grabbed the pole, helping the Joy Guardians to steady it. The column of pale light regained its direction, and the portal solidified once again.

"Thank God," Melanie moaned in relief.

"Move it, guys!" Lin and her friend Aihan rushed by us, then jumped into the black circle of the portal. It flared with a firework of golden sparks, swallowing both women.

More humans rushed by, jumping into the portal.

"Now." Melanie yanked on my hand.

But I couldn't move.

I stared at the prince who held the pole, keeping the portal open. He'd come after us. He chased us all the way from the palace. But instead of taking us back to Teneris, he was letting us go.

He was letting *me* go, setting me free.

Huffing and cursing, Kostya climbed up the hill.

"Get the fuck out of my way." He shoved past me.

Tripping over a rock, he fell, crashing into Melanie, who stood right in front of the portal. She fell in backwards and was swallowed whole by the cloud of black shadows and golden sparks of the portal. Kostya fell in halfway, his legs and backside still on this side.

"Melanie!" I froze in horror.

But my sister was gone. Gone from this world forever.

More people ran by me, tripping over themselves to make it

through the portal. The golden circle suddenly flickered and dimmed again.

I pivoted back to Rha and the Joy Guardians. The pole tipped sideways, held only by Rha now, who was on his knees, propping the pole with his shoulder. All four Joy Guardians lay on the ground, blood oozing out of the open wounds on their backs and chests.

Two dead thugs lay on the ground too. A bloodied sword was in the sand next to Rha. It looked like he had killed those who'd murdered the Joy Guardians. But he'd paid for it.

A dagger was sticking out from his back, just below his shoulders. The blade sparked with the red of Nerifir iron—the only metal deadly to fae. Swaying on his knees, he still kept the pole upright somehow.

"Hurry!" The married couple from the *sarai* climbed over Kostya, who was still struggling to get up with only half of his body inside the portal.

It was now or never.

Rha wouldn't be able to hold the pole much longer. The Nerifir iron of the dagger was poisoning his blood, killing him from the inside. There was no one to help him. His warriors were fighting our attackers, the battle moving farther away from him.

He'd fall. The portal would close, cutting me off from my world and my sister forever. And Rha would die.

Coming to this dark world had not been my decision. Escaping from Teneris hadn't been my idea, either. But as I took off in a mad dash down the hill toward the man bleeding on his knees for my freedom, I had no doubts. No matter what world I'd end up in, I realized, I would never be happy knowing Rha died and I let it happen.

It was that simple. I couldn't let him die.

I just hoped I wasn't too late already.

Rha swayed on his knees. The pole with the magical hexagon slipped from his shoulder and crashed to the ground, raising clouds of sand along its length.

The portal behind me closed.

Something rolled past me down the hill. A scream of horror stuck in my throat when I realized what it was—the lower part of Kostya's body. Dressed in pants he'd been so proud of getting from the Keepers, it was cut off at the waist, the charred flesh sizzling and sparkling with a gold shimmer of magic that had sliced him in two.

Hot air scorched my lungs. I gasped for every breath. My feet slid in the sand and tripped over patches of grass.

I fell to my knees at Rha's side. He bent forward, reaching behind him in search of the dagger, but he couldn't find it, already disoriented from the poison in his bloodstream.

Hugging his shoulders with one arm, I yanked the dagger out with the other. Blood gushed out from the wound, dark like wine.

My first instinct was to toss the weapon away, but I realized I needed it. I sliced a length of fabric off my skirt, then shoved the dagger behind my belt. Wrapping my arms around Rha, I pressed the ball of fabric to the wound on his back, trying to stop the blood from leaving his body.

"Dawn…" He tipped forward, leaning his forehead against my shoulder.

"Why did you do it?" I cried. "Why did you come here?"

"I had no choice. I'll always come for you…" his voice broke.

I pressed the side of my face to his. "Don't talk. Save your strength."

But he kept talking, as if needing to purge it all, "I woke up early. I couldn't sleep without you by my side. But your bed was empty. And so was the *sarai*. Kanjie told me where you headed. I was furious…" He heaved a labored breath. "Anger consumed me. You're mine. I had to get you back."

"But you didn't," I exhaled, reeling in disbelief. "You kept the portal open."

"When I saw you climbing up that hill, trying so desperately to get away from me, I realized something…" He lifted his head and found my eyes.

The movement cost him his balance. He swayed to the side, pushed by a gust of wind. The sky grew darker with black clouds choking the sunlight.

The storm thickened around us, hiding everything from view. I could no longer see either the men or their horses. I had no idea if the fighting was finished or who won. The storm had taken over, burying the dead bodies and the magical pole under a layer of sand. If we stayed out here, Rha and I risked being buried alive.

"We need to get out of here."

The only possible shelter was the massive structure of the temple that stood out like a monolith of darkness in the storm. The golden hexagon glistened faintly with receding magic like a beacon in the sand-filled air.

I scrambled to my feet, pulling Rha up with me. But he was too heavy for me to drag him through the sand.

"Help me, Rha. Can you walk? Please?"

He groaned, trying to get his feet under him. Half walking, half crawling, we made it to the black rocks of the entrance to the temple. One side of the tall, thick doors was open. The wind had already blown a thick layer of sand through it.

I helped Rha through the doors into what looked like the front room of the temple. A second, far more elaborate set of doors was opposite the entrance. But these doors were firmly closed. They wouldn't open when I pulled on the long carved-bone handle. Someone must have locked them from the inside. Not all Joy Guardians had been outside by the pole. Some must have stayed in the temple.

"We need help!" I slammed my fist against the doors, screaming, "Let us in, please!"

"They won't," Rha croaked. "Their purpose is to protect the Joy."

"Even at the expense of people's lives?"

"At the expense of everything, their own lives included."

"Well, fuck them then." I slammed my fist on the doors one last time. "Fuck you and your Joy!"

I helped Rha down to the ground, then rushed to close the outside door. The wind pushed against it, thwarting my efforts. I kicked the sand aside to give the door space to move, then shoved against it with all my strength, and it budged screeching closed. There was no lock on it from the inside, maybe because this room was intended to serve as a shelter from the storm, even as the Joy Guardians wouldn't let anyone inside the main building.

There could be more people, both humans and fae, needing to get away from the storm. Not all of them might be friendly to us. Pulling the dagger out from behind my belt, I laid it ready on the floor before sitting down next to Rha.

He slid sideways with his back against the wall. I helped him down, and he lay on his side, resting his head on my lap.

I removed the top layer of his garment from his head and brushed his hair down. My hand came back smeared with blood. Burgundy in color, it was considerably darker than human blood, but just as terrifying for me to see.

The wad of fabric had gotten lost somewhere, so I cut off a new one, then pressed it to his wound again. I ran the fingers of my free hand through his hair, stroking his head.

His tendrils appeared. Their ends slipped up my arms. Their familiar caress skittered with shivers along my skin.

"Are you sure you want to know what I'm feeling, Rha?"

"Always." He paused the tendrils over the ribbons of the harness around my arms. "May I?"

I shrugged. What difference did it make at this point?

"Go ahead."

He connected the tendrils. A familiar rush ran through my senses at the contact.

"You didn't leave," he whispered.

Reverence sounded in his voice, as if he still couldn't believe it. Just like I was still wrapping my mind around it all.

"What were you thinking?" I chastised, shaking my head. "You could've died. I mean you're not out of the woods yet."

"Let me tell you what I was thinking, my sweet, and what I

was feeling too. When I found you gone, I felt like my chest was ripped open and my heart was torn to pieces, leaving a bleeding, gaping hole that would never heal unless I got you back. But when I saw you on that hill out there. I knew that the only thing that mattered, the only thing I wished for, was for you to be happy. And if giving you what you wanted meant for my heart to remain crushed and bleeding for the rest of my life, so be it."

My heart ached, as if bleeding along with his.

"You were ready to die to give me what I wanted?"

"Yes." There was no doubt in his voice. "And that's how I knew I love you."

"You... What?" My next breath stuck in my throat.

"I love you, Dawn. No shadow fae wants to fall in love, but no one can prevent it from happening, either. And it happened to me. I love you, and I'd rather suffer without you than keep you by my side against your will. But you're not here against your will now, are you, my treasure?" A smile lit up his face the way it only ever did when we were connected like this. "You're here because you love me too."

"I do?" I choked out.

"Yes, my sweet, precious Dawn." He lifted a hand to touch my face but only brushed my cheek with the tips of his fingers before dropping it back to his side. "You came back to me."

I could tell him that I just didn't want him to die. I didn't want to see *anyone* die. But I knew why I ran down that hill. I needed Rha in my life more than anyone or anything I'd ever needed before.

"You love me, Dawn," he repeated with that annoying, all-seeing confidence of his. "And I'll wait for as long as it takes for you to admit it."

"Oh, shut up." I cradled his head in my arms and kissed his cheek. "Just shut up, Your Highness, and use that mighty fae magic of yours to heal as fast as you can."

DAWN

The storm raged outside the temple. The wind lashed against the doors like a feral beast trying to break in, and at times it felt like it might succeed.

The carving over the inner doors caught my eye. It must be old as the letters seemed worn by time with some words missing. I believed it said, *"Don't be afraid of the dawn. After a storm always comes peace."*

The words echoed what Rha had said to me back on the patio in Teneris when he was comforting me.

"After the storms of day, the calm of night will come."

He'd said these were the words of the First Priestess of Joy. And now, they rang more true than ever. Wait was all we could do.

Other than the storm, no one knocked on the doors leading outside or the ones leading inside the temple. Rha and I remained alone.

After a little while, Rha's eyes closed, but his breathing remained stable. I hoped he was indeed healing. Because it didn't look like there was help coming to him anytime soon.

Quite a few of the humans from the *sarai* had gone through the portal, including Melanie. I hoped she returned to the time she wanted to be. I hoped she made it and that she was safe and happy wherever and whenever she was now. We hadn't always seen eye to eye, but she'd forever remain my sister and my only family, even with the worlds between us now.

At the thought of Elaine, tears welled in my eyes. Her fate scared me. I'd seen the people who'd taken her, and I did not trust them to keep her safe.

I tightened my arms around Rha, as if someone was about to take him away from me too. At least he appeared to be resting peacefully, and I hoped the magic in his strong body was helping him heal.

THE STORM QUIETED. The beast was no longer pounding with sand and wind against the doors. Its howls had calmed.

Rha shifted in his sleep and groaned. His eyelids fluttered open. He blinked, looking momentarily disoriented.

"Did you sleep well?" I asked, brushing his hair out of his face.

His eyes found mine, and his features relaxed a little.

"It appears I did. Your emotions proved soothing, despite the worry racking you, my sweetest. But you don't need to worry about me." He stirred, wincing. "Has anyone tried to come in?"

"No. No one. Stay still." I leaned over and carefully removed the cloth I'd been pressing to his wound. The cloth was soaked in blood, but it looked old. No new blood seeped from the cut. "We should clean it somehow." I examined the wound for any signs of inflammation. "Do shadow fae get infections?"

"Since the iron hasn't killed me by now, I'll live." He sounded casual, almost dismissive, which eased my worry a little.

I helped him to sit up. He moved his shoulders tentatively, as if testing the toll the injury had taken on his body.

"How are you feeling?"

"I'll live," he repeated, with even more confidence than before.

"Okay. Can you answer some of my questions, then? Who were the people that attacked us?"

He made a face as if having bitten into a lemon. "Low-lifes, riffraff of the desert. Most of them are thieves. They'd take anything if given a chance. They must've found out you'd be here, and it's not surprising that they jumped on the chance to snatch Joy Vessels."

"What would they do with those they took?"

"Sell, most likely."

I sucked in air through my teeth. "They took Elaine."

"Your friend?" he asked.

"My *best* friend. Elaine has always been closer than a sister to me. Who do you think they'll sell her to?"

"To whomever pays the most." He cupped my cheek with his hand. "Joy Vessels are precious. Everyone wants one, but not many can pay what they're worth. I'll send the word out, offering a reward to anyone who returns my Joy Vessels to Teneris. We'll get Elaine back and everyone else who's been taken."

"Thank you." I felt better now but still far from relieved, not until I saw Elaine again, alive and well. "And then what?"

"What do you mean?" He arched an eyebrow in question.

"Rha, we ran away from you because we wanted to be free. People aren't meant to be anyone's property."

I thought he understood that when he'd held the portal open for us.

"I can't send them back, Dawn. This was the last portal possible between our worlds, and it's closed now."

"So it's true, then? There can't be any more?"

"No. The current spell has been used three times, and its magic is now gone."

The finality of his words settled heavily in my heart, but it didn't make me regret my decision. For once, I felt I was exactly where I was meant to be.

"The Joy Guardians who opened the portal, or the Watchers as they call themselves, didn't mean us harm, Rha. They simply wanted us gone." I thought about what the hag had said. "But who are the people who wear the flowers of golden hyacinth?"

His expression sharpened with focus. "The golden hyacinth is a dangerous flower, Dawn. Planting and gathering it is forbidden. Did you see someone wearing it?"

"The man who took Elaine had a small bunch of yellow flowers in his chest armor. Your hag warned me about them the morning I left Teneris. She said the Watchers want us out of the kingdom, but those who wear the golden hyacinth want to hurt us."

"Kanjie said that?"

"Yes. She's with the Watchers, by the way. Did you know? She has the same scorpion tattoo."

He frowned. "I've seen her tattoo. I never knew it was related to the Watchers."

"The guide who took us here sported the same wrist tattoo as well."

"Not much is known about the Watchers. I've only recently heard about them myself and that their goal is to preserve the purity of the Joy Source. Who knew that they would go so far for that goal as to defy the queen's orders." His frown deepened in concentration. "Last month, I saw a hyacinth flower next to the dead body of a man who killed himself under unexplained circumstances."

"What man was it?"

"A desert dweller just outside of the city walls. I didn't get to question him before he died."

"Maybe you should question Kanjie then? She also gave me these boots before I left." I stretched my leg out, demonstrating my fancy footwear. "Did she tell you about that?"

To my surprise, he nodded. "Yes. She told me everything."

"Even that she saw me this morning and didn't stop me from escaping?"

"Yes, that too. Kanjie vowed to serve me. Yet she still found a way to act behind my back, allowing you to escape into the desert filled with danger."

A dangerous glint in his golden eyes sent a chill down my spine. Aside from the mating fever, Rha's demeanor usually remained calm and even. He didn't roar or rage. His wrath ran cold but was as lethal as the curved blade of his sword.

"What did you do to the hag?" I asked. "Is she still alive?"

"Kanjie has been with us since I was born. This is her first offense. It is a grave one, however. Maybe she deserves to die for it. But no, I didn't execute her, just locked her in the dungeon before rushing to get to you."

I wasn't angry with the hag for ratting us out or with Rha for coming after us. Whatever relationship I had with my sister, I'd miss her for as long as I lived. It broke my heart to know I'd never see Melanie again. But at least now, I had a chance to find Elaine. And Rha was with me.

His ears twitched, and his brow furrowed in alarm. He turned to the doors leading outside.

"What is it, Rha? Are you hearing something—"

The doors flew open, shoved from the outside by much greater strength than my own.

With his arm hooked around my waist, Rha rose to his feet, taking me with him so quickly, I barely managed to grab the dagger from the floor.

"Whatever happens, stay close." He shouldered me behind him, standing between me and the people marching in through the open doors.

Dozens of armed men and women filled the small front room of the temple.

"He's here, Princess," one of them reported over his shoulder, then stepped aside, letting an elegant figure slide forward.

Tugging the protective fabric from her head, Princess Alzali cast a prodding glance up and down Rha's figure.

"Praised be the First Priestess, you're alive and well, Your Highness." She bowed gracefully.

"He isn't *well*," I said, relieved that Rha could finally get the help he needed. "He's been wounded and—"

Her orange, almond-shaped eyes squinted like those of a cat when she glanced at me. "You managed to hold on to at least one of your Joy Vessels, cousin. How fortunate."

Quick as lightning, she reached forward and placed an iron clip at the base of one of Rha's tendrils. It immediately fell limp, disconnecting from my arm. The guards surrounded us, leaving no route to escape.

Rha lowered his head, leveling his cousin with a heavy glare. "How dare you?"

"Queen's orders." Alzali casually took the bundle of clips from her belt and spoke while attaching them to all of his remaining tendrils, "You are to come with me to Kalmena to explain what the fuck has just happened out there." She tipped her chin at the open doors.

Rha rolled back his shoulders, wincing either from pain or from the situation in general. I gently touched his arm.

"Does it hurt?" My voice came out thick with worry. I glared at Alzali. "Did you not hear me? He's injured."

"And he looks to be taking it well." She didn't seem concerned. "You'll ride to Kalmena in the utmost comfort, my prince. We brought camels." If she meant it with sarcasm, I couldn't tell. She hid it well. "As for your sweet Joy Vessel..." Her eyes narrowed at me again.

Rha grabbed my hand, lacing his fingers through mine. "Dawn has no business with the queen."

"But the queen may like to have business with her," Alzali murmured.

"No." He shook his head adamantly. "She belongs in Teneris. With me."

"Very well, I shall send the Sweet One to Teneris with an escort." As accommodating as Alzali appeared to be, something in her cat-like eyes didn't sit well with me.

I pressed closer to Rha, squeezing his hand tightly. "I'll stay with Rha."

"Dawn..." He seemed hesitant, unwilling to drag me into whatever was waiting for him in Kalmena. On the other hand, he didn't trust Alzali's people to "escort" me back to Teneris, either.

"We should stay together," I said to him softly. "They can't hurt me, right?"

He released a long breath and nodded reluctantly.

"Dawn will come with me," he said to Alzali. "We'll travel together."

Twenty-Nine

RHA

It was dark outside when we left the shelter of the temple. The night fell, and with it the storm ended. The clouds had thinned, perforated by starlight. The haze of the heat was clearing too. The night breeze was too gentle to lift the sand high into the cooling air. Only the fine dust still curled over the crests of the dunes like silver mist.

The cooling air was fresh and light. So unlike the heavy weight pressing on my chest. I didn't know my mother well enough to predict what was waiting for us in Kalmena, and it bothered me.

Alzali moved her arm in a wide gesture at one of the camels waiting outside. "If you please, Your Highness."

I helped Dawn climb into the wide double seat before following her up as well. The dark, protective fabric around the frame had been pulled back, only the long gossamer curtains softly swayed in the breeze, framing the seat. My cousin hadn't lied when she said we'd ride in comfort.

The long caravan of the queen's warriors stretched behind us as far as the eye could see. In the front, there were only a few horses and the camel with Alzali. By etiquette, my cousin belonged behind me in a procession. The fact that she rode ahead proved I was not a guest or a visitor but a prisoner, detained and escorted to the queen.

"Do these hurt?" Dawn pointed at the clips on my tendrils.

"No, my treasure."

The iron clips were similar to those worn by Joy Keepers in the *sarai*. There was no pain from them, but my ego was bruised by the way Alzali slipped them on me without a warning or my consent.

I could've fought her and all those who'd come with her. Either way, I would've lost with so many warriors against me, but making it difficult for Alzali to detain me would've given me some satisfaction in the end. Except that Dawn was with me, and I couldn't put her in danger.

Curled against my side, she kept quiet. The iron clips around my tendrils incapacitated my magic, preventing me from dipping into her emotions. But I didn't need to use the tendrils to know that she was worried and scared.

I ran a soothing hand through her matted tresses. Normally soft and silky, her yellow hair was tangled and weighed down by storm dust clinging to it.

"Would you like to eat something?" I gestured at the basket with provisions the guards left for us.

The temple was about halfway between Teneris and Kalmena. We had a several-hour journey ahead of us. It was best to eat now to keep our strength up.

Dawn shook her head, then thought better of it.

"I should, shouldn't I? It's been a while since I ate last." She stirred, reaching for the basket. "You should have some food too."

I helped her move the heavy basket closer. It held a few meal packets and a large skin bag of water, but no food suitable for Joy Vessels. Irritation stirred in me. Dawn needed taste and flavor.

"This won't do." I leaned forward and flagged the closest

guard on horseback. "My woman can't eat *this*." I gestured at the basket. "Bring her something appropriate for a Joy Vessel."

The guard's eyes shifted under the cloth over his head. "I'm afraid that's all we have, Your Highness. We didn't bring any other food with us."

Holding back my anger, I gauged the distance between us to calculate whether I'd have a chance to wring his neck before the rest of them would stop me, but a gentle touch on my upper arm distracted me from my murderous plans.

"I'm okay, Rha," Dawn said. "Food is food. Who cares?"

I cared. After traveling through heat and storm all day, then sitting on the hard floor for hours, she deserved a bath, clean clothes, and an enjoyable meal—all of which I would've given her back in Teneris. Instead, we'd be tossed in the seat on the back of the camel for the better part of the upcoming night, and what awaited us upon our arrival to Kalmena remained unknown.

But she tugged on my arm, talking sweetly. "Come here. Have a drink of water with me. You must be thirsty."

The guard rode ahead, oblivious to the grim fate he'd so narrowly escaped courtesy of this sweet woman. She pressed the water bag into my hands, and I took a drink, washing the dust of the storm from my throat.

She handed me a meal packet next, taking one for herself too.

"Let's see what you guys eat. If it's snake meat, don't tell me. I'm hungry enough to eat anything, but I'd rather not know." She pulled back the parchment and took a bite from the pale substance inside.

I watched as she chewed and swallowed, her expression bland just like the food she was eating.

"And?" I prompted. "What do you think?"

"It's not terrible." She licked her lips, the tip of her pink tongue darting out of her mouth.

I ate it too—mashed root vegetables with minced meat pressed into a cube, then flattened to make it easier to hold and transport.

"It could really use some salt, though." She laughed. The sound brushed over my skin with a tingling sensation.

I tried to determine what this feeling could be, then realized that it was the echo of her pleasure—my memory of it. I knew what she normally felt when she laughed like that, and I remembered.

She ate a little more of her food as I finished mine quickly.

"How are you feeling?" she asked, leaning over to see my back.

The wound ached, pulling on the healing muscles when I moved. The layer of dried blood itched my skin, but the sharp pain was gone. After she'd yanked the iron out of my flesh, my body had been using its magic to heal.

"I'm feeling fine."

"Fine? Really? You had a knife stuck in your back." She packed her remaining food and put it back into the basket, then took the water sack out again. "Let me at least clean it."

I took the bag from her and drank from it instead.

"No need to waste water for that. When we get to Kalmena —" I paused, wondering what I could possibly promise her upon our arrival when I wasn't sure what to expect myself.

Dawn quietly drank some water, too, then put the bag away.

"Tell me about your mother," she said. "What is she like?"

Unease pricked my back. This was not a simple topic.

"I never knew the queen as a mother," I said slowly, choosing my words with care. "She never acted *motherly* toward me, not even when I was small. In fact, I could count on the fingers of one hand when she spent any time with me at all."

"But you're her only child."

"Not the one she wished to have," I replied.

"That's ridiculous. Children are to be loved, no matter their gender."

"Is that how it is in your world?"

She drew in some air to say something, then stopped.

"No," she admitted. "In my world, sadly, parental love sometimes comes with conditions too. Do you not have any good memories of you and your mother together?"

I didn't need to think long to answer.

"Just one. When I turned sixteen, the queen must've realized I was the only child she'd ever have and her only direct heir to the kingdom. I remember she joined me on a walk in the palace gardens. She asked me what the most important qualities a ruler of a kingdom should possess. I was so worried about giving her a wrong answer that I gave her none at all. She said there were two —a firm hand and compassion. The trick was to find the perfect balance between them. Then, she talked to me about the strategies she had employed during the centuries of being a queen. I remember every word she said then. It wasn't hard to do since she hardly spoke to me either before or after that walk."

"Did her attitude toward you not change even after that talk?"

I shook my head. "The queen accepted me as her successor but no more than that. After that talk in the gardens, she granted me access to the Royal Council meetings. When I turned eighteen, she started sending me with her army into battles, making sure I gained enough experience to eventually lead it."

"She groomed you as the future king, but she never cared for you as her son?"

The queen made no secret that she would've preferred to have a daughter instead of a son, but there was nothing I could do about being what I was. I'd learned to shrug off the guilt, but the bitterness always lingered.

"It's not just me. Queen Abeille doesn't let anyone close. Ever since my father's death, she's been actively avoiding any feelings toward anyone. It's common among my kind. Love often brings immeasurable pain, and it's natural to avoid any potential new source of suffering."

"Love can also bring the biggest joy, Rha. Even after it's gone, good memories help us cope with loss. It's a shame and grave injustice that shadow fae are incapable of experiencing that."

I was fortunate to have experienced her deep affection for me. I'd tasted it. Even while we'd waited for the storm to pass at the temple, a steady, warm glow of love flowed through my tendrils from her, aiding my healing.

Dawn had been fighting her love for me, but it proved stronger than her. And for that, I was grateful. I needed her love. For me, it alone balanced all the suffering in the world.

She placed a hand on my knee, and I leaned closer, craving the contact with her body since I could no longer connect to her soul. My tendrils lay motionless on the seat between us. Any sensation from them was gone, banished by the iron restraints.

Lifting my hand, I touched the side of her face. Her skin felt rougher than usual with traces of sandstorm clinging to it, but her eyes shone brighter than ever. Her lips parted, and I couldn't wait anymore.

"Kiss me. Please."

She shook her head. "You won't feel it, baby. Your tendrils—"

"But I'll remember the feeling. Please, kiss me."

I didn't wait for her to close the distance between us, putting my mouth on hers first. To my relief, she met me eagerly. Wrapping her arms around my neck, she pressed her body to mine.

And I did remember.

Every delicious morsel of joy she'd so generously shared with me had been carefully stored in my memories. The emotions rose from inside me, brought forward by her touch.

I knew what she was feeling at this moment. Tenderness must be flushing over her now. It'd be flowing through my tendrils had we been connected. Tantalizing tingles of lust would be twirling through it. Love burned deep inside me, radiating through my whole being. And I knew the same feeling resonated through her.

I drew her closer, deepening our kiss. The slide of my lips, the twirl of my tongue, every caress of my hands was bringing forward more of the joy inside her. I couldn't taste it, but I remembered it all.

Breaking the kiss, she leaned back. She saw my heavy breathing, my flushed skin, and the burning need for her in my eyes.

"You..." She cupped my face, smoothing my hair gently. "You're *feeling* it, aren't you? But how?"

"I *remember*, my sweet treasure. Once tasted, your joy is impossible to forget."

Thirty

DAWN

In the Alveari Kingdom, I was called a Joy Vessel. I was the source of happy emotions that shadow fae could not experience on their own. Only if so, then how did Rha give me so much happiness back?

Being in his arms healed me. His soft kisses and light caresses soothed the pain of loss and uncertainty. The journey to Kalmena was long, but not tedious or exhausting. The future no longer looked like an impenetrable black wall to me. It remained muddy and grim, but whatever came my way, I felt I could deal with it. And if Rha was with me, maybe dealing with anything would be that much easier?

Curled into his warm body and lulled by the steady swaying of the seat on the back of the camel, I must've dozed off at some point.

Noise woke me up. Clamoring of a crowd, trotting of hooves on stone tiles, clinking of tools and weapons. It was the general commotion of a big city.

I lifted my head from Rha's chest and rubbed my cheek.

"Are we here?"

The dark fabric was now drawn down over our seat, blocking the view of the city. With me no longer sprawling on top of him, Rha straightened in the seat too. The look in his eyes softened as he reached over to stroke my cheek.

"You have the pattern of my necklace imprinted on your face."

I rubbed my cheek again. "Great. Well, the pattern on your necklace is flawless. It may add some symmetry to my face at last, right?"

"No," he replied, brutally honest, like always. "It makes it even more grossly asymmetrical, since the imprint is only on one side." He took my chin in his fingers and brushed a feather-light kiss on my lips. "But I love your face, my treasure, just the way it is."

I smiled, not moving away. His affection was more than thrilling—it was utterly disarming.

"What will happen now, Rha? To us? And to you?"

His hand fell away from my face.

"I'll have to face the queen."

"What will she do to you?"

"That remains to be seen. But her judgement is usually fair."

I huffed. "What is she going to judge you for? What transpired wasn't your fault. You didn't know about our escape plans. And it's not like you sent those thugs after us."

The camel came to a stop, and I gripped Rha's hand, my anxiety surging.

He remained calm, visually at least. "My Joy Vessels are my responsibility. I should've known what was happening in my own *sarai*. The blame for their loss falls on me."

"Is the queen really going to punish you?" Dread chilled my insides.

The dark fabric was yanked up, revealing a spacious court in front of a metal gate. The golden filigree of the gate created a pattern of a honeycomb inlaid with tiny figurines of honeybees in a regular pattern.

Guards in black-and-gold uniforms lined up in two rows, forming a corridor between the gates and our camel. One of the guards stood on the ladder of our seat, holding up the fabric.

"Welcome, Your Highness," he said in a respectful but somber tone.

"Greetings, General Tanari," Rha replied. "It's good to see you again."

The general climbed down the ladder, allowing Rha and me to do the same.

"Queen Abeille wishes to see you immediately," the general informed Rha.

I hoped we'd get to wash the sand off and change into some clean clothes before the royal audience. But apparently the queen, who hadn't seen her son for years, was suddenly too impatient to reunite with him.

Rha didn't question her wishes. Or maybe he knew he had no choice. With a nod, he took my hand, then followed the general down the corridor formed by the guards.

General Tanari led us into the great hall of a grand palace. Intricate, gold, white, and green mosaics decorated the floor. Columns of golden filigree supported the arched ceiling that shone with a warm yellow light.

A figure appeared, moving toward us, as if darkness solidified into Princess Alzali in front of our eyes.

"Welcome to Kalmena, my prince." Alzali bowed gracefully, swaying the delicate golden chains in her ears.

Her tone and gestures remained perfectly respectful, but something about her rubbed me the wrong way. Maybe it was the flawless precision with which she always followed the etiquette in my presence. Everything about her just seemed so perfect. It gave me a feeling that at least something had to be fake.

I gripped Rha's hand tighter, shifting closer to him.

"Follow me." Alzali headed toward a wide arch between two columns to the left of the hall. When Rha and I moved to follow her, however, she whipped back. "Just you, Your Highness. Not the Joy Vessel."

Alarm shot through me. Rha appeared calm, however, holding my hand tightly.

"Dawn is with me. She goes where I go."

Alzali tilted her head.

"I'm afraid the queen's order was to bring you alone. Do you dare defy the order of Queen Abeille?" she asked softly, her voice coaxing the answer she longed to hear.

"Dawn will stay with me," Rha repeated firmly.

Satisfaction spread across his cousin's face. "Very well then."

She gave a signal, and a guard placed a hand on my shoulder. "You'll come with me, Sweet One."

"Get your hands off her," Rha hissed. Grabbing me around my waist, he snatched me out of the guard's reach. "Or I'll cut them off." In one smooth movement, he slid the guard's sword out of its sheath.

I gasped, and he quickly stepped back, pushing me behind him and raising the sword to meet the guards.

The swishing of blades being drawn filled the hall. Alzali stepped back, folding her arms across her chest. She looked like she'd gotten exactly what she wanted.

Dread descended upon me, pressing heavily on my chest.

A guard lunged in an attack on Rha. He easily deflected it, but two more guards leaped at him from the side. He pivoted around to meet them. His exposed tendrils fanned out in a spin around him. With them disabled by the iron clips, he couldn't even use his magic to disperse into shadow.

Maybe he could've run. He was fast and strong, with impressive skills in swordsmanship as it turned out. He could've fought his way out of this and run. But he wouldn't leave me.

Rha wasn't fighting for his freedom. He did it for us to stay together.

Alzali jumped toward him, her movements fluid like quicksilver. She grabbed one of his limp tendrils and yanked it back, knocking him off balance.

"No!" I rushed forward.

Alzali shot me a glare. Her decorum was gone now. Hatred was all that remained.

"Take her where she belongs!" she snapped at a guard as the rest of them swarmed my prince.

Rha launched forward, sinking his sword into the belly of a guard. Yanking the blade out, he sliced off another guard's arm. Dark blood splashed over the beautiful mosaic floor.

More guards rushed through the doors. Two of them grabbed me, dragging me away.

"Rha, stop! Please," I begged, terrified of what they'd do to him if he kept resisting. "Just go see the queen like they want you to. Please stay safe."

Alzali drew a long dagger from behind her belt. Winding Rha's tendril around her forearm, she yanked his head back, then pressed the dagger to his neck.

"Don't listen to her, cousin," she hissed. "Fight me. Give me a good reason to do what's right, in the name of the queen."

She wanted this. She'd waited for a chance to get rid of him all along. He couldn't give her the satisfaction.

"Don't, Rha," I pleaded as they dragged me away. "Do as they say. Stay alive, and I'll wait for you. Wherever you are, I'll wait for you to come for me."

Thirty-One

DAWN

The noise of the sword fight died in the distance, and I hoped it stopped with Rha unharmed.

I fought against the rough grip of the guards. Only there was no use. They were infinitely stronger than me, dragging me down a long corridor effortlessly.

We crossed a large, luscious garden. I wondered if it was the same place where Rha had that one and only walk with his mother.

What would she do to him?

I wished I knew more about that woman, but the little I'd learned about her didn't give me much hope.

We came to another golden gate. This one was even more heavily guarded than the entrance to the palace. Men and women dressed in the royal colors of gold and black lined along each side of the gate.

"Another Joy Vessel," a guard introduced me to them.

A woman stepped forward. All six of her tendrils were out, clipped with iron like was required from Joy Vessel Keepers.

"I'll take her in." She gestured to the guards to release me from their grip.

When they let go of me, however, I hesitated. I didn't know this woman or anyone else in here for that matter.

"You'll be safe, Sweet One," she murmured. "We'll take good care of you, the way every Joy Vessel should be cared for."

I fidgeted with the bottom edge of my necklace, not moving any further. "What exactly do you mean by *care?*"

She gave me a quick once-over. "Well, for one, you need a bath and some clean clothes."

My clothes were filthy, and my skin itched. The desert sand appeared to have gotten into every fold of the fabric and each crevice of my body. My own comfort was the least of my worries, however.

I shook my head. "I need to know what happens to Prince Rha."

The Keeper tossed a questioning glance at my guards.

"The prince is with the queen," one of them replied.

"I have to know when he's done," I said. "He'll be looking for me."

The Keeper took my arm gently. "The prince is with the queen, Sweet One. Neither you nor I can do anything about that, can we?"

"But—" I freed my arm from her fingers.

She deftly twined her both arms around mine again, like an ivy. "If the prince needs you when he's done, the royal *sarai* would be the first place he'd look. After all, this is where all our Joy Vessels are."

She made a point. With eight years to catch up on, the queen and Rha might take a while. Meanwhile, I had to wait somewhere.

"Fine. But I'm not staying. I'll leave as soon as he's done," I warned the Keeper, leaving her in possession of my arm this time. "Prince Rha will come for me."

"Of course, Sweet One," she purred, ever so subtly dragging me through the gate. "My name is Sefri. We'll brush your hair, get you a pretty skirt to wear. You must be hungry too. The queen's soldiers have no idea what to feed to a Joy Vessel. The tastes of the army brutes are far from refined."

A wide courtyard opened to my view. It was several times the size of the *sarai* garden in Teneris. The buildings around it were also a few floors taller. They spread out wider, arching over the passageways that appeared to lead into the branching-out sections of the yard.

An intricate system of water fixtures and flowerbeds connected the courtyard's grounds and the walls of the surrounding buildings, making the space look like the inside of a jewelry box filled with marble, colorful plants, and glowing insects.

But it wasn't the splendor of my surroundings that made me pause. People congregated in small groups inside the queen's *sarai*. And the more I looked at them, the more uneasy I felt.

A topless human woman lay on a plush rug between the flowers under a water feature. Her head rested on the lap of a shadow fae, who fed her candied figs from a dessert bowl. The two were attached by his tendrils with the fae sharing the enjoyment of the food with the human. She laughed, whipped cream dripping from her lips. It mixed with the wine she was drinking from the huge goblet held in her hand.

On the balcony to our left, another woman sprawled on thick floor cushions. Her upper body rested on the lap of a Joy Vessel Keeper, who massaged her naked breasts, rubbing her nipples. The woman's moans blended with the moans of a fae woman stretched in a recliner nearby with her tendrils attached to the human's *leilatha* harness.

A human man gripped the railing with both hands on the balcony next to theirs. The thick flower garlands draped over the balcony prevented me from seeing what was happening below the man's waist, but it was safe to say he wasn't alone. His head tossed back, his mouth slackened, he thrust his hips forward, pounding hard into someone's hand or mouth. A set of ink-black tendrils were attached to his harness too.

"What is this place exactly?" I took a step back into the shadows of the passageway under the arch.

Sefri's face lit up with pride. "It's Her Majesty's royal *sarai*. You'll be happy here. We'll make sure of it."

"I wouldn't be so sure..." I muttered, hiding in the walkway from the curious glances of both humans and fae.

People were bending over the balcony railings, peeking out of the open doors, and emerging from behind the shrubs and water fountains—curious about me, the newcomer. Their attention scraped against my nerves like an unwanted touch.

Sefri gave me the typical practiced smile of a Keeper— stretched lips and mirthless eyes. "We do everything to keep our Joy Vessels happy. The royal *sarai* is always brimming with joy."

I glanced back at the entrance. The guards had already closed and locked the gate behind us. The *sarai* was the first place where Rha would look for me after his meeting with the queen. Meanwhile, I could possibly talk to someone who knew Ciana, if these people ever took breaks from being pleasured long enough to talk.

"Come, Sweet One," Sefri coaxed. "Just think about how wonderful a bath would feel after your long and tiring journey through the desert. I'm sure you're all sweaty and covered in sand."

She led me to an open pool in the middle of the courtyard as I tried to avoid looking at all the half-naked people hanging around the gardens and to ignore the grunts and moans coming from every direction.

"Sefri, do you remember a human woman named Ciana?" I asked. "I've heard she was here until a few days ago when she ran away. She'd be the one with long pink braids—"

"No," the Keeper interrupted me promptly. "Our Joy Vessels have no reasons to run."

I believed General Oskura wouldn't lie to Rha about Ciana having been here. But maybe the general had been lied to herself?

"Are you sure she was never here? Or you just never met her?" I insisted.

Sefri's expression remained unchanged, with the wide smile plastered on her lips. "All Joy Vessels of Her Majesty are accounted for. We keep them in excellent spirits, happy and full of joy. Now," she nudged me toward the pool. "Why don't you take your clothes off, Sweet One? While I find you a suitable companion to take a bath."

I stopped in my tracks.

"Are you expecting me to bathe right here? In front of everyone? And what exactly do you mean by a *bath companion?*"

I'd been naked in public baths back in Teneris. Like now, there had been other people around. Like here, they all had been strangers. But there was one important difference.

Back then, the curiosity of the shadow fae was innocent enough. They looked at me because I was different, someone they hadn't seen before. After their curiosity had been satisfied, they moved their attention elsewhere, letting me be.

The attention of the shadow fae here was far more intrusive. There was a calculation in the assessing, scrutinizing stares burrowing into me, as if they already were planning all the ways to use me. I felt naked even with my clothes still on.

A few fae headed our way, beelining across the garden paths and through the flower beds.

"Humans are delightful creatures," Sefri purred into my ear. "They rejoice in giving. And what could be more rewarding than sharing your joy with those who can't have it on their own? It costs you nothing, and it means so much to someone like..." She gestured at the first man coming toward us. "Like Councilor Jerti here."

Her words flowed smoothly, like a well-practiced speech of a door-to-door salesman. I stiffened, realizing what she was trying to do.

"You can't force me," I said.

"But there is no need to force."

Holding my arm, she gently stroked the inside of my elbow with the tips of her fingers. The touch that would've been pleasant under different circumstances was mostly irritating now —an itch instead of a caress.

I scratched my arm, erasing the unpleasant sensation.

"Thanks, but I'd rather have a quick shower or even a sponge bath and some rest. Alone. Do I get my own room?"

Sefri heaved a long, regretful sigh.

"The poor thing is tired," she said apologetically in the direction of Councilor Jerti.

The man made a face, clearly displeased. To my relief, however, he retreated without a word of protest.

"They can't force me," I repeated in my head, calming my racing heart.

Forcing would kill the pleasure, and it's my joy that they were after. That thought helped me relax a little as I followed Sefri up a staircase to a room on the very top floor, right under the roof.

"I'll arrange for the tub to be brought in," Sefri informed me before turning to leave.

"No need. I'll be happy with a sponge bath."

She pivoted back to me.

"I can't allow for a Joy Vessel to be mistreated by denying her the utmost comfort in the *sarai*. You will enjoy your bath, even if you choose to hoard your pleasure all to yourself."

She stomped out of the room, leaving me to deal with the guilt she'd planted in my mind.

True, it would cost me nothing. But I had little joy to share. I felt anxious about the future, worried about both my sister and my best friend, apprehensive about Rha's meeting with the queen. All of this would be too distracting to focus on the bath and whatever pleasure it might give me, or to get naked in front of complete strangers. I just wanted to be left alone.

The Keepers brought a big metal tub in my room, then filled it with warm water. Sefri poured a fragrant oil into it, masterfully scattered flower petals over the water, then laid a folded towel on the edge for me to rest my head on.

"All is ready, Sweet One," she announced, as the other Keepers exited my room. "Do you still insist on bathing alone?"

Guilt stirred in me again. They had gone through all this trouble of carrying the heavy tub and buckets of water all the way to the top floor.

At the same time, I couldn't shake the feeling that all this had been designed to guilt me into submission. I didn't ask for a full bath, or for the oils, or for flower petals. I asked for privacy. And Sefri had been consistently pushing me to give it up.

It felt manipulative on her part, which did nothing to promote cooperation in me. They couldn't force me into submission, but they certainly tried hard to guilt and manipulate me into it.

"I'll bathe alone," I said firmly.

"As you wish." She pursed her lips, leaving the room.

I hastily inspected the small but functional room. It held a bed platform with cushy bedding. There was a vanity and a toilet in a niche in a wall, and a small trunk for personal belongings. Overall, this room was meant to be a bedroom but nothing more. There wasn't even a place to sit down other than on the bed. Any socializing, it appeared, was supposed to happen either outside or on the balcony off the room.

In other words, the Joy Vessels were encouraged to be in the open as much as possible, where they could be watched.

After a quick bath to scrub the dust off my skin and wash the sand out of my hair, I used the towel to dry off, then took the clean garment left for me by Sefri.

It was a single-layer skirt. Just a long piece of material attached to a leather belt with a metal buckle shaped like a rosette of gilded, semi-transparent insect wings. And that was it. No shirt, no underwear. Not a stitch of any other clothing.

I rummaged through the pile of my discarded clothes, looking for the least dusty piece I could wear as a top. I even briefly considered just wrapping the towel around myself. But my old clothes were too filthy and full of sand, and the towel was too wet and cold now.

After a brief consideration, I settled on my necklace to provide some coverage for my chest. Its beads were positioned close to each other, and the front panel stretched from my neck just past my breasts. With it on, I had a more modest outfit than most people around here, anyway.

I'd told Sefri I wanted to rest. But despite feeling tired, I wasn't sleepy. I couldn't quiet my worries long enough to rest.

Instead, I circled the room one more time, like a caged animal looking for an escape, then ventured out onto the balcony. With my room being on the highest floor, I could observe the courtyard while staying undetected by most.

The activities below remained the same, though the players had changed. The woman who'd had her breasts fondled was now napping in the cushions on her balcony. A Keeper was tidying up the blankets around her.

The woman on the rug below was still attached to the same shadow fae who had fed her figs earlier. Only now, he lay on the rug, too, his arms spread wide. He groaned in pleasure as two Keepers had their hands up the human woman's skirt.

Everywhere I looked, humans were fondled, caressed, or fed. The Keepers hurried around, carrying heavy wine carafes on their shoulders, ready to refill the goblets of anyone who had one in their hands.

The naked man who'd been jerked off or sucked off earlier was now standing on his balcony, smoking a cigarette. He appeared to be in his fifties, with his dark curls generously sprinkled with silver and his belly protruding slightly over his flaccid dick.

As if sensing me staring, he glanced up and smiled, waving at me. Unsure how to react so as not to give him any wrong signals, I smiled tightly but didn't wave back.

Suddenly, a familiar redhead caught my eye. Lucia was

promptly crossing the yard toward a fountain, holding a goblet in her hand.

"Lucia?" I was afraid to believe my eyes.

A Keeper with a wine carafe rushed to her, but she stopped him by holding up her hand.

"I just want some water, thank you very much."

"Lucia!" I leaned over the railing and waved both arms so hard, I risked falling over.

"Dawn?" She glanced up, shielding her eyes against the bright glow of the ceiling beams over the courtyard. "Is that really you? Holy fuck! Stay right there!" She ran toward the stairs. "Don't go anywhere. I'll be right up."

But I couldn't stay still. I ran out of the room to the stairs' landing as Lucia climbed up, breathless. She'd lost her goblet on the way somewhere and now grabbed me into a tight hug with both arms.

"I can't believe you fucking survived, girl!" She half-yelled in my ear.

I returned her hug with all my heart. "You didn't leave, after all."

She followed me into my room. "Nah. I never was keen on leaving, as you might've noticed. I just came along so as not to spoil it for everyone else."

Lucia was topless, like everyone else in here. Having her voluptuous chest on display didn't seem to bother her, though. She gave a quick glance around the room, then walked out onto the balcony with me.

We sat on the floor in the doorway. From this position, I could see the entrance to the courtyard through the balusters of the railing, while both of us remained unseen from the ground.

"So, you didn't even try to run for the portal?" I asked.

She shook her head.

"It kind of got crowded out there. Everyone was rushing. I just tried to stay out of the way. And then, well... You saw what happened to Kostya." She shuddered at the memory. "I mean, I couldn't stand the guy. He was such an obnoxious asshole, groping everyone in the *sarai* and talking shit. But what a horrible way to go. Even he didn't deserve that. After I saw that, I didn't stick around the hill."

"What did you do?"

"I saw Prince Rha came after us, so I ran down the hill and let the first Teneris guard I saw catch me. Except that then, we were attacked by those scruffy guys from the desert who came out of nowhere. They killed my captor-slash-savior guard, which was a shame, really. He seemed like a nice guy." She frowned, pushing a thick strand of her copper-colored hair away from her face.

"How did you get away from the desert dwellers?"

"Oh, they never caught me to begin with. I ran away while they were fighting the guard. I hid between the rocks on the hill-side and stayed hidden until all the baddies had left. I hitched a ride with another Teneris guard for a while until we met the queen's scouts, who then brought me here." She rubbed her forehead, wincing at her memories. "There was so much fighting in that storm. I saw you and the prince but briefly. I saw Elaine—"

"You did? What happened to her, do you know?" My heart raced as I waited for her answer. "Is she here in the *sarai* too?"

"No. One of those desert guys threw her over his horse's saddle and rode away. That's all I saw."

With my hopes crushed, I sat silent.

"Do you know who exactly those guys were?" Lucia asked. "Who attacked us?"

"I've no idea, other than Elaine is probably not safe with them," I replied in a hollow voice. "Rha promised to offer a reward for the safe return of his Joy Vessels. But he's been gone for a while now, and I'm afraid he may be in trouble himself."

"Where is he? How did you end up in Kalmena?"

"Princess Alzali brought us here."

"Well, that's nice of her."

I arched an eyebrow skeptically. "She didn't do it to be nice.

She said the queen wanted to see Rha. I fear queen Abeille will hold him responsible for losing his Joy Vessels."

"But he didn't lose us. We ran away."

"Somehow, that's still his fault."

"That's too bad." Lucia sighed sympathetically. "I like Prince Rha. It was chill and relaxing in his *sarai,* not like here." She lowered her voice. "Hey, what's the deal between you and the prince? I know you fucked him—"

"You do?"

Everyone seemed to be aware of that fact.

"Hey, people talk, you know? Kostya wined for days about how the prince nearly ripped out his throat for just talking to you. The prince clearly likes you. But are you guys together? Like a couple now?"

What exactly were we?

"He says he loves me."

She sucked in air with a whistle. "Wow. That didn't take him long."

"Shadow fae see love as a disease. He recognized the symptoms."

"Interesting. But how about you? Do you love him too?"

Rha believed that I did, though I never told him that. I remembered the feeling I had when running down the hill to him and away from the portal that would take me home. I remembered how certain I was about that spur-of-the-moment decision I'd made.

When I thought about Rha, my heart swelled with so much tenderness, I could barely contain it in my chest. I didn't want him hurt. But it was more than that. I didn't want to be in a world that didn't have Rha in it. We belonged together.

"I do," I said.

My head was spinning at that admission, but it was the truth.

She nodded. "If you said anything else, I'd think you're lying. I saw you running to him. I stayed in Alveari for food and shelter. But you stayed because of him."

I darted another glance toward the walkway that led out to the gate, waiting for Rha to walk through it any minute. But it remained empty. The longer Rha stayed away, the more my concern grew.

"I just hope he's okay," I muttered under my breath.

How long would the queen be talking to him? This was their first meeting in years. They probably had a lot to discuss.

Lucia followed my anxious gaze.

"Will you guys go back to Teneris?"

"I believe so. I'm waiting for him to come back. Have you met the queen yet?"

Lucia shook her head. "She hasn't come to the *sarai* since I arrived. A lot of fae have come and gone. Some I've seen twice already, but not her." She rolled her eyes at the steady choir of moans coming from the courtyard. "Everyone is looking for some joy."

"Where is your room?"

"In another courtyard, just around the corner that way." She gestured to the right. "I had to get out. There's even more noise there than here. I have people fucking nonstop on the balcony next to mine."

"Actually fucking? How? Shadow fae don't have sexual organs. Not unless they're having a mating fever."

"Oh, I know that. A Keeper kindly explained it to me back in Teneris when Prince Rha had you locked in his rooms for days." She grinned. "I guess you didn't mind that."

My face warmed at the memories of frantic, passionate sex with Rha. Butterflies fluttered in my stomach with a warm sensation spreading through my chest.

I cleared my throat. "It was intense. But I'd do it again in a heartbeat."

Someone groaned from below, panting through an orgasm by the sound of it.

Lucia made a face. "At least you guys did it in private. The couple next door to me are both humans. They've been fucking most of the night, with several fae joining them for each orgasm." She rubbed her sternum. "If you go back to Teneris, take me with you, okay? This place doesn't vibe with me. I mean, I love a good party. Who doesn't? But this is too much. They serve wine for breakfast, lunch, and dinner. If you ask for a drink, you'll get wine, unless you specifically insist on water. It's crazy. I haven't even spoken to anyone yet, other than you. Every human has a fae attached to them all the time. It's exhausting. One can't be happy all the time, so they pump them with wine to keep them permanently drunk. Kind of turns me off alcohol altogether." She exhaled a humorless laugh. "Never thought I'd say something like that. I've been a party girl all my life. But this... It's too much of the same. Like, there are many things people enjoy, aren't there? They could let them read, or paint, or knit, or do some other hobby. Humans like other things, too, not just fucking."

"*Like* isn't enough." I thought about Rha's puzzle design, about the necklace we made, and the extensive mosaics decorating almost every surface both in Kalmena and in Teneris. "Shadow fae can be creative on their own. They see harmony in beauty and are capable of experiencing peace when engaging in a hobby. They feel satisfaction from completing a project. They don't need us for that. They want us for pleasure—the more intense, the better. And it seems they've discovered that sex is a sure and quick way to get it."

"Well, back in Teneris, the prince had you for sex, and the Keepers left the rest of us alone. Here, they're way too pushy."

"They can't force you. Remember, they won't get pleasure by force."

Lucia heaved a sigh. "But they sure can be annoying as hell, trying to talk you into doing things you don't want to do."

Without a knock, the door to my room opened and Sefri entered, flanked by two male Keepers.

"Finished with your bath?" she murmured.

"Yes. Thank you," I replied icily.

The Keepers cleaned up after my bath, then took the tub out.

Sefri eyed the two of us sitting in the doorway to the balcony. "You should come down to the courtyard, Sweet Ones. Dinner will be served soon."

"Thanks," Lucia replied. "We'll be there in a minute."

Sefri gave us a long penetrating look but didn't argue, just inclined her head and left.

Lucia scowled at the door closed behind Sefri.

"They must be afraid we'd organize another escape or something," she said.

A question rose in my head at her words.

"How did you escape the *sarai* in Teneris? There were plenty of guards at the door."

"We didn't use the door." She smirked smugly. "We got out through the roof. After the sunrise, when the Keepers went to bed, we climbed up from the top-floor balcony, opened the roof shutters over the courtyard, and got out."

"Smart." I looked up at the domed ceiling above us.

The curved beams had cross bars that made them possible to climb. One would be hanging upside-down over the courtyard at the highest point of the ceiling, but it could be done.

"I know, right? Brilliant," Lucia agreed animatedly. "It was all your sister's idea. She is one smart cookie, I tell you."

Air left me in a long breath at her mentioning Melanie.

Lucia gave me a sympathetic look. "You miss her."

"I do. Melanie and I were never close. She said mean things, but she mostly did the right thing. No matter what, she's my only sister. My only family left. I just hope she's safe."

"Well, she got what she wanted, didn't she?"

"She did. Melanie always gets what she wants. If it didn't work out this time, she would've devised another plan somehow. She's strong and stubborn like that." It often used to infuriate me, but now I was glad my sister possessed the qualities that hopefully would help her survive wherever she was now. "I wonder where she ended up after all. It's killing me that I'll never know."

"Maybe you will, one day," Lucia said vaguely. "If there's

anything I've learned about this life, it's that it has tricks up its sleeve you won't see coming."

I couldn't argue with that. After all, here we were, in a world I knew nothing about only several weeks ago.

The moans and groans coming from below had finally stopped, replaced by the clinking of dishes and shuffling of feet.

"Dinner is here, I guess." Lucia climbed to her feet, then gave me a hand, helping me up too.

"I'm starving," I confessed.

Delicious smells wafted from below, making my stomach spasm and my mouth water. I hadn't eaten anything since that bland meal packet on the way here, which must've been hours ago.

"You know what?" Lucia said as we headed down the stairs. "I could use a drink, too, right now. I may actually have some of that wine they've been trying to shove down my throat ever since I arrived." She shrugged. "I mean, I got to see you again. We both survived. It's worth celebrating, right?"

"Right. There's a bright side to everything," I agreed.

We got two plates of food served by the Keepers in the courtyard and found a relatively quiet place on a bench in a recess by the wall. It took us some time to get rid of Sefri, who tried to hook up a couple of shadow fae to us for dinner.

"That woman just never quits." Lucia gave the Keeper a glare as she finally walked away from us, taking her disappointed clients with her.

"It's her job, I guess." Now, I miss Sigid and his friendly, non-intrusive presence.

"One can't even eat in peace around here," Lucia complained, digging into the food on her plate.

I didn't know if all the queen's Joy Vessels were out in the courtyard with us. Maybe some did eat in peace in the privacy of their rooms. But every single one I could see from my place on the bench had a fae next to them, their tendrils attached to the humans' *leilatha* harnesses.

I dipped a dumpling into a fragrant sauce, then took a bite. Dropping my eyelids, I chewed slowly before realizing that there was no need to savor it so thoroughly. Rha wasn't here to share it with me.

The time spent with Rha had taught me to pay attention to every tiny spark of joy. They were easily found even in the darkest of times, which was when we needed them the most.

The longer it was since I saw him last, the tighter worry squeezed around my chest. I knew he wouldn't just leave me here, and I doubted meeting with his mother would keep him that long, considering how little they had in common.

What if something bad happened?

Lucia handed me a goblet of wine.

"To us." She clinked her glass against mine. "And to our survival."

I took a sip mechanically but couldn't drink more. I usually drank alcohol when I was happy—to cheer, relax, and celebrate. Not when I was racked by worry like this.

"I'll get some water," I said to Lucia, getting up. "Do you want some?"

"No, thanks. I'm good with wine for now."

I made my way to the fountain promptly, feeling the stares of both humans and fae on me. Several fae wandered around without a free human to attach themselves to. They looked at me like at a dessert they wished to take a bite of.

I took a clean goblet from the tray on a stand by the fountain.

"More wine, Sweet One?" A Keeper with a wine carafe appeared seemingly out of nowhere.

"Thanks, but I already have some." I gestured in the direction of our bench.

The Keeper moved on in search of other empty goblets as I filled mine with clean water from the fountain.

"The execution is this morning, before the sunrise," a female voice came from behind the tall flower hedge to my right that separated the courtyard into sections.

I stilled, gripping my goblet tightly.

"The queen wants everyone present," the voice continued.

"Even the Joy Vessels?" a male voice replied.

These must be two Keepers talking, though I couldn't see them behind the hedge, and they couldn't see me.

"There is no need to upset the Joy Vessels," the woman replied. "The poor things are too emotional to handle something like that."

"Why? They don't know the prince to care much about his execution," the man argued.

The goblet slipped from my fingers, landing in the fountain with a splash. My legs shook, forcing me to sit down on the ledge of the fountain. My stomach churned, threatening to expel the food I'd just had.

What was the queen going to do to Rha?

Thirty-Two

RHA

The guards didn't dare restrain me when escorting me to the queen's private wing, but they hovered close to make it clear I wasn't free to leave. Only I would never leave without Dawn. I'd do anything to get her back, even face my mother.

Memories rose to the surface, with images popping in my mind like air bubbles as I walked the familiar corridors of Kalmena Palace. I'd played here as a child. I'd come this way to visit my father when he lay struck by the curse meant for my mother. The curse turned that strong man into a motionless corpse, with his spirit held prisoner to this world.

The familiar shiver of apprehension ran down my spine when we arrived at the doors of my mother's study. The guards opened them, letting me enter alone.

Shrouded in a dark-brown veil, Queen Abeille reclined in a low chaise piled high with silk cushions and backlit by high panels of glowing honeycomb. The panels edged her sitting area from three sides, filling the air with the sweet scent of honey.

I waited for a tug at my heart, for a wisp of tenderness, for some visceral reaction in my soul at seeing my mother after so many years away, but nothing stirred inside me. Whatever tender feelings I might've had for this woman had either long been gone or lay securely dormant.

"Your Majesty." I bent a knee as the etiquette required.

She heaved a long breath, watching from under her veil as I rose back to my feet.

"To mark your high standing in this kingdom," she said, her voice low and strained, "you received a *sarai* of Joy Vessels of your own." It wasn't a question, but she paused, as if expecting me to confirm.

"I did, Your Majesty."

Her pale-yellow eyes refused to meet mine, staring past me from under the embellished edge of the veil over her head.

"But you let them all go." Her disappointment permeated the room. Disappointment was the main and often the only emotion I caused in my mother.

I had managed to keep one Joy Vessel, the only one I wanted. But I sensed that mentioning that wouldn't make much difference at this point.

"You'll be punished publicly by sunrise. Go." The queen waved a dismissive hand. She sounded tired. "If recovered, all your Joy Vessels will become mine. You don't deserve the honor of having them. I'll gift them to whomever I please."

Alarm pierced the shroud of dull indifference that I held for my own fate. I had expected a punishment when coming here. I was prepared to deal with whatever the queen would shell out for me. But I was not going to part with Dawn.

"I will keep at least one," I said.

Queen Abeille raised her head slowly. For the first time since I came in here, she looked at me directly. The queen wasn't used to arguments, especially from her own son.

"What did you say?"

"I said you can't have my woman," I repeated just as loud and clear as the first time. "Dawn is mine."

Clinking with the chains that connected the rings on her fingers to the bangles around her wrists, the queen gripped the back of her chaise and pushed up, standing straight. A few beautiful but deadly golden bees rose into the air from the honeycomb panels with the queen's move.

"Do you dare question my judgement?" Her voice dropped threateningly low.

She didn't ask who Dawn was or what made her so special to me. That didn't matter. All that mattered to the queen was that I dared defy her.

"I'm not leaving Kalmena without her." I stood my ground.

"You devalued my royal gift." She headed my way, reciting my transgressions with every step. "You lost the Joy Vessels. Many of them escaped to their world, negating the effort it cost us to bring them here. Several are now dead. Others are stolen. They were your responsibility. Their loss is on you."

I stood straighter as she approached. "I agree. They were my responsibility, and I am prepared to answer for their loss. I'll accept whatever punishment you see fit. But Dawn will stay with me."

She glared at me from under her veil as one would look at an object standing in their way.

"It's no secret that I resented you from the day you were born," she said. "All your life, I waited for you to prove me right in my resentment. You were a quiet, contemplative child, and I thought you must be timid and weak. But then, you fearlessly headed my army, won battles, and brought glory to the crown." There was no praise in her voice, just the same old disappointment. "I thought that proved you must be a careless hothead, unable to govern. I sent you to Teneris, the city so overrun by disorder, poverty, and crime, I thought it'd eat you alive. But you turned it into one of the most prosperous cities of the kingdom. I waited for you to fail, but you managed to thrive at every turn. You have never been right for me, but I admitted you might be right for the kingdom. Alzali spent years in Kalmena, trying to convince me otherwise. She's good, but not as good as you." She slowly drew in the stifling, sweet air. "And now you did it. You finally made a mistake that both Alzali and I have been waiting for. You proved you aren't perfect. You let the Joy Vessels go."

She strolled along the honeycomb panels, their golden glow piercing through the veil around her body. Her bangles clinked as she raised her hand, letting a dangerous golden bee land on her finger.

"I should execute you," she spoke to me, keeping her eyes on the bee. "Alzali could be my successor. The kingdom would have a queen, as it should, and no traditions would be broken. But...*his* blood is in your veins..." Her voice broke. She dropped her hand, and the bee flew away with a buzz. The queen turned her head, staring at me over her shoulder. "No matter how disappointed I was on the day you were born, I could never truly despise you. You are a part of him. And now, you're all I have left of your father." She flinched. "You look like him, sound like him, you even act like him sometimes... But you are not him. It's like a cruel joke. A mockery. I can't stomach looking at you. It makes me ill."

She turned away again, unable to hold my gaze.

"You miss him," I said softly.

"I loved him." Her voice rose. "I still do. Even after all these years. I never stopped."

Hope fluttered its fragile wings inside my heart. "Then you should understand it. I love Dawn. I can never part from her."

The queen seemed speechless at my admission. Then she tilted her head back and laughed. It was a dry, mocking laughter without any mirth—the only kind of laughter that shadow fae could muster without the help of a Joy Vessel.

"What do you know about love, boy?" she scoffed.

The insult burned deep, blowing away my caution. The queen didn't just insult *me*. She mocked the connection Dawn and I had built. The connection I now held sacred.

"I know more than you do, my queen. My love is stronger than yours ever was." Her mouth dropped open at my audacity, but I continued. "You were so afraid of losing Father, you smothered him, taking away his free will."

I should've said it decades ago, instead of trying to be respectful of her mourning. Ever since Father died, the queen had allowed grief to consume her. She wore it proudly like the most splendid garment. Her grief had become her, blinding her to everything else. She never even realized how badly she hurt Father while he was still alive.

Her eyes narrowed. The look in them turned sharp like a blade.

"How dare you—"

But I refused to stop now.

"Father was a seasoned warrior when you met him. He tracked through the desert, slept under the dunes, and weathered the day storms. He thrived outside in fresh air, and you locked him here, in your perfumed royal chambers. Every time I returned to the palace after a trip, he begged me to describe how the moon looked that night and what the air smelled like outside of these walls. You took away everything that brought him peace."

"He loved me," she protested.

"He did, as much as one can love their jailer. That's why he gave up everything for you. But he was miserable. Believe me, he would've given up the crown for just one more mission outside of the palace walls."

Her anger exploded.

"Kalmena was the only safe place for him! And you know it. I did everything to protect him, but death still found him. Even here, in the palace, despite my best efforts, it found him..." Her voice broke, and her chin trembled.

I felt her sorrow. And her regret. Her guilt too.

"I know you blame yourself for his death, Your Majesty, but no one else does. No one could've predicted that attack or what your sister managed to do with the juice of the golden hyacinth. Father did what any loyal husband and subject would do. He protected his queen and his wife with his life and died, forever the hero of our kingdom. I don't blame you for his death, Mother. But I disapprove of what you did to him after."

She heaved a breath, setting her mouth in a stubborn line. "He didn't die that night."

"Yes, he did. He was on his way to leave this world, and it would've been a mercy to let him go. But you ordered to leave the dagger in his back. You had a shrine built around his body. You trapped him in death as you had him trapped in life."

She fisted her hands, the beaded chains straining over her knuckles.

"I will not apologize for that, boy. I loved your father with every tendril of my being. I would not part from him. You know it too. That's why you're fighting me, risking your life, just to keep that sweet little Joy Vessel of yours."

"It's not the same." I shook my head.

"It is exactly the same. You are no better than me."

She wasn't far from the truth. We were similar, except for where it truly mattered.

"It's true," I said. "I stole Dawn from her world and brought her here against her will. I wished to keep her at all costs. In that way, you and I are alike. But in the end, I let Dawn go. I bled for her freedom, and I would've died for it. Do you know why? Because loving someone, really loving them, means putting their happiness first. She wished to be free, and I made it happen. All she had to do was take one more step away from me, and she would've been free from me forever. But she came back. She chose to stay with me. She realized she wanted us to be together. And now, I'll do everything to make that wish of hers come true. Dawn is mine. As I am hers. We belong together."

The queen smirked, mocking. "Your little Joy Vessel allowed you a taste of pleasure, and now you think you're in love?"

"I know I am. Because I know what love is. Love is not entrapping someone just because it hurts when they're not with you. It is not holding on to their dead body even after their spirit has left it."

She sucked in a breath with a sob. "As long as I had his body, I had hope."

"There was no hope, Mother. We proved it, but you refused to accept it. We caught the hag who'd brewed the poison and the priest who'd unearthed the ancient curse to go with it. The casts of their heads are still displayed on the spears at the city entrance, along with that of Father's murderer, who used the dagger they had prepared for him and his wife, your younger sister. All four are now cursed for eternity after what you've done to them. The recipe for the poison and the exact wording of the curse have been recovered. We learned everything. We all knew, without a doubt, that Father could never come back. His spirit no longer belonged to this world, but it remained tethered to his body that would not decay for as long as the dagger was still lodged in it. He couldn't cross into the afterlife because you couldn't bear to part with his corpse. You chose to let him suffer just so that you could ease your grief."

"It was all I had!" she repeated stubbornly. "He was the love of my life. He was mine..." She drew in a shuddering breath. "I grieved his loss. I'll never stop grieving."

"I mourned him too. I still miss him terribly. And back then, I wished with all my heart to hold on. But that meant keeping his spirit suspended in torture between two worlds. You insisted on that. Even in death, you refused to give him peace."

"So, you think I should've let him go?" Her eyes narrowed, pinning me in place.

I sensed a threatening note in her voice, but the warning came too late. Her veil fluttered open in the front, releasing her tendrils. They lashed forward like whips, their ends momentarily merging with the ends of mine.

With my tendrils clipped, I couldn't withdraw them. The queen didn't suffer to stay connected to me for longer than a second. But even that second proved enough for her to find what she searched for. I had no regret over what I'd done, and she saw that.

"You!" Her eyes opened wide like two golden saucers. "It was you who pulled out the dagger."

She lunged at me. And I didn't stop her, making no attempt to protect myself. She slapped me across my face. My skin burned with long scratches from her nails. Her heavy rings bruised my cheekbones. But I didn't fight it, letting her take her anguish out on me.

"You killed him!"

"My uncle did," I corrected. "His own brother-in-law was the one who plunged the dagger into Father's heart. That was the moment he died. He was dead for decades while you cried over his body in the shrine of your making. All I did was set his spirit free."

Snarling like a wild animal, she punched me in the chest with both fists. The pain didn't stop the memories from rising in my mind.

Every night, I came to the bedroom where the queen kept my father's body. He lay on his front, with the dagger piercing his heart from the back. It hurt to see the man who had been miserable while trapped in the palace to continue being trapped after his death too. Standing there, looking at the corpse that was nothing but the empty husk of my father, I'd tried to envision the invisible thread connected to his spirit.

The thread was stronger than a chain. Unbreakable. Unless someone was brave enough to pull the cursed dagger laced with forbidden magic out of his heart.

No one had dared to touch it for over four decades. Not even me. The queen had tortured the four people responsible for her husband's death, including her own sister. There was no doubt the same fate awaited anyone who'd dare take his body away from her.

For a while, I'd also hoped Father could be brought back to life. But that hope diminished after I'd carefully studied everything about the curse and the poison.

My uncle knew he had but one chance at it, and my aunt

found a weapon more effective than Nerifir iron. Even if he'd missed the heart, a shallow wound from the dagger would've turned the queen into a mindless doll, breathing and moving but with no will of her own. The dagger never reached the queen. Her husband launched himself between her and the weapon, shielding her with his body. It entered his heart instead, and he died that very moment.

Forty-three years later, I stood over the corpse of my father, thinking about the unimaginable torture his spirit was going through night after night, decade after decade. I thought about how many years of that still lay ahead of him, and I knew I had to stop it. Even the queen's wrath no longer mattered. My father deserved peace.

So, I gave it to him. I pulled the dagger out and placed it gently on Father's back, saying my last goodbye.

"We'll meet again," I remembered whispering.

And at that moment, the weight that had been pressing down on my chest for decades had lifted. Father's spirit left this plane of existence, joining the shadows on the other side. He was finally free.

I'd been prepared to deal with the consequences of my action, but by the time the queen found out what happened, Father's body had partially decomposed. Parts of the flesh had turned to shadows, with the dagger lying among the remains. Everyone believed that time did its job, that the body started deteriorating despite the dagger being in it. No one was blamed then. But now...

Now she knew.

Part of the reason I'd kept it a secret was that I knew it'd devastate the queen. And it did. She howled as if I'd stabbed a dagger through her own chest. As she raised her fist to slam it against me again, her veil fell away. Long strands of her hair fanned back, like wisps of ink-black clouds. They floated over her shoulders—hair strands mixed with shadows.

"Mother?" I caught her wrist mid-strike. "You're aging."

It was no mistake. Filaments of black shadows clung to her temples. They spread through her hair like smoke from an incense. Looking closely, I noticed the fine lines around her eyes and in the corners of her mouth that she tried to hide under the veil.

Now, I felt that tug of longing that'd been missing from my heart before. My mother's days in this world were coming to an end. She might have months left. Maybe a few years. But the countdown had already begun. Her aging process had started, taking a toll on her looks.

"I'm so sorry," I said, feeling it with all my heart.

Sorrow descended upon me. Most of my life, my mother had spent in mourning and isolation, grieving the dead and already lost to the living. But soon, I would lose her for good.

She freed her arm from my grip, then adjusted her veil, hiding her hair and face again.

"You won't leave Kalmena," she said, frightenedly calm. "You will be punished for the loss of the Joy Vessels harshly, as you deserve."

She yanked on the chain of the bell by the door, summoning the guards.

"Mother, please, listen to me." I took a step toward her, but she backed away from me as if I were the evil itself.

"Take him," she ordered the guards. "Let Princess Alzali carry out the punishment ceremony as planned. Then leave him in the courtyard for as many days as how many Joy Vessels he lost."

I had eighteen Joy Vessels to begin with. I only managed to keep one. My mother was condemning me to spend seventeen days under the direct exposure of the sun. Without water or shade, half of those days would be enough to kill a shadow fae.

Dread gripped my throat. My mother sentenced me to the slow death by torture with thirst and heat.

"You're not punishing me for the loss of the Joy Vessels," I said. "It's revenge for setting Father's spirit free."

"A life for a life," she hissed, staring at me with so much hatred, I wondered how it didn't burn me on the spot.

I shook my head. "Executing me won't bring Father back. It will only make you my murderer."

Dawn was right all along. There was no balance in murder. No matter how many people my mother killed trying to avenge my father, he would never be alive again. And she would never find peace.

Thirty-Three

DAWN

*P*rince...

Execution...

The words rang in my head, pounding like a hammer inside my skull as I stumbled back to the bench under an arch of flower garlands.

Lucia caught the change in me immediately.

"Dawn, what happened? You're white as a ghost. And where is your water?"

I'd left the goblet in the fountain.

"I'm fine," I mumbled mechanically.

I had to find a way out of here. But I couldn't tell that to Lucia. If I got caught, I didn't want her to get in trouble as my accomplice. It was best if she knew nothing.

Plopping on the bench next to her, I picked up my plate again and poked at the remaining food, but my appetite was gone.

Inside, I felt like a glass filled to the brim with horror. I was afraid to move, lest it spill over and explode with panic.

"Are you sure you're okay?" Lucia prodded. "You don't look so good."

"Just tired. I should go to bed early today."

"Yeah, I should too." She finished her food. "I didn't sleep much, either. With everything that happened, my sleep has been all over the place. Let's just hope the loud fucking will stop for a while. Not sure how much more moaning I can take to hear."

Giving up on finishing my dinner. I handed my plate back to a Keeper, then said goodbye to Lucia and retreated to my room. Here, I sat on the floor of the balcony, watching through the balusters as the Keepers cleaned up after the dinner.

The fae visitors eventually left, but humans mingled around the courtyard for a while longer.

The sky was still pitch dark outside as I waited for the Keepers to climb up the dome to close the skylight. I hoped they'd show me the best path to do so. Unfortunately, they let the guards do it instead.

The guards dissolved into shadows that floated up to the ceiling, turned to people again to shutter and lock the skylight, then dropped back down to the ground as shadows again.

No one climbed anything. Yet the beams running along the ceiling toward the skylight had horizontal pegs that looked like they were meant for climbing. Maybe that was the backup way for the Keepers to reach the skylight when needed, since the iron clips on their tendrils prevented them from dissolving into shadows.

Shortly after, the Keepers ushered the remaining humans into their rooms for the day's rest. The courtyard was cleared. The guards returned to their posts outside the gate, and the Keepers left, probably to attend the execution as per the queen's order.

Was she really going to execute her own son?

I never met the woman, but it seemed too extreme to do for a mother, even if an estranged one. Maybe I'd misunderstood the conversation I'd overheard? I hoped that was the case. Yet my heart pounded frantically with worry and fear.

Sleep was out of the question. Rha never came for me. And I feared if I went to sleep, I might never see him again. I had to get out of here to find out what was going on.

I waited for a little while longer to make sure the Keepers were really gone and the humans were hopefully in their beds, recharging for another night of pleasure and debauchery.

The golden glow of the pillars around the courtyard illuminated the space under the dome as bright as ever. But everyone seemed to have left at last. I got up from my spot on the floor and tied my long skirt up, threading the fabric between my legs to get it out of the way.

After that, I came to the wall and climbed onto the railing of the balcony.

My room was right under the ceiling. I easily reached the first rung of the closest beam that ran in an arch between my balcony and the hexagonal skylight. Pushing off the railing, I moved up the beam, using the horizontal rungs like a ladder.

As the beam curved, my body eventually transitioned from a vertical into a nearly horizontal position. I had to hook my legs over the pegs, hanging off them with my knees bent. Keeping the entire weight of my body suspended from the ceiling took a toll on my strength. My hands felt sweaty. I feared they'd slip, sending me plunging to the ground.

I refused to look down. But then, a long, slow whistle came from below. Hugging the beam with all four limbs, I glanced down over my shoulder.

The naked man I'd seen earlier was standing on his balcony again. He wasn't smoking this time. Instead, he had a large goblet in his hand, probably finishing the last of his wine before going to bed.

Grinning, he lifted his goblet as if in a toast, then tilted his head to the side, trying to get a better look up my skirt. The knot I'd made between my legs had loosened somewhat. And since I wasn't wearing any underwear, he probably got a good view of my bare ass hanging out while I was clinging to the beam like a monkey.

I didn't dare yell at him, afraid to bring any extra attention to myself. At least he remained quiet, just grinning at me with glee. Setting his goblet down, he gave me two thumbs up.

Rolling my eyes, I ignored him and continued to climb. My muscles started to cramp, making my arms shake. I couldn't waste any time. Every second I remained hanging like that drained my strength. Falling from this height would certainly kill me.

I reached the edge of the skylight. Wrapping my legs and one arm tightly around the beam, I used my other hand to open the latch on the shutter. When I pushed against it, the shutter lifted, creating an opening possibly big enough for me to squeeze through. Except that now, I had to climb vertically up and out.

Hugging the beam with all my limbs, I breathed in, then counted to three before grabbing the edge of the skylight with one hand, then the other. Clinging to it, I carefully hooked my right leg around the very last peg. I lifted my left leg to move it next to the right, but it slipped.

My heart pounded high in my throat. My fingers went numb, gripping the edge of the skylight. My left leg dangled over the courtyard, and my right one was slipping too. If it did, I'd hang by my hands only, which meant I'd crash within seconds. I didn't have the upper body strength of an action movie star to pull myself up from that position.

Straining every muscle in my body, I felt for a rung with my left foot. The moment I found purchase with it, I shoved against the peg and flexed my arms, pushing my torso through the opening and onto the roof.

The rounded roof was made of smooth polished stone. But a low, solid banister ran around the skylight a short distance away from the opening, possibly for preventing sand and small animals from falling in.

Stretching toward it, I managed to hook my fingers over the banister, then pulled myself up and dragged my legs out through the opening and into the calm, early morning.

Before the wooden shutter fell back into place behind me, I heard the drunk, naked guy cheer for me from the inside.

"There you go, girl! You made it!"

Exhausted, I didn't feel annoyed at him. If he were here, I'd probably even hug him, to celebrate being alive instead of lying in a blood puddle on the courtyard tiles below.

For a few heartbeats, I just lay there, catching my breath and taking inventory of my limbs and functions. I could breathe. After gathering my arms and legs under me, I knew I could move. Then, I pushed to my feet and looked around me.

The early morning was still dark. There wasn't even a hairline of light on the horizon yet. They had sent the Joy Vessels to their beds early in their hurry to comply with the queen's order to attend the execution.

Now, I had to figure out where it was taking place. And I hoped I wasn't too late.

The domed roof of the *sarai* was only one of many. From the outside, the roofs of the city buildings looked like wide, low mounds over the surface of the giant hill of Kalmena. They poked out from the tall grass like bald spots. And I had no idea which one was the queen's palace or where Rha might be.

I scrambled down the *sarai* dome, then climbed up another one to take a better look around. The morning appeared to glow behind the next group of domes, so I headed out that way.

The wispy ends of the grass tickled my face as I pushed ahead, but its stems were hard and rough, scratching against my arms and bare legs. I missed the hag's boots. Though, climbing up the beam in the *sarai* would've been more difficult with them on.

As I approached the glow, the sound of the crowd clamoring broke through the darkness.

The roof over the city parted in this location, opening to a plaza below. The surrounding buildings formed a hexagon around it. I crouched down to stay out of sight, then lay on my belly and crawled to the edge of the roof to look below.

Shadow fae filled the plaza, the crowd spilling into the side streets nearby. The windows and balconies of the surrounding buildings were bursting with spectators too. Tall pillars met in arches over the narrow side streets, illuminating the plaza with bright, golden light.

The flying insects that normally seemed to be comfortable around people rose away from the crowd, hiding in the grass on the roofs. A few of the silver moths and iridescent butterflies fluttered around my head.

In the center of the plaza stood a tower-like platform. Taller than the crowd, it reached the height of the second-floor balconies. On the top of the platform, two tall, ornate posts rose from the opposite sides with thick chains wound around each.

A man in a long shimmering skirt and strands of gemstones over his chest descended the stairs of the platform. He held a partially unwound scroll in his hand, looking like he might've read from it to the crowd, and I'd just missed his speech.

Two rows of guards created a live corridor between the stairs of the platform and the gates of the queen's palace, letting a small group walk through.

My stomach sank.

Rha walked toward the platform, flanked by at least a dozen guards. The crown prince was bound in chains. Six guards held the ends of the chains, three on each side, as if they really needed that many to contain one man.

His crown circlet was still on his head that he held high. But my doubt was gone. This was *his* execution. He was the one being punished.

Panic shook me. I frantically searched the roof and the walls for a way to climb down.

But what would I do once I was there?

How could I help? Attack the guards? Make a scene? Demand to see the queen?

Deep inside, I knew none of it would probably make any difference. But I couldn't just sit here and watch. I crawled on all fours toward the closest balcony. But it was already filled with people. Thankfully, they were too absorbed by the events on the plaza to look up and notice me.

The guards brought Rha to the base of the platform and stood back, stretching the chains. Princess Alzali marched from the palace gate, carrying a wide sickle. The curved silver blade of the tool glistened in the golden light of the pillars around the plaza. The sickle wasn't made from the dark and deadly Nerifir iron. Still, my stomach sickened with apprehension.

What was she going to do?

Alzali circled the prince. He followed her with his gaze until she stepped too far behind his back.

Tossing the sickle up, as if in play, she caught it by its short handle again, the sharp side of the blade turned toward her. With the dull edge, she hit Rha on the back of his knees.

The crowd gasped as their prince fell to his knees. With his arms bound to his torso by the chains, he nearly lost his balance, lurching forward. With a clank, the guards yanked on the chains, keeping him in straight.

A cry lodged in my throat, and I slammed both hands over my mouth to stop myself from screaming.

Holding the sickle in her right hand, Alzali collected Rha's incapacitated tendrils in her left. She wound them around her wrist and pulled. Rha arched back, tilting his face up. For a moment, it looked like he might see me hiding among the grass on the roof, but the distance was too great and the light on the plaza too bright for him to spot me in the shadows.

Swinging the sickle through the air, Alzali sliced through Rha's tendrils, cutting them off at their base. The iron clips fell to the ground from the cut-off ends.

A tortured roar shook Rha's body.

Instead of blood, black, heavy shadows spread from the wounds on his arms and back. They trickled in rivulets down his skin and dripped like thick inkblots on the pale marble of the plaza.

I stared in horror, unable to comprehend the pain he was going through. Shadow fae's tendrils weren't just a physical part of them. They connected to their emotions, to their very soul.

Losing them wouldn't result in just physical pain. The torture he must be enduring was unimaginable.

Rha lurched forward, yanking the chains from the hands of three guards out of six. They scrambled to grab them and pulled to get the prince up to his feet. Half-leading him, half-dragging, they hauled him up the stairs of the platform.

Here, they unwound the chains from around him and spread his arms wide to place his wrists into the manacles of the chains from the poles.

"Poor prince." A woman on the balcony below me sighed. "I remember him playing on this very plaza when he was little. And now, there he is, destined to die on it."

"It's a shame," a man chimed in. "He would've been a great king. The city of Teneris has been thriving under him. It used to be such a shithole filled with low-lifes and starving beggars before he took over."

"Honestly, death seems too harsh a punishment for losing a few Joy Vessels," another woman said. "It's not like he intentionally hurt them."

"What can I say," the man grunted, "the nobles obviously want their joy. And now that the last portal has been opened and closed, the Joy Vessels are irreplaceable."

"Well, what's done is done," another man said. "The sun will be up soon. We should shutter the windows and doors."

There were no shutters to protect Rha on the platform that was too high to stay in the shade during the day.

Rha's execution wasn't complete yet. His torture had just begun.

Thirty-Four

DAWN

Doors were slamming closed all around the plaza. There was no ceiling or shutters over it. The plaza remained exposed to the heat and storms of the day. All doors and windows facing it had to be secured and shuttered.

The moment the people on the balcony below me left, I climbed down to it, then looked for a way to get to the ground. Knocking on the door and asking to use the stairs was out of the question. I didn't escape the *sarai* to be captured now and put right back in there. Instead, I climbed over the railing, then down to the balcony below, using the vines and the support pillars.

Once I made it all the way down to the plaza, I hid in the shadows of the vines and watched.

The doors were locked; the windows shuttered. People took planters inside. Some drew thick shrouds over the gates, hedges, and archways to protect them from the sun and sand damage.

Only the prince on top of the platform remained completely unprotected. As the sky lightened over Kalmena, Rha had no cover from the rising sun.

The few guards who remained on the plaza with him hid in

the shade of his platform. They propped their weapons against it and lounged on the floor, passing a bag of water between them.

Staying close to the walls, I circled the plaza to get out of the guards' view. Scanning the windows and balconies, I made sure no one was watching me before sprinting for the platform. I reached its stairs and even jumped onto the first one, when a hand gripped my neck from behind.

"And where do you think you're going?" A guard spun me around to face him. "A Joy Vessel?" he gasped, his mouth falling open. "What are *you* doing here?"

"Please," I croaked. "I have to talk to Prince Rha."

"Why?"

Rha had to know I was here. Maybe he'd tell me what I could do to save him, but the guard didn't need to hear that.

I decided to bet on his compassion. "I'm from his *sarai*. I knew him well. I want to say goodbye. Please, just a few minutes."

That turned out to be a losing bet. The guard clearly lacked any compassion.

He smirked. "And what will I get if I let you up there?"

"Anything," I pleaded. "I'll do anything. What do you want?"

He couldn't hurt me, could he? His eyelids dropped a little, which gave his smirk a lewd expression. Except that how could it be? He couldn't just randomly feel lust for me, could he? He didn't even have a dick, for goodness' sake.

He dragged me from the stairs and to the shade on the side.

"Stay right here," he ordered. "If you move even a step in either direction, the deal is off."

"What deal?" I mumbled, but he was already gone.

He returned a moment later, bringing a small package wrapped in a piece of oily paper. He unwrapped it, revealing a crème-filled pastry.

"I want you to eat this." He shoved the pastry in my hand.

"Now?" I blinked at him, confused.

"Yes."

With a quick glance around the plaza, he shoved the fabric of his shroud behind his shoulders. Black shadows extended from his upper arms, snaking toward me. I stilled, halting my breath, my eyes fixed on the undulating shadows braiding into tendrils.

"That's the food normally served to Joy Vessels," the guard explained, tipping his chin at the pastry in my hand. "Eat it. I want to feel your pleasure."

I swallowed hard. The sweet scent of the pastry made my stomach roil. Which was not the pastry's fault. It smelled nice. It probably tasted good too. But my stomach was tied in knots from nerves, and there was nothing I could do about it.

"If I do... If I eat it, will you let me see the prince?" I asked.

"That's the deal."

His tendrils plunged into the openings of the harness around my arms. Two more appeared from behind his back and slipped around me, connecting with the *leilathas* on my back. No one but Rha had done it to me before.

"Now be a good girl and eat it." He panted in anticipation. His mouth opened as he watched me bring the pastry to my lips.

The guard's presence invaded my emotions. The eager prodding of his tendrils around my feelings was almost physical, like the greedy fingers of a stranger exploring the hidden, private layers of my psyche. I had the strong urge to yank them out and run away, but I needed the deal with the guard to work. He stood in my way to Rha.

Slowly, I opened my mouth and took a bite.

I tried, I really tried, to give the guard what he wanted. Being with Rha had taught me to find pleasure in little things and enjoy every moment. I tried to focus on the flakiness of the pastry dough as it broke and crunched under my teeth. On the flavor of the sweet crème melting on my tongue. But it mostly felt like tasteless clay to me.

All I could think about was Rha chained just above us and me being down here, unable to help him. I felt scared, helpless, anxious, and impatient. If there was any joy inside me, it was buried so deeply below worries and fear, even I couldn't find it.

"What the fuck is this?" the guard growled, grabbing the bitten pastry out of my hand. "What kind of a Joy Vessel are you? If I wanted to feel anxious and terrified, I'd stick to my own emotions. I don't need to break the law for this shit and risk my head."

Begrudgingly, he withdrew his tendrils and packed away his precious pastry that he must've stolen from the kitchen at some point.

"Can I see the prince?" I couldn't give up.

"Fuck off." The guard gave me a shove toward the nearest side street. "Go back to the *sarai* before I report you and have you whipped for escaping."

Disappointment crushed me. I dragged my feet, making a few slow steps toward the archway of the street. I wasn't going to return to the *sarai*, of course, but I couldn't figure out what else to do to get on that platform.

The sun was rising, and with it the wind. A day storm was approaching. If I just waited somewhere, maybe I could sneak up on the platform later? After all, I tolerated the sunlight much better than the shadow fae did.

"Greetings, Your Highness," came from behind me.

Your Highness?

I tripped over my feet. For a moment, I believed the guard was talking to Rha. That the prince got free somehow.

As I whipped around, however, Princess Alzali approached the guards. Her slim, sleek figure was draped into a full-body shroud, complete with a hood that was drawn low over her eyes and a scarf that covered the lower part of her face. The thin, dense fabric of the black shroud hugged her body like melted tar, glistening with gold in its folds. She wore the circlet of her crown over the hood, so there was no mistaking who she was.

Her orange eyes narrowed at me from the shadow of her hood.

"What is *she* doing here?"

The guard with the pastry in his belt satchel fidgeted, adjusting his uniform.

"She escaped the *sarai*, Your Highness. I was just about to call for the Joy Vessel Keepers..."

The princess had been Rha's executioner. She was the one who'd cut his tendrils off. He didn't trust her. I had no reason to count on her leniency, either. But she had the authority over the guards.

Desperation urged me to step forward. "I need to see Prince Rha, Your Highness. Please allow me to speak with him. Just for a minute."

"She says she wants to say goodbye," the guard offered reluctantly.

The princess tilted her head. The focus in her eyes sharpened with a long, assessing look.

"Of course," she said, and I stilled, afraid to hope. "You're Cousin Rha's favorite little treat, aren't you? I'm sure he'll appreciate seeing you. Come." She grabbed my arm, heading toward the stairs. "I'll take you up there myself."

"Um..." The guard cleared his throat, looking uneasy. "No one is allowed up there, Your Highness. Queen Abeille's order."

"Surely, we can't refuse the Joy Vessel's plea to say goodbye to her beloved master," Alzali purred. "Besides, I need to make sure the prince's restraints are locked properly." She moved aside her shroud, revealing a key attached to her belt.

The golden key rested against her hip. It was hanging by a hook, not a keyring, for practical reasons, I assumed. It was easier to remove it from a hook. Much easier than from a keyring.

The key must be a sign of added authority, because at the sight of it, the guard nodded and stepped aside, letting us pass.

I preferred to speak with Rha in private, but just a moment ago, I didn't believe I'd see him at all. I couldn't miss this chance. Silently, I followed Alzali up the stairs.

The morning sun pleasantly stroked my bare arms with warmth as we ascended the stairs. Despite the strong wind, I would've enjoyed this morning had my mind not been so preoccupied with worries and with the thoughts of that key that glistened in the sunshine so close to me.

Tripping over a step, I bumped into the princess and gripped her shroud for balance.

"I'm so sorry," I muttered, sliding my hand down her side and quickly swiping the key off her belt. I had no idea if I'd have a chance to use it. But I had to try. "I haven't eaten well, feeling a bit lightheaded." I gave her a meek smile.

"Poor thing," she hissed, yanking me up and away from her. "It'll be over soon."

She shoved me forward, ahead of her, and I ran up to the top of the platform.

Rha was on his knees. The chains stretched from the manacles around his wrists to the pillars on each side of him. They held his arms spread wide, not allowing him to sit down or lie on the platform.

He squinted against the sunlight. "Dawn?"

"Rha, baby..." I dropped to my knees in front of him.

Thick, black smoke streamed from the wounds on his arms. It trickled down to the ground, pooling in a black puddle on the stark white platform. When I lifted the top layer of his long skirt to pull it over his head for protection from the sun, the smoke seeped through the fabric on his back. It trickled between my fingers, leaving a layer of fine, black soot on my skin.

"It hurts?" I whispered, holding back tears.

"You make it all better." Incredibly, his lips stretched into a smile, one that reflected with warmth in his eyes. Shadow fae couldn't do it on their own. It was my emotions that had taught him to smile like that, with all his heart.

"Rha." I cupped his face and pressed my forehead to his.

My chest was full with love, compassion, fear, and longing that grew inside me so strong, I feared I'd burst or melt into another puddle at his knees.

"Why are you here, my treasure?" The relief at seeing me gave way to concern in his voice.

Alzali joined us on the platform. "She wished to say goodbye. Isn't that sweet, cousin?"

Wind tore at the fabric of her skirt and shroud, but her hood remained on, held by the circlet of her crown. She brought a hand to her belt, to the opposite side where the key used to be, then swept the plaza with her gaze, turning around.

Using the moment, I shifted to the left and grabbed Rha's manacle.

"You'll have to tell me what to do next, okay?" I whispered, quickly shoving the key in the lock.

If I set him free, together we could find our way out of this.

"Dawn, no!" His eyes opened wide with alarm, focused on something behind me.

I turned around.

Princess Alzali held a dagger in her hand. She didn't raise it, just holding it casually while sliding a finger along its curved, dark blade. The metal sparkled with red where she touched it—Nerifir iron.

I moved closer to Rha, as if I could protect him somehow.

"It was very fortunate to find you here, sweet little Joy Vessel," the princess murmured.

"Why? What do you want?"

She bent over and took my hand, yanking me up to my feet.

"I want you to attack me." She placed the dagger in my hand.

"Don't, Dawn," Rha warned.

I took a step back from her. "I'm not going to fight you."

If I did, I wouldn't win. My human strength was no match for the fae power. The princess wouldn't give me the dagger if there was any chance of me using it against her successfully. It felt like a trap.

She seized my wrist.

"But you did attack me. Oh, look!"

She moved my wrist, slashing with the dagger clutched in my

hand. The blade pierced through the fabric of her shroud, leaving a long, ragged tear in it.

Alzali yanked me closer, speaking straight into my face, "I don't want to kill you, Sweet One. Joy Vessels are rare and now irreplaceable. But I have to get rid of Rha before his ill-tempered general does something stupid, like organizing a rescue mission. If you do as I say, I'll let you live."

"You can't kill me," I snapped. "If you do, you'll end up here, in Rha's place."

"No, poor thing." She shook her head, looking at me with pity. "Not if you die due to an unfortunate accident, while the two of you attacked me, and I fought for my life."

"But that's a lie! I'm not fighting you."

"Every lie can be true if enough people believe it. The guards will confirm that I allowed you to see the prince out of the kindness of my heart. And in turn, you betrayed me."

She had a cruel plan. And the worst part was that it might work. There were just the three of us up here. No witnesses, and no one to stop her.

I twisted my arm, trying to free my wrist, but she held tightly, so I unclenched my fingers from around the handle, letting the dagger drop.

"I'll take it as a no," Alzali stated flatly. She jerked my arm back and gripped my throat. "So, the little sweet bee thinks she can sting? But you are so gravely mistaken. You'll die by 'accidentally' falling off the platform and breaking your neck. Except that I'll break your neck first, just to make sure."

She squeezed my throat, cutting off my airway. Blood rushed to my brain, blurring my vision. My heartbeat thundered in my ears so loudly, I barely heard a clunk of metal dropping to the marble tiles of the platform floor.

A chain rattled.

Darkness fringed my awareness as my mind swam, deprived of oxygen. I staggered back, my knees buckling and my legs crumbling under me. Alzali bent over me, arching me backwards.

With a strangled gasp, her grip on my neck suddenly weakened. She swayed backwards as a strong arm wrapped around my middle, yanking me out of her reach.

Unimpeded, she lurched farther back, tipping over the edge of the platform. She plummeted down, the handle of her own dagger sticking out from between her ribs. The weapon was sunk all the way to its hilt.

As an experienced warrior, Rha knew exactly where to strike to make Alzali's death certain and quick. He'd hit from the side, going straight for her heart. And he did it with his right wrist still chained to the pole.

His left manacle lay open on the platform, with the key in its lock. I'd unlocked it when Alzali startled me. I just never had the chance to open the restraint. But Rha had. He'd opened it, freed his arm, then grabbed the dagger I'd dropped.

He flexed his arm around my waist, drawing me to him.

"Dawn. My treasure. My one ray of joy."

I threw my arms around his neck, catching my breath.

He pressed the side of his face to mine. As much as I wished we could stay like this forever, we needed to hurry. The guards could walk around the platform any minute now. They'd see Alzali's dead body.

"We have to run, baby." I grabbed the open manacle and wrenched the key out of the lock. "I'll unlock the other one, then we'll go."

"No, my sweet."

He took the key from me and tossed it off the platform, the way Alzali had gone.

"What have you done?" I shouted over the wind, shaking in shock. "Why?"

"There are guards below."

"Not that many."

"The queen's guards are on every street of this city, day and night. There is a small army of them at the gate. We won't get far."

"We can climb up a wall." I frantically gestured at the buildings around the plaza. "I got down like that already. We can climb up."

He shook his head. "It'll take time. Enough time for them to catch us. You'll be tried as my accomplice in both the murder and the escape."

"They can't hurt a Joy Vessel," I repeated as a mantra.

"The queen can do whatever she wants, even if it's just to make an example of you for the others. She will punish you," he said with conviction that clearly came from experience.

The queen had condemned her own son to torture. Why would she care about me?

"I can't let it happen, Dawn. I can't let her hurt you."

"But I can't leave you here to die," I cried in anguish.

"The most important thing is that you'll be safe, my treasure." He pulled me tighter into his chest, talking in an urgent half-whisper. "It was *I* who killed the princess. *I* tried to escape. You had nothing to do with it. You're innocent. They can't do anything to you."

His words gutted me. My chest ached as if the dagger was lodged in me, not in Alzali. Voices came from below. Surprised shouts. The guards must have found their dead princess.

"I can't leave you..." I pleaded.

"But you must. You can't die with me."

Despite everything, he remained calm and stoic, like always, while I was a sobbing, miserable mess, clinging to him.

"No...Rha. Please come with me. We'll be together. We'll dance again. We'll make another necklace. I need you..." I cried openly now.

"Kiss me," he said softly. "It always feels better when *you* do it."

Tears streamed down my face, making our kiss taste salty and stinging my wind-burned lips.

"Thank you for giving me a taste of true happiness," he said. "My one regret is that I failed to make you happy in return."

"But you did make me happy, Rha. I've never been happier

than when I was with you." If only I'd appreciated what we had back in Teneris more. If only I'd enjoyed it fully, without any doubt or guilt.

The guards appeared at the top of the stairs. I flexed my arms, holding Rha tighter to me. But he dropped his arm from around me.

"Go, my love. Live. There is joy in life, waiting to be found by you."

My throat closed. I could barely breathe in short, shuddering gasps as the guards pulled me away from him. Tears blurred my vision. The world turned into a disorienting ball of light, wind, and heat.

I was barely aware of the guards dragging me down the stairs. Grief clouded my mind, painfully familiar, like an old nightmare. Once again, I was losing someone I loved. Again, I wished to curl into myself and let sorrow take me. Because fighting it hurt.

Unlike my family, however, Rha wasn't gone yet. I could still do something to save him.

I must do something.

The undying hope burned through the suffocating helplessness. My awareness sharpened. I strained my brain to think, frantically roaming my gaze around the plaza in search of a solution.

The golden gate caught my eye. There, behind the polished-gold honeycomb, Queen Abeille must be going to sleep in her luxurious royal bed. Like a queen bee, she hid inside her beehive while her son was dying.

She was the one in charge of his life.

"Take me to the queen," I demanded, stopping in my tracks.

"What?" a guard scoffed. "The queen has better things to do."

The second guard gave me no answer whatsoever, silently dragging me ahead toward the street that led back to the *sarai*.

"I need to speak to the queen." I wouldn't give up. "Trust me, she'll want to hear what I have to say."

The first guard huffed impatiently. "The queen is long in bed already. No one is going to wake her because of you."

"Are you saying no one is going to report the death of Princess Alzali to Queen Abeille? Her one and only remaining heiress?"

I jerked my chin at the small crowd of guards gathering around the execution platform. Some of them ran up the stairs, others kneeled by the body of the princess. Black wisps of shadows were already clouding the wound on Alzali's side as her body began to decompose.

Four guards opened the golden gates and ran into the palace, undoubtedly bringing the report to the queen.

"Looks like the queen will have to wake up after all." I pointed at the open gates. "Don't you think she'll want to know exactly what happened?"

One of the guards flicked his ear. "Everyone knows what happened. Prince Rha stabbed Princess Alzali with a dagger."

"Prince Rha didn't have a dagger on him, did he? Neither did he have the key to unlock his restraints," I retorted promptly.

The guards exchanged uncertain looks with each other.

"I know exactly what happened and how," I kept pushing. "Because I was there. I am the only eyewitness, aside from Prince Rha." I propped my hands on my hips. "Don't you think Queen Abeille will want to speak with me as soon as possible?"

One of the guards crossed his arms over his chest, taking a wide stance. "Tell us what you saw. We'll relay it to the queen."

I mimicked his pose, hiking my chin up. "I'll tell it to the queen and no one else."

The guard blew out a frustrated breath.

The other guard reached for me. "Fine. Let's take her to the queen. If Her Majesty doesn't want to see her, we'll take her back to the *sarai* then."

But there was one more thing I had to do before they would take me away from the plaza. I'd shared every single emotion with Rha. I couldn't leave here without sharing my hope with him too.

Folding my hands into a funnel, I brought them to my mouth.

"I love you, Rha!" I screamed toward the platform.

The wind tore my words from my mouth, whisking them away. Maybe it took them all the way up to my prince, or maybe it didn't. But somehow, I knew that he heard me. I felt a firm tug of reassurance in response, as if we were still connected through his tendrils.

I took a deep breath, feeling stronger and ready to face anything.

"All right." I thrust out my arms to the guards for them to take me away. "Now, lead me to the queen."

Thirty-Five

DAWN

Queen Abeille was alone when I entered her private sitting room. The only light came from the three tall panels of golden hexagons. They stood around a low chaise piled up with silk cushions. Each hexagonal frame in the panel of many was about the size of a dinner plate. It was filled with a thick amber substance that glowed, illuminating the room.

The queen stood by a side panel, turned mostly with her back to me. She was shorter than I'd expected, looking rather frail.

A semi-transparent, chocolate-brown veil stitched with gold covered her head-to-toe, draping all the way down to the floor. It was held by a tall crown of hollow hexagons fitted together, with tall amber-colored spikes rising from the top corners of the hexagons.

Something flew from one of the honeycombs and zoomed my way with a buzzing sound. I ducked with a gasp.

"Careful," the queen said in a quiet voice without turning. "The sting of a golden bee will surely kill a weak little human like yourself."

Only then did I notice the large bees sitting on the panels. Most of them didn't move at all and could be easily mistaken for decoration, especially since their wings appeared to be made from paper-thin iridescent crystal fitted into golden filigree frames.

The queen slowly turned to face me. The veil covered her forehead, hair, and shoulders, leaving her eyes in the shade. In a heavily bejeweled hand, she held a narrow spoon with a long handle.

I opened my mouth to plead Rha's case, but she spoke first. "Tell me what you think about the honey they make."

Was she for real?

Her son was out there, burning alive under the scorching sun, and she wanted to do a honey tasting with me?

I felt torn between wishing to yell at her, to shake her until she came to her senses, or to fall to her feet and plead for Rha's life. But I'd made too many mistakes in my life, big and small, and I could not afford to make any right now. A wrong word or even a gesture could lead to her kicking me out of this room, sealing Rha's fate.

She was my last resort. My only chance.

I couldn't rush it.

I reined in my impatience, bridled my anxiety, and just stood there, rooted in place while watching the queen tap the golden spoon against the thin, clear barrier that held the amber liquid inside the hexagonal frame. The barrier cracked like glass, but it appeared to be made from caramelized sugar. She removed a shard of it from the frame, then dipped the spoon into the shimmering honey inside.

"Taste it." She lifted the spoon to my mouth.

I parted my lips obediently, allowing her to slide the spoon between them. The veil over her upper arm moved, as if a tendril was emerging. I braced for another invasion of my senses, but the tendril never made it from under the fabric.

Instead, the queen waited for me to take the honey from the spoon as she stared at me. Her lips curved slightly.

"You have the most peculiar eyes. And my son has the most unusual taste, it seems." She glanced aside. "So, what do you think about the honey?"

The honey was sweet. Probably. Though, I couldn't say much about its taste. The bitterness in my chest spoiled everything. My mind was so far away from this untimely tasting session, I couldn't focus on analyzing the flavor or even the texture.

"It's good," I squeezed through my throat coated with the sticky substance.

"You know, they say the lily honey from the Wetlands of Lorsan from Above is the best in Nerifir. I wonder what they would say if they had a chance to try this one." She gave me a penetrating look, with the eyes of the same pale gold shade as Rha's. "I wonder which one you would prefer if you tasted them both." She sighed. "Too bad I don't have any Lorsan honey for you to try. The shadow tunnels we used to travel to Above have long been sealed. You see, the fae from Above fear us. They believe we have the ability to suck out their souls."

"Have you ever tried talking to them, to explain yourselves?"

She shook her head. "It's hard to speak when they cut your head off before you even get a chance to open your mouth."

How did I get myself into this conversation?

Why were we talking about things that had absolutely no relevance to Rha?

"Um... Your Majesty," I started.

She dropped the used spoon into a tall vase on a stand next to the honeycombs. Her hand jerked as she did it. The spoon clinked against the hammered metal vase, the sound reverberating through the room like the ringing of a bell.

The queen's fingers trembled, and she balled her hand into a fist. Her lips quivered, and she bit the bottom one in an attempt to stop the tremor. With a long, shaky breath, she composed herself.

"So." She turned to me again, her voice calm and steady like before. "They say you're a dancer?"

Another unrelated topic. But I believed I now understood what she was doing. The queen was very much aware of her son dying a slow death out there. This room, with all these honeycombs and the bees, was just a tool for her to deal with that awareness. She had them for the same purpose Rha had his never-ending puzzle or his very discriminating pet cat.

In a world with no joy, calm was treasured above all. It required effort and special tools to achieve it, especially in a situation like we were in right now.

Our idle conversation was just a distraction, something to occupy the time until the queen would find the strength to hopefully speak about what really mattered.

Did that mean she cared?

Could I allow myself to hope that she did?

"Yes," I replied tentatively. "I'm a professional dancer. Or used to be, back in my world."

I wondered how the queen knew about that. She probably found it out from Alzali, who must've learned about my dancing on her visit to Teneris. That meant that the queen had spoken to her about me. Did she also know what Rha and I meant to each other?

"Maybe we'll see you dance one day," she said casually.

"I dance the best when I'm happy."

"Is that so?" She arched an eyebrow. "And what makes you happy, Sweet One?"

"Your son made me the happiest I've ever been."

She sucked in a breath, pursing her lips. I'd struck a nerve, and it didn't look like it was in my favor.

"My son is dead. You'll have to find another source of happiness now."

"It's not too late to save him." I stepped closer to her, wringing my hands as nerves racked me. "Spare his life. Give him back to me."

She glared at me from under her veil.

"And who will give me back *my* love?"

"Killing Rha won't bring his father back. But you can still have your son."

"He's hardly been a son of mine."

"You never gave him that chance. Save him. Learn to love him—he's so worthy of your love. Rha is a son to be proud of."

She raised her hand, her chest rising and falling rapidly as her breathing sped up in agitation.

"How old are you, child? What do you know about me or my son? You know nothing about what he's done."

"He was born a boy when you wished for a girl. That was his first transgression. You hated him the moment he drew his first breath, and it all went down the hill from there, didn't it? No matter what Rha did, he never could do anything right by you. You ended up favoring that snake-faced Alzali over him. Admit it, you wished she'd be your successor over him—" I cut myself short, afraid I'd gone too far.

Laying blame and accusations was not the way to win the queen's favor.

My chest filled with worry. I wanted her to understand how much she'd missed by casting Rha out of her life, but I was afraid to push too hard or I'd spoil it all. I feared I might've spoiled it already.

"Insolence is ugly, child," the queen snapped. "It's extremely unbecoming in a Joy Vessel."

This was my one and only chance to save Rha, and I saw it slip through my fingers as the queen withdrew. She wasn't interested in hearing about Rha. She didn't even care about my eyewitness account about Alzali's death. She hadn't brought it up at all. She seemed done with this conversation and was about to call the guards in.

"Please, Your Majesty. If only you knew Rha better... If only you saw the man he truly is," I rambled, words tripping over each other. Desperate, I followed the queen and grabbed her hands. "If only you could see him the way I do."

The queen shrank away from me but didn't reclaim her hands, staring at my arms instead.

Thin filaments of black smoke drifted from the *leilatha* openings of my harness. I froze, watching in shock as they stretched down my arms. The smoky strands grew thicker, curling and braiding into a thicker one—a tendril.

Real shadow fae tendrils appeared from my arms. They grew. Their wispy ends slipped under the queen's veil.

"It can't be…" she muttered, looking just as shocked as I was.

Her own tendrils were moving under her veils. And somehow, the ends of hers found the ends of mine. Or maybe it was mine that trapped hers. I wasn't sure how it happened exactly. I had no physical awareness of my tendrils. They weren't like my limbs that I could move at will. They seemed to be the embodiment of my fervent wish to connect with the queen on some level.

And now, our connection was deeper than I could ever imagine having with a stranger. Her emotions slammed into me like a freight train, sending a shudder through my body.

Queen Abeille's inner world lay open to me like a map. And it was a dark journey. Grief saturated her very being, practically becoming her. It was blended with hatred so thick, I feared nothing could ever penetrate it.

I couldn't read her thoughts, but if her grief was for her husband and the hatred was for her son, then I'd already lost. Anything I could possibly say would be insignificant. Words were useless against this deep, all-consuming, long-enduring despair.

A thin white streak of pity unexpectedly struck across the darkness. It fluttered like a white rose petal, tossed into the wind.

I snapped my gaze to hers, finding the pity reflecting in her eyes directed at me.

"You truly love him," she said.

While I'd studied her emotions, she clearly had sifted through mine.

"I do."

"Hm." She nodded. "I hoped, for your sake, that it was just

some light, brief infatuation, but it looks real. Your love is new, but it proved strong enough to form a bond. Humans have the ability to bond with us through their love, I've heard. And now I see that it's true." She tipped her chin at my tendrils. "That's my son's magic you're using now."

I couldn't even begin to wrap my mind around the magical aspect of it. But one word from what she was saying stuck with me—real.

"Of course it's real, Your Majesty. What Rha and I share is very real. He isn't dying out there because of your orders. I gave him a chance to run, but he refused to put my life in danger. He'd rather die than put me at risk. Do you know how it feels?"

"Yes." She freed her hands from mine and retrieved her tendrils, breaking every connection between us. "I know exactly how it feels, child. And I pity you."

She raised her hand and pulled on a thick chain by the door. A bell rang out there somewhere. Then the guards entered the room.

"Your Majesty, please..." I moved her way, realizing the guards were here to take me away. "Please have mercy on your son."

Deep inside, I knew my meeting with the queen was over. I failed to save the man I loved. Anguish tore through me. But the queen remained unmoved.

"Sweet child, you have nothing but grief and misery ahead of you," she said as the guards dragged me out the door. "As a human bonded with a fae, you won't survive him for long. You'll die mourning him, but at least your sorrow will be short. That is the blessing I never got."

Thirty-Six

DAWN

I sat on the floor with my back against the door. I didn't remember how I got here or where exactly in Kalmena this room was.

Ever since the guards shoved me in here and locked me in, I'd been yelling for them to let me out while thrashing against the door with the fury of a caged animal. Every second I spent here, Rha was being tortured by the burning sun.

The urgency shook me. I had to do something. Except that yelling and thrashing got me nowhere. All I had to show for it were a hoarse voice and bruised knuckles. The door remained closed, and no one came to even check on me.

I rocked on the floor, hugging my knees. My mind drowned in sorrow and helplessness. Horror spread, threatening to tear me apart. Only where would I be if I broke down now? What good would that do to Rha? Or to Elaine, who was still out there somewhere, needing help?

I had to tame the chaos that consumed me from the inside, and I wished so badly for some of Rha's composure.

I slid my palms down my upper arms. Like always, I

couldn't feel the harness or the *leilathas* by touch. The awareness of them was much deeper, coming from within. It felt like my very being expanded beyond my body, reaching further than ever before.

A black curl of wispy magic filtered between my fingers pressed to my arm over the *leilatha* opening. I jerked my hand away, and the tendril solidified, growing thicker and longer.

"It's my son's magic you're using," the queen had said.

I closed my eyes, opened my mind, and...*felt* him.

Rha's longing reached out to me eagerly, as if he'd been searching for me in the darkness all along. The connection snapped in place, unbreakable. I felt his worry and his exhaustion. But there was no more pain. There was hope. And it gave me strength, too, as if he were right here with me.

Terror receded, allowing me to function again. I got off the floor and used the small bathroom niche in the room. I washed my face and hands, brushed my teeth, then smoothed and braided my hair the best I could.

My mind turned to more productive thoughts. Not all was lost. Alzali had shown up at the platform for a reason. She feared that Rha would be freed before his execution was over. Her concerns might be valid. After all, Rha was a prince. He had his own army, led by the fierce and loyal General Oskura.

The general might be on her way already. Instead of melting into a puddle of panicky mess on the floor, I had to figure out how to get out of this room. Then maybe I could find a way to let Rha's army into the city.

Hope was a wonderful thing. It sharpened my mind and gave me a burst of energy. I decided to inspect my room, so I could figure out how to get out of here, when the door suddenly opened.

Two of the queen's guards stood on the threshold.

"Come, Sweet One," one of them said.

I backed away from them, cautiously. "Come where?"

"Prince Rha wishes to say goodbye to you."

That was enough for me to follow them out of the room with no arguments. But my mind reeled from a twister of questions.

"Why does he want to say goodbye? Is he leaving? Where?" I bombarded the guards as they led me down a narrow corridor with walls and a ceiling of roughly hewn rock. My room must be a cell, because this place looked very much like a dungeon cut into the rock below the city.

Worry tormented me anew.

What did they mean "to say goodbye"?

Had the queen changed his sentence from death to exile?

Or had she decided to speed up his execution? Maybe she'd learned about General Oskura moving on Kalmena and, like Alzali, decided not to risk Rha being freed?

As we crossed an underground courtyard, one of the guards finally took pity on me to answer some of my questions.

"Prince Rha is banished from Kalmena," he said. "But he's allowed to see you before he leaves. To say goodbye."

Rha's life was no longer in danger. I was afraid to believe. Afraid to breathe in relief.

But I still had to part from him.

Hope and anguish warred in my heart as I hurried up several sets of stairs, trying to catch up with the guards' long strides.

Eventually, we entered the front hall of the queen's palace, and I saw him. Rha was standing by the golden entrance gate, flanked by dozens of guards on each side.

I was robbed of breath at the sight of him. He was dressed for a journey across the desert, wearing high boots, a wide silk scarf wound loosely around his neck, and a heavy satchel with provisions on his shoulder.

The thin rivulets of thick smoke still trickled faintly down his arms.

His skin, normally smooth like velvet, looked rough and scarred on his high cheekbones—scorched by sunlight and abraded by the wind. However, his golden eyes lit aglow, and his chapped lips curved into a smile the moment he saw me.

After a few tentative steps toward him, I moved faster, then ran across the hall, eager to feel his arms around me.

The guards around him proved faster than me, however. Two of them crossed their swords between us, stopping me barely two steps away from him.

"Rha..." I whispered, breathless.

His body swayed toward me, but his feet remained rooted in place. Only his eyes locked with mine, betraying the passion that raged inside him, restrained by the impenetrable armor of his self-control.

"Hello, Dawn," he said so calmly, it sounded almost unnatural, considering the circumstances.

"She released you? You're leaving?" Not possessing anything close to his composure, I nervously wrung my hands and restlessly shifted from foot to foot.

"Yes. The queen wants me out of Kalmena. I am to leave for Teneris immediately, with the escort she provided. I'm allowed to bring along nothing but the most essential supplies to cross the desert. And only as much as I can carry."

I drew in a shaky breath, fighting tears that burned behind my eyelids.

He was alive. Death was no longer looming over him. That had to be enough. I should be happy he survived. Only I felt nothing but misery at having to let him go, without even a chance for a hug.

Seeing as we weren't trying to fight them, the guards lowered their swords.

A wild spark flashed in Rha's eyes. A cocky smirk momentarily lifted a corner of his mouth as he lunged forward, sleek like a shadow. In the blink of an eye, I was in his arms. And not just in a hug. He lifted me off the ground, holding me like he was never letting me go.

Without questioning it, I snapped my arms and legs around him so tightly it would take an army to pry us apart.

"I've got you," he murmured.

I buried my face in the silk of his scarf, breathing in his familiar scent. He was alive, and I couldn't believe I got to hold him again. Touch him. Breathe him in.

The sound of blades drawn out of their sheaths circled us. The guards surrounded us.

General Tanari stepped forward. "The Joy Vessel stays here. Please release her, Your Highness."

I stiffened, bracing for the worst. Rha calmly shifted me to the side to see the general, not showing any intention of setting me down.

"I'm taking Dawn with me, General. On the queen's orders."

The general's bushy eyebrows jerked up in shock.

"But Queen Abeille decreed all Joy Vessels, including those from your *sarai,* now belong to her."

Rha nodded. "Absolutely. You're right. All Joy Vessels belong to the queen, just like everything else in Kalmena belongs to her, including the supplies I have in my satchel. The queen, however, allowed me to take anything from her possessions that I can carry, and I'm taking Dawn. Rest assured, General, I will carry her all the way out of Kalmena as per the queen's wishes. I'll carry her all the way to Teneris if I have to. I'll never let her go."

The general squinted at Rha, looking impressed by his logic, though still somewhat doubtful.

"Surely, Her Majesty meant for you to take only the essential supplies necessary for your survival in the desert," he said.

"But Dawn is the most essential of them all," Rha retorted firmly. "I can make the entire journey from here to Teneris with no food and very little water. But I refuse to spend another second without her."

The general rubbed the back of his neck, then lowered his weapon. He seemed to have no personal dislike of Rha. The prince's explanation sounded logical enough for him, it appeared.

"May the gods protect you during your journey and beyond." The general made a gesture to the guards, and they stepped back, letting Rha pass.

The golden gates opened, and Rha carried me out of the palace.

My heart raced as he crossed the plaza with the tall platform, the place of his torment. He didn't spare it a glance, taking me to a street behind it that led to the city gate.

"You're trembling." He planted a kiss in my hair, sliding a soothing hand up and down my back while supporting me with the other.

"I still can't believe it," I breathed out. "I...I'm afraid they'll stop us any minute."

"They won't dare go against the queen's orders."

I sighed, wishing I had his confidence. "Was it her order, though? What exactly did she say?"

"She never spoke to me. I didn't even see the queen after that first meeting upon our arrival in Kalmena. General Tanari was the one who released me. But I made it clear to her earlier that I would never leave Kalmena without you. She knew, and she still ordered my release and exile. She won't stop us now. You're safe." He nuzzled the side of my face, pressing me tighter to him.

"Why do you think she changed her mind?" I asked.

"I'm not sure. She does have a very good reason to hate me."

"Does she?"

His chest expanded with a deep breath. "The queen blames me for my father's death. I was the one who removed the dagger from his body, allowing his spirit to cross into the afterlife when she wanted to keep him here forever."

"Is there really an afterlife?" I asked, running my fingers over his hair. It'd been washed and braided into a single plait, instead of his usual hairstyle.

"In Nerifir, there is."

"How do you know?"

"Because people have returned from it before. Some have even met the gods," he replied simply, as if it was a well-known fact. "Maybe Mother understood it, after all. Maybe she doesn't hate me as much as she thought she did."

I'd seen the hatred in the queen's heart. I'd felt it. It was too dark and heavy, too solid to disappear in the short time since we spoke.

The only humane emotion in the queen had been her pity for me, and I wondered if that was what had changed her mind in the end. She couldn't forgive her own son. But she could relate closely to the suffering she'd be condemning me to if he died.

I could be wrong, of course, so I kept it to myself. Whatever the queen's motivation was, it led to Rha being free and alive, and to us being together now.

The guards at the city gate blocked our way, but General Tanari, who was escorting us, gestured to them to let us pass. The heavy gate opened, and Rha carried me out into the desert night beyond. A camel and several horses waited for us at the gate, for Rha and his escort. The queen was sending her guards with us, to make sure Rha made it to Teneris and stayed there.

Rha helped me up the ladder and into the seat on the camel's back, then wrapped an arm around me, pulling me close again. With the other hand, he sat his satchel down as our small caravan headed on its way.

"Hungry?" he asked.

"No." I shook my head, taking a full breath for the first time in what felt like forever. "I should be. But I'm still too over-whelmed."

For one long moment, he looked at me intensely, his eyes searching my face.

"My treasure," he exhaled, taking my face between his hands. "I didn't think I'd see you again."

He kissed my forehead, then my eyes, one after the other, then my cheeks. His kisses were light, with a soft scrape of his rough, damaged skin against mine.

"I didn't think I'd ever get to ask you to kiss me again," he whispered, his lips just a breath away from mine.

I didn't wait for him to ask. I kissed his mouth, putting every-thing I felt into it. Even after the kiss ended, neither of us was willing to take our hands off each other. Rha ran his fingers over my necklace, then kissed the spot on my neck where a chain of the necklace circled it.

With the tips of my fingers, I gently traced the rough, sun-burned patches of skin on his face, arms, and shoulders. The sight of his injuries made my chest ache.

"We'll need to get you some good cream for this," I said, swallowing the tears.

"It'll heal soon enough." He slipped a hand under my necklace, cupping my breast. "As will the tendrils."

"Will they grow back?" I arched into his touch. Everything momentarily became secondary to that. His hands on me felt real, tangible, and true—we were both alive. And we were together.

"Mhm," he hummed, kissing my neck while kneading my breast gently. His other hand hiked up my skirt. Finding me naked under it, he leaned back. "Dawn." His throat moved with a swallow. "What happened to you in the queen's *sarai*? How did they treat you there?"

A dark undercurrent rolled through his deep voice, as if he'd launch into vengeance if I said a word against the Keepers or the queen herself.

"It's all good, baby." I adjusted my hips on his lap to give him better access to all of me. "I wasn't mistreated. No need to worry. I—" I inhaled sharply as he flicked my nipple, desire sparkling through my body. "Oh God, Rha... I've missed you."

"They didn't hurt you?"

"Only when they took you away from me." Placing a knee on each side of his thighs, I rocked against his hand.

I opened the closure of my necklace and let it drop to the seat next to us. With his arm around my waist, he brought me closer and dragged his tongue over my nipple. His fangs scraped against my skin, sending sparks of excitement down to my core.

Desire pooled low in my belly. Pressure was building up. I whimpered, rocking my hips against his abs.

"I know where you want me," Rha murmured, slipping a finger inside me.

I'd missed him so much. I craved his touch. But then I remembered he had no way of enjoying it with me now. I was using him solely for my pleasure.

The sobering thought came like a bucket of cold water over my sizzling desire. I jerked away from him.

"Rha... I'm sorry."

He wouldn't let go of me, however, drawing me to him again. His eyes hooded by eyelids, his mouth slacked, he ran his tongue over his lips like he'd been enjoying a fine dessert before I took it from him.

"Please let me, my treasure." He flicked his tongue over my other nipple. "I want you to come on my hand."

He found his way between my thighs again, stroking my hot, swollen clit with his fingers. A shiver of pleasure rushed through me. I wanted it badly. But doubts still weighed on my mind, sabotaging my joy.

"You can't feel this," I said as he gently lifted my breast, sucking and nibbling on the tip.

"Of course I can." He moaned against my skin, rubbing hard between my legs, as if his own orgasm depended on it.

"But how?"

"Because I remember."

He pressed my hand to his abs, then slid it down to his groin. I sucked in a breath in shock. His feelers had come to life, pushing against the fabric of his skirt. I shoved the fabric aside, finding the magnificent, glowing cluster of the slick, undulating tendrils in all their glory.

"How can it be?"

He looked slightly dazed, grinning at me. "It doesn't feel like a mating fever, sweetheart. There is no pain or desperate urgency. I can feel your need with all its delightful facets. And it's so good, Dawn. It shimmers with pleasure."

"You *remember* it all, do you?" I ran my fingers between his thighs. "You have a heck of a memory, my prince."

His delicate feelers caressed my fingers, winding and unwinding themselves around my hand. Their golden glow shone brightly between us. He moaned softly, with a shudder running through him.

I longed to know what he was feeling, and then I remembered that I probably could. I reached for Rha through my mind, my heart, and my soul. Tendrils of magic appeared from my *leilathas*. They grew as he stared at them in wonder.

"They say we share a bond." I smiled. "That's your magic, my love, but it looks like I can borrow it. May I?" I tilted my head, asking for his permission, the way he'd asked for mine before.

"This is incredible." He stroked a tendril with his fingers.

Warm tingles rushed me, popping along my skin like Champagne bubbles.

"I want to feel you." He brought the end of the tendril to the black gaping wound on his arm.

This wasn't like connecting to another tendril or to a harness. Rha had raw wounds, still fresh and possibly painful.

"What if it hurts?" I hesitated.

"It's *my* magic, my sweet. How can it ever hurt me?" He pressed the end of my tendril to his arm, and I let the connection happen.

Rha's emotions blended with mine, making us whole. It felt like coming home after a long absence. Love and comfort embraced me, wrapping around my heart like a warm blanket. I rose over his lap, letting some of his cluster slip inside me. Our bodies entangled as our emotions merged, making our connection complete.

Straddling his lap, I rocked against him.

"I love you." I pressed the side of my face to his.

"I feel it. Your love is the biggest treasure of all, Dawn. As long as I have it, I can weather any storm."

He gripped my hips, thrusting up into me. His feelers caressed my inner walls. Those that didn't fit inside me stroked me from the outside, fanning my desire.

When the pleasure crested with orgasm, it wasn't mine or his —it was ours. My moans mingled with Rha's. Our bodies rocked against each other. My inner muscles spasmed around the length of his feelers. Every shudder of pleasure rocked through us both.

I relaxed in his arms, feeling completely spent and delightfully elated.

"I love you." He kissed my hair, my temple, then the side of my face as I rested my head on his shoulder. "I love you, my treasure, my light. My one and only Joy."

Epilogue

DAWN

"This way, Your Highness." General Oskura ducked to fit under a low door frame that led us into a narrow corridor one floor below the palace.

This was the real dungeon, nothing like the room where I was held the day of my arrival in Alveari Kingdom. The dark walls and packed-dirt floor created the gloomy space where the Prince of Teneris held those who had wronged him or his people.

It also served as a reminder that the man, who could be poignantly gentle and heartbreakingly vulnerable with me, was a mighty ruler with means to administer harsh punishment to those who disobeyed his laws.

General Oskura stopped in front of one of several heavy doors in the corridor.

"Unlock it," she ordered to one of the guards who'd come with us.

We'd returned to Teneris only a few minutes earlier. The first thing Rha had to do upon our arrival was talk with the royal hag. Personally, I held no grudge against the woman and hoped Rha would release her from the dungeon. But I had a few questions to ask her, too, that I hoped she'd answer.

The guard unlocked the door. Golden sparks splattered from the spots where his fingers brushed the wood, marking the area protected by wards of magic. The wards here allowed people to enter the cells but prevented them from leaving unless Rha released them.

The hinges screeched as the guard shoved the door open. The air inside was damp and chilly. I hugged myself, peeking from around Rha's bicep into the cell.

"His Highness Prince Rha is—" General Oskura announced, cutting it short with a deep frown.

The small, dingy room was empty, save for two piles of charred clothes on the floor. The hag's gray cloak was in one pile, with a curved sword stabbed through it and her bracelets scattered around.

The second pile consisted of a black skirt like the Teneris guards' uniforms, a heavy chest armor dropped on top of it, with a pair of sandals peeking from underneath.

With a heavy sigh, Rha propped a hand in the door frame.

I hugged his arm, leaning closer. "What does it mean? Where is Kanjie?"

"Whose chest armor is this?" General Oskura asked the guards.

"Ulzur's," one of them replied, somberly.

The scene still made no sense to me.

"All experienced hags wear a protection spell," Rha explained. "It eviscerates their bodies on the spot if they're killed. But the one who dared murder them would die instantly too."

"Ulzur knew that," the guard said.

The general nodded. "Everyone knows that. It was suicide on his part. He knew he wouldn't leave the cell once he entered it."

"But why would he do that?" I asked.

The muscles in Rha's jaws flexed. "To protect something she knew."

I couldn't believe my ears. "Ulzur killed her, dying in the process, too, just to stop her from answering your questions?"

The general clenched her hands into fists. "The Watchers have reached deep into Teneris, Your Highness."

I OPENED my eyes at the soft whirring of the wall clock turning. With a quiet click, the golden bee shifted to a new position, indicating six o'clock in the evening.

Since our return to Teneris, I'd moved to Rha's bedroom permanently. Last morning, however, we started kissing in the baths and somehow ended up having sex in the golden room, where we then fell asleep in my old bed.

My tendrils were still out, some connected to Rha, others not —all tangled with our limbs. I retracted them all carefully, so as not to wake him up.

Somehow, my prince managed to look even more beautiful in his sleep. His black hair spread over the pillow like a spill of dark magic. It glistened with gold in his long braids. Without jewels covering his chest, his strong torso was fully on display with all its ridged landscape of well-defined muscles. Rha's wound on his back had closed and was healing well. All that he'd gone through was now behind us.

My heart overflowing with love for him, I placed a light kiss on Rha's shoulder. He made a soft rumbling noise in his throat and rolled onto his side but thankfully didn't wake up.

I slipped out of bed and picked up my folded nightgown that I'd never gotten a chance to put on before going to bed. After slipping it on, I wrapped a long, thin shawl around my shoulders, then shoved my feet into a pair of fabric slippers and padded out of the room.

As I ascended the stairs to the floor above, the day guard stood to attention.

"Evening, Sweet—" He blinked and promptly corrected himself, "my lady."

The status of a Joy Vessel was a tricky one. We were rare and treasured, but at the price of our freedom and often of our free will.

From the moment we returned to Teneris, Rha made it clear to his court and the entire city that I was not his Joy Vessel but his bonded mate. Our bond was created through my love for him, but our commitment to each other was because we both chose to make it.

From now on, the Court of Teneris had to address me accordingly. Though some still let the old honorifics slip, like this guard did.

"Evening, Edan," I said, heading toward Rha's private sitting room. "I'll be outside if anyone asks."

"Would you like to take your breakfast now, my lady?" Edan asked. "Coffee maybe?"

"Not right now. When Sigid is up, tell him to bring my coffee out to the patio. But there's no need to wake him."

I moved aside the tall window shutter. It was bright outside. The sun was out, though its edge had almost touched the horizon already. I'd had a nap after midnight, planning to get up early enough to catch the sunset, and I got here just in time.

With a short purr and liquid grace, Zala jumped from the cushion and weaved between my legs. I bent down to pet her.

"Evening, kitty cat. Sleep well?"

She rubbed her head against my hand in greeting, then slipped through the open window outside and promptly disappeared into the wall of grass growing just below the parapet around the patio. No rodent was now safe with that cat out.

It must've been a relatively calm day. The wind had already quieted down, and only a thin layer of sand covered the patio stones. The heat of the day remained scorching for now. But I didn't mind it. I had missed the sun.

I shook out the sand from the cushions of the swing, then

stretched on the seat. Taking my shawl off and lifting the hem of my sleeping shirt up above my knees, I soaked up the sunshine and enjoyed the peace of the late evening.

Most of Teneris was still asleep. Even the birds and insects remained in hiding for now, escaping the heat. There was peace in the quiet. The unrest came from my thoughts alone.

True to his promise, Rha had sent word out, offering a generous reward for the safe return of his escaped Joy Vessels. So far, no one had been located. There had been no word on Elaine's whereabouts, either. I hoped most of the people from the *sarai* had escaped safely through the portal. But I knew for a fact that a few remained, including Elaine.

Rha gave the entire *sarai* building to me to do with as I pleased. All Joy Vessel Keepers were now in my direct service as well. The prince declared he'd own no Joy Vessels anymore. Those who'd return would stay in Teneris as guests, keeping full control of their bodies and emotions.

It pained me to know that Lucia was still in Kalmena when she'd asked me to take her back to Teneris. But as per the queen's orders, Rha remained largely a prisoner in his own city and could make no demands of the queen to return Lucia.

The sun steadily crawled down as the night advanced. Sigid brought me a cup of coffee and a glass of ice water.

"Would you like your breakfast, too, my lady?"

"No. I'll wait for His Highness to wake up first."

I loved sharing all my pleasures with Rha, big and small. It felt like a waste to even drink coffee without him. But I couldn't wait any longer, taking that most wonderful first sip of the invigorating liquid on my own.

As the sun descended lower, the lacy shadow of the grass wall stretched across the patio to cover my legs. The sky dripped with vivid colors that splashed over the torn remnants of the storm clouds.

A soft crunch of sand under someone's soles alerted me to a

visitor. I smiled, turning over my shoulder. With the stealth of a shadow, Rha crossed the patio toward me.

He squinted at the bright colors of the sunset from under the fabric pulled low over his head. "What a mess."

"You're up early. It's not dark enough yet." I removed my feet from the swing's seat to make space for him.

He took the seat but caught my feet before I could put them down and placed them on his lap instead. "The sleep isn't quite the same without you."

"Well, the coffee isn't quite the same without you, either." I sat my empty cup down. "That bond is rather annoying, isn't it?"

He took my hand in his and brought it to his lips for a kiss, raking his gaze over me. I smoothed my hair and jerked the skirt of my sleeping shirt down.

"I'm a mess." I smiled apologetically. "Just got out of bed."

Unlike me, Rha looked fresh and was fully dressed already. Only his hair hadn't been re-braided yet.

"Mhm, a mess," he agreed. "You are my beautiful, brave, chaotic mess, Dawn. And I wouldn't change a thing about you."

I might not have had the best judgement of people or situations. I'd made mistakes. I'd made many questionable decisions in my life. Some turned out okay, others, not so much. I'd battled uncertainty and self-doubt all of my life.

But there was one decision I stood behind without a shadow of regret. The decision to run down that hill toward the man who was ready to die for me, instead of running up to the portal that would take me away from him.

"I love you." I kissed him, because I knew he loved my kisses more than anything else in the world.

Patreon

For an early access to the next book in the series, bonus material, and illustrations, including NSFW art, please join the author's Patreon:

More in the River of Mists world

Joyless Kingdom Trilogy

Somber Prince

Joy Guardian

Pleasure Trader

Wingless Crow Duet

Wingless Crow

Crownless King

Fire in Stone Duet

Fire in Stone

Hearts of Fire

Serpent's Touch Duet

Serpent's Touch

Serpent's Claim

<u>*Madame Tan's Freakshow Trilogy*</u>

Call of Water

Madness of the Moon

Power of Rage

A Look in the Mirror

Downfall of a Princess
Rise of a Fallen Man
War of Smoke and Mirrors

Seven Horny Sins

Let Me Claim You
Let Me Win You
Let me Feed You

More by Marina Simcoe

PARANORMAL ROMANCE

Demons (Complete Series)

Demon Mine

The Forgotten

Grand Master

The Last Unforgiven - Cursed

The Last Unforgiven - Freed

Stand Alone Novels

The Real Thing

To Love A Monster

Midnight Coven Author Group

Wicked Warlock (Cursed Coven)

More by Marina Simcoe

SCIENCE-FICTION ROMANCE

My Holiday Tails

Married to Krampus

My Tiny Giant

My Birthday Getaway

New Year, New Planet

Mail Order Mom

My Pumpkin

What Makes an Alien a Dad?

Dark Anomaly Trilogy

Gravity

Power

Explosion

Stand Alone Novels

Experiment

Enduring (Valos Of Sonhadra)

About the Author

Marina Simcoe likes to write love stories with human heroines and non-human heroes who just can't live without them. She firmly believes that our contemporary world could always use a little bit of the extraordinary.

She has lots of fun exploring how her out-of-this-world characters with their own beliefs, values, and aspirations fit into our every-day life.

She lives in Canada with her very own extraordinary hero, their three little offspring, and a cat who is definitely out of this world.

facebook.com/MarinaSimcoeAuthor

instagram.com/marinasimcoeauthor

amazon.com/author/marinasimcoe

bookbub.com/profile/marina-simcoe

goodreads.com/MarinaSimcoe